SHROUDED BY DARKNESS
TALES OF TERROR

W9-APR-369

SHROUDED BY DARKNESS
TALES OF TERROR

Edited by Alison L R Davies

First published in England in 2006 by
Telos Publishing Ltd

61 Elgar Avenue, Tolworth, Surrey, KT5 9JP, England
www.telos.co.uk

Telos Publishing Ltd values feedback. Please e-mail us with any
comments you may have about this book to: feedback@telos.co.uk

ISBN: 1-84583-046-6 (paperback)
ISBN: 1-84583-047-4 (hardback)

For individual contributor copyright information please
see page 389

The moral rights of the authors have been asserted.

All royalties from this book are being donated to DebRA

Printed in India

1 2 3 4 5 6 7 8 9 10 11 12 13 14 15

British Library Cataloguing in Publication Data.
A catalogue record for this book is available from the British
Library.

This book is sold subject to the condition that it shall not by way of
trade or otherwise, be lent, resold, hired out or otherwise circulated
without the publisher's prior written consent in any form of binding
or cover other than that in which it is published and without a similar
condition including this condition being imposed on the subsequent
purchaser.

This book is dedicated to all the Butterfly Children in the world.

INTRODUCTION

I wasn't lucky enough to meet Jonny Kennedy, but I felt like I knew him after watching his incredibly moving documentary *The Boy Whose Skin Fell Off*. The film, which portrayed Jonny in the last few months of his life, left me with an enormous admiration for his amazing bravery and spirit. Those who have seen it will know what I mean and those who haven't have missed a glimpse of a truly remarkable young man. It was Jonny that motivated me to raise money and awareness for the charity DebRA. It was also Jonny that inspired me to put together a collection of horror stories, in essence this book. (I'm sure he would have enjoyed the read.) It was Jonny that moved me to approach some of the world's best writers in the hope that they too would recognise this as a worthy cause. Finally, it was Jonny that pushed me to succeed in getting a publisher interested, and I'm so glad he did, because this collection has exceeded all my expectations.

I'd like to thank the writers for their wonderful contributions. I'd like to thank Telos for taking the time and care to publish this book. I'd like to thank the folks at DebRA for their tireless work for sufferers of Epidermolysis Bullosa. And I'd like to thank you for buying this collection and supporting the charity.

Alison L R Davies
Nottingham
April 2006

If you wish to make a donation to DebRA, please send cheques or postal orders made payable to DebRA to:

DebRA House,
13 Wellington Business Park,
Dukes Ride,
Crowthorne,
Berkshire. RG45 6LS.
debra@debra.org.uk
Charity registration number is: 1084958

CONTENTS

Foreword

Stephen Jones

All of us who contribute to the horror genre – writers, artists, editors and publishers – are acutely aware that we are producing works of fiction.

Our aim is to entertain the audience with stories of supernatural monsters or crazed psychotic killers that will – hopefully – disturb, terrify and even revolt the reader or viewer. However, when our tales are finally told, you can close the pages of a book or magazine, turn off the television, or leave the movie theatre, locking those gruesome images and dreadful concepts away in the dark corners of your mind, where they rightly belong.

But out there in the real world, the situation is very different. For many people, there are far worse things than vampires, werewolves or malevolent ghosts.

***

Epidermolysis Bullosa (EB) is a rare inherited genetic condition that causes extremely fragile skin and internal body linings to erupt and blister at the slightest friction or trauma. In the more severe cases, these wounds heal very slowly, resulting in permanent scarring, physical deformity and life-long disability.

Those suffering from the more extreme types of EB have a high risk of developing skin cancers, shortening their lives by thirty to forty years. In its very worst form, the condition is fatal in infancy.

Although not contagious, it is estimated to affect around 1 in 17,000 births in Britain and 1 in 50,000 births in the United States. This extremely painful disorder occurs in every ethnic and racial group throughout the world and is found equally in both sexes. There are currently some 5,000 people living with EB in Britain and around 12,000 children and adults suffering in the United States.

First-time parents are often unaware that they are carriers and have no prior warning that their child will be affected until birth.

Founded in 1978 by a group of parents whose children were affected by EB, DebRA was created to raise awareness, establish a range of specialist support services and fund medical research into this horrific and potentially fatal disease. The charity is now established in more than thirty countries and exists entirely as a result of voluntary donations.

A great deal of progress has been made in recent years in understanding and identifying the genes that cause EB. However, there is not as yet an effective treatment or cure.

***

The many excellent contributors to this present volume have donated their work for free to support the work of DebRA and raise awareness of this awful condition.

Despite our reputation for working in the dark side of the arts, the horror community is no less caring than any other of the creative fields when it comes to helping our fellow human beings.

Our avowed aim may be to scare you – to mess with your mind and emotions in various grim and bizarre ways – but none of us want to see that suffering and pain continue over into the world that surrounds us.

So sit back, enjoy the many fine stories that follow, and prepare to be entertained by some of the most talented practitioners that our genre has to offer.

But when all is said and done, and you eventually close the pages of this book (hopefully with a shudder), I urge you to recall why this volume was put together in the first place.

Please spare a thought for those children too small or too defenceless to understand what is happening to them, or the many adults forced to live with this debilitating condition every day of their lives – and remember that not all horrors come from the imagination.

Stephen Jones
London, England
May, 2006

Cenobite
©Clive Barker

Hell Came Down
Tim Lebbon

I went looking for him where it was dry and parched, where the skeletons of cattle decorated the outskirts of town like grotesque, bleached baubles, where children lay on pavements and breathed shallowly, painfully as their mothers tried to squeeze a drop of moisture from sagging breasts, where the sun had leeched all colour and the façades of buildings presented a uniform paleness, where stream-beds were crazy paving punctuated here and there with dead weeds, where people wandered in a haze to and from the watering hole that was little more than mud now, mud that could be squeezed for a few precious drops, sometimes, if they were lucky. A place where death was sometimes a release, and cadavers were never put to waste. Dead fathers gave their children a source of sustenance for a day or two. They would have wanted it that way. I knew that Lucien would be here. Where better to find a rain-maker?

Heads turned my way as I entered the town. The dying people heard the slosh of water in my canteen, a sound that doubtless haunted their dreams, waking and sleeping. Some looked pleadingly, others scheming. They saw the rifle across my shoulders and perhaps thought better of it, but even without that I would not have been concerned. I had other ways of protecting myself.

I looked for signs of his presence. It was no use asking, because they all thought he was trying to help them: Lucien, bringing down rain onto parched lands, urging the clouds to form and the droplets to condense, conjure life back into a dead place and a dying people.

They thought this even though he had yet to bring a storm ... of rain, at least. In Birmingham, a shower of frogs had emerged from the clear blue skies and splattered across the ground around him. I had not seen it happen, but I had heard others talk of it. In Bristol, dogs and cats, clogging the remaining streams and watering holes with rancid bodies crawling with fleas and God knew what else. Some of the cats had two tails. Some of the dogs were new breeds. Still, they worshipped him.

I stopped at a bakery devoid of bread. It was selling dried potatoes, their skins wrinkled around withered insides. I picked one up and it rattled like an egg containing a mummified chick.

'A drink from your canteen,' the man in the shop said. He was still in his twenties, I guessed, but he looked 50.

'It would kill you.' I touched the metal canister on my belt, then briefly adjusted the gun across my shoulders. It was not what I meant ... I wouldn't shoot him, the water itself would finish him because it was not of this world ... but he got the message.

'Well then, what will you trade me?'

'For these?' I picked up a handful of potatoes and weighed them. There was hardly any mass there at all. Certainly no goodness.

'They're all I have,' he said wretchedly.

I looked around the shop and saw old posters displaying rich cakes, thick with cream and bleeding with jam. 'I used to work for a baker,' I lied. 'He was a good man. Jesus was a baker, you know.'

The young-old man frowned, confused. He licked his dry lips with a drier tongue. I heard it, like a boot scraping across sandy ground.

I tried a smile. 'You help me, and I'll do what I can to help you.'

'What do you mean?' Still he glanced at the canteen on my hip.

'I told you that will kill you. But I have other water ... purified. Filtered.'

'Where?'

'Help me first.' I sat on the inside window sill, wondering how many had rested there in the past waiting for their order of bread and doughnuts. In the street someone was wailing, but it was a common sound now, as regular as the beating of the sun. 'I'm looking for the rainmaker.'

'Lucien!' The baker's tired eyes brightened.

'You've seen him?' I sat forward. The black water moved in the canteen, shifting it against my leg like a living thing.

'I fed him!' the man said. 'He came to me and took some food, and gave me –. something in return.'

'What?'

The man shrugged, looking as embarrassed as a man slowly dying of thirst and hunger could. 'A frog.' He had eaten it, his expression made that clear. Its blood, its mucus, its fluids – moisture of a kind.

'I need to find him,' I said. 'He's making all this worse.'

'No, he's making it better!'

'Then where are the rains?' I roared, standing and advancing on the man, angry and desperate and so willing to cause pain … though I had caused enough already. The trail of Lucien's devastation across the land displayed that so well. 'Show me how he's helped!'

'He said … he said that if I talked –'

'I'll give you water!'

'No, I can't, he said –'

I grabbed him by the shirt, lifted him and pressed him against an old poster for Chelsea buns. 'Tell me where he is!'

'The courthouse. Last I heard he … he was …' The baker gagged, his eyes turned up in his head, he bit straight through the end of his own tongue.

I dropped him. I didn't want to be covered in his mess.

The young man who looked so old slipped to the dusty tiled floor of his shop, twitching and twisting himself into unnatural shapes, arms and legs entwining as whatever was inside sought escape. His eyes bulged, as did his stomach. He screeched, a high keening sound that scared the few remaining birds outside into flight and set a rabid dog growling somewhere in the distance. His hands clawed. I backed away. His nails scored into his throat and chest as he ripped at himself. I was standing outside on the pavement when his stomach ruptured and a sickly grey mess spilled across the floor, steaming precious fluids to condense and dry on the walls of his shop. He twitched one more time, then was still. Lucien was covering his tracks well, but not well enough. Perhaps, despite all his powers, he was not expecting me. I had to find the courts.

***

I was not a bad teacher. It was Lucien who was a poor pupil. My real mistake was in not seeing that, and this is why I had to pursue him across the country, closing in day by day, until that time I confronted him in the old courts in Usk. He had come to me as a boy and begged to be shown the weird ways, and even then he displayed some level of barely restrained potency that made me seem an amateur. I took him in. He had fled his family years before, his peculiar gift effectively ostracising him even from them. He had worshipped, venerated and heeded me, absorbing what I taught, listening when I warned. He was a strong young man haunted by what his mind contained. And that should have been my first warning: it haunted him, but did not control him. He fought it. He fought his gift from God. I should have killed him there and then.

I walked along the town's main street, trying to smile at one or two people but seeing only pain and fear sent back at me. The heat had been so great for so long that some of the buildings were crumbling, their brick and stonework destroyed from within, heated and expanded and cracked to ruin. On the left, an old antiques store had lost its window and surround. The sign still hung above, letters faded and forgotten, but all it housed now was a mountain of yellowed books. A fire waiting to happen. And indeed, further along the street there was a charred gap in the row of shops, a place where fire had come and taken its due. A few roof members had survived, protruding from the black mass of stone and concrete, thinned out by the flames. There was something else lying there as well, in amongst the wreckage. It glinted white, but only because carrion creatures had picked its cooked bones clean. Carrion creatures and, perhaps, carrion humans as well.

I reached an intersection of two roads. There was a banner strung across the street from years before, a bitter in-joke that the townsfolk seemed still to be playing upon themselves. It read: *Usk in Bloom*. They had been gardeners, flower growers, feeding into the ground the water that they so craved now. It had not rained for over a year. The country was in ruin.

I saw a bank, a restaurant, a clothes shop, all totally redundant now that famine and disease were grinding the last dregs of humanity into the soil. Some people still tried to keep a hold of what they had once been, and I was sure I saw the shadowy movement of someone behind the bank's counter. Perhaps even now they counted useless millions and slipped out with a secret note here, a note there, slowly accumulating a fortune as worthless as the dry river bed, or the underground water pipes that had cracked in the heat and given their final precious drops to the dry earth.

'You!' someone shouted. 'Hey, you!'

I could not locate the caller at first, so I closed my eyes and found them in my mind. Above and behind. I turned and looked up at an open window. There was a woman leaning out, naked and filthy, hair knotted and skin cracked beneath the dirt. Dried blood clotted around her joints. Her eyes were wild, at least the one I could see, squinting at me along the length of a shotgun.

'The water. Throw it up.'

'You really think it will save you?'

'You think I give a fuck? It's for my baby.' She was mad with thirst and hunger, I could tell that much at least, but her aim never wavered: my head. I could see right into the barrels.

I closed my eyes again and moved up to her, felt into the gun, saw that it was loaded. No bluffing, then. She really meant it. I opened my eyes and leaned slowly against the wall beside me. I made certain that my hands stayed at my sides. There was no way I could reach my rifle in time. Besides, there were other ways of stopping her.

'Don't make me kill you,' I said quietly.

She laughed. 'Your head will be all over the road before you even touch that gun. Now throw up the canteen and you can go on. I mean it. I won't kill you.'

'I know you won't,' I said, 'but the water will kill your baby. It's black water.'

'He's drunk dirty water before.'

'Never black.'

I closed my eyes one more time and moved back up there, fingering my way into her mind this time, desperate not to see what was inside there but more desperate not to have to kill her. I knew how risky this was. I could spend precious seconds convincing her, or I could just slip in and throw a switch, kill her painlessly and without a sound, drop her to the floor and go on my way. I had killed before, many times. I would do so again, soon, when I found Lucien. But it was ironic that now, with my own head framed by a shotgun's line of fire, one more life seemed so precious amongst a billion dead.

She was mad. There were visions in there that terrified me, perverted truths that lied even to themselves, a fragrant paranoia that stank of neglect and pain and decades of abuse, stemming from long before the drought and famine, rooted in a past so dark that even the black water would taste sweet in comparison. I closed my mind to these places and tried to pass through, feeling the soapy touch of terror attempting to drag me from my path and lose me in the depths, places where direction was lost and simply being was all there was, being awed, being feared, being trapped.

At last I found the centre of her, the place where all sanity had been driven and where, even now, madness was eating away at its edges like an eternally patient caterpillar chewing at the boundaries of the mightiest forest. She had been a good woman once, a mother and a wife and a librarian, fighting a difficult past by revelling in a content present, little suspecting what the future held.

Then I showed her the black water.

'Get that fucking shit away from me!' she screeched, seeing instantly, not giving me a chance to withdraw before panicking. I pulled out and went back to myself, opened my eyes, stunned by her quick reaction and suddenly knowing my mistake. She may be mad, yes, but she was desperate as well. She had a child to save when her own life was already wasted. I had time to slip inches down the wall before she pulled the trigger.

Most of the shot struck the brickwork directly where my head had been a second before. Shattered brick rained down on my head and shoulders, and I felt something plucking at my forehead and right eye, something that felt cold but quickly turned hot, white hot, burning its way into my head and down through my neck. I screamed, fell to the ground and put my hands to my face. The ruin of my eye was leaking from its socket. My good eye was blinded by the pain. The blood and fluid was thick and slimy like a broken, raw egg.

Any normal man would have died or curled up with the pain. I stood, unslung the rifle from my pack and opened up at the window. I tried to probe at the woman but the pain was too great, I could not detach properly, and besides, I had the feeling she had fled. The sight returned slowly to my left eye, fading in from a bright white to a semblance of what was around me, and I emptied the clip at the window and those either side of it. Glass smashed, stonework spat out powdered eruptions, a bullet ricocheted along the street and starred the windscreen of an abandoned car.

Then I turned and ran. In my blinding agony I ran without direction. I automatically replaced the magazine in the rifle, but no-one seemed keen to stop or tackle me. I must have presented a fearsome sight, a big man with bloodied face, ragged eye socket, water canteen and rifle, sprinting along streets where nowadays people could barely crawl.

I ran for five minutes. My blood pumped, my heart thumped, I bled out the pain. By the time I stopped, my eye had ceased bleeding and was already scabbing over. The pain had reduced to a bright throb, flashing into my head as if my eye was still there and I was looking directly at the sun. I slumped against a garden wall, unhooked the canteen and took a swig of the black water. It tasted awful, but it invigorated me, giving sustenance and strength and power of mind and will with one swig.

And I suddenly realised the truth. Things had come to a head without me even instigating it. I had to catch Lucien now, within the next few minutes, because he would have heard the shooting, and if he'd learnt anything good from me it was an aggressive instinct for self-preservation. Wherever he was, whatever he was doing, he would be readying to leave. If I lost track of him now, it would take me weeks, or even months, to find him again, wounded as I was. Weeks or months may be far too late for this place. I may not even have days.

In Devon, I had found a whole village killed by the scorpions Lucien had brought down from the sky when he was trying to conjure rain.

When I arrived, the air was still tainted with his pain, his guilt, his growing madness. He was trying, trying again, striving to get it right, but wherever he went, things were getting worse, the manifestations matching his increasing frustration. There were over five hundred bodies in that place. They were swollen and bloated and burst from the effects of the scorpions' poison. Some of the creatures had been as big as my hand. Many had possessed a sting at both ends. It could only get worse.

I pushed myself from the wall and went to the nearest house showing signs of habitation. I probed inside, saw that they had no weapons of threat to me, smashed on the door until it gave way. There was no time for niceties. A little girl scampered into a room to my left. Her father stepped into the corridor, a short-bladed knife in his hand and a look of resigned terror in his eyes. He was ready to die for her. He looked about set to die anyway, all the signs of hunger and thirst evident on his face. It was obvious that he had been giving all the food and drink he could scrounge or steal to his daughter.

I grabbed him, shoved him against the wall, knocked the knife aside.

'I'll let you live if you tell me where the old courts are in the next three seconds.'

'Your ... your eye.'

'One.'

I was choking him. He could barely talk.

'Two.'

'I ... I ...'

'Three.'

'Show you ... I'll show you ...'

I let him slide down until his feet touched carpet, then I let go. He looked down at the knife on the floor but obviously thought better of it. Rubbing at his bruised neck, he glanced into the room at his daughter, tried to smile at her. She cried at his grimace.

'That way,' he said, pointing out the front door and to my right. 'Two streets along, then turn left. Iron railings. But I don't know what you want with the courts ... they're haunted.'

'I know,' I said, and although I was lying – I didn't know whether they were haunted or not – I was sure they soon would be. I turned to leave. 'Sorry,' I muttered. I felt the man's stare, felt him beginning to crumple. His daughter ran to him and he was trying to hide his tears, but he was nearing the end of a life of weakness and loss, hopelessness and shame.

Sometimes I saw far too much to bear.

Lucien was still there. As I neared the courts, I saw signs. Cracked paving slabs at first, whatever falling things that had caused their destruction long since vanished. A row of houses with shattered slates, the holes in the roofs adorned with wispy material, flickering like spider-web in the subtle breeze. It could have been roof lining, or dusty webs snagged on the broken timbers, or skin. Then living things: a beetle with two heads, scurrying along the gutter on twelve legs; a butterfly spiralling in lazy, pointless circles, its wings a death mask with bleeding eyes; a hummingbird, probing at withered flowers in its useless quest for sustenance. Alien animals to these shores, perhaps even alien to this world. Especially the rat. It was as big as a tomcat, and as it ran across the road, I saw traces of bloodied ginger fur around its jaws. A tomcat's match as well, evidently. It had a horn protruding from the centre of its forehead, serving no purpose other than to give it a hateful appearance.

I turned away and jogged along the street. Each footfall provoked a spike of pain in my head from my destroyed eye socket, but I welcomed it. It told me that I was still alive. The chaos Lucien had caused was my fault, and if half-blindness and constant pain was all the punishment I would receive for such a heinous mistake, then it was light indeed, for I was as guilty as sin.

The courts were large and imposing. Columns graced the entrance, leaded windows on either side stared out like grey, dead eyes, iron railings contained the building within its gardens, once lush but now brown and dry and dead. There was an old fountain in the front courtyard with a body curved around its central spout. Perhaps whoever had crawled here to die had believed that, if a miracle did occur and water flowed again, they would be revived. Most of the flesh had been chewed away. A denim jacket covered the ribcage. Rings, a silver necklace and a glittering anklet all touched bone.

I probed inside, carefully so that Lucien would not sense me. He was powerful, but mad with it, a twisted genius. If I was careful, he would not notice me.

I gasped. There were things in there … I had felt ghosts before, but never like this, never in such profusion. And the strangest thing was, they were all new, all recently dead, all inhabiting the same place in this doomed town.

Here, an old woman wandering in a circle, in and out of this world, seeking her husband both here and elsewhere. *Have you seen my Gerald?* she asked. *He's a farmer …*

A young girl too, barely into her teens, crawling around the ceilings inside as if too afraid to touch the ground. Her mouth was open in a permanent scream. Her skin was raised in grotesque humps, each of them capped with a poison-filled pustule. *The ants, the ants, the ants, the ants …*

A man and a woman, husband and wife, twisted together and merged where something had gored them to death. *I love you … love … love you …* their voices entwined madly, neither of them realising that they had no reason to haunt.

Lucien's dead, I knew: those who had perished because of his failed efforts, killed by creatures they knew or monsters they did not. I probed further, trying to ignore the anguish and the pain and the resentment that only the dead can truly feel. I sensed old ghosts too, ground back into the shadowy realms of this place by the new, fresh anger of the recently dead. And then I found him: Lucien, sitting at a table in the old library, reading from a book written in Latin, able to understand if he so desired but merely skimming the pages, relishing the peace to muster his energies.

I realised how late I had left all this. He was going to try again in minutes, try one more time to put things right where he had done so much wrong. I opened my good eye and glanced at the sky. Thunderheads were forming from nowhere as his energies converged, darkening the sky and bringing yet another false promise of rain. Guilt should have driven me after him sooner, but pride had held me back. The two had torn me apart. They were still tearing, deep inside, sparring with accusatory feelings and a dreadful home truth:

that I had created a monster.

You. He had sensed my furtive probings. I withdrew quickly and ran to the front doors, unslinging the rifle. So damn clumsy of me! If he hadn't found me, I could have slipped into his mind, distracted him, shot him through a window then torn him apart inside as he lay there bleeding. I did not want to do it. I hated to have to kill him. But like all mistakes, if I let him live, I knew he would only come back to haunt me again. And there really was no other way to stop him.

I kicked open the doors and ran into the lobby, already lifting the rifle, ready to fire as soon as I burst into the library. Surprise had gone, but I had speed and strength – which I knew, instantaneously, to be outforced. He slammed me back against a wall without touching me. The rifle tumbled from my hands and disappeared beneath a bench in the lobby. The ghosts screamed and I tried to shut them from my mind, but I felt Lucien's fingers in there, rooting around and opening up all the routes to my self, letting in his victims, giving him respite as they poured their rage into me.

I screamed. My wounds bled again. He emerged from the library. 'You,' he said, standing before me.

'Lucien, you have to stop!'

'The world is dying! And what have you done to help it? Nothing.'

'You'll kill it yourself,' I shouted, barely hearing myself above the screams of the dead.

'I'm giving it life,' he said. 'I'm bringing a storm. A flood. Can't you feel it brewing? Can't you feel the electricity in the air, the hairs on yours arms standing on end, your teeth tingling? A storm to wash away the bad and bring goodness once again.'

Somehow, I formed words around all the pains in my head, forcing them out, not knowing whether they made sense or not. 'Lucien … help me help you. I made a mistake with you, I admit it –'

'Admit this, old man! That you're proud and arrogant, and you cannot – for – a – second believe that I've taught myself more.'

He pressed me harder against the wall, and I felt my lungs compressing, my heart being forced flat, blood pounding in my ears and pouring from my eye.

'Your dead are screaming at me!' I tried to shout, not even knowing if my voice was working any more. 'How many more are you going to make?'

The noise stopped. I fell to the floor. I hugged myself, trying to make sure all my parts were still there.

'Look at me,' he said.

I looked up. There was the Lucien I had known, a thin, short man with long hair and a face to match, down-turned eyes that gave him a begging-puppy look, clothes that never seemed to fit. Someone who had never seemed able to leave the angst of his teens behind. Someone with so much power, but who looked so weak.

'I'm a good man,' he whispered. 'You told me that. I'm here to bring good. I'm going to bring rain and end the famine, because I'm the rainmaker. You told me that, too.'

I went to say that he was wrong – that I had been wrong – but my voice did not work. It had gone dark, an instant dusk. 'The storm's beginning,' he said. Then he turned his back on me and went outside.

I heard it from where I lay, unable to move, paralysed by fear and defeat. Lucien roared. I imagined him standing out there with his arms outstretched, his palms facing skyward as he invoked what he thought would be a downpour to save this blighted land. I sensed the ghosts in the building cowering from the fury he imparted, hiding themselves away, the dead fearing something far worse than death. I tried to stand. I could not. Perhaps it was failure, because I knew even then that I could not stop him. He was right. I was arrogant. I had not for a second believed that he could face me and win.

For a time, I thought he had prevailed. There was a glass atrium in the courthouse's lobby, and for a long few seconds something pattered wetly onto the frosted glass canopy above me. I lay on my back and so wished that he had succeeded, but then I knew that was not the case. Rain did not crack glass. Rain did not leave bloody smears behind. Most of all, rain did not scurry away after it had landed, searching for dark places in which to hide.

No, I felt Lucien say in my mind. He must have seen something horrible coming down. I resisted the temptation to say I'd told him so; it was too much effort, and I had no energy left.

No... Something massive hit the ground outside. The lobby windows blew in, letting in a terrible stench of rot and insides turned out.

Oh no, Lucien said again. *I'm sorry* ... Perhaps he was even talking to me.

Other things began to fall, bigger and smaller, growling or roaring when they hit. Many of their calls halted instantly, but some went on. Some survived. I sensed Lucien extinguished like an ant beneath the foot of a giant. His death should have stopped it. It did not. The storm went on all night.

Lucien was right. He did cause a flood. I managed to crawl to a place of safety while that long night brought chaos down to earth. I remained hidden in the basement of the old courts for two days, recuperating and using my battered powers to hide myself when anything came inside to investigate. Once, I heard a creature on two feet drag something across the mosaic tiled floor above me. It grunted, chewed, spat. Sniffed the air. Held still. I closed my eyes and had to use all my energy to turn it away from me. Its mind was revolting. And victorious.

When I left the courts, I fled the town as quickly as I could, shielding myself from view with simple but energy-consuming invisibility. The flood was diminishing, but only because the things that had fallen that night were spreading out. I saw a tiger strolling carelessly along the main street; a bulging black mass hanging from a telegraph pole, dropping spiders as big as my head to the ground; something that looked like an alligator but had wings; a wolf and a bear hunting together. I saw carcasses stripped clean, and the living results of Lucien's final storm were well-fed.

The town was obliterated. Every building was damaged, most completely shattered, and as for the inhabitants – a limb here, a blood-smeared pavement there. Most of the things that had come down, I knew, were carnivorous. Lucien's final, desperate, anguished attempts had made them so.

***

I've been hiding in the hills for several weeks, hiding like a criminal ... and I suppose I am. I trained the person that ended the world, after all.

Sometimes I sense Lucien, a wandering ghost whose powers are ineffectual now that he has moved far, far on. But he still cries, and I cry with him. He was an innocent. I'm the one to blame.

When the things that fell that night finally find me, it will be only what I deserve.

Making A Noise In This World
Charles de Lint

I'm driving up from the city when I spot a flock of crows near the chained gates of the old gravel pit that sits on the left side of the highway, about halfway to the rez. It's that time of the morning when the night's mostly a memory, but the sun's still blinking the sleep from its eyes as it gets ready to shine us into another day.

Me, I'm on my way to bed. I have a take-out coffee in my free hand, a cigarette burning between the tobacco-stained fingers of the one holding the wheel. A plastic bag full of aerosol paint cans, half of them empty, rattles on the floor on the passenger's side every time I hit a bump. Behind me, I've left freight cars painted with thunderbirds and buffalo heads and whatever other icons I could think up tonight to tell the world that the Indians have counted another coup, hi-ya-ya-ya. I draw the line at dream-catchers, though I suppose some people might mistake my spiderwebs for them.

My favourite tonight has become sort of a personal trademark: a big crow, its wings spread wide like the traditional thunderbird and running the whole length of the boxcar, but it's got that crow beak you can't mistake and a sly, kind of laughing look in its eyes. Tonight I painted that bird fire engine red with black markings. On its belly I made the old Kickaha sign for *Bín-ji-gú-sân,* the sacred medicine bag: a snake, with luck lines radiating from its head and back.

I've been doing that crow ever since I woke one morning from a dream where I was painting graffiti on a 747 at the airport, smiling because this time my bird was really going to fly. I opened my eyes to hear the crows outside my window, squawking and gossiping, and there were three black feathers on the pillow beside me.

***

Out on the highway now, I ease up on the gas and try to see what's got these birds up so early. Crows are sacred on the rez – at least with the Aunts and the other elders. Most of my generation's just happy to make it through the day, never mind getting mystical about it. But I've always liked them. Crows and coyotes. Like the Aunts say, they're the smart ones. They never had anything for the white men to take away and they sure do hold their own against them. Shoot them, poison them, do your best. You manage to kill one and a couple more'll show up to take its place. If we'd been as wily, we'd never have lost our lands.

It's a cold morning. My hands are still stinging from when I was painting those boxcars, all night long. Though some of that time was spent hiding from the railroad rent-a-cops and warming up outside the freight yard where some hobo skins had them a fire burning in a big metal drum. Half the time, the paints just clogged up in the cans. If I'd been in the wind, I doubt they'd have worked at all.

The colours I use are blacks and reds, greens and yellows, oranges and purples. No blues – the sky's already got them. Maybe some of the Aunts' spirit talk's worn off on me, because when I'm trainpainting, I don't want to insult the Grandfather Thunders. Blue's their colour, at least among my people.

My tag's *Crow*. I was born James Raven, but Aunt Nancy says I've got too much crow in me. No respect for anything, just like my black-winged brothers. And then there's those feathers I found on my pillow that morning. Maybe that's why I pull over. Because in my head, we're kin. Same clan, anyway.

There's times later when maybe I wished I hadn't. I'm still weighing that on a day-to-day basis. But my life's sure on the road to nowhere I could've planned, because of that impulse.

The birds don't leave when I get out of the car, leaving my coffee on the dash. I take a last drag on my cigarette and flick the butt into the snow. Jesus, but it's cold. A *lot* colder here than it was in the freight yards. There I had the cars blocking the wind most of the time. Out here, it comes roaring at me from about as far north as the cold can come. It must be 20, 30 below out here, factoring in the wind chill.

I start to walk towards where the birds have gathered and I go a little colder still, but this time it's inside, like there's frost on my heart.

They've found themselves a man. A dead skin, just lying here in the snow. I don't know what killed him, but I can make an educated guess, considering all he's wearing is a thin, unzipped windbreaker over a T-shirt and chinos. Running shoes on his feet, no socks.

He must've frozen to death.

The crows don't fly off when I approach, which makes me think maybe the dead man's kin, too. That they're here not to eat him, but to see him on his way, like in the old stories. I crouch down beside him, snow crunching under my knee. I can see now he's been in a fight. I take off my paint-stained gloves and reach for his throat, looking for a pulse, but not expecting to find one. He twitches at my touch. I almost fall over backwards when those frosted eyelashes suddenly crack open and he's looking right at me.

He has pale blue eyes – unusual for a skin. They study me for a moment. I see an alcohol haze just on the other side of their calm, lucid gaze. What strikes me at that moment is that I don't see any pain.

Words creep out of his mouth. 'Who – who was it that said, "It is a good day to die"?'

'I don't know,' I find myself answering. 'Some famous chief, I guess. Sitting Bull, maybe.'

Then I realise what I'm doing, having a conversation with a dying man. 'We've got to get you to a hospital.'

'It's bullshit,' he says.

I think he's going to lose his hands. They're blue with the cold. I can't see his feet, but in those thin running shoes, they can't be in much better condition.

'No, you'll be okay,' I lie. 'The doctors'll have you fixed up in no time.'

But he's not talking about the hospital.

'It's never a good day to die,' he tells me. 'You tell Turk that for me.'

My pulse quickens at the name. Everybody on the rez knows Tom McGurk. He's a detective with the NPD that's got this constant hard-on for Indians. He goes out of his way to break our heads, bust the skin hookers, roust the hobo bloods. On the rez, they even say he's killed him a few skins, took their scalps like some old Indian hunter, but I know that's bullshit. Something like that, it would've made the papers. Not because it was skins dying, but for the gory details of the story.

'He did this to you?' I ask. 'Turk did this?'

Now it doesn't seem so odd, finding this drunk brave dying here in the snow. Cops like to beat on us, and I've heard about this before, how they grab some skin, usually drunk, beat the crap out of him, then drive him 20 miles or so out of town and dump him. Let him walk back to the city if he's up for some more punishment.

But on a night like this …

The dying man tries to grab my arm, but his frozen fingers don't work anymore. It's like all he's got is this lump on the end of his arm, hard as a branch, banging against me. It brings a sour taste up my throat.

'My name,' he says, 'is John Walking Elk. My father was an Oglala Sioux from the Pine Ridge rez and my mother was a Kickaha from just up the road. Don't let me be forgotten.'

'I … I won't.'

'Be a warrior for me.'

I figure he wants his revenge on Turk, the one he can't take for himself, and I find myself nodding. Me, who's never won a fight in his life. By the time I realise we have different definitions for the word 'warrior,' my life's completely changed.

***

I remember the look on my mom's face the first time I got arrested for vandalism. She didn't know whether to be happy or mad. See, she never had to worry about me drinking or doing drugs. And while she knew that trainpainting was against the law, she understood that I saw it as bringing Beauty into the world.

'At least you're not a drunk like your father's brother was,' she finally said.

Uncle Frank was an alcoholic who died in the city, choking on his own puke after an all-night bender. We've no idea what ever happened to my father, Frank's brother. One day we woke up and he was gone, vanished like the promises in all those treaties the chiefs signed.

'But why can't you paint on canvases like other artists do?' she wanted to know.

I don't know where to begin to explain.

Part of it's got to do with the transitory nature of painting freight cars. Nobody can stand there and criticise it the way you can a painting hanging in a gallery or a museum, or even a mural on the side of some building. By the time you realise you're looking at a painting on the side of a boxcar, the locomotive's already pulled that car out of your sight and further on down the line. All you're left with is the memory of it; what you saw, and what you have to fill in from your own imagination.

Part of it's got to do with the act itself. Sneaking into the freight yards, taking the chance on getting beat up or arrested by the rent-a-cops, having to work so fast. But if you pull it off, you've put a piece of Beauty back into the world, a piece of art that'll go travelling right across the continent. Most artists are lucky to get a show in one gallery. But trainpainters … our work's being shown from New York City to LA and every place in between.

And I guess part of it's got to with the self-image you get to carry around inside you. You're an outlaw, like the chiefs of old, making a stand against the big white machine that just rolls across the country, knocking down anything that gets in its way.

So it fills something in my life, but even with the trainpainting, I've always felt like there was something missing, and I don't mean my father. Though trainpainting's the only time I feel complete, it's still like I'm doing the right thing, but for the wrong reason. Too much me, not enough everything else that's in the world.

***

I'm holding John Walking Elk in my arms when he dies. I'm about to pick him up when this rattle goes through his chest and his head sags away from me, hanging at an unnatural angle. I feel something in that moment, like a breath touching the inside of my skin, passing through me. That's when I know for sure he's gone.

I sit there until the cold starts to work its way through my coat, then I get a firmer grip on the dead man and stagger back to my car with him. I don't take him back to the city, report his death to the same authorities that killed him. Instead, I gather my courage and take him to Jack Whiteduck.

I don't know how much I really buy into the mysteries. I mean, I like the idea of them, the way you hear about them in the old stories. Honouring the Creator and the Grandfather Thunders, taking care of this world we've all found ourselves living in, thinking crows can be kin, being respectful to the spirits, that kind of thing. But it's usually an intellectual appreciation, not something I feel in my gut. Like I said, trainpainting's about the only time it's real for me. Finding Beauty, creating Beauty, painting her face on the side of a freight car.

But with Jack Whiteduck it's different. He makes you believe. Makes you see with the heart instead of the eye. Everybody feels that way about him, though if you ask most people, they'll just say he makes them nervous. The corporate braves who run the casino, the kids sniffing glue and gasoline under the highway bridge and making fun of the elders, the drunks hitting the bars off the rez – press them hard enough and even they'll admit, yeah, something about the old man puts a hole in their party that all the good times run out of.

He makes you remember, though what you're remembering is hard to put into words. Just that things could be different, I guess. That once our lives were different, and they could be that way again, if we give the old ways a chance. White people, they think of us as either the noble savage, or the drunk in the gutter, puking on their shoes. They'll come to the powwows, take their pictures and buy some souvenirs, sample the frybread, maybe try to dance. They'll walk by us in the city, not able to meet our gaze, either because they're scared we'll try to rob them, or hurt them, or they just don't want to accept our misery, don't want to allow that it exists in the same perfect world they live in.

We're one or the other to them, and they don't see a whole lot of range in between. Trouble is, a lot of us see ourselves the same way. Whiteduck doesn't let you. As a people, we were never perfect – nobody is – but there's something about him that tells us we don't have to be losers either.

Whiteduck's not the oldest of the elders on the rez, but he's the one everybody goes to when they've got a problem nobody else can solve.

So I drive out to his cabin, up past Pineback Road, drive in as far as I can, then I get out and walk the rest of the way, carrying John Walking Elk's body in my arms, following the narrow path that leads through the drifts to Whiteduck's cabin. I don't know where I get the strength.

There's a glow spilling out of the windows – a flickering light of some kind. Oil lamp, I'm guessing, or a candle. Whiteduck doesn't have electricity. Doesn't have a phone or running water either. The door opens before I reach it and Whiteduck stands silhouetted against the yellow light like he's expecting me. I feel a pinprick of nervousness settle in between my shoulder blades as I keep walking forward, boots crunching in the snow.

He's not as tall as I remember, but when I think about it, that's always been the case, the few times I've seen him. I guess I build him up in my mind. He's got the broad Kickaha face, but there's no fat on his body. Pushing close to 70 now, his features are a roadmap of brown wrinkles, surrounding a pair of eyes that are darker than the wings of the crows that pulled me into this in the first place.

'Heard you were coming,' he says.

I guess my face reflects my confusion.

'I saw the dead man's spirit pass by on the morning wind,' he explains, 'and the manitou told me you were bringing his body to me. You did the right thing. After what the whites did to him, they've got no more business with this poor dead skin.'

He steps aside to let me go in, and I angle the body so I can get it through the door. Whiteduck indicates that I should lay it out on his bed.

There's not much to the place. A pot-bellied cast-iron stove with a fire burning in it. A wooden table with a couple of chairs, all of them handmade from cedar. A kind of counter running along one wall with a sink in it and a pail underneath to catch the run-off. A chest under the counter that holds his food, I'm guessing, since his clothes are hanging from pegs on the wall above his bed. Bunches of herbs are drying over the counter, tied together with thin strips of leather. In the far corner is a pile of furs, mostly beaver.

The oil lamp's sitting on the table, but moment by moment, it becomes less necessary as the sun keeps rising outside.

'*Mico'mis*,' I begin, giving him the honorific, but I don't know where to go with my words past it.

'That's good,' he says. 'Too many boys your age don't have respect for their elders.'

I'd take offence at the designation of 'boy' – I'll be 21 in the spring – but compared with him, I guess that's what I am.

'What will you do with the body?' I ask.

'That's not a body,' he tells me. 'It's a man, got pushed off the wheel before his time. I'm going to make sure his spirit knows where it needs to go next.'

'But – what will you do with what he's left behind?'

'Maybe a better question would be, what will you do with yourself?'

I remember John Walking Elk's dying words. *Be a warrior for me.*

'I'm going to set things right,' I say.

Whiteduck looks at me, and all that nervousness that's been hiding somewhere just between my shoulder blades comes flooding through me. I get the feeling he can read my every thought and feeling. I get the feeling he can see the whole of my life laid out, what's been and what's to come, and that he's going to tell me how to live it right. But he only nods.

'There's some things we need to learn for ourselves,' he says finally. 'But you think on this, James Raven. There's more than one way to be a warrior. You can, and should, fight for the people, but being a warrior also means a way of living. It's something you forge in your heart to make the spirit strong and it doesn't mean you have to go out and kill anything, even when it's vermin that you feel need exterminating. Everything we do comes back to us – goes for whites the same as skins.'

I was wrong. He does have advice.

'You're saying I should just let this slide?' I ask. 'That Turk gets away with killing another one of us?'

'I'm saying, do what your heart tells you you must do, *no'cicen*. Listen to it, not to some old man living by himself in a cabin in the woods.'

'But –'

'Now go,' he says, firm but not unfriendly. 'We both have tasks ahead of us.'

***

I leave there feeling confused. Like I said, I'm not a fighter. Whenever I have gotten into a fight, I got my ass kicked. But there's something just not right about letting Turk get away with this. Finding the dying man has lodged a hot coal of anger in my head, put a shiver of ice through my heart.

I figure what I need now is a gun, and I know where to get it.

***

'I don't know,' Jackson says. 'I'm not really in the business of selling weapons. What do you want a gun for anyway?'

That Jackson Red Dog has never been in prison is an ongoing mystery on the rez. It's an open secret that he has variously been, and by all accounts still is, a bootlegger, a drug dealer, a fence, a smuggler, and pretty much anything else against the law that's on this side of murder and mayhem. 'I draw the line at killing people,' he's said. 'There's no percentage in it. Today's enemy could be tomorrow's customer.'

He's in his fifties now, a dark-skinned Indian with a greying ponytail, standing about six-two with a linebacker's build and hands so big he can hold a cantaloupe the way you or I might hold an apple. He lives on the southern edge of the rez and works out of the back of that general store on the highway, just inside the boundaries of the rez, where he can comfortably do business with our people and anybody willing to drive up from the city.

'I figure it's something I need,' I tell him. 'You got any that can't be traced?'

He laughs. 'You watch too much TV, kid.'

'I'm serious,' I say. 'I've got the money. Cash.'

I'd cleaned out my savings account before driving over to the store. I found Jackson in the back as usual, holding court in a smoky room filled with skins his age and older, sitting around a pot-bellied stove, none of them saying much. This is his office, though come spring, it moves out onto the front porch. When I said I needed to talk to him, he took me outside and lit a cigarette, offered me one.

'How much money?' Jackson asks.

'How much is the gun?' I reply.

I'm not stupid. I tell him what I've got in my pocket – basically enough to cover next month's rent and a couple of cases of beer – and that's what he'll be charging me. He looks me over, then gives me a slow nod.

'Maybe I could put you in touch with a guy that can get you a gun,' he says.

Which I translate as, 'We can do business.'

'Just tell me,' he adds. 'Who're you planning to kill?'

'Nobody you'd know.'

'I know everybody.'

All things considered, that's probably true.

'Nobody you'd care about,' I tell him.

'That's good enough for me.'

There's laughter in his eyes, like he knows more than he's letting on, but I can't figure out what it is.

***

The gun's heavy in my pocket as I leave the store and drive south to the city. I don't know any more about handguns than I do fighting, but Jackson offers me some advice as he counts my money.

'You ever shoot one of these before?' he asks.

I shake my head.

'What you've got there's a .38 Smith and Wesson. It's got a kick, and to tell you the truth, the barrel's been cut down some and it's had a ramp foresight added. Whoever did the work, wasn't exactly a gunsmith. The sight's off, so even if you were some fancy shot, you'd have trouble with it. Best thing you can do is notch a few crosses on the tips of your bullets and aim for the body. Bullet goes in and makes a tiny hole, comes back out again and takes away half the guy's back.'

I feel a little sick, listening to him, but then I think of John Walking Elk dying in the snow, of Turk sitting in his precinct, laughing it off. I wonder how many others he's left to die the way he did Walking Elk. I get to thinking about some of the other drunks I've heard of that were supposed to have died of exposure, nobody quite sure what they were doing out in the middle of nowhere, or how they got there.

'You planning to come out of this alive?' Jackson asks when I'm leaving.

'It's not essential.'

He gives me another of those slow nods of his. 'That'll make it easier. You got the time, tell Turk it's been a long time coming.'

That stops me in the doorway.

'How'd you know it was Turk?' I ask.

He laughs. 'Christ, kid. This is the rez. Everybody here knows your business before you do. What, did you think you were excused?'

I think about that on the drive down to the city, how gossip travels from one end of the rez to the other. It's like my paintings, travelling across the country. I don't plan where they go, how they go, they just go. It's not something you can control.

I'm not worried about anybody up here knowing what I'm planning. I can't think of a single skin who would save Turk's life if they came upon him dying, even if all they had to do was toss him a nickel. I'm just hoping my mom doesn't hear about it too soon. I'd like to explain to her why I'm doing this, but I'm not entirely sure myself, and I know if I go to her before I do it, she'll talk me out of it. And if that doesn't work, she'll sit on me until the impulse goes away.

***

There are crows lined up on the power lines and leafing the trees for miles down the road. Dozens of them, more than I've ever seen. I know their roost is up around Pineback Road, near Whiteduck's cabin. A rez inside the rez. But they're safe there. Nobody on the rez takes pot shots at our black-feathered cousins.

When I come up on the entrance to the gravel pit, I see the crows are still there as well. I stand on the brakes and the car goes slewing towards the ditch. I only just manage to keep it on the road. Then I sit there looking in my rearview mirror. I see a man standing there among the crows, John Walking Elk, leaning on the gate at the entrance and big as life.

I back up until I'm abreast the gates and look out the passenger window at him. He smiles and gives me a wave. He's still wearing that thin windbreaker, the T-shirt and chinos, the running shoes without socks. The big difference is, he's not dead. He's not even dying.

I light a cigarette with shaking hands and look at him for a long moment before I finally open my door. I walk around the car, the wind knifing through my jacket, but Walking Elk's not even shivering. The weight of the gun in my pocket makes me feel like I'm walking at an angle, tilted over on one side.

'Don't worry,' he says when I get near. 'You're not losing it. I'm still dead.'

And seeing a walking, talking dead man isn't losing it?

'Only why'd you have to go leave me with that shaman?' he adds.

My throat's as dry and thick as it was when I did my first two vision quests. I haven't done the other two yet. Trainpainting's distracted me from them.

'I ... I thought it was the right thing to do,' I manage after a long moment.

'I suppose. But he's shaking his rattle and burning smudge sticks, singing the death songs that'll see me on my way. Makes it hard not to go.'

I'm feeling a little confused. 'And that's a bad thing because ...?'

He shrugs. 'I'm kind of enjoying this chance to walk around one last time.'

I think I understand. Nobody knows what's waiting for us when we die. It's fine to be all stoic and talk about wheels turning and everything, but if it was me, I don't think I'd be in any hurry to go either.

'So you're going to shoot Turk, are you?' the dead man says.

'What, is it written on my forehead or something?'

Walking Elk laughs. 'You know the rez ...'

'Everybody knows everybody else's business.'

He nods. 'You think it's bad on the rez, you should try the spiritworld.'

'No thanks.'

'You try and kill Turk,' he says, 'you might be finding out firsthand, whether you want to or not.' He gives a slow shake of his head. 'I've got to give it to you, though. I don't think I'd have the balls to see it through.'

'I don't know that I do either,' I admit. 'It just seems like a thing I've got to do.'

'Won't bring me back,' Walking Elk says. 'Once the shaman finishes his ceremony, I'll be out of here.'

'It's not just for you,' I tell him. 'It's for the others he might kill.'

The dead man only shakes his head at that. 'You think it starts and stops with Tom McGurk? Hell, this happens anyplace you got a cold climate and white cops. They just get tired of dealing with us. I had a cousin who died the same way up in Saskatchewan, another in Colorado. And when they haven't got the winter to do their job for them, they find other ways.'

'That's why they've got to be held accountable,' I say.

'You got some special sight that'll tell you which cop's decent and which isn't?'

I know there are good cops. Hell, Chief Morningstar's brother is a detective with the NPD. But we only ever seem to get to deal with the ones that have a hard-on for us.

I shake my head. 'But I know Turk hasn't got any redeeming qualities.'

He sighs. 'Wish I could have one of those cigarettes of yours.'

I shake one out of the pack and light it for him, surprised that he can hold it, that he can suck in the smoke and blow it out again, just like a living man. I wonder if this is like offering tobacco to the manitou.

'How come you're trying to talk me out of this?' I ask him. 'You're the one who told me to be a warrior for you.'

He blows out another lungful of smoke. 'You think killing's what makes a warrior?'

'Now you sound like Whiteduck.'

He laughs. 'I've been compared to a lot of things, but never a shaman.'

'So what is it you want from me?' I ask. 'Why'd you ask me to be a warrior for you?'

'You look like a good kid,' he says. 'I didn't want to see you turn out like me. I want you to be a good man, somebody to make your parents proud. Make yourself proud.'

I've no idea what would make my father proud. But my mom, all she wants is for me to get a decent job and stay out of trouble. I can't seem to manage the first and here I am, walking straight into the second. But he's annoying me all the same. Funny how fast you can go from feeling awed to being fed up.

'You don't think I have any pride?' I ask.

'I don't know the first damn thing about you,' he says, 'except you were decent enough to stop for a dying man.'

He takes a last drag and drops his butt in the snow. Studies something behind me, over my shoulder, but I don't turn. He's got a look I recognise – his gaze is turned inward.

'See, someone told me that once,' he goes on, his gaze coming back to me, 'except I didn't listen. I worked hard, figured I'd earned the right to play hard, too. Trouble is, I played too hard. Lost my job. Lost my family. Lost my pride. It's funny how quick you can lose everything and never see it coming.'

I think about my uncle Frank, but I don't say anything.

'I guess it was my grandma told me,' the dead man says, 'how there's no use in bringing hurt into the world. We do that well enough on our own. You meet someone, you try to give them a little life instead. Let them take something positive away from whatever time they spend with you. Makes the world a better place in the short and the long haul.'

I nod. 'Putting Beauty in the world.'

'That's a warrior's way, too. Stand up for what's right. Ya-ha-hey. Make a noise. I can remember powwow dancing, there'd be so many of us out there, following the drumbeat and the singing, you'd swear you could feel the ground tremble and shake underfoot. But these last few years, I've been too drunk to dance and the only noise I make is when I'm puking.'

I know what he means about the powwows, that feeling you can't get anywhere else except maybe a sweat, and that's a more contemplative kind of a thing. In a powwow, it's all rhythm and dancing, everybody individual, but we're all part of something bigger than us at the same time. There's nothing like it in the world.

'Yeah,' the dead man says. 'We used to be a proud people for good reason. We can still be a proud people, but sometimes our reasons aren't so good anymore. Sometimes it's not for how we stand tall and honour the ancestors and the spirits with grace and beauty. Sometimes it's for how we beat the enemy at their own game.'

'You're starting to sound pretty old school for a drunk,' I tell him.

He shakes his head. 'I'm just repeating things I was told when I was growing up. Things I didn't feel were important enough to pay attention to.'

'I pay attention,' I say. 'At least I try to.'

He gives me a considering look. 'I'm not saying it's right or wrong, but what part of what you were taught has to do with that gun in your pocket?'

'The part about standing up for ourselves. The part about defending our people.'

'I suppose.'

'I hear what you're saying,' I tell him. 'But I still have to go down to the city.'

He gives me a nod.

'Sure you do,' he says. 'Why would you listen to a dead drunk like me?' He chuckles. 'And I mean dead in the strictest sense of the word.' He pushes away from the gates. 'Time I was going. Whiteduck's doing a hell of a job with his singing. I can feel the pull of that someplace else getting stronger and stronger.'

I don't know what to say. Good luck? Goodbye?

'Spare another of those smokes?' he asks.

'Sure.'

I shake another one free and light it for him. He pats my cheek. The touch of his hand is still cold, but there's movement in all the fingers. It's not like the block of ice that tried to grab my sleeve this morning.

'You're a good kid,' he says.

And then he fades away.

I stand there for a long time, looking at the gate, at the crows, feeling the wind on my face, bitter and cold. Then I walk back to my car.

***

Before I first started trainpainting, I thought graffiti was just vandalism, a crime that might include a little creativity, but a crime nonetheless. Then one day I was driving back to the rez and I had to wait at a crossing for a freight train to go by. It was the one near Brendon Road, where the tracks go uphill and the freights tend to slow down because of the incline.

So I'm sitting there, bored, a little impatient more than anything else, and suddenly I see all this art going by. Huge murals painted on the sides of the boxcars and all I can do is stare, thinking, where's all that coming from? Who did these amazing paintings?

And then, just like that, there's this collision of the synchronicity at seeing those painted cars and this feeling I've had of wanting to do something different with the iconology I grew up with on the rez – you know, like the bead patterns my mom sews on her powwow dresses. I turn my car back around and drive for the freight yards, stopping off at a hardware store along the way.

I felt a kinship to whoever it was that was painting those boxcars, a complete understanding of what they'd done and why they'd done it. And I wanted to send them a message back. I wanted to tell them, I've seen your work and here's my side of the conversation.

That was the day Crow was born and my first thunderbird joined that ongoing hobo gallery that the freights take from city to city, across the country.

***

It's a long ride down to the city. I leave the crows behind, but the winter comes with me, wind blowing snow down the highway behind my car, howling like the cries of dying buffalo. It's full night by the time I'm in the downtown core. It's so cold, there's nobody out, not even the hookers. I drive until I reach the precinct house where Turk works and park across the street from it. And then I sit there, my hand in my pocket, fingers wrapped around the handle of the gun. Comes to me, I can't kill a man, not even a man like Turk. Maybe if he was standing right in front of me and we were fighting. Maybe if he was threatening my mom. Maybe I could do it in the heat of the moment. But not like this, waiting to ambush him like in some Hollywood Western. But I know I've got to do something.

My gaze travels from the precinct house to the stores alongside the street where I'm parked. I don't even hesitate. I reach in the back for a plastic bag full of unused spray cans and I get out of the car to meet that cold wind head on.

I don't know how long I've got, so I work even faster than usual. It's not a boxcar, but the paint goes on the bricks and glass as easily as it does on wooden slats. It doesn't even clog up in the muzzle – maybe the Grandfather Thunders are giving me a helping hand. I do the crow first, thunderbird style, a yellow one to make the black and red words stand out when I write them along the spread of its wings.

TOM McGURK KILLS INDIANS.

I add a roughly-rendered brave with the daubed clay of a ghostdancer masking his features. He's lying face-up to the sky, power lines flowing up out of his head as his spirit leaves his body, a row of crosses behind him – not Christian crosses, but ours, the ones that stand for the four quarters of the world.

HE HAULS THEM OUT OF TOWN, I write in big sloppy letters, AND LEAVES THEM TO DIE IN THE COLD.

I'm starting a monster, a cannibal windigo all white fur and blood, raging in the middle of a winter storm, when a couple of cops stop their squad car abreast of where I parked my own. They're on their way back to the precinct, I guess, ending their shift and look what they've found. I keep spraying the paint, my fingers frozen into a locked position from the cold.

'Okay, Tonto,' one of them says. 'Drop the can and assume the position.'

I couldn't drop the can if I wanted to. I can barely move my fingers. So I keep spraying on the paint until one of them gives me a sucker punch in the kidneys, knocks me down, kicks me as I'm falling. I lose the spray can and it goes rattling across the sidewalk. I lose the gun, too, which I forgot I was carrying.

There's a long moment of silence as we're all three staring at that gun lying there on the pavement.

They really work me over then.

***

So as I sit here in County, waiting for my trial, I think back on all this and find I'm not sorry that I didn't try to shoot Turk. I'm not sorry that I got busted in the middle of vandalising a building right across the street from the precinct house, either. But I do regret not getting rid of the gun first.

The charges against me are vandalism, possession of an unlicensed weapon, carrying a concealed weapon, and resisting arrest. I'll be doing some time, heading up to the pen, but I won't be alone in there. Like Leonard Peltier says on that song he does with Robbie Robertson, 'It's the fastest growing rez in the country,' and he should know, they've kept him locked up long enough.

But something good came out of all of this. The police didn't have time to get rid of my graffiti before the press showed up. I guess it was a slow news day because pictures of those paintings showed up on the front page of all three of the daily papers, and made the news on every channel. You might think, what's good about that? It's like prime evidence against me. But I'm not denying I painted those images and words, and the good thing is, people started coming forward, talking about how the same thing had happened to them. Cops would pick them up when the bars closed and would dump them, ten, 20 miles out of town. They identified Turk and a half dozen others by name.

So I'm sitting in county, and I don't know where Turk is, but he's been suspended without pay while the investigation goes on, and it looks like they've got to deal with this fair and square, because everybody's on their case now, right across the city – whites, blacks, skins, everybody. They're all watching what the authorities do, writing editorials, writing letters to the editor, holding protest demonstrations.

This isn't going away.

So if I've got to do some jail time, I'm thinking the sacrifice is worth it.

My cousin Tommy drives my mom down from the rez on a regular basis to visit me. The first time she comes, she stands there looking at me and I don't know what she's thinking, but I wait for the blast I'm sure's coming my way. But all she says is, 'Couldn't you have stuck with the boxcars?' Then she holds me a long while, tells me I'm stupid, but how she's so proud of me. Go figure.

Some of the Creek aunts have connections in the city and they found me a good lawyer, so I'm not stuck with some public defender. I like him. His name's Marty Caine and I can tell he doesn't care what colour my skin is. He tells me that what I did was 'morally correct, if legally indefensible, but we'll do our damnedest to get you out of this anyway.' But nobody's fooled. We all know that whatever happens to the cops, they're still going to make a lesson with me. When it comes to skins, they always do.

***

I see Walking Elk one more time before the trial. I'm lying on my bunk, staring up at the ceiling, thinking how, when I get out, I'm going on those last two vision quests. I need to be centred. I need to talk to the

Creator and find out what my place is in the world, who I'm supposed to be so that my being here in this world makes a difference to what happens to the people in my life, to the ground I walk on and the spirits that share this world with us.

I hear a rustle of cloth and turn my head to see John Walking Elk sitting on the other bunk. He's still wearing the clothes he died in. I assume he's still dead. This time he's got the smokes and he offers me one.

I swing my feet to the floor and take the cigarette, let him light it for me.

'How come you're still here?' I ask.

He shrugs. 'Maybe I'm not,' he says. 'Maybe Whiteduck sent my spirit on and you're just dreaming.'

I smile. 'You'd think if I was going to dream, I'd dream myself out of this place.'

'You'd think.'

We smoke our cigarettes for a while.

'I'm in all the papers,' Walking Elk says after awhile. 'And that's your doing. They wrote about how Whiteduck sent my body down to the city, how the cops drove me up there and dumped me in the snow. Family I didn't even know I had anymore came to the funeral. From the rez, from Pine Ridge, hell, from places I never even heard of before.'

I wasn't there, but I heard about it. Skins came from all over the country to show their solidarity. Mom told me that the Warriors' Society up on the rez organised it.

'Yeah, I heard it was some turnout,' I say. 'Made the cover of *Time* and everything.'

Walking Elk nods. 'You came through for me,' he says. 'On both counts.'

I know what he's talking about. I can hear his voice against the northern winds that were blowing that day without even trying.

Don't let me be forgotten.

Be a warrior for me.

But I don't know what to say.

'Even counted some coup for yourself,' he adds.

'Wasn't about that,' I tell him.

'I know. I just wanted to thank you. I had to come by to tell you that. I lived a lot of years, just looking for something in the bottom of a bottle. There was nothing else left for me. Didn't think anybody'd ever look at me like I was a man again. But you did. And those people that came to the funeral? They were remembering me as a man, too, not just some drunk who got himself killed by a cop.'

He stands up. I'm curious. Is he going to walk away through the wall, or just fade away like he did before?

'Any plans for when you get out?' he asks.

I think about that for a moment.

'I was thinking of going back to painting boxcars,' I say. 'You see where painting buildings got me.'

'There's worse places to be,' he tells me. 'You could be dead.'

I don't know if I blinked, or woke up, but the next thing I know, he's gone and I'm alone in my cell. But I hear an echo of laughter and I've still got the last of that cigarette he gave me smouldering in my hand.

'Ya-ha-hey,' I say softly and butt it out in the ashtray.

Then I stretch out on the bed again and contemplate the ceiling some more.

I think maybe I was dead, or half-dead, anyway, before I found John Walking Elk dying in the snow. I was going through the motions of life, instead of really living, and there's no excuse for that. It's not something I'll let happen to me again.

Going Bad
Alison L R Davies

Feeling like no other as the tender meat of my womb expands and threads of vein act like glue to rotting gristle. Something moves, but not in a separate way. No, it almost leeches upon this watery cavern; this gummed up tissue hole in the deepest part of my belly. I'm waiting for the blood to come, in discoloured pools, in a vomit-beaded thatch of hair and a trickle that could be a stream of urine. The pain is beside itself, and I am just a vessel for what went wrong, but it hasn't always been this way.

As a girl in my daisy slip print with nothing but the pinkest buds of breast, I was protected from this pain. And even when the first rains began staining my panties with speckles of iron, even then I could stand it. It was a righteous agony, it was clean and fresh and it made me cry. It meant I was turning, and that had to be a good thing. Mama would rest a reddened hand upon my shoulder, and whisper assurances. *You're a big girl now, you'll see, it's all for the best.* At night when the dark shadow came I held onto her words. But as I sit here rocking in the darkness, feet acting as a pivot and nothing but a broken radio sound for comfort, I wonder. Because really, that was when it happened, when it all turned sour.

There is no distinct moment that presents itself; instead it is a gathering of events, of words left to fester. The years have added their weight, pressing the swell of my abdomen with their cruel considerations. As I grew, I learned that this place within me could be so brutal and yet provide such pleasure. It was not just the seat of my womanhood, or some morbid monthly sacrifice. It was everything essential to my being. I am going bad from the inside. I have always known this. And as I pummel the pastry of my belly, I hope for an end.

***

When Martin comes home he finds me stretched, a pale linen torso pointing at diagonals along the bed. He nuzzles my hair with his nose and plants a kiss on the back of my head.

'Is it bad again?'

Again. Said without hostility and yet I know that he is tiring of my monthly rituals.

'Is there anything I can do?' He continues.

'No.' The word sinks into the pillow, and I try to turn over. Martin stares down, concern makes his forehead appear unusually large.

'No. I'll be okay once the tablets kick in.'

'Of course you will, dear,' he says.

You see, nobody believes me, and that's the real tragedy of it. Not that they think I make it up; it's obvious what I go through. But they look at me with sympathetic smiles, synthetic in their sadness, when I tell them what is really happening. I've had all the usual tests; the ones where they cut you open just below the naval and insert a telescopic tube. I've got the scar; a mini crucifix raised in lumpy white, it acts as a reminder that I must be going mad.

'There's nothing to worry about, Mrs Snider.' The doctor's told me. But I beg to differ.

'Just because they didn't find anything, doesn't mean that it's not happening,' I told Martin the day we left the hospital.

'Sshhh dear. It's over now. You just need to rest and try the new medication they've prescribed.'

But it didn't do any good. I knew it wouldn't.

We have dinner together that night; me forcing the food down my gullet, feeling each broken morsel. It might as well be salted glass as it sticks to the back of my throat. But Martin doesn't notice; the zealous way he clears his plate has to be an act. He's over-compensating for my sour presence.

'Why don't we try again?' he says, licking his lips.

I feel sick and nudge my plate in his direction.

'A baby could the be answer to all our problems.' He smiles.

'You mean it could be the answer for me, could stop me from imagining I'm going bad.'

'Well yes, and that too.'

'It will never happen,' I say, and I bite my lip. It's the only way I can control the raging tears inside.

'There's something not right in here.' I press my stomach. 'I can tell.'

'But we've been there before, you've had all the tests.'

'That doesn't matter,' I snap. 'They must have missed something.'

'You want to have our baby don't you?'

I nod. I'm afraid if I speak it will all come out.

He smiles then, and I see the tiny purple veins of his eyes flex. 'It has to be worth a try.'

Yes, anything's worth a try if it will make me feel human again. I offer him my hand and he leads me to the bedroom.

I can't pretend what follows doesn't soothe my heart, but inside, my womb breaks open and another part of her fibre extends a sticky finger beneath my flesh. It pokes at the fat, at the heaving coat that I have become, and as my husband enters me, I am separated from this inner sanctum. He might as well have slipped a length of wire, a hooked coat hanger end up inside my slippery shaft, because that's what I feel. The piercing of a needle, the weeping of tissue engulfed in flame, it's all there in my throbbing tubes. I scream, but he mistakes it for pleasure. I push and thrash, but my movements are likened to those in a dance of animal passion. There is nothing I can do until his seed is dispelled.

'Bastard,' I whisper as he comes. Bastard, bastard, bastard. But then I remind myself that this curse is not his doing. He kisses me hard, his slick tongue caressing the warmth of my mouth. I hate sex.

***

Four months later and the sewage that has become my womb is not alone. The gluey substance that drips a continual path smells of phlegm and earth and rot. I watch as my stomach distends, an awkward ruddy balloon that pushes my belly button inside out. All the time I'm greeted by smiles, by looks of admiration from passers-by who cannot possibly know of my plight. They think this is something to rejoice. Their gaping mouths and sugary words inflame me.

'How lovely; when's it due?'

'Oh you must be so happy.'

'You're positively blooming.'

I want to bang their heads together, such silly people, can they not see the decay that weeps down my legs? Can they not smell the sour rubbish stink as this new wart grows inside? I want to cut it out. I want to show the world what is really going on here, but I know that they would only think me mad, and I'm much cleverer than that.

Martin came with me on that first visit. We sat in china walls, enclosed and supported by people in white cotton uniforms. He held my hand, *so proud*, he kept saying, *I'm so very proud of you*. When they showed us in, I felt an enormous pressure on my bladder, as if everything was being pushed aside by the evil. I sat in brown leather, feeling like a sack of potatoes. I watched the thin lines, like scratches, around the doctor's mouth as he spoke, but nothing seemed to sink in.

'Once you've had your baby, you should find the painful symptoms of your period decrease. It's quite common in cases like yours. I'm sure you'll be glad to know that.'

'I don't think so,' I said, but Martin tweaked my hand and mouth into silence.

'So everything looks okay?' he asked.

'Yes, Mr Snider, everything looks fine. Your wife is expecting a perfectly healthy baby.'

Perfectly. I couldn't think of anything further from the truth.

'Congratulations to you both,' the doctor added.

I didn't smile, and I could see that he felt uncomfortable with that. Why would I not provide the usual accompaniment of pleasure that was expected on these occasions? Because I knew nothing could change the rot inside, and now that something shared the space, something small and needy and desperate for nurture, things were bound to get messy.

***

That night I dreamt of Armageddon, of sweet decay in all its glory. I saw the fortress in me break and the castle walls crumble, and with it came a rush of seedlings, hungry-faced ogres spilling blood upon the cobbled surface. There was no time to run. I was trapped, swamped in the stampede. And there, appraising the destruction from the battlements, he stood, the angry warlord of my torment. He had no face of which to speak. There was only a hole that folded in on itself, and skin that rippled like a shrivelled date, turning and twisting and seething with venom. Then I realised, it wasn't a head at all but a thing that represented my sex, an abomination with withered petals and bruised flaps that drooped in the sunlight. It beckoned me close, it offered itself on the brow of the hill, unravelling until I was so close I could smell the rot and I wanted to push my fingers in deep, to scrape the badness out.

Facing my secret place, I had nowhere to run. I watched as a trickle of spittle smoothed a path down this sluggish creature. And then the spittle became richer, heavier, stained with things that should never have seen the light of day. Projectile, it extended a stream of bitter, colourless fluid that drenched me, and I screamed, my voice rising up with all the others who were slaughtered by this evil army. When I awoke, my husband was bearing down on me, his warm body smothering me in kisses.

'*Just a nightmare, that's all. Just a silly nightmare.*'

Nightmares are funny things. They have a way of getting under your skin. I remember one in particular as a girl.

I was about 13 at the time. It was recurring, a train of events that left me feeling broken and bruised. But always I followed the journey; the fusty carriage became the sheets around my head, like an oily turban holding everything in. Then came the gentle motion at first hypnotic and then picking up speed like thundering tracks, and the fusion of steely energy. Sparks, always sparks, screeching on iron girders and me feeling sick, knowing that something was wrong. But how could I stop it? I was only a child, and like most journeys, I couldn't quite remember where it went. It moved so fast and never seemed to end. Until, gasping for air, my tattered breath sought the comfort of furry darkness and I would wake up. Above me, there were voices that snaked their content in whispers, reassuring and then joining to form one familiar sound. 'Ssh now. It's all right. No need to worry or wake your Ma.'

Daddy was right. I was a silly girl who needed to grow up. But it didn't stop the tears. There were always plenty of those to dampen my pillow and leave me snivelling into the night.

***

It is six months now. Six brittle-edged months, travelling on nerves, on eggshells of my own making. It is still too early for the main event, and yet I will it with all my heart. Martin no longer regards me with kindness. I can see he is waiting, only waiting for the day I produce his heir, and then I'll be gone. Out on my heel with all my foolish machinations. I have become what I feared, a machine for human flesh. But no-one can see the disease that breeds, or the fact that my seedling feeding on the rot inside will only make it worse than I. It moves within me, charging at my bladder, at my tired intestinal wall. I cannot sleep, and food revolts me. Everything smells of vomit and tastes like the gritty phlegm at the back of my throat. The pain still comes in angry waves, demonic surges of power that grip the boundaries of my mind. I must have it out. I must …

When in the choked light of early morning I feel something split, and the lip extends to reveal a flood of juice, I know that it is coming. At last, I have no care that it is way too early. I just want it over. I tumble from my bed, all arms and raggedy legs, like some overweight ball of clown rolling to the bathroom. I lock the door and squeeze myself in.

Give up, it urges. *Give up the fight.*

But there is no fight left in me.

The pain is ticking the minutes off, serrating the edges of my gut in short, perfectly timed bursts. It doesn't matter. I am hoping that the birth of this thing will bring with it the decay of years. Outside, someone is shouting. I recognise Martin's throaty tones. He is scared, but not for me.

'Let me in, baby,' he says.

My stomach jerks. I scream, but it is drowned by a dull banging, a jabbing sound of bone and wood. Air rushes, air and something else that chills. My hips ache. They long for the cool freedom of release that only a cloud of breath can provide. My hands massage the lump beneath my skin, and my fingers are no longer encouraging. They are savage as they push and stretch. I squeeze hard, biting my wrist to blot out the pain. There is no time for polite intervention or emotion. And then, in a sudden surge of exhaustion, it is there before me, peering without eyes into my sweaty face. It is jelly, red and steaming, with snail-like tendrils that reach up. It is twisted, torn at the root from this rotten source of nourishment; an obscenity rejected from my diseased womb.

At last I have proof. I watch as it wriggles; a fat, bloodied worm on my lap. No-one can deny this deformity.

I am yours, it says. *I have suckled on your decay and it has made me this way.*

'No,' I say, but my voice is ruined.

Hold me, it begs. *I am a part of you.*

'Not if I can help it!' I roar.

I do not feel the razor slice my fingers. I don't even know how it got in my hands. I am consumed by an altogether different hurt. I'm amazed at how the ripened surface emits only a thin strain of blood. At how such a tiny, delicate thing can have so many strands, so many cotton veins that knot and weave together. It is even uglier on the inside, but I expected that. And the smell, the terrible, earthy stink of rubbish, of something long dead like the shoots inside me; it was not meant to survive, not on the putrefied scraps my body supplied.

'It is a blessing,' I say.

But is it enough? How can I stop this from ever happening again? Corrosion spreads; it multiplies in mouldy cells; it coagulates and strengthens, leeching off living tissue. This cannot be matched or fought by mortal hand. It is as natural as evolution and equally as dangerous.

The banging sound is getting louder; it fills my head.

'Let me in!' screams Martin. 'Just fucking let me in!'

But I've never really done that, and why should I start now? He has always been an onlooker to circumstance, always audience and never part of the show.

The door shivers, the weight of another hit and he'll be through and able to see the mess that I've created. Maybe then he will believe me.

Go on, it says, whatever *it* might be.

Go on.

***

Once more I am a child, my pretty sheaths of dress about me in a swirl of cherry brightness, a limp doll at my feet, nothing but pale moon skin and glistening rubies. I am free without the weight of adult implication. Nothing can infiltrate my shallow breathing, and I gasp as thin, pre-pubescent bones move with ease.

'Look at me daddy! Look how I fly!'

And I'm spinning now as the eyes above me shake with fear, eyes that split the door in two.

***

'What have you done? What have you done?'

But I ignore the questions.

'It no longer hurts.' I smile.

'But you've killed it. You've killed our child.'

'No, only the badness. It was already dead. It wasn't meant to live.'

Below, my feet slide on a veil of roses, and I glide like a princess; *my princess*, that's what daddy always said. I'm a skater, twirling with the elegance of a child. The river is changing, no longer smooth, and my toes snag on lumps, on swollen clots that I never noticed.

'Oh shit!' It's Martin's face upon me, Martin's tears that tickle my cheeks. 'You're bleeding.'

'It's only the bad stuff,' I whisper. 'Only the rot that I told you about.'

But he doesn't hear. He presses his slippery face against my neck, and I smell a mixture of bed sheets and sweat and lavender oil.

'Don't cry. It's over now,' I say, and I let my petticoats swing again, let the ice tremors find a path up my skirt.

Daddy would be proud of me. He always said I was going bad, that there was something wrong with me inside, because that's what made him do it. If I hadn't been nasty or so filled with pain it would never have happened. Well, there's nothing left now, nothing to probe or hurt or feel. No darkened corners or secrets in the night. The journey is finally over.

'Going bad, Martin,' I say. 'Just going bad, that's all …'

Neighbours From Hell
Graham Masterton

You hear about these people, how they've experienced something so terrible that they totally blank it out, and don't remember that it ever happened at all. Like, they see their sister crushed in an auto accident, and when you ask them about it a couple of years later, they stare at you and say, 'What sister?'

I never personally believed that people could do that. I was convinced that if something really, truly terrible happened to me, I'd be sweating about it every waking moment for the rest of my natural life.

But –

***

It was pretty horrible the way my grandmother died. I was working in The Blue Turtle Bar in Fort Lauderdale last summer when the phone rang and it was Mr Szponder, the super in my mother's apartment building. He said in his rusty old voice that she'd tumbled into a bath of scalding water and that she was now in intensive care at St Philomena's.

'Oh, God. How bad is it?'

'Bad. Thirty percent third-degree burns, that's what they told me. They don't expect her to make it. Not at her age.'

'I'll catch the next flight, okay?'

I asked Eugene for the rest of the week off. Eugene had greasy black curls right down to the collar of his red-and-yellow Hawaiian shirt and a face like somebody had been using a pumpkin for a dartboard. He hefted his big hairy arm around my shoulders and said, 'Jimmy – you take as long as you like.'

'Thanks, Eugene.'

'In fact, why don't you take forever?'

'What do you mean? You're *canning* me? This is my grandmother I'm talking about here. This is the woman who raised me.'

'This is also the middle of the season, and if it's a choice between profit and compassion – well, let's just say that there isn't a Cadillac dealership in town that takes compassion in exchange for late-model Sevilles.'

I could see by the look in his pebbly little eyes that he wasn't going to give way, and it wasn't even worth saying 'Screw you, Eugene.' It just wasn't.

I went back to the tattily-furnished house I was sharing on Broward Street with three inarticulate musicians from Boise, Idaho, and a wide-eyed brunette called Wendiii who thought that the capital of Florida was 'F'.

'Hey, you leaving us, man?' asked the lead guitarist, peering at me through curtains of straggly, sun-bleached hair.

'My grandma's had an accident. They think she's probably going to die.'

'Bummer.'

'Yeah. She practically raised me single-handed after my mom died.'

'You coming back?'

I looked around at the bare-boarded living-room with its broken blinds and its rucked-up rug and every available surface crowded with empty Coors cans. Somehow it seemed as if all the romance had gone out of the Fort Lauderdale lifestyle, as if the sun had gone behind a cloud and a chilly breeze had suddenly started to blow.

'Maybe,' I said.

Wendiii came out of the john, buttoning up her tiny denim shorts. 'You take care, you hear?' she told me, and gave me a long, wet, open-mouthed kiss. 'It's such a pity that you and me never got it on.'

Now she tells me, I thought. But my taxi had drawn up outside, and it was time to go. She lifted her elbows and took a little silver crucifix from around her neck and gave it to me.

'I can't take this.'

'Then borrow it, and bring it back safe.'

***

In Chicago, the sky was dark and the rain came clattering down like bucketfuls of nails. I hurried across the sidewalk outside St Philomena's with a copy of *Newsweek* on top of my head, but it didn't stop water from pouring down the back of my neck. The hospital lobby was lit like a migraine and the corridors were crowded with gurneys and wheelchairs and people arguing and old folks staring into space and nodding as if they absolutely definitely agreed that life wasn't worth living.

A tall, black nurse led me up to intensive care, loping along in front of me with all the loopy grace of a giraffe. My grandmother lay in greenish gloom, her head and her hands wrapped in bandages. Her face was waxy and blotched and her cheeks had collapsed so that you could see the skull underneath. She looked as if she were dead already.

I sat down beside her. 'Grandma? It's me, Jimmy.'

It was a long time before her eyes flickered open, and when they did, I had a chilly feeling of dread. All the blue seemed to have drained from her irises – did you ever see eyes with no colour at all? – and it was obvious that she knew that death was only hours away.

'Jimmy –'

'Mr Szponder told me what happened, Grandma. Oh, Jesus, what can I say?'

'They're keeping me comfortable, Jimmy, don't you worry.'

She gave a feeble, sticky cough. 'Plenty of morphine to stop me from hurting.'

'Grandma – you should have had somebody looking after you. How many times did I tell you that?'

'I never needed anybody to look after me, Jimmy. I was always the looker-afterer.'

'Well, you sure looked after me good. Nobody could have raised me better.'

Grandma coughed again. 'Promise me one thing, Jimmy. You will promise me, won't you?'

'Anything. Just say the word.'

She tried to raise her head, but the effort and the pain were too much for her. 'Promise me you won't think bad of your mother.'

I frowned at her and shook my head. 'Why should I think bad of her? It wasn't her fault that she died.'

'Try to understand, that's all I'm saying.'

'Grandma, I don't get it. Try to understand *what*?'

She looked at me for a long time, but she didn't say anything else. After a while, she closed her eyes and I left her to sleep.

I met her gingery-haired doctor on the way out.

'What chances does she have?' I asked him.

He took off his eyeglasses and gave me a shrug. 'There are times when I have to say that patients would be better off if they could come to some conclusion.'

'*Conclusion*? She's a human being, not a fucking book.'

I took a taxi over to her apartment building on the South Side, in one of the few surviving streets of narrow four-storey Victorian houses, overshadowed by the Dan Ryan Expressway. It was still raining and the expressway traffic was deafening.

I opened the scabby front door and went inside, carrying a brown paper shopping sack with six cans of Heineken and a turkey sandwich. The hallway was dark, with a brown linoleum floor and an old-fashioned umbrella stand. There was a strong smell of lavender floor-polish and frying garlic. Somewhere a television was playing at top volume, and a baby was crying. It was hard to believe that I used to think of this building as home.

A door opened and Mr Szponder came out, with his rounded face and his saggy grey cardigan. His grey hair was swept back so that he looked like a porcupine.

'Jimmy – what can I say?' He held me in his arms and slapped my back as if he were trying to bring up my wind. 'I always tried to look out for your grandma, you know – but she was such a proud lady.'

'Thanks, Mr Szponder.'

'You can call me Wladislaw. What do you like? Tea? Vodka?'

'Nothing, thanks. I could use a little sleep, that's all.'

'Okay, but anything you need.'

He gave me a final rib-crushing squeeze and breathed onions into my face.

Up on the fourth floor, grandma's apartment was silent and gloomy and damp. It seemed so much more cramped than it had when I was young, but very little had changed. The sagging brown velvet couch was still taking up too much space in front of the hearth, and the stuffed owl still stared at me from the mantelpiece as if it wanted to peck out my eyes. A framed photograph of a sad-looking seven-year-old boy stood next to the owl, and that was me. I went through to the narrow kitchen and opened the tiny icebox. I was almost brought to tears by Grandma's pathetic little collection of left-overs, all on saucers and neatly covered with Saran-wrap.

I popped open a can of beer and went back to the living-room. So many memories were here. So many voices from the past. Grandpa singing at Christmas; Grandma telling me stories about children who got lost in the deep dark forest, and could only find their way out by leaving trails of breadcrumbs. They looked after me as if I were some kind of little prince, those two, and when Grandpa died in 1989, he left me a letter that said, '*There aren't any ghosts, Jimmy. Always remember that the past can't hurt you.*' To be honest, I never knew what the hell he was trying to tell me.

I tried to eat my turkey sandwich, but it tasted like brown velvet couch and lavender polish, and after two or three bites I wrapped it up again and threw it in the trash. I switched on the huge, old Zenith television and watched this movie about a woman who thinks that her children are possessed. The rain spattered against the window and the traffic streamed along the Dan Ryan Expressway with an endless swishing noise, and out on the lake a steamer sounded its horn like the saddest creature you ever heard.

I woke up with a jolt. It was dark outside, and the apartment was illuminated only by the flickering light of *Wheel of Fortune*. The audience were screaming with laughter, but I was sure that I had heard somebody else screaming, too. There's a difference between a roller-coaster scream of hilarity and a scream of absolute terror.

I turned the volume down and listened. Nothing at first, except the traffic, and the muffled sound of a television from downstairs. I waited and waited and there was still nothing. But then I heard it again. It was a child screaming, a little boy, and when I say screaming, this was a total freezing fear-of-death scream. I felt as if I had dropped into cold water right up to my neck.

I stood up, trying to work out where the screaming was coming from. It wasn't underneath me. It wasn't the next-door apartment, either. And this was the top storey, so there was nobody living above.

Suddenly I heard it again, and this time I could make out part of what the child was screaming. *'Mommy! Mommy! No Mommy you can't! Mommy you can't, you can't, you can't!* NO MOMMY YOU CAN'T!'

I went quickly through to Grandma's bedroom, where the covers were still turned neatly back, and Grandma's nightdress was still lying ready on the quilt. The screaming went on and on, and I could tell now that it was coming from the top-storey apartment of the house next door. I thumped on the wall with my fist and yelled out, 'What's happening? What the hell are you doing?'

The screaming stopped for a second, but then the child let out a high, shrill shriek, almost inhuman, more like a bird than a child. I hurried out of the apartment and ran downstairs, three and four stairs at a time. When I got to the hallway, I banged on Mr Szponder's door.

'Mr Szponder! Mr Szponder!'

He opened his door in his vest and suspenders with a half-eaten submarine sandwich in his hand. 'Jimmy? Whatsa matter?'

'Call the cops! It's next door, that side, there's some mother who's hurting a kid! Tell them to hurry, it sounds like she's practically killing him! Top floor!'

'Hunh?' said Mr Szponder. 'What do you mean, killing?'

'Just dial 911 and do it now! I'm going up there!'

'Okay, okay.' Mr Szponder dithered for a moment, uncertain of what to do with his sandwich. In the end he put it down on the seat of a chair and went off to find his telephone.

I ran down the front steps into the rain. The house next door was different from the house in which my grandma had lived. It was narrower, with a hooded porch, and dark, rain-soaked rendering. I bounded up to the front door and pressed the top floor bellpush. Then I hammered on the knocker and shouted out, 'Open up! Open up! I've called the cops! Open the fucking door!'

Nobody answered, so I pressed every single bellpush, and there were at least a dozen of them. After a long while, a man's voice came over the intercom. '*Who is this*?'

'I live next door. You have to let me in. There's a kid screaming on the top floor. Can't you hear him?'

'*What do you mean, kid*?'

'There's a kid screaming for help. Sounds like his mother's hurting him. For Christ's sake open the door, will you?'

'*I don't hear no screaming.*'

'Well, maybe he's stopped, but he was screaming before. He could be hurt.'

'*So what's it got to do with me?*'

'It doesn't have to have anything to do with you. Just open the goddamned door, will you? That's all I'm asking you to do.'

'*I don't even know who you are. You sound like a maniac.*'

'Listen to me – if you don't let me in and that kid dies, then it's going to be your fault. Got it?'

There was a lengthy silence.

'Hello?' I called, and pressed every bellpush all over again. 'Hello? Can anybody hear me?'

I was still pushing the bells and banging on the door when a police cruiser arrived with its lights flashing. Two cops climbed out, a man and a woman, and came up the steps. The man was tall and thin, but the woman looked as if she could have gone nine rounds with Jesse Ventura. The raindrops sparkled on their transparent plastic cap-covers.

'What's the problem?'

'I was next door – staying in my grandmother's place. I heard a kid screaming. I think it's the top floor apartment.'

The woman cop pressed all the buttons again, and eventually the same man answered. '*Look – I told you – I didn't hear no screaming and this is nothing to do with me, so stop ringing my bell or else I'm going to call the cops.*'

'I am the cops, sir. Open the door.'

Immediately, there was a dull buzz and the door swung open. The cops stepped inside and I tried to follow them, but the woman cop stopped me. 'You wait here, sir. We'll deal with this.'

They disappeared up the rickety stairs and I was left standing in the hallway. There was a mottled mirror on the hallstand opposite me and it made me look like a ghost. Pale face, sticking-up hair, skinny shoulders like a wire coathanger. Just like the seven-year-old boy on grandma's mantelpiece.

It was strange, but there was something vaguely familiar about this hallway. Maybe it was the beige-and-white diamond-patterned tiles on the floor, or the waist-high wooden panelling. There must have been tens of thousands of old town houses that were decorated like that. Yet it wasn't just the décor. There was something about the *smell*, too. Not damp and garlicky like next door, but dry and herby, like pot-pourri that has almost lost its scent.

I waited for almost ten minutes while the police officers went from floor to floor, knocking on every door. I could hear them talking and people complaining. Eventually they came back down again.

'Well?' I said.

'There's no kid in this building, sir.'

'What? I heard him with my own ears.'

'Nobody has a kid in this building, sir. We've been through every apartment.'

'It was the top floor. I swear to God. He was screaming something like, "Mommy, Mommy, you can't" – over and over.'

'The top floor apartment is vacant, sir. Has been for years. The landlord uses it for storage, that's all.'

'You're sure?'

'Absolutely. We're going to check the two buildings either side, just to make sure, but I seriously think you must have been mistaken. Probably somebody's television turned up too loud. You know what these old folks are like. Deaf as ducks.'

I followed them down the steps. Mr Szponder stood in his open doorway watching me.

'Well, what's happening?' he asked me, as the cops started ringing bells next door.

'They looked through the house from top to bottom. No kid.'

'Maybe your imagination, Jimmy.'

'Yeah, maybe.'

'Better your imagination than some kid *really* getting hurt. Think about it.'

I nodded. I couldn't think of anything to say.

The next morning, while I was washing my teeth, the telephone rang. It was the gingery-haired doctor from St Philomena's.

'I'm sorry to tell you that your grandmother reached her conclusion just a few minutes ago. She didn't suffer.'

'I see,' I said, with a mouthful of minty foam.

I called a couple of my cousins to tell them what had happened, but none of them seemed to be very upset. Cousin Dick lived in Milwaukee and could easily have come to Chicago to meet me, but he said he had a 'gonad-cruncher' of a business meeting with Wisconsin Cuneo Press. Cousin Erwin sounded, quite frankly, as if he were stoned out of his brain. He kept saying, '*There you are, Jimmy – another milestone bites the dust.*'

Cousin Frances was more sympathetic. I had always liked Cousin Frances. She was about the same age as me and worked for Bloomingdales in New York. When I called her, she was on her lunch break, and she was so upset that she started to cough and couldn't stop coughing.

'Listen,' she said, 'when are you going back to Florida?'

'I'm not in any hurry. I was fired for taking time off.'

'Why don't you stop over in New York (*cough*)? I'd love to see you again.'

'I don't know. Have a drink of water.'

Pause. More coughing. Then, 'Just call me when you get to La Guardia.'

***

Cousin Frances lived in a terraced brownstone on E17 Street in the Village. The street itself was pretty crummy and run down, but her loft was airy and beautifully decorated as you'd expect from somebody who made a living designing window-displays. Three walls were plastered and painted magnolia, the fourth had been stripped back to its natural brick, with all kinds of strange artifacts on it, like driftwood antlers from the Hamptons and a Native American medicine-stick from Wyoming.

Cousin Frances herself was very thin and highly groomed, with a shining blonde bob and a line in silky blouses and slinky pyjama-like pants. She was the youngest daughter of my mother's sister Irene, and in a certain light she looked very much like my mother, or at least the two or three photographs that I still had of my mother. High forehead, wide-apart eyes, distinctive cheekbones, but a rather lipless mouth, which made her look colder than she actually was.

She poured me a cold glass of Stag's Leap chardonnay and elegantly unfolded herself on the maroon leather couch. 'It's been so long. How long has it been? But you haven't changed a bit. You don't look a day over 22.'

'I don't know whether that's a compliment or not.'

'Of course! Are you still working on that novel of yours?'

'Now and then. More then than now.'

'Writer's block?' I could smell her perfume now; Issy Miyaki.

I shrugged. 'I think you have to have a sense of direction to write a novel. A sense that you're going someplace … developing, changing, growing up.'

'And you don't feel that?'

'I don't know. I feel like everybody else got on the train but I dropped my ticket and when I looked up the train was already leaving the station. So here I am, still standing on the platform. Suitcase all packed but not a train in sight.'

She looked at me for a long time with those wide-apart eyes. In the end, she said, 'She didn't suffer, did she?'

'Grandma? I hope not. The last time I saw her, she was sleeping.'

'I would have come to the funeral, but –'

'It doesn't matter. We had a few of her friends there. The super from her building. An Italian guy from the grocery store on the corner. It was okay. Very quiet. Very …'

'Lonely?' she suggested.

'Yes,' I said. 'Lonely.' But I wasn't sure who she was really talking about.

She had a date to go out later that evening to some drinks party, but all the same she made us some supper. She stood in the small designer kitchen and mixed up *conchiglie alla puttanesca* in a blue earthenware bowl. 'Tomatoes, capers, black Gaeta olives, crushed red chillies, all mixed up with extra-virgin olive oil and pasta … they call it "harlot's sauce."'

I forked a few pasta shells out of the bowl and tasted them. 'That's good. My compliments to the harlot.'

'Do you cook, Jimmy?'

'Me? No, never.'

'*Never*? Not even meatballs?'

'I have a thing about ovens.'

She shook her head in bewilderment. 'I've heard of people being afraid of heights, or cats, or water. But *ovens*? That must be a first.'

'Stove-o-phobia, I guess. Don't ask me why.'

We ate together at the kitchen counter and talked about grandma and about the sisters who had been our mothers. Mine had died suddenly when I was five. Frances's mother had contracted breast cancer at the age of 37 and died an appalling, lingering death that went on for months and months.

'So, we're orphans now, you and me,' said Frances, and laid her hand on top of mine.

Just after nine o'clock the doorbell rang. It was a wiry-haired guy in a black velvet coat and a black silk shirt. 'Frances? You ready?' he said, eyeing me suspiciously.

'Almost, just got to put my shoes on. Nick – meet my cousin Jimmy. Jimmy, this is Nick. He's the inspirational half of Inspirational Plaster Mouldings, Inc.'

'Good to know you,' I said. 'Glad you're not the plastered half.'

'You're welcome to come along,' Frances told me. 'They usually have organic wine and rice cakes, and all kinds of malicious gossip about dadoes and suspended ceilings.'

'Think I'll pass, if it's all the same to you.'

After Frances and Nick had gone, I undressed and went for a long, hot shower. It had taken a lot out of me, emotionally, seeing Grandma die. When I shampooed my hair and closed my eyes, I could still see her sitting on the end of my bed, her head a little tilted to one side, smiling at me.

'Grandma, why did Mommy die?'

'God wanted her back, that's all, to help in heaven.'

'Didn't she love me?'

'Of course she loved you. You'll never know how much. But when God calls you, you have to go, whoever you are, and no matter how much you like living on earth.'

I was still soaping myself when I thought I heard a cry. I guessed it was probably a pair of copulating cats in the yard outside, and so I didn't pay it much attention. But then I heard it again, much louder, and this time it didn't sound like cats at all. It sounded like a child, calling for help.

Immediately I shut off the faucets and listened. There was silence for almost half a minute, apart from the honking of the traffic outside and the steady dripping of water onto the shower-tray. No, I must have imagined it. I stepped out of the shower and wrapped a towel around my waist. Then my God the child was screaming and screaming and I ran into the living-area and it seemed like it was all around me. '*Mommy! Mommy! You can't! Stop it Mommy you can't, you can't!* STOP IT MOMMY YOU CAN'T!'

I tugged on my jeans, my wet legs sticking to the denim. Then I dragged on my sweater and shoved my feet into my shoes, squashing the backs down because I didn't have time to loosen the laces. I opened the loft door and wedged a book into the gap so that it wouldn't swing shut behind me. On the landing, I pressed the button for the elevator, and it seemed to take forever before I heard the motor click and bang, and the car come slowly whining upward.

I ran out into the street. The wind was up and it was wild, with newspapers and cardboard boxes and paper cups whirling in the air. I hurried up the steps of the next-door house and started jabbing at the doorbells. I was so frantic that it took me 16 or 17 heartbeats before I realised that these were the same doorbells that I had been pressing in Chicago.

I stopped. I took a step back. I couldn't believe what I was looking at. Not only was I pressing the same doorbells, but I was standing in front of the same house. It had the same black-painted front door, the same hooded porch, the same damp-stained rendering. I felt a kind of *compressed* sensation inside my head, as if the whole world was collapsing, and I was the centre of gravity. How could it be the exact same house? How could that happen? Chicago was nearly a thousand miles away, and what were the chances that I was staying right next door to a house that looked identical to the one that was next door to Grandma's?

For a moment, I didn't know what to do. Then a man's voice came over the intercom. '*Who's there?*' I couldn't tell if it was the same voice that I had heard in Chicago.

'I – ah – do you think could you open the door for me, please?'

'*Who is this?*'

'Listen, I think there's a child in trouble on the top floor.'

'*What child? The top floor's empty. No children live here.*'

'Do you mind if I just take a look. I work for the ASPCC.'

'*The what?*'

'Child cruelty prevention officer.'

'*I told you. No children live here.*'

I was unnerved, but I didn't want to give up. Even if I couldn't work out how this building was the same building from Chicago, I still wanted to know what all that screaming was. 'Just open the door, okay?'

Silence.

'Just open the fucking door, okay?'

Still silence.

I waited for a while, wondering what to do, and then I held onto the porch railing and gave the door a hefty kick. The frame cracked, so I kicked it again, and again, and again, and then a large piece of wood around the lock gave way and the door juddered open.

I went inside. The hallway was dark, but I managed to find the light switch. The walls were panelled in darkly-varnished wood, waist-high, and the floor was patterned in beige-and-white diamonds. There was a hall stand with a blotchy mirror in it, and there was a dry, barely-perceptible smell of dead roses.

I climbed the stairs. They were creaky but thickly covered in heavy-duty hessian carpet. Chinks of light shone from almost every door, and I could hear televisions and people talking and arguing and scraping dishes. A woman said, *'There should be a law against it – haven't I always said that?'* and a man replied, *'What are you talking about? How can you have a law against body odour?'*

I reached the second storey and looked up toward the third. Without warning, the lights clicked off and left me in darkness, and it took me quite a few moments of fumbling before I found the time switch. When the lights came on again, there was a man standing at the top of the stairs. It was impossible to see his face, because there was a bare light bulb hanging right behind him, but I could see that he was bulky and bald and wearing a thick sweater.

'Who are you?' he demanded.

'Child cruelty prevention officer.'

'That was you I was talking to before?'

'That's right.'

'Don't you hear good? There's no children live here. Now get out before I throw you out.'

'You didn't hear any screaming? A little boy, screaming?'

He didn't answer.

'Listen,' I insisted, 'I'm going to call the police, and if they find out you've been abusing some kid –'

'Go,' he interrupted me. 'Just turn around and go.'

'I heard a boy screaming, I swear to God.'

'*Go*. There are some things in life you don't want to go looking for.'

'If you think that I'm going to –'

'Go, Jimmy. Let it lie.'

I shielded my eyes with my hand, trying to see the man's face, but I couldn't. How the hell did he know my name? What was he trying to say to me? Let it lie? Let *what* lie? But he stayed where he was, guarding the top of the third-storey stairs, and I knew that I wasn't going to get past him and I wasn't sure that I really wanted to.

I lowered my hand and said, 'Okay, okay,' and backed off along the landing. Out in the street, I stood in the wind wondering what to do. A squad car drove slowly past me, but I didn't try to hail it. I realised by then that this wasn't a matter for the cops. This was a matter of madness, or metaphysics, or who the hell knew what.

'What do you know about your neighbours?' I asked Cousin Frances, over breakfast.

'Nothing. Why?'

'Ever give you any trouble? You know – parties, noise, that kind of thing?'

She frowned at me as she nibbled the corner of her croissant. 'Never. I mean like there's nobody there. Only the picture-framing store. I think they use the upstairs as a workshop.'

'No, no. I mean your neighbours that way.'

'That's right.'

Without a word, I put down my cup of espresso, walked out of the apartment and pressed the button to summon the elevator.

Cousin Frances called after me, 'What? What did I say?' I didn't answer, couldn't, not until I saw for myself. But when I got out into the street, I saw that she was right. The building next door housed a picture-framing gallery called A Sense of Gilt. No narrow house with a hooded porch; no peeling black door; no doorbells.

I came back to my coffee. 'I'm sorry. I think I need to go back to Florida.'

***

There were thunderstorms all the way down the Atlantic coast from Norfolk to Savannah, and my flight was delayed for over six hours. I tried to sleep on a bench next to the benign and watchful bust of Fiorello La Guardia, but I couldn't get that screaming out of my mind, nor that narrow house with its damp-stained rendering.

What were the options? None, really, except that I was suffering from grief. Houses can't move from one city to another. My grandmother's death must have triggered some kind of breakdown that caused me to have hallucinations, or hyper-realistic dreams. But why was I hallucinating about a child screaming, and what significance did the house have? There was something faintly familiar about it, but nothing that I could put my finger on.

We were supposed to fly directly into Fort Lauderdale, but the storms were so severe that we were diverted to Charleston. We didn't get there till 1.35 am, and the weather was still rising, so United Airlines bussed us into the city to put us up for the night. The woman sitting next to me kept sniffing and wiping her eyes. 'I was supposed to see my son today. I haven't seen my son in 15 years.' Rain quivered on the windows, and turned the streetlights to stars.

When we reached the Radisson Hotel on Lockwood Drive, I found over a hundred exhausted passengers crowded around the reception desk. I wearily joined the back of the line, nudging my battered old bag along with my foot. Jesus. It was nearly 2.30 in the morning and there were still about 70 people in front of me.

It was then that a woman in a black dress came walking across the lobby. I don't know why I noticed her. She was, what, 32 or 33. Her brunette hair was cut in a kind of dated Jackie Kennedy look, and her dress came just below her knee. She was wearing gloves, too; black gloves. She came right up to me and said, 'You don't want to wait here. I'll show you where to stay.'

'Excuse me?'

She said, 'Come on. You're tired, aren't you?'

I thought: *hello – hooker*. But she didn't actually *look* like a hooker. She was dressed too plainly and too cheaply, and what hooker wears little pearl earrings and a little pearl brooch on her dress? She looked more like somebody's mother.

I picked up my bag and followed her out of the Radisson and onto Lockwood. Although it was stormy, the night was still warm, and I could smell the ocean and that distinctive sub-tropical aroma of moss and mould. In the distance, lightning was crackling like electric hair.

The woman led me quickly along the street, walking two or three steps in front of me.

'I don't know what I owe the honour of this to,' I said.

She half-turned her head. 'It's easy to get lost. It's not so easy to find out where you're supposed to be going. Sometimes you need somebody to help you.'

'Okay,' I said. I was totally baffled, but I was too damned tired to argue.

After about five minutes' walking we reached the corner of Broad Street, in the city's historic district. She pointed across the street at a row of old terraced houses, their stucco painted in faded pinks and primrose yellows and powder-blues, with the shadows of yucca trees dancing across the front of them.

'That one,' she said. 'Mrs Woodward's house. She takes in guests.'

'That's very nice of you, thank you.'

She hesitated, looking at me narrowly, as if she always wanted to remember me. Then she turned and started to walk away.

'Hey!' I called. 'What can I do to thank you?'

She didn't turn around. She walked into the shadows at the end of the next block, and then she wasn't there at all.

Mrs Woodward answered the door in hairpins and no make-up and a flowery robe, and I could tell that she wasn't entirely thrilled about being woken up at nearly 3.00 am by a tired and sweaty guy wanting a bed and a shower.

'You were highly recommended,' I said, trying to make her feel better.

'Oh, yes? Well, you'd better come in, I suppose. But I've only the attic room remaining.'

'I need someplace comfortable to sleep, that's all.'

'All right. You can sign the register in the morning.'

The house dated from the 18th Century and was crowded with mahogany antiques and heavy, suffocating tapestries. In the hallway hung a gloomy oil portrait of a pointy-nosed man in a colonial navy uniform with a telescope under his arm. Mrs Woodward led me up three flights of tilting stairs and into a small bedroom with a sloping ceiling and a twinkling view of Charleston through the skylight.

I dropped my bag on the mat and sat down on the quilted bed. 'This is great. I'd still be waiting to check into the Radisson if I hadn't found this place.'

'You want a cup of hot chocolate?'

'No, no thanks. Don't go to any trouble.'

'Bathroom's on the floor below. I'd appreciate it if you'd wait until the morning before you took a shower. The plumbing's a little thunderous.'

I washed myself in the tiny basin under the eaves, and dried myself with a towel the size of a Kleenex while I looked out over the city. Although it was clear, the wind had risen almost to hurricane force and the draught seethed in through the crevices all around my window.

Eventually, ass-weary, I climbed into bed. There was a guide to the National Maritime Museum on the nightstand, and I tried to read it, but my left eye kept drooping. I switched off the light, bundled myself up in the quilt, and fell asleep.

'*Mommy, you can't! Mommy, you can't! Please, Mommy, you can't!* NO MOMMY YOU CAN'T!'

I jerked up in bed and I was slathered in sweat. For a second, I couldn't think where I was, but then I heard the storm shuddering across the roof and the city lights of Charleston through the window. Jesus. Dreaming again. Dreaming about screaming. I eased myself out of bed and went to fill my toothbrush glass with water. Jesus.

I was filling up my glass a second time when I heard the child screaming again. '*No, Mommy, don't! No Mommy you can't!* PLEASE NO MOMMY PLEASE!'

I switched on the light. There was a small, antique mirror on the bureau, so small that I could only see my eyes in it. The boy was screaming, I could hear him. This wasn't any dream. This wasn't any hallucination. I could hear him, and he was screaming from the house next door. Either this was real, or else I was suffering from schizophrenia, which is when you can genuinely hear people talking and screaming on the other side of walls. But when you're suffering from schizophrenia, you don't think, 'I could be suffering from schizophrenia.' You believe it's real. And the difference was, I *knew* this was real.

'Mommy no Mommy no Mommy you can't please don't please don't please.'

I dressed, and he was still screaming and pleading while I laced up my shoes. Very carefully, I opened the door of my attic bedroom and started to creep downstairs. Those stairs sounded like the Hallelujah Chorus, every one of them creaking and squeaking in harmony. At last I reached the hall, where a long-case clock was ticking our lives away beat by beat.

Outside, on Broad Street, the wind was buffeting and blustering and there was nobody around. I made my way to the house next door, and there it was, with its hooded porch and its damp-stained rendering, narrow and dark and telling me nothing. I stood and stared at it, my hair lifted by the wind. This time I wasn't going to try ringing the doorbells, and I wasn't going to try to force my way inside. This house had a secret, and the secret was meant especially for me, even if it didn't want me to know it.

I went back to Mrs Woodward's, locking the street door behind me. As quickly and as quietly as I could, I climbed the stairs to my attic bedroom. I thought at first that the boy might have stopped screaming, but as I went to the window I heard a piercing shriek. The window-frame was old and rotten and badly swollen with the rain and the sub-tropical humidity. I tried to push it open with my hand, but in the end I had to take my shoulder to it, and two of the panes snapped. All the same, I managed to swing it wide open and latch it, and then I climbed up onto the bureau and carefully manoeuvred myself onto the roof. Christ, not as young as I used to be. The wind was so strong that I was almost swept off, especially since it came in violent, unexpected gusts. The chimneystacks were howling and the TV antenna was having an epileptic fit.

I edged my way along the parapet to the roof of the house next door. There was no doubt that it was the same house, the hooded-porch house, because it was covered with 19th Century slates and it didn't have a colonial-style parapet. I didn't even question the logic of how it had come to be here, in the centre of historic Charleston. I was too concerned with not falling 75 feet into the garden. The noise of the storm was deafening, and lightning was still crackling in the distance, over toward Charles Towne Landing, but the boy kept on screaming and begging, and now I knew that I was very close.

There was a skylight in the centre of the next-door roof, and it was brightly lit. I wedged my right foot into the rain-gutter, then my left, and crawled crabwise toward it, keeping myself pressed close to the slates in case a sudden whirlwind lifted me away.

'*Mommy you can't! Please Mommy no!* NO MOMMY YOU CAN'T YOU CAN'T!'

Grunting with effort, I reached the skylight. I wiped the rain away with my hand and peered down into the room below.

It was a kitchen, with a green linoleum floor and a cream-and-green painted hutch. On the right-hand side stood a heavy, 1950s-style gas range, and just below me there were tables and chairs, also painted cream-and-green. Two of the chairs had been knocked over, as well as a child's high-chair.

At first there was nobody in sight, in spite of the screaming, but then a young boy suddenly appeared. He was about five or six years old, wearing faded blue pyjamas, and his face was scarlet with crying and distress. A second later, a woman in a cheap pink dress came into view, her hair in wild disarray, carrying a struggling child in her arms. The child was no more than 18 months old, a girl, and she was naked and bruised.

The woman was shouting something, very harshly. The boy in the blue pyjamas danced around her, still screaming and catching at her dress.

'*No, Mommy! You can't! You can't! No Mommy you can't!*'

His voice rose to a shriek, and he jumped up and tried to pull the little girl out of his mother's arms. But the woman swung her arm and slapped him so hard that he tumbled over one of the fallen chairs and knocked his head against the table.

Now the mother opened the oven door. Even from where I was clinging onto the roof, I could see that the gas was lit. She knelt down in front of the oven and held the screaming, thrashing child toward it.

'*No!*' I shouted, thumping on the skylight. '*No you can't do that! No!*'

The woman didn't hear me, or didn't want to hear me. She hesitated for a long moment, and then she forced the little girl into the oven. The little girl thrashed and screamed, but the woman crammed her arms and legs inside and slammed the door.

I was in total shock. I couldn't believe what I had seen. The woman stood up, staggered, and backed away from the range, running one hand distractedly through her hair. The boy got up, too, and stood beside her. He had stopped screaming now. He just stared at the oven door, shivering, his face as white as paper.

'*Open the oven!*' I yelled. '*Open the oven! For God's sake, open it!*'

The woman still took no notice, but the boy looked up at me as if he couldn't understand where all the shouting and thumping was coming from.

As soon as he looked up, I recognised him. He was the boy in the photograph that had stood on my grandmother's mantelpiece.

He was me.

***

I don't know how I managed to get down from that roof without killing myself. It took me almost five minutes of sweating and grunting, and at one point I felt the guttering start to give way. In the end, however, I managed to get back to the comparative safety of Mrs Woodward's parapet, and climb back in through my attic window. I limped downstairs and into the street, but I guess I knew all along what I would find there. The house next door was a flat-fronted three-storey dwelling, painted yellow, with a white door and the date 1784 over the lintel. The house with the hooded porch had gone, although God alone knew where, or how.

***

Three weeks later, when I was back in Fort Lauderdale, working at The Scorpion Lounge, I received a package of photographs and letters from my grandmother's attorneys.

'Your late grandmother's legacy will be settled within the next three months. Meanwhile, we thought you would like to have her various papers.'

I opened them up that evening, on the veranda of my rented cottage on Sunview Street. Most of the letters were routine – thank-you notes from children and cousins, bills from plumbers and carpet-fitters. But then I came across a letter from my dad, dated 26 years earlier, and handwritten, which was very unusual for him.

Dear Margaret,

It's very difficult for me to write to you this way because Ellie is your daughter and obviously you feel protective toward her. I know you don't think much of me for walking out on her and the kids but believe me I didn't know what else to do.

I talked to her on the phone last night and I'm *very* concerned about her state of mind. She's talking about little Janie being sent from hell to make her life a misery by crying and crying and never stopping and always wetting the bed. I don't think the Ellie I know would hurt her children intentionally, but she doesn't sound like herself at all.

Please can I ask you to call around and talk to her and make sure that everything's okay. I wouldn't ask you this in the normal way of things as you know but I am very anxious.

All the best,
Travers.

Fastened to this letter by a paper-clip was a yellowed cutting from the *Chicago Sun-Times*, dated 11 days later. MOTHER ROASTS BABY. Underneath the banner headline there was a photograph of the house with the hooded porch, and another photograph of the woman who had pushed her child into the oven. It was the same woman who had guided me from the Radisson Hotel to Mrs Woodward's lodging-house. It was my mother.

There was also a cutting from the *Tribune*, with another photograph of my mother, with me standing beside her, and a little, curly-headed girl sitting on her lap. 'Eleanor Parker with baby Jane and son, five-year-old son James, who witnessed the tragedy.'

Finally, there was a neatly-typed letter to my grandparents from Dr Abraham Lowenstein, head of the Psychiatric Department at St Vincent's Memorial Hospital. It read:

Dear Mr and Mrs Harman,

We have concluded our psychiatric examination of your grandson James. All of our specialists are of the same opinion: that the shock he suffered from witnessing the death of his sister has caused him to suffer selective amnesia, which is likely to last for the rest of his life.

In lay terms, selective amnesia is a way in which the mind protects itself from experiences that are too damaging to be coped with by the usual processes of grieving and emotional closure. It is our belief that further treatment will be of little practical effect and will only expose James to unnecessary anxiety and stress.

So it was true. People *can* forget terrible experiences, totally, as if they never happened at all. But what Dr Lowenstein couldn't explain was how the experience itself could come looking for the person who had forgotten it – trying to remind him of what had happened – as if it *needed* to be remembered. Or why I shall never give Wendiii her crucifix back, because I still wake up in the night, hearing a young boy screaming, '*No, Mommy, you can't! No, Mommy, please, you can't!* NO MOMMY YOU CAN'T!' And I have to have something to hold on to.

An Unremarkable Man
Justina Robson

The imp Saclides, second only to the Hell Lord Androcus, wearied under the weight of his burden. The locked box in his hands was cold as ice. The steel of its making was rimed with frost that spread from the shards of human bone that pitted its surface and made Saclides' hands bleed as he carried it. The further he had flown, the lighter it had become, at least for the first two hundred miles, but now its weight was steadily increasing. Lower and lower he dropped, out of the high stratus and into the low clouds over the cities beneath, and still the box dragged him down and the frost bit deeper. The changes meant only one thing: his attempt to steal it had failed. He was seen, and the master of the box was coming to claim his rightful property.

Below him, the dotted trails of yellow lights showed roads where the humans ran their cars up and down, white lights streaming one way and red the other like the flow of cells in veins. Saclides grimly thought of blood and conjuring with it. He used his own wounds to bring heat into his hands and nearly passed out with the pain of returning sensation. As if in response, the box became yet colder and shards of ice formed on it as Saclides fell through the clouds. They broke and plummeted down, only just faster than he did as the box itself doubled its gravity and sucked Saclides towards the unwelcome Earth.

Behind him he thought he could sense the pressure wave and late boom of the flap of giant, spectral wings, which meant there was no time to lose if he were going to survive. He stopped trying to flee and began to search for a good hiding place.

As he came tumbling out of the sky onto some domestic lane in a town he didn't even know the name of, he cast a cloak on himself and was lost to human sight, but not to the sight of the box's master. That he could feel like a prickle on his back.

Saclides looked up and down. Houses, houses all the same, little boxes on a little lane of similar lanes, clustered together in meaningless rows ... Where better than someplace like this to hide a treasure such as the one in the box? All so anonymous. All so dull ... And then he saw it.

It was almost dawn, and on the step of a house a few metres away a red box sat waiting to be found alongside the milk delivery. It was just the right size.

Fumbling, his hands covered in green heating flames, Saclides dragged the box he carried to the step and set it down. The new box was sturdy red cardboard in the shape of a heart, and it contained a sizeable array of medium-priced chocolates. It was the work of a few moments to open the lid, open his mouth and consume the lot in a single inhalation. He was small, but he could eat elephants if he wanted to.

The imp put the freezing box inside the heart and closed the lid. To conceal it in a mundane object! He felt the touch of genius. As soon as the card lid had shut, the biting cold and pressure stopped. So flimsy – but it hid the thing completely from all arcane sight. Even he would not have been able to find it now – not like before –

An almost gentle beat, like the stroke of a blow on a distant drum, brushed across his senses. He ran. He flew. He dashed and dodged. He led a merry dance through city streets and country lanes, along hedgerows and beside vast buildings full of sleeping machines, all while the gentle beats grew closer and stronger until one of them was so full it struck him out of the air onto the muddy ground of a football field. It was dawn, and in the faint light Saclides saw traffic speeding on motorways just over the hill. He saw it through the spectral form of the box's master, as that form stretched out one of its many hands, at the tip of one finger a bead of darkness so complete that the growing day seemed to rush into it and be swallowed there.

'Thief,' said a quiet voice. The finger touched Saclides and he expected death, but it was not his death that came. Instead, screaming and howling, it was Androcus who was pulled through his minion, torn to pieces on the simple wish of this master's darkness. Androcus passed through Saclides in bits and vanished into the void at the master's centre; a howl of rage and fury the only thing left long after his essence was gone.

Saclides, unhurt, looked up into the shifting form above him; barely more than a veil over the softening blue of the growing light, it cast a pall of grey like the settling of dust in an abandoned room.

'I can get it back,' he offered, surprised he could speak, for the grey had sapped him of almost all his will. It seemed to him that it would be better now to turn away from life, and he could not remember what it was he had thought he could ever gain by stealing this power for his Lord, nor why his Lord could want it. Death was preferable to another moment of this powdery fall.

'Let it lie,' said the master. 'If I cannot see it, then who will?'

The finger returned and touched Saclides with gentleness. There was no pain and no confusion, no final angry glare, no moment of grief or gladness, only his end.

***

Laura heard the post arrive and went to get it. She opened the door to fetch the milk in and almost tripped over a red box on the step. It skidded a few feet after her toes caught it, and she cursed and stood there rubbing her foot and giving it a baleful stare.

Red heart. Oh dear. Robert was getting desperate. She looked at it with annoyance and a growing dislike of all things romantic. Also, it had felt light, and after the last week of handwringing, angsty text messages and midnight calls she felt the least she deserved was a seriously heavy freight of something extremely Belgian and preferably hand-dipped.

She tucked the letters under her arm and took the milk inside. Was it un-modern and feeble of her to want to pack Robert in simply because he was boring? Boring wasn't a crime. It was barely ranking on the list of hideous possible faults you could have in a boyfriend. He was nice. He was polite. He had courted her with the utmost care and thoughtfulness, escalating his gifts from the traditional starting point of a single flower, through bunches of flowers belled fat with chrysanthemums, then gradually evolving into roses and after the roses little bits of jewellery, nothing too flashy, only cute pieces and later … but she had forgotten the list before she got to the end, there being nothing memorable or personal on it.

And then yesterday, to say that he had been seeing Celia. And thinking of her a lot. And hoping that Laura wouldn't mind too much but things were looking altogether better with Celia, who shared his love of spending every weekend sitting in windswept grandstands listening to the whine of tortured metal all for the occasional flash of colour as a formula one car fled through the straight just as you had bent down to pick up your overpriced plastic carton of beer and thought about how you could have been walking in the sunshine with a nice pub lunch ahead of you instead…Oh that was so nice!

Laura went back for the cardboard heart, ready to kick it into next week. There was a note attached to it. She decided she would read it. And if it was wet and boring, she would simply text the same words to Robert's phone as the final verdict on a completely pointless exercise. She ground her teeth as she thought of the hours of patience she had wasted on him, foolishly and selfishly, because she thought he was lonely and needed her, and how it was so nice to be needed, even if he couldn't seem to manage *wanted*, and now, all her kindness was repaid with Celia, who had been lurking around in the background all along, Celia with her beige twin-set and her Prada handbag and her passion for inhaling kerosene.

The box stared at her. You deserve me, it seemed to say. You were being Miss Bountiful and here I am, full of Bounty. Go on. Wallow in self pity and take me in. She bent down to it and opened the note with one finger. Inside, Robert's strange habit of always writing in BLOCK CAPITALS proved it to be his work, but the paper was strangely scorched and warped, making it hard to read.

LAURA – it screamed at maximum volume – *I NEVER MEANT TO HURT YOU. I REGRET NOT TELLING YOU EARLIER ABOUT CEE*

AND ME. I HOPE WE CAN STILL BE FRIENDS. WITH LOVE FROM ROBERT X.

Laura felt a smile of deep satisfaction stretch over her face. Now she could legitimately hate him with all her heart. Friends indeed. With love from. X. She prided herself on her broad mind and forgiving nature, but that could wait another few hours.

She picked up the box with a fondness and warm regard for it she had never experienced for Robert and took it with her into the house, thinking it was strangely light and suspecting darkly that no doubt he had wished to save for Celia's massive engagement ring and had probably bought her the showy set of chocolates that was all lovely on the top but had a completely false bottom. A perfect end to a hugely stupid relationship. What had she been thinking?

She set it on the kitchen counter and eased the top off. There were no chocolates inside, although there was a whiff of chocolate. Instead, there was a small, heart-shaped chest the size of a large fist, made of some kind of dull grey metal, bound with leather and studded with nubs of ivory. It was dirty, as though it had recently been dug out of the ground, and a heavy, cold smell emanated from it, redolent of old gold, the graves of heroes and the death of empires. An object of power!

Laura rammed the lid back on as fast as she could. As with all natural materials, the cardboard of the box hid the magic of its contents perfectly, and she breathed a sigh of relief, followed by a deep breath of worried contemplation.

Had she made a terrible mistake? Was Robert's dull front simply that – a mask of mundane humanity over the face of an unspeakably corrupted agent for the nether gods? Could he have been stringing her along all the time with his square cut sandwiches, his thermos flasks, his Tupperware? No. Tupperware was the devil's work, she reminded herself sternly – look at how the lid always went missing to the piece you wanted to use, and then, when you found it, inexplicably, it would not fit over the last corner of the box, no matter how hard you pushed and pulled, so that bread went stale anyway and mayonnaise leaked all over the inside of your bag. No demon would consider using it as part of a cover story.

Laura sat with her breakfast forgotten, holding the box between her hands, wondering if she dared risk another peek. It had been a long time since she had smelled that smell of ancient forces, and that had been in a church in the wilds of North Yorkshire where something old had been hidden under a tombstone. It was still buried there, probably inside the ribcage of a priest, for safekeeping. Like this one, it had been concealed by wards of bone, earth, grass and stone, but the frosts of winters had cracked the stone cover and she had felt it as she lingered there one autumn day. Like this one, it shimmered with promises of infinite pain to those who disturbed it, though that was only to be expected when the contents were so precious.

She thought she knew what it was. She would have to check with Sophie first though. Just to be sure. She flipped open her phone and texted Sophie's number. *Mt me now, Sbux by libry, vvvvvimptnt.*

Laura put the box into a plastic carrier bag and went to get dressed.

Sophie was standing in the queue at Starbucks by the time Laura arrived looking cool and interesting in pastels. Her necklace with its tiny silver cross glinted warmly.

'Hi,' Laura said. 'Look at this.'

Sophie glanced down into the bag that Laura held open. 'Big deal. Valentine's Day. He got you chocolates. Is that it?' She had the weary look of someone who has lied to get out of work and regrets the effort.

'Not chocolates,' Laura said, and ordered a double espresso with another espresso in it and a hot chocolate on the side, no cream.

She leant into Sophie and whispered, 'I think it's a *Viscus Diabolique*.'

Sophie almost dropped her mint tea. She looked down at the bag. 'Oh my.'

There were no free tables – not, that was, until Sophie smiled her soft smile at the couple in the corner spot with the armchairs and they found that they suddenly wanted to go out into the drizzle and walk.

'Not very PC of you,' Laura said gratefully. She handed the bag to Sophie, who put it on the table and took a peek under the box lid. As she did so, a soft chime like the ring of tubular bells in a distant cathedral rang out across the shop, and a wave of cold air gusted around their legs.

'Sophie!'

'Sorry ...' Sophie closed the lid as various people reached around to check their phones. 'Well. Whoever's it is knows now that it's been found.'

Laura tried not to be annoyed, or terrified. 'Can you open it?'

Sophie stared at her as if she had asked for a lightly warmed giraffe.

'Come on Soph,' Laura encouraged, holding her espresso with two hands. 'You picked open the Gates of Jericho. You can do it.'

'Laura, what is wrong with you? Are you insane?' Sophie furled the bag in her hands, whispering through the rustle it made.

'Sophie,' Laura whispered back. 'I just spent three months dating the world's most boring human because I felt sorry for him. I thought I could change him. Bring some interest to his life. Fall in love with him and rest in the dullness because it was a nice change from having to fight on against the ordinary everyday evils ...'

'But ... where did it come from ... what are you going to do with it?'

Sophie rustled the bag some more, and they both tried not to notice a chill creeping around their table.

'Change of path,' Laura said. 'Look. Robert didn't give me it. I have no idea how it got there. Someone might even be planning to come back for it. But this is a chance for me ...'

'Chance?' Sophie's blue eyes, used to giving blessings of wisdom, were huge in her gentle face, and not with the grace of sages but with the astonishment of the truly startled.

'To get out of sales,' Laura smiled winningly at Sophie, giving her best smile.

'Now I have heard enough,' Sophie hissed, giving Laura a look of motherly sternness. 'We must destroy it. It is our duty.'

'Ah, come on, even you know nothing is black and white like that.'

Laura felt her espresso cooling and knocked it back before it could go stone cold. 'These things you find once in an eternity ... and get hold of even less often ...'

'Laura ... are you ... you can't mean ...?'

The table, loaded with a tea, a chocolate, a coffee, Sophie's elbows and the box, creaked suddenly. Sophie tugged surreptitiously at the bag. It didn't budge.

'They're *close*!' she hissed at Laura. 'My hands are freezing. We have to re-hide it ...'

'The box is the problem,' Laura whispered. 'Open it and I'll do the rest.'

Sophie looked at her with great misgiving, her eyes turning grey with anxiety, but Laura was right. The box was the magnet, the telltale, the mine and the problem. The contents were ... a whole different problem. Whatever they were. Her eyes sparkled with excitement in spite of her reservations: Laura knew that she wasn't the only one long-wearied by the ages of mankind and their rapid progress from unconscious to barely functional. 'All right. But if it's one of the Old Ones, you're on your own here, Laura my girl.'

'Okay!'

The table legs shifted a few millimetres apart on the false tile of the floor and the cheap wood creaked again. Sophie dived into her handbag and took out a small square of silk. It unrolled, displaying neatly stitched pouches, each containing a tiny bone. She extracted a long and delicate fishbone with her dainty fingers and plunged her hands into the plastic carrier bag. She closed her eyes and her face became still and serene as a plaster saint's.

A man came and sat down at the table with them, though there had been no spare chair there until he sat in it and no man approaching across the cafe a second before he was there, his long coat sighing in a heavy fall of silk around him, his gloves laid down upon the table top to reveal rough and ready carpenter's hands.

'Ladies,' he said in a voice low as a bull's. 'Please let my heart alone.'

Around them the chink of china, the low hubbub of general chat, the sounds of the coffee machines and the distant noise of traffic continued. Sophie and Laura turned their faces to see who had come.

He had no particular look. His hair was of a nondescript colour, possibly some shade of brown. His face was bland and unremarkable, his eyes middling in the ranges of earthy tones, his skin a sallow mixture of any number of racial inputs that couldn't be placed as one thing or another. He sat with calm, and in manner and posture that were inoffensive, somewhere between assertive and gentle. He looked at neither of them, only at the carrier bag.

Sophie withdrew her hands, palming the fishbone as she did so.

Laura reasoned that the box was open, else he would simply have taken it. But with the release of its lock, its powers were severely diminished. Also, it was in her possession, and until she relinquished it, he could not claim it or its contents.

He had said 'heart.' It was, as she had hoped, a relic of extreme power. Creatures such as he were vulnerable to only certain fates, death not among them, but of those fates, some were to be feared more than simply a mortal end: banishment, imprisonment and eternal suffering were the top of that list, and each of these afflictions was cast upon the victim's heart. Hence smart cookies had long since removed their hearts and put them away for safe keeping beyond the reach of enemies who might be capable of such a charm.

'I've got a deal for you,' Laura said, fuelled by the espresso entering her blood.

The unremarkable man looked at her for the first time, although his steady gaze informed her that he knew she was the temporary owner. He might have considered her an unworthy opponent – it was hard to tell when they didn't know each other – but if he did, he showed none of it on his face. He was good, Laura thought.

'I am listening.'

'This box,' Laura indicated the bag with a tip of her head. 'Lasted only two seconds until Soph opened it. That's not much of a safe.'

'It has served for the last millennium. She is the greatest lockpick left of the ancient world. Unluckily for me.'

He gave Sophie the slightest of nods, a concession to her skill. With a slight gesture of one finger, he unspelled the box itself, and the table cracked as normal weights and temperatures returned.

'Well, the ancient world is long buried in time,' Laura said as a preamble, 'and I was wondering whether or not you'd be considering a new form of long term storage?'

Sophie gave her a Significant Look that said You Are Mad.

The unremarkable man stared at Laura with almost complete disinterest.

'Your words are frivolous. The modern age suits you well, Laura the Honoured, First Among Equals.' A slight smile may have crossed the man's face.

He reached across the table into the bag and took out the heart box.

'I sense your boredom, the ennui of the spoiled, wealthy classes, the angst of those to whom everything comes too easily. You were victorious in many battles. You rode the winds and hunted down all the lesser demons so far beneath you. Glory was yours. Yet love was not; for who can love such easy perfections? You don't even know my name.'

His voice was soft as old paper that has been thumbed many times, a page of a prayer book, one whose owner has sought solace in its pages and found none.

Sophie had no amusement in her face now. She looked at Laura and shook her head. From her expression, it was clear that even she did not know who this was, or what infernal power his heart might hold, except that it was the obvious vessel of his life.

Laura felt herself insulted by his words, but they had struck something in her she had not liked recently, and so she said nothing, only watched, looking into the heart-shaped box as he put his hand to the chest and opened its small lid on the single hinge.

Inside, the chest was lined with silvery lead. A heart, human sized, lay in its cold, poisonous embrace. Severed cleanly at aorta and veins, its sheaths glinting wetly, it beat a steady, slow, relentless rhythm. In her mind, Laura heard the march of soldiers' feet down defeated roads, the shuffle of slippers across worn carpets, the hopeless tread of prisoners and slaves, soft like the clap of dove wings.

The light diminished as he took the heart out and placed it onto his open palm. A little blood leaked around the inside of the box. He held it out to Laura and spoke in a voice that was the dead calm of the doldrums.

'Yours. If you want it. It is, after all, St Valentine's day. Lady's prerogative.'

Behind the service counter, one of the coffee machines made a wrong noise and slowly sputtered out.

Sophie said quietly, looking down at the heart. 'You are of the old world?'

Laura knew she was thinking of modern monsters, wondering if they had misjudged this one, thinking he was old when he was not. If they had forgotten someone …

'I am as old as any,' he said. 'Come. Trade if you will. One for another. I would like an easy victory. I would like to know the pleasure of winning, of elation and the terror of the fall. I would like to know fear, and boredom.'

'What is your power?' Laura asked, not sure now that she wanted it, even if it was a connection to all that had passed in time, the ages when they had been greater than mere humans instead of mingling among them like equals. She had thought – and it seemed very frivolous now – that an Ancient One's strength, even borrowed, might restore that old feeling of glory … but as she looked at this unremarkable man, she was reminded only of Robert: though now Robert seemed positively electric by comparison.

'What is your name?' whispered Sophie, who had never in her life been stuck for an answer. Laura looked at her with real misgiving. She wished she had not found the box.

'Your heart for mine and you shall know all,' he said to Laura. His voice was like the whisper of pens signing unwanted divorce papers. 'A fair exchange is no robbery.'

He made a gentle motion of his free hand over the heart, and its empty beat stopped. It became suddenly solid, and a fresh colour of rich, dark brown crept across it. It became chocolate. He glanced at Laura and she felt no sense of connection, as though he was a robot and no-one looked at her. He tipped his hand over her hot chocolate mug, and the heart fell into the steaming, milky liquid and began to melt.

'Laura,' Sophie said in a warning tone. Laura looked at her and saw in her old friend's eyes the same feelings she felt in her own heart. They longed for things so lost that they were almost unknown to them now – the days of gods and monsters. This heart charm was no more than an ancient narcotic, a trick of exchanging powers to give life to palates jaded by too much of their own euphoria. The long years wore on, and there was no change in the temper of humans, only the surfaces altered. Laura and Sophie, Honour and Wisdom ... empty idols all. Oh she wanted it, that charge of power, the rush of it. And it would go back one day and leave her just as she was now, waiting and empty and hungry ... Sophie's eyes were as flat as the salt pans of dry kingdoms.

Laura looked at the unremarkable man. If he had been anyone else, someone she knew, she would have said no. She picked up the hot chocolate mug and drank down the contents. It was so warm, and so sweet.

Immediately there was silence, or not true silence but the fogging of sound, as though everything was at a new distance from her, a distance very slight, no more than a hair's breadth, but at the same time unbridgeable. She felt herself separate out from the world, disconnect. When she looked at Sophie, she could see only the outward form, nothing inside made her feel better, as it used to. The table was as interesting, as real, as any human being in existence.

'Oh,' she said, as the world became unreal and her isolation complete.

In the seat beside her, the unremarkable man nodded and held out his hand to her. As she shook it, he smiled warmly at her and said, 'Easy victory,' with something like wonder, something like elation. He looked like he was waking from a bad dream.

'Yes,' she whispered, and knew she had traded with the most insidious and powerful of the agents of extinction, Death In Life, the master of self doubt and depression. By contrast, the powers he had received were ephemeral and small. She could feel oceans moving inside her, vast and unquenchable lakes of grey lava, the turning stone of hopelessness grinding on itself forever.

'Oh,' she said again. 'Oh no.'

The man pushed his chair back with a scrape and stood up and stretched, a smile crossing his rather handsome features.

'You know,' he said brightly, 'I think I'm going to treat myself and have a muffin ... Not a chocolate one, though.'

He smiled at both of them, bowed and walked off towards the counter.

'Laura?' Sophie asked faintly.

Laura shrugged. 'Win some ...' Across the world she could feel billions of hearts touched by her various blights. Their silence echoed to the distant stars. It was too late to go back. She would have given anything even to be bored. Anything.

The taste of chocolate lingered, but did not satisfy.

'Laura?' Sophie said.

The handsome man at the counter nodded and winked jauntily at Laura as he paid for his cake.

Laura watched him and felt within herself the power to sap a million lives.

'I'll have another chocolate,' she said. 'Cream and extra sugar.'

Life's A Beach
Darren Shan

Summer + the weekend + me aged 8 = beach! A long, beautiful stretch of golden sandy dreams, an hour and a half's drive from where I lived. Stunning, chilling cliff caves to explore. Choppy waves to surf on or break. Ice-cream, candy-floss, the arcades afterwards. Heaven!

The gang – me, Mum and Dad, my younger brother Declan, two older cousins, an aunt and her boyfriend, and my grandfather, Paddywhack. Squashed into Dad's big white Datsun, adults in the seats, kids in a boot the size of a whale's stomach.

Bombing along the road to Ballybunion, the adults chatting, the kids bored in the boot. Killing time. Singing songs. Telling stories. 'I spy with my little eye …'

We spotted the sea from the road a few miles out of town, an incredible expanse of blue, stretching on into eternity. The smell hit us next, the air aflame with salt. Finally the shrieks and laughter of those on the beach. Our desperation to escape the confines of the boot and be part of the crowd increased to the point of outright mutiny. 'Faster, Dad, faster!!!' Dad just laughed and slowed down, teasing us rotten.

We parked on top of the cliff and ambled down to the beach, making slow progress because of Paddywhack, who walked with the aid of a walking stick. Finally, after what felt like half a day … the beach! I threw myself into a bank of hot sand as if it was a bath and thrashed around wildly, drawing worried stares from the nearest families. One harsh threat from Mum later and I was back on my feet, grinning like a loon, spitting out sand.

We found a relatively quiet spot near the smaller cliffs on the left, the boring ones without caves. Laid out a blanket and located swimming costumes and towels. Cue lots of complicated changing, shouting and arguing.

Five minutes later, a race to the water. 'Last one in's a rotten egg!' My older cousins made lots of noise and ran in up to their knees, but were soon back on the beach, teeth chattering, waiting for the sun to heat the water. They'd have a long wait!

Dad came with my brother (he was too young to go swimming by himself) and kicked water at us, Declan squealing in his arms. Within seconds, we were all at it, soaking each other, roaring from the shock of the freezing water. A minute of that and we were used to the cold, ready to fall in, fight the waves, splash about – maybe even swim!

Later. Roasting. Mum rubbed sun-tan lotion all over me. I gobbled ice cream while she worked. The others were off exploring the caves, but I was saving them for later – the day was young and I didn't want to burn out early. I sat with Mum, my aunt and Paddywhack. Paddywhack looked bored and was fidgeting a lot, digging out his pocket watch every few minutes to check the time. He wasn't fond of beaches. I'm not sure why he came in the first place.

Mum suggested to Paddywhack that he play with me. I didn't want to – with his bad leg, he couldn't play football, tennis or anything good. I started to sulk. Paddywhack wasn't keen either. He tried telling Mum he was happy just sitting there, but she wouldn't listen.

Then Mum suggested I bury Paddywhack in the sand. That sparked my interest! I nodded eagerly, smiled and pulled my granddad up by the arm when he resisted.

Giving in, Paddywhack led me away from the crowd, out of the sun, into the shadow of the cliffs where it was quiet. Everybody was either swimming, sun-bathing or exploring the interesting cliffs on the other side of the beach. It was almost deserted over here.

It took us a long time to dig a hole big enough for Paddywhack to lie down in. I did most of the work, using my hands and spade to scrape the sand away. Whenever I complained that he wasn't helping, Paddywhack chuckled and said, 'Every job needs a foreman.'

When the hole was ready, Paddywhack put his hat down, took his jacket off, even loosened his braces a notch or two. Wild man! Then he eased himself into the hole and I shovelled sand back over him, Paddywhack warning me not to spill any on his face.

My granddad played along beautifully at first, kept perfectly still and breathed lightly so the sand could settle around him. But then, with his legs and most of his stomach covered, he suddenly gasped and began to jerk about. He pulled a frightening face, shook and heaved upwards, cracking the previously smooth mound.

I was having none of it. He wasn't escaping so easily, not after all the hard work and time I'd put into digging the hole. I spread myself out on his chest and pinned him down. 'No you don't!' I grunted.

Paddywhack struggled, choking and panting, wheezing like a dog, but I wasn't fooled. I knew he was only playing. If I let him up, he'd hobble away, laughing at me for being such a soft touch and letting him limp free.

The old man was stronger than me, of course, but I had the advantage of my superior position. Plus the weight of the sand played in my favour. He tried to push me off, but his fingers were twisted and weak. I hadn't seen them like that before. I guessed they must have shrivelled slightly in the sun.

Eventually he stopped struggling. There wasn't even a shiver out of him after that, and I swiftly finished covering him with sand, completing the job. When I'd patted the sand into place, I looked at his face. It was eerily calm and expressionless. I'd have said he was asleep, except his eyes were open. His mouth too. For fun I poured some sand in, to see him splutter and rage. I was ready to run for my life if he roared at me angrily, but he didn't react. Frowning, I poured more in – nothing. He didn't even spit it out.

I let some sand trickle into his eyes, knowing I shouldn't, that he'd really give me hell for doing that. But he didn't even blink! A bit more … more … Soon his entire face was covered – and still he didn't move! How was he breathing? It was incredible, a truly brilliant trick. I'd make him teach it to me later, so I could do it with my cousins.

When he didn't surface after ten minutes, I got bored and decided to leave him. I joined my cousins and Dad – Declan was with Mum and my aunt – and we played football and built sandcastles. Then we went for another swim and finished off the last of the sandwiches when we came out. We were having a great time. I forgot all about Paddywhack until Mum asked where he was. I said he was over by the cliff, performing a magic trick. She frowned, looking around for him, and asked *exactly* where he was. I pointed to the mound of sand.

The tide was coming in and had licked away at the base of the small, sandy hill. From where we were, we could just make out the yellow glare of Paddywhack's corn-stubbled toes. Mum stared at them, confused. Then she leapt to her feet and ran. She hurdled over kids and ploughed through sandcastles. Reaching the mound, she collapsed on her knees and scrabbled sand away from around Paddywhack's face. I was going to yell at her to stop – she was spoiling the trick – but my throat suddenly went skeleton dry. I sensed something awful in the air. Trouble was brewing.

Getting up, I hobbled after her, a sick feeling in my belly, and stopped a few feet away, watching silently, not sure what I'd done wrong, but certain I'd crossed some sort of a line. Mum cleared the veil away from Paddywhack's face. His eyes and mouth were full of dry, crusty sand. My bad feeling got worse – like when I'd broken a window at home a few weeks earlier, playing football. Mum stared at Paddywhack. Then she turned around and stared at me.

The waves were rolling in behind us. Families were packing up for the day and going home. A few latecomers were only just arriving. Ice-cream and candy-floss were being sold. Seagulls were swooping and children were splashing and shouting. But all I could see was the horror in Mum's eyes. All I could hear was the beating of my heart. And all I could feel were tears trickling down my sand-encrusted cheeks, though I had no idea why.

Of The Wild And Berserk Prince Drakula
Paul Finch

Professor Lexington was a well-groomed sort of chap, with a neat line in breast-pocket handkerchiefs and gleaming diamond tie-pins, and a head of immaculate white hair. He was also camp and insufferably pompous. When pronouncing foreign-language terms or names, he had the tendency to revert to the mother-accent of the foreign land it came from. Hence, Poienari became a pantomime *Pw-an-aa-ri*, and Drakula a ludicrous *Drrrr-aa-kl*.

'*Pw-an-aa-ri*,' he declared, as the next slide came onto the lecture-theatre screen. 'The scene of *Drrrr-aa-kl*'s most fearsome act of vengeance.'

Kate gazed up at the stark image. Against a background of shredded grey cloud, a crumbling medieval edifice was visible atop a bleak and rocky crag. Ivy clad its once-castellated walls. Its aura was one of solitude and utter desolation. Startling, she thought, how closely it matched her idealised perception of the fictional Dracula's decayed stronghold.

'The fortress was a ruin when *Drrrr-aa-kl* first came to power in *Waa-aa-la-chh-ia*,' the professor added, 'but he valued its military significance and he determined to rebuild it. Operations commenced in 1457, but not in the normal way. *Drrrr-aa-kl* began by rounding up all those boyars he suspected of complicity in his brother's murder – several hundred at least – and drove them, naked and on foot, to *Pw-an-aa-ri*, where under whip and chain they provided slave-labour. Working at an inhuman pace, they rebuilt the powerful structure within two months, though most died in the process. Those who didn't, *Drrrr-aa-kl* then personally killed.'

There were mutters around the darkened hall. Most of the students on Professor Lexington's night-school course in European Studies were approaching middle-age and seeking belated educational qualification. They weren't as *au fait* with the celebrated tyrants of history as their younger compatriots might be, and were mildly shocked by what they were hearing. Kate, still only 33, was less so, though the true facts behind the Dracula myth had up until this point eluded her.

'Worse was to follow,' the professor went on, calling another slide to the screen. An old wood-cut appeared, depicting a bearded nobleman feasting beside a phalanx of sharpened spears, on which writhing prisoners were transfixed. In the foreground, a burly henchman seemed to whistle as he hacked up corpses.

'*Teii-pesh*,' said Lexington. 'Impalement. It was his favourite method of execution, and befell vast numbers during the long years of his reign. But it wasn't only the *Waa-aa-la-chh-ian* aristocracy who suffered. Also … German merchant communities, which he sought to extort money from, the many poor of his country, whom he assembled at a gigantic feast at *Tree-guv-eeste*, then locked in a wooden hall packed with fuel and burned to death, and of course, the Turks. Under Sultan *Meh-med* II, they tried to extend Ottoman power into the Balkans, but in *Drrrr-aa-kl* found an implacable foe. On one occasion, an entire Turkish army – 20,000 strong – was captured and impaled alive. Other prisoners were dismembered, flayed, roasted to death in kilns. At least 100,000 died hideous deaths at his command.'

Such was the amazed mumbling of the audience after this, that for a short while they didn't notice the next slide, which depicted Drakula himself. Kate stared at it. It was another 15th Century print, this one displaying a fierce, barbaric countenance: long, straggling hair; narrowed eyes under heavy brows; the overall features sharp and pinched, as if chipped from stone. She was mesmerised by the viciousness implicit, even in a simple line-drawing. It just went to show, she reasoned, there was always somebody worse than her Kenny, currently residing on D-Block, Barlinni Violent Offenders' Wing.

'So is it true he was a vampire?' she asked, for a fleeting, fatal second thinking aloud.

There was a silence. The professor looked round at her, startled. Then he grinned – one of his affectionate, if slightly patronising grins. 'No more so,' he said, 'than it's true a dinosaur has survived 70 million years and is still swimming about in a cold lake in your country, *ma wee lassie!*'

Kate flushed. Stifled sniggers came from seats to the rear.

***

She could still have kicked herself half an hour later, when the lecture closed. What had possessed her to ask such a dumb question? It was common knowledge, even to the uneducated, that Dracula the vampire was a work of 19th Century fiction. Good God, there'd been enough documentaries on the telly about it … usually more interested in the dark side of Gothic romance, in unspoken Victorian desires and sexual repression, than the real-life Vlad Drakula of Wallachia. She shook her head as she pulled her coat on over her denims and set out into the chill London night.

A few moments later, she was on the platform at New Cross Station, keeping as far as possible from the shabby, drunken man talking to himself in the waiting room door. It wasn't an uncommon sight in this neck of the woods, but the best method was usually to ignore it. Kate glanced up at the towering blocks of flats over Cold Blow Lane. Faceless things of cement, they were. Only a few lights were visible in their myriad tiny windows. They reminded her discomfortingly of Glasgow.

'You are not wrong,' someone suddenly said, in a curious accent.

Kate turned. A pale-faced man, dressed in a leather jacket and jeans, had appeared beside her.

He smiled. 'About Drakula.'

Kate quickly decided she didn't like that smile. It was toothy and cat-like.

'I'm sorry,' she said, backing away a step. 'Do I know you?'

'Ah, forgive me.' He offered her his hand. 'Slaken. Grigori Slaken. I was in the lecture too.'

'I see,' she said, pointedly avoiding physical contact.

Just then, a train came rumbling in. Its doors hissed open almost immediately. Kate felt relief flood through her. Grigori Slaken didn't seem to notice, however. He was still talking about the lecture. 'I understand these things, you see,' he added. 'I am Romanian.'

'Yeah,' she said, 'and I'm Mary, Queen of Scots.'

And without another word, she stepped aboard the train and made her way down the compartment until she found a suitable seat. A moment later, the vehicle lurched forwards again.

'*I ... am ... Romanian.*' Yes, of course. It was hardly an original line, she thought, and since she'd enrolled at college, she'd heard quite a few. Kate might be 33, but she was still trim and shapely. Her flowing, dark-brown hair nicely set off her sultry features. Her complexion, since the last crop of bruises had faded, had finally returned to its creamy lustre. It was pleasant to be made to feel attractive again, but after 11 years of marriage to Kenny, Kate knew better than most what men were really like. '*I am Romanian*' – Jesus wept, she'd heard it all!

She glanced back along the train, just to make sure the jerk hadn't come aboard as well. There was no sign of him. But then there wouldn't be, because the carriage was empty. In itself, that wasn't a particularly pleasing thought. Not at 9.30 at night, on the East London Line. Born and raised in Glasgow's unforgiving Gorbals district, Kate knew what deprived inner cities were all about, but that didn't make them any the less frightening. And there was something about this district – she glanced out as they slid into the next station, which was Surrey Docks – that was more frightening than most, mainly the sheer size of it. The train dallied for a minute, nobody climbing on or off, then pulled out again. Beyond the dirty window-panes, vast black monoliths of buildings drifted past. Between them, narrow, ill-lit streets wallowed in litter. Here and there a burned-out car stood skew-whiff by a kerb.

She couldn't suppress a shudder at the thought that when she disembarked at Whitechapel, she still faced a ten-minute walk. And that was a name to conjure with, wasn't it ... *Whitechapel*. The very word could be written in blood and no-one would notice anything odd.

Twenty minutes later, she arrived there. Whitechapel Station – in keeping with all those on the District Line – was modern, clean and mercifully free from graffiti. But it was the streets above that Kate was less happy about. Needless to say, she couldn't afford a cab, and even if she could, there was none around to hail. So she set off on foot, briskly, her bag over her shoulder.

As April nights went, this one was rather chilly, and a grey miasma had risen, hanging like a curtain in the cramped alley-ways, smothering the stretches of wasteground between the brownstone tenements. Kate did her best to put it from her mind as she walked. Good Lord, it wasn't as if she was the only person about. The pubs seemed full – perhaps not with the most wholesome people, but full nevertheless – while plenty of traffic was moving. When she rounded the corner into Stepney Way, she saw that the Spar was still open. That was good – she needed some odds and ends. On her way towards it, though, she saw two men standing against the wall outside, slugging from tins of lager. Their heads were shaven to the bone, their faces brutish and ape-like, and they wore a uniform as distinctive and chilling as anything the Third Reich had ever clad its official storm-troopers in: khaki jackets, tight, stone-washed jeans and heavy, steel-toed bovver-boots. Just to complete the picture, though, in case anyone still misunderstood, one of them had a swastika tattooed on the side of his neck. They were talking quietly together, but fell silent as she passed them. Kate felt the same pang of fear that she used to feel when Kenny came barging in at three o'clock in the morning, shouting for food. Hurriedly, she entered the shop, the bell jangling loudly.

It was warm and bright in there, and the fact that the young Asian guy behind the counter seemed unfazed by the proximity of the neoliths outside, helped to steel her. Perhaps it was all for show then? An appearance of danger, rather than a promise? She still wanted to linger, however – to hang on for as long as she could, on the off-chance the two hoodlums would wander away – but she knew that wasn't the answer.

She selected a few items and took them to the counter to pay, but then heard the bell again … and sensed a menacing presence come up behind her. For a second she went rigid. She didn't need to look to know that it was one of the skinheads, and now she had her purse open … with three five-pound notes on view. Not only that, but she was bound to have to converse with the guy on the till ... in those dulcet Scottish tones of hers. Mind you, she thought, nobody could be worse than Kenny, and she'd survived 11 years of him. And why the hell should she be afraid of speaking anyway? It was a free country.

'Is that right?' she asked loudly, when the price rang up. 'One pound, 98 pence?'

The Asian guy nodded indifferently, and Kate paid, then left the shop with her goods, and a fierce Celtic pride burning in her breast. The blood of the clans ran in her veins, she told herself, as she rounded the next corner into a cut-through alley. She was damned if she was going to let two in-bred throwbacks like that scare her. A second later, however, the picture changed dramatically.

'Oy! Ya Scotch tart!'

The voice was guttural, aggressively Cockney, and echoed along the alley from behind. She looked wildly back. As she might have guessed, it was the two skinheads, side by side, approaching quickly.

Kate froze like a rabbit in headlights. Suddenly her heart was in her mouth. *She hadn't believed, she hadn't really imagined* – and then a thousand things occurred to her at once: the savage beatings handed out to Scottish football fans in London during the Euro '96 competition; the trouble at tournaments abroad; the reported rise of English neo-fascist groups; the knifing to death of the black teenager Stephen Lawrence. All these things were real – *real*.

Frantically, she began to run – but it wasn't easy in her platform soles, carrying a bag of books and a bag of shopping. And now, with thunderous footfalls, those two bastards were coming after her. She made it to the end of the alley, but found a misty and deserted roadway in front of her. All of a sudden there was *no* traffic, there were *no* pubs packed with drinkers. She tottered across the tarmac all the same, hardly daring to shout for help in case her accent betrayed her to yet more predators of the night.

'Bitch!' one of the skinheads screamed, his voice infused with hatred. 'A'w fackin' kiw ya!'

As she staggered along, Kate considered throwing her purse over her shoulder – casting meat to the wolves, so to speak – but in her heart of hearts she knew that wasn't what they were after. Would they *really* kill her? Would they rape her? *God, oh dear God* ...

On the far side of the road she tripped over the pavement. She almost went sprawling, but sheer terror kept her on her feet. Directly in front, another dark passage loomed, filled with overflowing dustbins. It was by far the most sinister place she'd seen yet, but in that split-second it was the only avenue of escape. She barged down it, crashing through the bins, sending them flying. All manner of rubble tangled around her feet. She kicked it aside and blundered on, wondering despairingly where she was going, hoping to Jesus that it wasn't a dead-end. A moment later, however, she found herself descending steps – stone ones, very steep and coated with slippery moss. She skidded several times as she went down, but still managed to stay upright. Her lungs were raw bags in her chest, her heart banging like a drum. Then – from nowhere, a hand caught hold of her arm.

The scream locked in Kate's throat. *Dear Jesus – she hadn't realised they were so close* ...

But they weren't.

With a strength she hadn't thought it possible for any man to possess, she was yanked sideways off her feet and through a narrow entrance that she hadn't even noticed in the gloom. Before she knew it, she was in a rubbish-cluttered yard, and whoever had dragged her there had slammed a wooden gate shut, plunging them both into complete darkness.

'Who ... who are ...?' she stammered.

'Shhhhh,' was all he said, in a whisper.

Kate did as she was told, though she was still breathing hoarsely. Her blood was pumping so hard, it seemed inconceivable nobody else could hear it. After what seemed a lifetime of waiting, the two skinheads came clomping down the flight of steps, cursing and muttering. A minute later, however, they'd gone, passing the closed gate without paying it any attention.

Kate leaned back against the brick wall, still gasping, hardly able to believe that her ordeal was over. Of course, she wasn't entirely sure that it was. It was still too dim in that tiny, unlit space to see who her saviour was, though that became apparent when he spoke.

'Dare I say it,' he began, in his heavily-accented voice. 'But I think I know this city better than its natives.'

It was *him* ... the Romanian, or whatever it was he was supposed to be. For a moment, Kate's hair prickled. How was this possible? She'd left him at New Cross ...

'You've got a lot of questions, I don't doubt,' he said, almost as if he'd read her mind. 'But I think maybe we leave them 'til later, no? Those guys ... they're not finished yet.'

In all that fear, madness and confusion, that at least made sense. Kate nodded and swallowed. She was now perspiring hard, her limbs aching. It was good just to rest for a minute, in the cool darkness, not talking, not even thinking.

***

'It's true what I tell you,' he said later on, as he walked her down Sidney Street. 'I live in London for eight years. This city is my home now.' He seemed proud of the fact.

'You've obviously settled in,' Kate replied, still uncertain of him, but sticking as close as she could.

Grigori Slaken – for that indeed was his name, he assured her – shrugged. 'Hey ... you got to be ready to meet new cultures on their own terms. Not like Prince Drakula, huh?' He looked round at her and grinned.

'What ... Oh, no.' She half-laughed.

'Sorry I scared you at the station,' he said. 'But I wanted to speak to you after you asked that question in the lecture. It seemed to me you didn't get an answer.'

'I think you're right.'

Slaken nodded. 'Drakula ... yeah, he *was* deemed vampire. Even by his own people. But that was not because of the killing. You see, to please the Hungarian royal family, Drakula converted from Greek Orthodox to the Roman Catholic. In Wallachia, this was great heresy, and heretics, when they die ... were believed to be *nosferatu*.'

'I see.'

Slaken smiled again. 'So, Professor Lexington got it wrong, yeah.

Not for the first time, I might say. His accents … they leave a little bit
to be desired, huh?'

Kate chuckled. There was no doubting that. She glanced more
closely at Slaken. He was waxy-pale in complexion, but his features
were handsome and strongly boned, and framed either side by rich,
black sideburns. His hair, also thick, and almost oily in its blackness,
was a rich mass, currently tied back in a long pony-tail. When he
smiled, he pursed his lips slightly, revealing healthy white teeth. She
wasn't sure what colour his eyes were – in the sodium street-light it
was impossible to tell – but she imagined blue-grey. That would suit
him best.

She stopped and turned to face him, not wanting him to accompany
her much further, to see that she lived in a refuge for battered women.
'Listen, my name is Kate McCleod,' she said. 'I should thank you.
You looked after me back there.'

He waved that aside, then a thoughtful look stole over him. 'Maybe
you can make it up to me?' He grinned again, but now in a crafty sort
of way. 'Let me buy you a drink.'

'Oh, I don't know …'

'Hey ..' He took her by the hands. A tremor went through her. 'Just
a drink. No strings. What you say?'

Despite her inclinations, Kate went along with him. He was far
from unfanciable, and his easy, relaxed manner had reduced her
suspicions almost to zero. If they were genuinely on the same course
together, it was perhaps odd that she hadn't spotted him before, but
then her attendance at lectures was not all it should be – she'd only
started the course to fill her long, empty hours while she waited to be
re-housed, and occasionally it was hard to maintain interest.

They found a smart wine bar off Whitechapel Road, and tucked
themselves away in a quiet corner where heavy satin drapes and
armchairs of deep, crushed velvet created a decadent atmosphere.
Slaken ordered a bottle of Chablis, which was delivered with two crystal
goblets and a horrifying bill for £45, though the price didn't seem to
worry him.

Once again, he was eulogising on the Dracula myth: 'Bela Lugosi.
My countryman, well … nearly. He sort of lisped a lot and twisted his

face around. I don't think he did the Count justice. Your Christopher Lee … he was basically an English lord, was he not. Tall, elegant, shouting voice. And all these evening suits they put these guys in. I tell you, the Carpathian Mountains are not a place for evening suits.'

'You've seen them?' Kate asked.

'Oh yeah. Many times. It's a beautiful land. Or *was*. Much of it is now spoiled.'

'So I hear,' she said, recalling one of Professor Lexington's earlier lectures, and his grim revelation that Transylvania's skies were now so vilely polluted that it wasn't uncommon in winter for black snow to fall. *Black snow*. The thought of that still sent a shudder through her, though in a dark and spooky sort of way it seemed highly appropriate.

'Is Drakula still well known over there?' she asked. 'I mean, do people talk about him?'

'Hey,' he said. 'In my country, Drakula is the national hero. What they never teach you in the West is that as well as a tyrant, he was also a statesman and a great soldier. He held the Danube frontier for many years against the Turks, who threatened to swamp all our Christian lands.'

'Oh, come on,' she replied. 'He was evil … a savage.'

Slaken took a sip of wine. 'Well – in my experience, national pride can bring out the worst in any person. Your own hero, for example – William Wallace. Was he not a monster too?'

'Och, man – he was not,' she said, mildly stung.

Slaken wagged a finger at her. 'Ah-ah. I think, if you look at the fact – not the Hollywood fact, but the *real* fact – you will see the brute in him. Did he not skin and burn his captives? Did he not put sword to every person he could who understood the English tongue?'

'Wallace was a true patriot,' she told him firmly.

Slaken sniffed. 'Did we not meet two true patriots early on? Those skinheads?'

She waved that aside. 'They were just fascist thugs.'

He sat back, smiling. 'That sounds like it's okay for the Scottish to be nationalist, but not the English?'

'It's not the same thing at all,' she protested.

'I don't know.' He shook his head. 'Pride is a strong emotion. It motivates us in crazy ways. Of course, that doesn't excuse Drakula his hundred-thousand victims. You want to know what I think about that?'

'What?' Kate asked. She was enjoying the conversation immensely, though the wine was starting to go to her head.

Slaken looked thoughtful and leaned forward, his voice a throaty whisper. 'I think Drakula – he *wanted* to be a vampire. I think the killing, the torture, all this depravity – is proof that he had the desire to damn himself, you know, to get himself cast out. To be *nosferatu* would have solved a lot of that guy's problems – on all sides, he had enemies. And, of course, he was a believer. As they all were in those days.' Slaken raised a charcoal-black eyebrow. 'As *you* are too, I think?'

Kate blushed. 'Well, I've read some books, seen some films.'

Slaken sat back. 'Hey listen, your books and movies are not so far off the mark. In the myths of my people, the vampire is a kind of dark angel, a powerful aristocrat of the night. A hunter, a beast – but also a thing to be approached in awe, with respect as much as loathing.'

Kate felt a warm tingle when he said this. She'd never been able to accept the mythological assertion that vampires were basically blood-sucking ghosts that hung around graveyards, thinking only of quenching their insatiable thirst. It was the headier, more romantic vision she clung to – a funereal world of ruined castles and gloomy vaults maybe, but a strangely passionate one too, where a tastefully-clad and perfectly-mannered nobility brooded in shadowed places, mourning its lost existence.

Slaken, meanwhile, was still expounding his own theory. 'This, I think, is what Drakula had in mind. And – you know, I think others thought that, too. When they found his body, he had been brutally mutilated. He was hacked and torn and stabbed many times through the heart. And his head had been cut off. And not only that – whoever did it, and they never found out who, they tried to weigh him down in the swamp with stones. To me, those guys were really making sure – trying to destroy him both as human *and* vampire. I guess *nosferatu* was bad enough, but the idea of Vlad Drakula joining that unholy legion

– wow!' He looked up at Kate and grinned. 'No wonder it caught your Bram Stoker's imagination.'

***

Later on that night, after he'd walked her safely back to the hostel, Slaken began to prowl. He didn't have to search hard to find what he was looking for. They were in a dank underpass, perhaps half a mile from the shop where they had first begun to chase the girl. Now they had a girl of their own, and three confederates with them. *Five*, he thought, as he walked down the stone corridor towards them. Well – even five would be relatively easy meat. They only noticed him when he was close. An immensely fat skinhead, who hadn't been with the group before, was the first. He broke off his conversation and nodded in Slaken's direction. One by one, the others turned.

Jesus, but they were ugly, thought the Romanian. Why did they affect that convict look? Even the girl had done everything possible to dehumanise herself, covering her female form with a bulky flak-jacket and zip-up combat trousers. On her feet she wore boots, through her nose an iron ring. Her hair, she'd shaved down to the bristles. She too sported Nazi tattoos – crossed daggers on either temple. No doubt they still fucked her, he thought, but then who else could they get, looking like gorillas as they did?

'Hey boys,' he said, as he walked up to them.

All were now facing him. The closest was drinking from a bottle of Jack Daniels, and without warning, Slaken lashed out at *him* first, smashing it into his face. The others reacted quickly, but compared to the Romanian, they were sluggish. A lightning flat-hand blow slammed a nose-bone backwards into a brain; a sweeping karate chop shattered a windpipe. The fat one launched a hay-maker, but Slaken wove past it and hammered six quick punches into the broad, pudgy face. Then the girl attacked, swinging in a big kick. He caught her easily by the ankle, swung her up into the air and dropped her hard, the back of her skull impacting on the concrete pavement. In the space of a second, only one of them was left – he was young and lean. In his tight-fitted denim drainpipes, he looked ridiculous. When he tried to run, it was with a lanky, spidery gait, and the Romanian was able to overhaul him with ease. The youth gibbered for mercy, but was pinned face-first against the wall while Slaken rummaged through his jacket pockets. A couple of seconds later, he found what he was looking for – a seven-inch flick-knife. It was a crude weapon, but it would serve. He sprang it open, then plunged it into the skinhead's back, roughly on line with the right kidney, ripping it upwards and sideways until it jarred on the spinal column …

Five minutes later, he'd laid them all out side-by-side. Only two were still alive – the fat one and the girl. He could use the girl, so he threw her over his shoulder. Then he stamped on the skull of the remaining male, compressing it with his heel until it cracked. Shortly afterwards, he found a disused stairway, now grilled off and filled to half its depth with stinking refuse. Prying the grill loose, Slaken hauled his captive inside and laid her down on the garbage. She groaned, made faint gesticulations with her hands. That impressed him. Brain damaged or not, she was undoubtedly a tough one. Still, there was no time for sentiment. Flicking open the blade again, he pushed her head back and slashed her carotid artery. A hot, crimson flow came forth, pulsing out in thick, looping jets. Slaken caught it in mouthfuls, guzzling it down voraciously.

Only after several minutes did he stagger back, and smear the gore with his sleeve across his sweaty, ashen face. He doubted that he'd drained her completely, but she was certainly dead, and satisfied with that, he lurched away down the underpass, eventually emerging on barren, brick-strewn wasteland near Tower Hamlets Cemetery. He walked almost drunkenly towards it, finally coming up against railings of corroded iron. Beyond them, unkempt vegetation ran riot over the crooked forms of sepulchres and gravestones.

'Are you happy now?' he shouted into the night, in his own language. 'Surely, even *you* can not ignore this? Am I not invincible?'

He rattled the fence. Rust showered off it; prongs snapped. Still, though, the midnight hush remained.

'Take me now!' Slaken roared. 'It is my right! By ancestry, by blood, by nationality! Well? Come then! Come for me!'

A sickness was now rising in his guts – swift and relentless, overpowering even to a man of his steel-thewed frame. Beyond the old fence, only wind stirred the rank vegetation. Litter breezed down a weedy footpath.

'You bastards!' he shrieked. 'You cowards! I'll never forgive you, if you … fail me. I demand this – I order it. I …'

He slumped down onto his knees. His head was suddenly swimming. Then, pint after pint of blood surged up from his retching stomach, splattering and steaming on the cindery floor. Around him, the wind sighed emptily.

***

That night, despite her narrow bunk, and the fact that she shared a small, stuffy room with two other women, one of whom – a brazen-voiced Mancunian – chunnered endlessly through the night, begging someone called Charlie not to do it to her again, Kate dreamed vividly that she was far away, in another land if not another time.

Her dream opened as she stepped ashore a small island from a rowing-boat, which swayed uneasily in silt-dark water. For some reason, she was barefoot and clad only in a filmy white shift. The air was chill and rank, with a noxious chemical odour. Unsure where she was, Kate followed a path that snaked ahead through skeletal willows, and came at last to a chapel. It had been built in the exotic Baroque style so popular in the Eastern Orthodox culture, but now was sorely dilapidated, the frescoes on its outer walls decayed and black with soot, its carved saints faceless lumps of mouldering stone.

Unwilling, but unable to resist, Kate was drawn towards and then inside the mournful structure. An ornate wooden door creaked open of its own accord, admitting her to an inner sanctum, which though wide and airy was also claustrophobic and damp and filled with deep, foetid shadows. Here and there, candles flickered, revealing faded tapestries on the walls and golden icons set in niches. Some glittered; most, though, were coated in dust and webs. In the very centre of the room, almost on an altar of its own, with a vase of dead flowers set at one end and a silver chalice, stained brown around its rim, at the other, lay a heavy tombstone that was perhaps six feet by three. Cyrillic lettering covered much of it, and to one side, propped up by two rusted daggers, there was a framed portrait of a cruel and wicked face, which Kate clearly recognised from the lecture-theatre screen.

Now she knew where she was. There was no mistake. This was Snagov Monastery, where Vlad Tepes, the Drakula of truth rather than legend, had finally been laid to rest. This was the very place, still kept as a shrine and unquestioningly revered by the people whose ancestors he'd so zealously both protected and slaughtered. Then, as Kate stared down at the arcane inscriptions, wondering if they rendered a blessing or a curse, the candles began to flicker and an icy wind blew up from some hidden recess.

Almost inevitably, with a slow, grating sound, the tombstone began to shift. Kate was rooted to the spot. Colossal in weight though it doubtless was, the great slab of rock was inexorably rising. It was a scene she had witnessed on a multitude of occasions before, in any number of movies – but now it was *real*, and a terror more acute than anything she'd believed possible seized her. Instinctively she knew that whatever lay beneath that stone was neither handsome, nor sad, nor noble – but unimaginably foul; a shapeless, corrupted thing of ancient, destructive evil. Its stench flowed out like poisonous gas, threatening to suffocate her even as she backed away.

In a fog of blind panic, Kate turned and stumbled towards the chapel entrance, the heavy wooden door of which even now was swinging shut. With a mighty effort, she buffeted it aside, and threw herself out into the open air. No reviving freshness awaited her, however. The vile fumes of rot and death were all-engulfing. The chill had risen to a new, searing level, numbing her to near-paralysis. Unable to move, even to whimper, she could only listen in dread as slithering, dragging feet drew towards the chapel door behind her. And then, she realised – snow was falling. But not the plump, fleecy down she was used to in Scotland. As Professor Lexington had warned, this snow was *black*, tumbling from a smeared and leaden sky like the torn-off feathers of a million crows …

Kate awoke shuddering, staring wild-eyed at the water-marked ceiling a foot above her. Only after several breathless seconds was she able to look around and think clearly again. She realised the morning had come. Its weak, milky light was leaking through the net curtains. For the first time in a long time, she was glad to see that cramped, grotty room.

The relief was short-lived however, for later on, over breakfast, someone handed her a letter. At first Kate assumed it would be from her sister, Johanna, the only person who knew her address here, but then she saw that it had been left on the doorstep rather than posted, and that worried her. Unless it had come from Grigori. But then she glanced at the envelope again. It was rose-pink and scented with lavender; her name was written on the front in dark, reddish ink, in a delicate, artistic hand. In view of that, she thought, perhaps it wasn't from Grigori after all. As a man, he didn't strike her as being beyond romantic gesture, yet this was somehow 'feminine.' More to the point, when she finally opened the letter, it was *about* him, not from him. And it contained only three words. They read: *Slaken is dangerous.*

Involuntarily, she dropped the paper onto the breakfast-table. It lay there, face up, its accusing words staring at her. If this was a joke, she thought, it was in poor taste. But what could it mean? And who was it from? Someone else on the course? Maybe someone who'd seen them speaking together at New Cross Station, or in the wine bar? But that was ridiculous. She knew nobody at the college well enough.

'Everything all right, love?' asked the Mancunian girl from across the table.

'Yes,' Kate began uncertainly, her mouth dry. 'Well – no. I've met this guy, but …'

'Oh Jesus! There but for the grace of God go all of us. Forget him, chuck. Whoever he is. Just ditch him. Save yourself the grief.'

Kate nodded. She didn't bother finishing what she'd been going to say. It would make no sense to them. She glanced back at the letter, no longer wanting to touch it but knowing that she couldn't leave it there. After a moment, she picked it up, folded it and slipped it into her jeans pocket. It was all the more distressing, of course, as she'd been due to meet Grigori again that evening. They'd left things well the night before. Not so much as a kiss, but she'd found his company invigorating, his attention flattering. The sexual chemistry had been right. And now this. She wondered if it was in any way conceivable that Kenny might be involved. But how? As far as she knew, he was still in his cell. He wasn't due to be considered for parole for at least another year. In any case, something like this – cryptic, subtle – was surely beyond her husband, who was only good it seemed for spur-of-the-moment street-robberies, usually when he was inebriated. No, Kenny, it could not be.

It nagged her for much of the day. She took out the note, re-read it, then re-read it again. Still, it made no sense. She even travelled down to the college that afternoon, wandering through its libraries and arched corridors, which as always were bustling. In the central hall, musicians were at practise. The Students' Union office throbbed with activity – a demo march was being planned for that weekend, against the Allied bombing of Serbia. But nowhere, in the midst of all that chaos, did she spot Grigori – or anyone else she recognised.

She returned to Whitechapel lost and confused, still knowing nothing but feeling deeply betrayed. Was it a genuine warning, or a malevolent trick? Did her suitor have another woman in tow? Was that it? It would certainly explain the perfume, but even from a woman scorned, this message was meaningless. One thing *was* certain – Kate needed to know what it meant, because as long as she didn't, she'd have no option but to view the Romanian as another male vulture out to abuse her in some way.

It wasn't going to be pleasant, but she *had* to know.

***

They dined that night at the Astarte Hotel, which was sumptuous in the extreme all high oak-panelled rooms, adorned with paintings and exotic plants, though Kate was mildly intimidated by such extravagance. Having testified for the prosecution at Kenny's trial, and then fled Scotland with only an overnight bag, she hadn't managed to bring much with her in the way of clothes. She could still trick herself pretty when she wanted to, though. A touch of pink lip-gloss and a little green shade over her hazel eyes brought her looks out to perfection, and she did have one nice outfit, a blue trouser-suit that had recently been pressed and cleaned. Grigori had also risen to the occasion, and wore a smart, collarless shirt and jacket of purple, patterned silk. His hair was loose and hung past his shoulders in thick, shiny-black tresses. This time, however, the girl was determined not to be won over by his looks, or his charm – at least, not yet.

They ate in style. Kate chose smoked haddock soup with lentils, followed by roast lamb in mustard and breadcrumbs. Grigori selected red pepper mousse, then veal in Madeira sauce. It went as smoothly and pleasantly as the previous night, and afterwards, over coffee and cognac, they snuggled together on a sofa. But it was still a fallacy as far as Kate was concerned. A fallacy that couldn't last. Grigori, showing great knowledge and enthusiasm, was discussing Celtic FC's future without Fergus McCann, when she suddenly interrupted him

'You don't really want to talk about football,' she said. It wasn't so much a question as a statement.

He glanced round curiously. 'I'm sorry?'

'I wonder if you are.'

He smiled, but seemed puzzled. 'You lost me.'

She watched him carefully. 'Your part of the world is in flames, Grigori. Even now, British and American bombers are flying missions to try and smash Serbia.'

He shrugged politely. 'What would you have me do about it?'

'Well … nothing. It just seems funny you haven't commented.'

'*My* part of the world is past comment, Kate,' he replied. 'You say these NATO bombers are out to smash Serbia. Well … Romania has *already* been smashed. Many years ago. I loved my country, but these days it's in ruins. It's a wasteland.'

'But does that really upset you, Grigori? It doesn't seem to.'

Now he was returning her gaze hard. 'What is it you think you know, I wonder?'

'That you're mysterious,' she said. 'That you're interesting and fun, but that you never … never really talk about yourself.'

'And what would you have me tell you?'

'Tell me about this.' And clumsy through drink, but determined all the same, she produced the letter, opened it and thrust it towards him.

After a moment, he took it and gazed down at the simple wording. If it upset or shocked him, he didn't show it. He showed no emotion at all.

This, Slaken knew, was not the time for an insane rage.

Insane rages had served him well in the past: when he'd interrogated dissidents in the dark basements of Ceausescu's presidential palace; when he and his squad had broken up their secret meetings in school classrooms or newspaper offices; when yard by yard, he'd fought his way out through the labyrinthine passages under Bucharest, cutting down the rebel troops in swathes, and when his Kalashnikov ran dry, blasting them with his Nagan, then his big, experienced fists. But most often in those days, the cooler head had ruled. To rise through the ranks of the *Securitate*, there was no other way. Calculating efficiency was the thing the dictator had sought most in his elite security-police. Was there any other way to root out skilled moles, assassinate foreign interventionists, pinpoint the leaders of dissent and remove them with swift and surgical precision?

So Slaken kept his temper, and a few seconds later was able to look the girl in the eye again.

'Where did you get this?' he quietly asked her.

'It was delivered to my door this morning. I don't know who by.'

He nodded. 'I'm afraid *I* do.' Abruptly, he stood. 'We should leave. I'll pay.'

'Wait ... Grigori, I ...'

He put a gentle finger to her lips. 'I'll tell you everything, I promise. But not here.'

She nodded, taking him at his word, and a few moments later they were outside together, walking along the pavement towards a distant taxi-rank.

'It's a long story,' he said, after a moment.

'I've got plenty of time,' she replied.

He glanced round at her. 'More than you realise.'

Then, shoving her backwards into an alley, he struck her violently on the head.

***

Slaken prepared his gift in a dismal chasm beneath the railway arches at Mile End. Here, amid a welter of shattered, abandoned vehicles, smashed furniture and clutches of vagrants swathed in tatters and huddled together for warmth, he stripped the lifeless body, then laid it out on two packing-cases. After that, he waited. Rats scuttled in the heaped trash; water dripped; a train roared overhead, its echoes crashing like cannon-fire. Yet, nothing out of the ordinary stirred. Slaken bit his bottom lip until his filed-sharp teeth drew trickles of blood.

'I am waiting!' he finally bellowed, once again in the Romanian tongue. 'This time I give you not one, but *two* lives. In all senses perfect.' With a sweeping gesture, he revealed his offering, her handsome contours gleaming like marble in the filtered moonlight. 'Is she not choice?' he cried. He ran a hand across her flat belly, then leaned forward, and with a lapping tongue, took possession of her jutting nipples, bringing them to firm, erect points. When he looked up again, his chin glistened with saliva. 'Is she not ideal? Is she not *worth* immortalising? I tell you, *she is* – for there is more than you can see.' He gave a bass laugh. 'She is *a believer*. Yes – in this day and age, a believer. Not only that, she is a worshipper. I can sense it. *I know it.* In addition, she is strong – of pure tribal stock. The blood of warriors flows through her. Come then! Take her. And me. We are ready.'

Still only rags and litter rustled on the adjacent lot. Slaken could hardly conceal his rage.

'In the name of Lucifer, why do you hesitate? Who will miss her? As well as all these other things, she is a loner – she has no friends, no family. Come now ...'

And in that moment, a faint shuffle – as of some dead-weight being dragged painfully forwards – caught his attention. He turned, his eyes narrowing. A thing was moving out there. But what? For a moment, it was as if some formless gobbet of darkness had detached itself from the main bulk and was now sliding slug-like towards him over the sea of rubble and broken glass. Slaken gazed at it, perplexed. Then he spied a second one, some seven or eight yards behind the first; then a third, homing in from a different direction. All at once he realised they were on every side, perhaps 20 of them in total; and in that same instant, he realised what they were – *the derelicts, the vagrants.* Swaddled like mummies in their leprous shreds, they crawled and inched forwards, blind, mindless things, feeling their way with wizened claws.

Slaken knew nothing of fear, and indeed he didn't feel it now, though bewilderment was certainly there; this was something he had never seen before – and then a stunning realisation struck him. His bafflement became first astonishment, then wrathful glee. His heart leapt in his chest. 'So!' he shouted. 'You come at last. And about time.'

As one, the slug-like things halted. 'Yes, Grigori,' came a breathy, chuckling whisper. 'We come at last. And yes –' With a sudden shout, the nearest of them sprung upright, flinging off its dirty cloak '– *it is about time!*'

Disbelief caught in Slaken's throat. He wasn't sure which astonished him more: the pale, bearded face so recognisable to him, or the slim-barrelled Mauser now levelled on his chest. As he stood there, dumbfounded, the rest of the creatures threw off their disguises. There was a loud snapping and clicking as firearms were cocked. The Romanian's gaze flicked from one face to another, until at last it came back to the first.

'Kyuryatki!' he snarled. His hand went to his hip, but of course his Nagan wasn't there – as it hadn't been for many years. Such was the price of incognito.

Kyuryatki gave a lupine grin. 'You thought you could escape us forever, Grigori? After the things you have done?'

'You bastard!' Slaken spat. 'You betrayed us!'

'Ohhhh, no,' said his former lieutenant, in mock outrage. 'I won't have that. I saw the light, that is all. As did many others, when the hour came for us to choose.'

Slaken sensed them closing in. He glared around at them. 'You fucking traitors!'

The Mauser barked, and lead ripped his thigh, smashing the femur and pitching him hard onto his back. Unbearable pain lanced upwards through his body …

'Don't call us names, Grigori,' warned Kyuryatki. 'You'll only make things worse for yourself.'

'Son – son of a bitch,' Slaken choked, curling and twisting in agony, clamping his fingers to the two wounds in his leg – the entrance and exit – both now spurting hot fluid. 'You – you'll pay for this!'

Kyuryatki shook his head. 'You're the one who's going to pay – when we get you home.'

From a hidden place somewhere to their left, an engine rumbled into life. Lights came on, and then a heavy vehicle was lumbering backwards – a van of some sort. Slaken glanced up at it, and saw that its rear doors were already swinging open. Inside it, there was total blackness.

'No!' he shrieked, and struggled to get free as they reached down for him, but a smashing blow to his left temple put paid to all that.

'You know how we found you, Grigori?' said Kyuryatki into his ear, as they lifted his dazed body. '*They* told us.' The agent gave an oily, gloating chuckle. 'Yes – *them*. The ones you seek to join. A bloodless corpse here and there was an easy enough trail to follow, but without *their* help, we'd never have closed in so quickly. It seems they don't want you, Grigori. *Not at any price!*'

***

When Kate finally came round, she was in a sleepy, dream-like state. She had the notion she'd been there for some time, and though she was lying naked beneath the Gothic arches of the railway line, in that most villainous corner of the city, for some reason she felt neither cold nor frightened. In fact, if anything, she felt safe, secure.

When she eventually sat up, she understood why, because she saw that she wasn't alone. The others with her weren't easy to pick out, but they were definitely there – in their ones and two, on the furthest realms of her vision, posed and silent like mime-dancers in a shadow-play. To some degree, they encircled her, but she didn't feel trapped by them. Far from it. When she climbed to her feet, and walked unsteadily towards them, they seemed to recede – ethereal, translucent things, more mist than flesh.

Then a light fell across her, and Kate turned, and where there hadn't been one before, far back among the stanchions of the railway, there was now a portal – a tall, narrow aperture, as if two great sections of stage-scenery had shifted apart for a moment. A warm, ruby glow spilled out – enticing, comforting, and with a vague fragrance of lavender. Warily, Kate approached it, and as she did, she sensed those nether-beings closing ranks behind her. But there was still no threat from them. Only a gentle, whispered coaxing.

And the promise of a place where berserkers feared to tread.

Feeders And Eaters
Neil Gaiman

This is a true story, pretty much. As far as that goes, and whatever good it does anybody.

***

It was late one night, and I was cold, in a city where I had no right to be. Not at that time of night, anyway. I won't tell you which city. I'd missed my last train, and I wasn't sleepy, so I prowled the streets around the station until I found an all-night café. Somewhere warm to sit.

You know the kind of place; you've been there: café's name on a Pepsi sign above a dirty plate-glass window, dried egg residue between the tines of all their forks. I wasn't hungry, but I bought a slice of toast and a mug of greasy tea, so they'd leave me alone.

There were a couple of other people in there, sitting alone at their tables, derelicts and insomniacs huddled over their empty plates. Dirty coats and donkey jackets, buttoned up to the neck.

I was walking back from the counter with my tray when somebody said, 'Hey.' It was a man's voice. 'You,' the voice said, and I knew he was talking to me, not to the room. 'I know you. Come here. Sit over here.'

I ignored it. You don't want to get involved, not with anyone you'd run into in a place like that. Then he said my name, and I turned and looked at him. When someone knows your name, you don't have any option.

'Don't you know me?' he asked. I shook my head. I didn't know anyone who looked like that. You don't forget something like that. 'It's me,' he said, his voice a pleading whisper. 'Eddie Barrow. Come on, mate. You know me.'

And when he said his name I did know him, more or less. I mean, I knew Eddie Barrow. We had worked on a building site together, ten years back, during my only real flirtation with manual work.

Eddie Barrow was tall, and heavily muscled, with a movie star smile and lazy good looks. He was ex-police. Sometimes he'd tell me stories, true tales of fitting-up and doing over, of punishment and crime. He had left the force after some trouble between him and one of the top brass. He said it was the Chief Superintendent's wife forced him to leave. Eddie was always getting into trouble with women. They really liked him, women.

When we were working together on the building site they'd hunt him down, give him sandwiches, little presents, whatever. He never seemed to *do* anything to make them like him; they just liked him. I used to watch him to see how he did it, but it didn't seem to be anything he did. Eventually, I decided it was just the way he was: big, strong, not very bright, and terribly, terribly good-looking.

But that was ten years ago.

The man sitting at the Formica table wasn't good-looking. His eyes were dull, and rimmed with red, and they stared down at the table-top, without hope. His skin was grey. He was too thin, obscenely thin. I could see his scalp through his filthy hair. I said, 'What happened to you?'

'How d'you mean?'

'You look a bit rough,' I said, although he looked worse than rough; he looked dead. Eddie Barrow had been a big guy. Now he'd collapsed in on himself. All bones and flaking skin.

'Yeah,' he said. Or maybe 'Yeah?' I couldn't tell. Then, resigned, flatly, 'Happens to us all in the end.'

He gestured with his left hand, pointed at the seat opposite him. His right arm hung stiffly at his side, his right hand safe in the pocket of his coat.

123

Eddie's table was by the window, where anyone walking past could see you. Not somewhere I'd sit by choice, not if it was up to me. But it was too late now. I sat down facing him and I sipped my tea. I didn't say anything, which could have been a mistake. Small talk might have kept his demons at a distance. But I cradled my mug and said nothing, so I suppose he must have thought that I wanted to know more, that I cared. I didn't care. I had enough problems of my own. I didn't want to know about his struggle with whatever it was that had brought him to this state – drink, or drugs, or disease – but he started to talk, in a grey voice, and I listened.

'I came here a few years back, when they were building the bypass. Stuck around after, the way you do. Got a room in an old place around the back of Prince Regent's Street. Room in the attic. It was a family house, really. They only rented out the top floor, so there were just the two boarders, me and Miss Corvier. We were both up in the attic, but in separate rooms, next door to each other. I'd hear her moving about. And there was a cat. It was the family cat, but it came upstairs to say hello, every now and again, which was more than the family ever did.

'I always had my meals with the family, but Miss Corvier, she didn't ever come down for meals, so it was a week before I met her. She was coming out of the upstairs lavvy. She looked so old. Wrinkled face, like an old, old monkey. But long hair, down to her waist, like a young girl.

'It's funny, with old people, you don't think they feel things like we do. I mean, here's her, old enough to be my granny and ...' He stopped. Licked his lips with a grey tongue. 'Anyway ... I came up to the room one night and there's a brown paper bag of mushrooms outside my door on the ground. It was a present, I knew that straight off. A present for me. Not normal mushrooms, though. So I knocked on her door.

'I says, "Are these for me?"

'"Picked them meself, Mister Barrow," she says.

'"They aren't like toadstools or anything?" I asked. "Y'know, poisonous? Or funny mushrooms?"

'She just laughs. Cackles even. "They're for eating," she says. "They're fine. Shaggy inkcaps, they are. Eat them soon, now. They go off quick. They're best fried up with a little butter and garlic."

'I say, "Are you having some too?" She says, "No." She says, "I used to be a proper one for mushrooms, but not any more, not with my stomach. But they're lovely. Nothing better than a young, shaggy inkcap mushroom. It's astonishing the things that people don't eat. All the things around them that people could eat, if only they knew it."

'I said, "Thanks," and went back into my half of the attic. They'd done the conversion a few years before, nice job really. I put the mushrooms down by the sink. After a few days, they dissolved into black stuff, like ink, and I had to put the whole mess into a plastic bag and throw it away.

'I'm on my way downstairs with the plastic bag, and I run into her on the stairs. She says, "Hello Mister B." I say, "Hello Miss Corvier."

'"Call me Effie," she says. "How were the mushrooms?"

'"Very nice, thank you," I said. "They were lovely."

'She'd leave me other things after that, little presents, flowers in old milk-bottles, things like that, then nothing. I was a bit relieved when the presents suddenly stopped.

'So I'm down at dinner with the family, the lad at the poly, he was home for the holidays. It was August. Really hot. And someone says they hadn't seen her for about a week, and could I look in on her. I said I didn't mind. So I did. The door wasn't locked. She was in bed. She had a thin sheet over her, but you could see she was naked under the sheet. Not that I was trying to see anything; it'd be like looking at your gran in the altogether. This old lady. But she looked so pleased to see me.

'"Do you need a doctor?" I says.

'She shakes her head. "I'm not ill," she says. "I'm hungry. That's all."

'"Are you sure?" I say. "Because I can call someone, it's not a bother. They'll come out for old people."

'She says, "Edward? I don't want to be a burden on anyone, but I'm so hungry."

'"Right. I'll get you something to eat," I said. "Something easy on your tummy," I says. That's when she surprises me. She looks embarrassed. Then she says, very quietly, *meat*. "It's got to be fresh meat, and raw. I won't let anyone else cook for me. Meat. Please, Edward."

'"Not a problem," I says, and I go downstairs. I thought for a moment about nicking it from the cat's bowl, but of course I didn't. It was like, I knew she wanted it, so I had to do it. I had no choice. I went down to Safeways, and I bought her a readipak of best ground sirloin.

'The cat smelled it. Followed me up the stairs. I said, "You get down, puss. It's not for you," I said. "It's for Miss Corvier, and she's not feeling well, and she's going to need it for her supper," and the thing mewed at me as if it hadn't been fed in a week, which I knew wasn't true because its bowl was still half-full. Stupid, that cat was.

'I knock on her door, she says, "Come in." She's still in the bed, and I give her the pack of meat, and she says, "Thank you Edward, you've got a good heart." And she starts to tear off the plastic wrap, there in the bed. There's a puddle of brown blood under the plastic tray, and it drips onto her sheet, but she doesn't notice. Makes me shiver.

'I'm going out the door, and I can already hear her starting to eat with her fingers, cramming the raw mince into her mouth. And she hadn't got out of bed. But the next day, she's up and about, and from there on, she's in and out at all hours, in spite of her age, and I think, "There you are. They say red meat's bad for you, but it did her the world of good." And raw, well, it's just steak tartare, isn't it? You ever eaten raw meat?'

The question came as a surprise. I said, 'Me?'

Eddie looked at me with his dead eyes, and he said, 'Nobody else at this table.'

'Yes. A little. When I was a small boy – four, five years old – my grandmother would take me to the butcher's with her, and he'd give me slices of raw liver, and I'd just eat them, there in the shop, like that. And everyone would laugh.'

I hadn't thought of that in 20 years. But it was true.

I still like my liver rare, and sometimes, if I'm cooking and if nobody else is around, I'll cut a thin slice of raw liver before I season it, and I'll eat it, relishing the texture and the naked, iron taste.

'Not me,' he said. 'I liked my meat properly cooked. So the next thing that happened was Thompson went missing.'

'Thompson?'

'The cat. Somebody said there used to be two of them, and they called them Thomson and Thompson. I don't know why. Stupid, giving them both the same name. The first one was squashed by a lorry.' He pushed at a small mound of sugar on the Formica top with a finger tip. His left hand, still. I was beginning to wonder whether he had a right arm. Maybe the sleeve was empty. Not that it was any of my business. Nobody gets through life without losing a few things on the way.

I was trying to think of some way of telling him I didn't have any money, just in case he was going to ask me for something when he got to the end of his story. I didn't have any money: just a train ticket and enough pennies for the bus ticket home.

'I was never much of a one for cats,' he said suddenly. 'Not really. I liked dogs. Big, faithful things. You knew where you were with a dog. Not cats. Go off for days on end, you don't see them. When I was a lad, we had a cat, it was called Ginger. There was a family down the street, they had a cat they called Marmalade. Turned out it was the same cat, getting fed by all of us. Well, I mean. Sneaky little buggers. You can't trust them.

'That was why I didn't think anything when Thompson went away. The family was worried. Not me. I knew it'd come back. They always do.

'Anyway, a few nights later, I heard it. I was trying to sleep, and I couldn't. It was the middle of the night, and I heard this mewing. Going on, and on, and on. It wasn't loud, but when you can't sleep, these things just get on your nerves. I thought maybe it was stuck up in the rafters, or out on the roof outside. Wherever it was, there wasn't any point in trying to sleep through it. I knew that. So I got up, and I got dressed, even put my boots on in case I was going to be climbing out onto the roof, and I went looking for the cat. I went out in the corridor. It was coming from Miss Corvier's room on the other side of the attic. I knocked on her door, but no-one answered. Tried the door. It wasn't locked. So I went in. I thought maybe that the cat was stuck somewhere. Or hurt. I don't know. I just wanted to help, really.

'Miss Corvier wasn't there. I mean, you know sometimes if there's anyone in a room, and that room was empty. Except there's something on the floor in the corner going *Mrie, Mrie ...* And I turned on the light to see what it was.'

He stopped then for almost a minute, the fingers of his left hand picking at the black goo that had crusted around the neck of the ketchup bottle. It was shaped like a large tomato. Then he said, 'What I didn't understand was how it could still be alive. I mean, it was. And from the chest up, it was alive, and breathing, and fur and everything. But its back legs, its rib cage. Like a chicken carcass. Just bones. And what are they called, sinews? And, it lifted its head, and it looked at me. It may have been a cat, but I knew what it wanted. It was in its eyes. I mean.' He stopped. 'Well, I just knew. I'd never seen eyes like that. You would have known what it wanted, all it wanted, if you'd seen those eyes. I did what it wanted. You'd have to be a monster, not to.'

'What did you do?'

'I used my boots.' Pause. 'There wasn't much blood. Not really. I just stamped, and stamped on its head, until there wasn't really anything much left that looked like anything. If you'd seen it looking at you like that, you would have done what I did.'

I didn't say anything.

'And then I heard someone coming up the stairs to the attic, and I thought I ought to do something, I mean, it didn't look good, I don't know what it must have looked like really, but I just stood there, feeling stupid, with a stinking mess on my boots, and when the door opens, it's Miss Corvier. And she sees it all. She looks at me. And she says, "You killed him." I can hear something funny in her voice, and for a moment, I don't know what it is, and then she comes closer, and I realise that she's crying.

'That's something about old people, when they cry like children, you don't know where to look, do you? And she says, "He was all I had to keep me going, and you killed him. After all I've done," she says, "making it so the meat stays fresh, so the life stays on. After all I've done. I'm an old woman," she says. "I need my meat." I didn't know what to say.

'She's wiping her eyes with her hand. "I don't want to be a burden on anybody," she says. She's crying now. And she's looking at me. She says, "I never wanted to be a burden." She says, "That was my meat. Now," she says, "who's going to feed me now?"'

He stopped, rested his grey face in his left hand, as if he was tired. Tired of talking to me, tired of the story, tired of life. Then he shook his head, and looked at me, and said, 'If you'd seen that cat, you would have done what I did. Anyone would have done.'

He raised his head then, for the first time in his story, looked me in the eyes. I thought I saw an appeal for help in his eyes, something he was too proud to say aloud.

Here it comes, I thought. This is where he asks me for money.

Somebody outside tapped on the window of the café. It wasn't a loud tapping, but Eddie jumped. He said, 'I have to go now. That means I have to go.'

I just nodded. He got up from the table. He was still a tall man, which almost surprised me: he'd collapsed in on himself in so many other ways. He pushed the table away as he got up, and as he got up he took his right hand out of his coat-pocket. For balance, I suppose. I don't know. Maybe he wanted me to see it. But if he wanted me to see it, why did he keep it in his pocket the whole time? No, I don't think he wanted me to see it. I think it was an accident.

He wasn't wearing a shirt or a jumper under his coat, so I could see his arm, and his wrist. Nothing wrong with either of them. He had a normal wrist. It was only when you looked below the wrist that you saw most of the flesh had been picked from the bones, chewed like chicken wings, leaving only dried morsels of meat, scraps and crumbs, and little else. He had only three fingers left, and most of a thumb. I suppose the other finger-bones must have just fallen right off, with no skin or flesh to hold them on.

That was what I saw. Only for a moment, then he put his hand back in his pocket, and pushed out of the door, into the chilly night.

I watched him then, through the dirty plate-glass of the café window. It was funny. From everything he'd said, I'd imagined Miss Corvier to be an old woman. But the woman waiting for him, outside, on the pavement, couldn't have been much over 30. She had long, long hair, though. The kind of hair you can sit on, as they say, although that always sounds faintly like a line from a dirty joke. She looked a bit like a hippy, I suppose. Sort of pretty, in a hungry kind of way. She took his arm, and looked up into his eyes, and they walked away out of the café's light for all the world like a couple of teenagers who were just beginning to realise that they were in love.

I went back up to the counter and bought another cup of tea, and a couple of packets of crisps to see me through until the morning, and I sat and thought about the expression on his face when he'd looked at me that last time.

***

On the milk-train back to the big city, I sat opposite a woman carrying a baby. It was floating in formaldehyde, in a heavy glass container. She needed to sell it, rather urgently, and although I was extremely tired, we talked about her reasons for selling it, and about other things, for the rest of the journey.

Feather
Gary Greenwood

In a small cupboard, tucked away in a corner, sat an old shoe box, its once-sharp corners scuffed and blunted, the remains of a sticky label on one side, partially torn and rubbed off, the black marker ink smudged and faded. An industrious, if slightly hopeful, spider had woven a thin web attaching the box to the worn wooden panel of the cupboard and had succeeded in catching only dust, eventually moving on to more fruitful pastures, leaving behind only the web and the dead and relinquished shell of its body.

The box looked unassuming, tucked away in its little corner, undisturbed for who knew how long until one bright summer's morning when the cupboard, complete with the shoe box and the few other contents, was taken from the wall of the house where it had hung for many years and was carried away by an antiques dealer to his shop.

There, the cupboard was emptied in preparation for its cleaning. The shoe box, and other little odds and ends, were unceremoniously dumped on to a small table at the back of the shop, where it was destined to sit amongst the other rubbish and oddments, until the old man found time to look through everything and sort out what, if anything, was of any use.

***

So it was that a week after it had found its way onto the back table, the shoe box, still with the tatters of the dusty spider's web clinging valiantly to its side, was discovered by Sarah, a young girl who helped the antiques dealer in the summer months when there was no school.

'What's this?' she asked, holding up the box.

'Ach, it's just an old shoe box. Zrow it avay,' the dealer replied in his foreign accent.

'Can I have it?' Sarah asked, turning the box this way and that.

'*Ja, ja,*' the dealer muttered, turning back to something he was working on. Sarah took the box out into the back garden of the shop and lay on her front on the grass, feeling the cool breeze through her legs as she waved them idly in the air, holding her head in her hands and staring at the box. Turning to make sure the antiques dealer was still busy in his shop, Sarah reached out and slowly opened the box, lifting the lid carefully away from the body.

She moved forward, peered inside and saw a small piece of white card. Lifting that away, she found a single feather, perhaps three inches long and brilliantly white, flecked with gold and silver sparkles. Her eyes wide, Sarah carefully picked it up, marvelling at how delicate it was, the stem tapering to an almost invisible point, the filaments fine and graceful. Turning it gently, she smiled as the sun was reflected back from the gold and silver that permeated the feather, sending sparks of light flying off into the sky.

Quickly, Sarah stood and ran back inside the shop, hiding the feather from the old man almost guiltily, and into the toilet up the stairs. Putting the lid down, she sat on the toilet and with the hand that wasn't holding the feather, pulled a few sheets of toilet paper from the roll and spread them on her lap. She placed the feather onto them and very carefully folded the sheets over one another, gently making a parcel. When she had finished, she tucked the tissue paper, the feather safely inside, into the pocket of her dress and returned downstairs.

'Is it okay if I go home a little early today?' she asked the antiques dealer.

'*Ja, ja.* Zat is fine. No vorries, heh?' He chuckled, and it seemed to her ears that even his laughter carried an accent.

When Sarah got home, she rushed up to her small bedroom, barely pausing to shout hello to her mother, and closed the door behind her, taking the tissue parcel out of her pocket. She sat on her bed and unwrapped the tissue, looking at the feather as it sat in her lap. Once more she picked it up and turned it this way and that, smiling at the reflections the afternoon sun made on its surface.

She looked around her room, wondering where she could put it. Something as pretty as this, she thought, ought to be displayed, but where and how? The last thing she wanted to do was pin it to something – using a needle or drawing pin seemed too much like stabbing it, and she certainly didn't want to use sellotape or blutack. She noticed the small potted plant on the windowsill that her grandmother had bought her for her birthday the month before. It was a tall plant, with its flowers and leaves high up its stem, leaving the bottom relatively free. Smiling at her cleverness, Sarah placed the tip of the feather gently into the soil of the pot, leaning it against the plant's stem. She stepped back and admired it for a few minutes, then lay on her bed and began to read a book. Within ten minutes, she had completely forgotten about it.

***

'Here. You left zis out in ze garden yesterday.' The antiques dealer handed Sarah the old shoe box, now empty and slightly damp from that morning's dew. 'Vas dere anyzing exciting inside?'

Sarah was normally an honest child, straightforward and truthful, and it came as a great surprise to her when she said, 'No, nothing at all, really,' and placed the old box onto the pile of rubbish in the corner of the workroom. The old man muttered something in agreement, then asked her to pass him a screwdriver, took it from her and bent back to the clock that he had been working on.

For the rest of the morning, as Sarah helped him, she couldn't stop wondering why she had lied to him; she never had before, so why now over a feather? And how could she have forgotten the feather the previous evening? After she had been reading for half an hour, her mother had called her down to the kitchen for her tea, and after finishing that, she had watched television before going to bed. During the day, the feather had entranced and intrigued her so much, but as soon as she had placed it in the plant pot, she had forgotten all about it.

Returning home for lunch, once more calling hello to her mother as she ran up the stairs, Sarah went straight to her room and the plant pot on the windowsill. The feather stood there, in exactly the same position as she had left it, the tip pressed into the soft soil, its shiny filaments catching the sunlight as it slipped in through the half open curtains. Gently, Sarah stroked it for a moment, then pulled it up out of the soil to hold it once more, frowning as she realised it had become heavier.

Hanging from the end of the feather, growing from it, was a man. Small, only half an inch long, curled up into the foetal position and unmistakably human, hung the pink form of a man. She stared at it, her mouth open, her eyes wide, turning the feather slowly from side to side until the tiny figure moved, one of its arms lifting to cover its head, as if to shield its eyes from the sun. Quickly Sarah replaced the feather and its passenger into the small hole that had been made when she had lifted it out, and gently patted the earth back over the man with her little finger, wondering whether she had done any damage by removing it.

Sarah ran back to the antiques shop, determined to tell the old man about the box and the feather and how it had somehow set down human roots in her plant pot, but when she arrived, she was alarmed to find an ambulance on the drive, its lights flashing, engine running. Stepping around it, walking towards the shop itself, where a handful of people stood watching, Sarah saw the antiques dealer being pushed to the ambulance on a trolley, a red blanket covering his body, an oxygen mask over his face.

'What happened?' she asked one of the medics.

'You a friend?' Sarah nodded. 'He had a heart attack, love. One of his customers found him. We're taking him to hospital.'

She watched as he was loaded into the back of the ambulance, hoping that he would see or hear her, but the doors closed and it drove off, siren blaring.

***

The days seemed infinitely longer to Sarah. Occasionally she would play with her friends, or help her mother around the house, but nothing seemed to compare to watching the old antiques dealer repair a watch or strip the varnish from a chest of drawers, passing him a rag or a bottle when he asked. Twice she pushed the soil away from the root of the feather and stared at the figure that still nestled there, no bigger than it had been, still apparently sleeping. More than once she wanted to talk about it to someone, but her friends would think her a liar, and her mother ... well, she had no idea how her mother would react to her growing a man on her window sill.

Not that she thought it was a man anymore. If she could make it grow to full size, she was sure that the feather sprouting from its back would become one of many, shining and sparkling in the brilliant sunshine as they turned into two strong wings, capable of carrying the figure up into the sky, back to its home, back to heaven. Sarah was convinced an angel was growing in her room.

She visited the old man the day after he came out of intensive care. He was still unconscious and, the doctors told her mother in hushed tones, they didn't hold out much hope for him. His nephew, a polite older gentleman who wore a three piece suit and a monocle, told Sarah that his uncle had often talked about her and that she was welcome to help him in the shop, as he would be looking after it until his uncle was well again. Sarah cried as she looked at the tubes leading into the antique-dealer's old body, into his arm and up his nose, dribbling fluids into him in an attempt to make him better. Her mother took her home.

That evening, she stared at the plant pot and at the feather that gleamed even in the pale moonlight, and made up her mind.

***

'I've brought you something,' she whispered into the old man's ear the next day. The ward in which he lay was full of other visitors sitting next to their relatives or friends, who either lay or sat up in bed and talked with each other, the entire ward seeming to hum gently as words floated around the sterile room like bees. 'I hope it'll help you,' Sarah said as she placed the potted plant on the cupboard next to his bed. Glancing around furtively, she took a hold of the feather and gently pulled it free, the figure, the angel, still hanging from it. With one hand, and feeling a little embarrassed, she opened his pyjama jacket and placed the feather and its cargo onto his chest, above his heart.

Nothing happened. Sarah looked around the room again, then back at the feather. Slowly, as if waking from a long sleep, the tiny man uncurled himself and stretched, making the feather wave about in the air. Carefully, he stood up and looked directly at Sarah and smiled. Pushing aside the wiry grey hairs in his way, the small figure began to walk up the antiques dealer's chest, trailing the feather along behind him, occasionally having to swing it back and forth to free it from a hair that had snagged it, until he came to the old man's neck. Without pausing, he reached up and grabbed a minute handful of wrinkled skin, dug his feet into a fold and began climbing. He pulled himself up by using either the old man's flesh or a patch of stubble that the nurses had missed when shaving him, until, with what seemed like a sigh of relief to Sarah, he stood on the old man's chin, the feather almost painfully visible, to Sarah's mind. Once more she looked around, but could see no-one paying any attention to her or her friend.

When she turned back to the old man, the small figure, the angel, was pushing his lips apart, easing himself in between them ,and Sarah thought that she caught more than one grunt of exertion or irritation as the lips fell back into place as soon as he relinquished any pressure. Carefully, she reached out and held the antiques dealer's lips back, exposing his pink gums. For the second and last time, the angel looked up at her and smiled, then slipped into the old man's mouth, the feather standing upright for a second before disappearing altogether. Sarah let his lips fall back into place and sat back, staring at him, watching as his throat worked once or twice as if trying to swallow something.

She sat and watched him, saying nothing, doing nothing, until a nurse's voice announced over the intercom that visiting hour would be finishing in five minutes. Around the ward, people began to say their goodbyes, leaning over their friends or relatives and pecking them on the cheek, or shaking their hands, or, in one or two cases, hugging them and crying. Slowly, bit by bit, the room began to empty.

'Almost time to go, love,' a nurse said as she walked past the old man's bed. Sarah nodded, picked up her coat and looked at the antiques dealer.

'I'll visit you tomorrow,' she said quietly, wondering if she had imagined everything with the feather and the figure, the angel. 'Get well soon.' She held his hand and turned to leave.

He coughed once, gently. Sarah stepped back to him, holding his hand as he coughed again. His mouth worked, swallowing and chewing until, with a third cough, he spat out a small white feather, the filaments stuck together with his spittle and speckled with a tiny amount of blood. There was nothing on the end of it.

The old man drew in a deep breath, released it, and for the first time in over a week, began to sleep peacefully. Unaware of the tears rolling down her cheeks, Sarah reached out and picked up the feather, wondering what had happened to the angel, where he had gone. Smiling, she pulled the plant pot nearer and made to replace the feather when the old man's hand grabbed hers, making her turn and stare.

His eyes were open and glowed brilliant white, flecked with gold and silver, the light shining through the dry skin of the old man's face, illuminating blood vessels and muscle.

'Don't do it. The blood will make it grow bad. Burn it,' he said, without the trace of an accent, then collapsed, the light winking out as quickly as it had appeared, leaving only an old man sleeping in a hospital bed.

Sarah looked at the feather, at the small smears of blood on it, and felt it pull her hand towards the pot, as if the feather itself wished to be planted. For a moment she was curious as to what would grow, but then she glanced at the antiques dealer and thrust it into her pocket.

'Time to go now, love,' the same nurse said. This time she stayed at the foot of the bed, making sure Sarah was leaving. She leaned over the old man and pecked him on the cheek, thanked the nurse and left.

***

Two days later, Sarah stood in the antiques shop, looking around at everything. The nephew pottered around in the workroom, trying to make sense of his uncle's haphazard way of storage and filing, and didn't hear the shop door open. A young couple walked in hand in hand, smiled at Sarah, and looked around the shop.

'I'll get the boss for you,' Sarah said, and walked into the workroom. At the mention of potential customers, the nephew hurried out, plastering on his best smile. She looked around the place, still missing the antiques dealer, but she knew that he would be back in a day or two. Just like in a movie or TV programme, the doctors were muttering about 'miracle cures' and 'never having seen anything like it' and 'a couple of days for observation.'

Wandering around, she found a small pile of rubbish in a corner and, sat on top of it, the old, scuffed shoe box she had found the feather in, the top still on. After leaving the hospital that night, Sarah had gone straight home and thrust the feather into the fire, using the poker to hold it in place while it was quickly reduced to a small piece of ash. Now, looking at the box, she found herself wondering if it had been the only feather. She picked it up and held it in both hands. Gently, Sarah opened it and looked inside. A piece of card, white with gold and silver flecks, sat at the bottom. From the angle at which it lay, Sarah thought there could be something beneath it.

Walking out into the shop, carrying the box, the top back on, she saw the couple writing out a cheque and heard the nephew extolling the virtues of the Welsh dresser they had just bought. He handed them a receipt, took their cheque and their address and promised to have it delivered that evening. They thanked him and left, arms around each other, and the nephew returned to the workroom.

Quickly, Sarah stepped over to the dresser and knelt in front of it, opening one of the cupboard doors. With a last, wishful look at the shoe box, she placed it inside and closed the door. Humming to herself, she followed the nephew into the workroom and asked if she could make him a cup of tea.

Cutting Criticism
James Lovegrove

Dear Friend,

First of all, may I say how gratified I am that you have chosen to send your narrative and images to Incisive Comments. When I started this service all those years ago, I had no idea it would grow in quite the way it has. What was originally conceived as a hobby to pass an idle hour or two and earn me a little pin-money has burgeoned into a full-time occupation, one which I realise now to be my life's work. Not only did I underestimate the number of potential clients out there, I underestimated it by a huge factor. I tapped a vein, and it turned out to be a major artery.

All of which is a roundabout way of apologising for the tardiness of this reply. I have been snowed under with submissions lately, and only now do I seem to be making some headway. Thank you for your patience. It is much appreciated.

Much appreciated, too, is the quality of your submission. The Polaroids and accompanying text are evidence of a mind at once lively and logical, mischievous and at the same time possessed of a healthy sense of tradition. It is immediately clear to me that you have, with your first outing, discovered your 'voice.' (At least, I am assuming this is your first outing, since I have not heard from or of you before.) For many novices, there is often only failure and disappointment. The event does not go as planned, or does not reward them with the satisfaction they were expecting. I recall one correspondent of mine, a young American fellow, whose maiden effort in a sorority dorm was both ill-prepared and poorly executed. The girls simply would not behave as planned, outsmarting him at every turn, avoiding all the traps and lures he laid – clumsily – for them. He, I should point out, has since gone on to bigger and better things, and I like to think that in some small way, my advice has helped steer him onto the path of success and keep him there. I mention him now merely as an example of someone who did not instinctively possess the skills of his craft but had to learn them *en route*. This would appear not to be the case with you. You are of that fortunate breed who spring into artistic being, like Athena from Zeus's brow, complete and fully-formed, brandishing your weapons.

Your use of an anniversary date amply demonstrates an adherence to both the theatrical aspects of and the conventions of your craft. April 1st has, of course, already been employed by others, but then so have all of the major public holidays and calendar events. The adoption of a thematic date is in itself somewhat slightly passé, but that does not matter when the interpretation of the theme is fresh and innovative, and in this respect you have come up trumps. I take it that April 1st has some personal significance for you? No matter if it does not. I enquire simply because your work has the hallmarks of a private, deeply-held passion. In its honesty, its directness, I see that sublime fusion of self and self-expression that invariably gives rise to great art. Hence I am drawn to the conclusion that, for you, All Fools' Day represents more than just an iconography to plunder; that its associations have provided the key to the actualisation of your psyche.

I am impressed with the content of all your photographs, but two of them in particular, nos. 5 and 7, stand out. I like the way no. 7 – the young man in overalls with the mouthful of Swarfega and the adjustable wrench embedded in his skull – offers a neat commentary on that hoary old building-site trick of sending the apprentice off to fetch a left-handed spanner or a can of elbow grease. As for no. 5, the girl whom you have drowned by thrusting a hosepipe down her throat and turning the tap on full, the nod to the oft-reiterated 'powdered water' hoax of television fame is noted and enjoyed.

I enjoyed also your account of how you set up and executed each piece. Nowadays, while kitchen knives, meat-hooks and machetes are all the rage, meticulousness and imagination are, alas, rare commodities. As I think I have made clear, I am not averse to tradition, but it must be leavened with an admixture of flair, or at the very least of morbid humour. Your third subject is a perfect example of what I mean. Yes, he died by a knife wound, but the knife was held in the hands of the puppet in a jack-in-the-box and driven through his eyeball by the impetus of the puppet's spring. Great art is a question of inventing new variations, of taking things one step further. Lazy minds recycle clichés; great minds invent the motifs that will become the clichés of the future.

One small suggestion. Your self-portrait – photo no. 11, yourself in the mirror – shows that you wear a jester mask while plying your trade. A mask has, of course, become *de rigueur* for those who follow your vocation, necessary both to intimidate subjects and to maintain anonymity. Since you have adopted the jester as your visual 'signature,' and since you do not at the moment have a *nom de meurtre* with which to identify yourself, might I propose the Fool or the Fool-Killer as suitable soubriquets?

Whatever you choose to call yourself, what really matters is the high standard of your work, so let me conclude by saying again how impressed I am with what you have achieved so far. I look forward to your next offering, which, I assume, I will be receiving a few months from now, after another April 1st has passed.

By the way, I am on e-mail – address at the top of this letter – so if you have online capability, why not get in touch with me that way in future? If it's any incentive, I tend to get round to responding to e-mail submissions more quickly than those that come through the post. You might also like to visit the Incisive Comments website, where you will be able to view your own work featured along with that of your peers. Contact me if you want the password.

All the very best,
X

***

Shrouded By Darkness

Dear Fool-Killer,

Has April been and gone already? Time really does fly these days!

Thank you for your new batch of pictures and attendant letter. Don't apologise for not owning a computer. The old methods of communication still work fine. Besides, for those like you who pay me in cash, there is no alternative but the post office, is there?

I must say that I have been looking forward with some eagerness to seeing what you would come up with for your follow-up, and on the whole I am not disappointed. You have managed to avoid the many pitfalls that tend to bedevil sophomore efforts. You have not repeated yourself. You have come up with fresh techniques. You have resisted the temptation to revisit the location of your previous foray. These are all laudable points. They indicate someone not content to rest on his laurels, someone still keen to, as the Americans have it, 'push the envelope.' You would not believe how many times a second attempt turns out to be a limp rehash of the first, if not a downright carbon-copy.

As before, your methods of despatch show verve and wit and attention to detail. I grinned mercilessly at the picture of the Frenchman clubbed to death with a frozen trout – *poisson d'Avril* indeed! – and laughed aloud at the shot of the television journalist hanged from a tree with lengths of white washing-line, a neat consonance of expediency and form there, ridding yourself of, as you put it, 'that meddlesome snoop' while at the same time referencing the famous *Panorama* hoax about spaghetti trees. It is obvious that you are continuing to invest a lot of thought into what you do, and that you are happy to broaden your range of subjects to include people only tangentially related to the incident, whatever it was, that initially inspired your creativity. That shows determination and adaptability, both admirable traits.

It is on the, as it were, subject of your subjects, however, that I feel obliged to offer one small criticism. Rereading my copy of the comments I sent you last time, I notice that I made no mention of the young lady whom you allowed to survive your first night of mayhem. I heartily approve of leaving someone alive to tell the tale – it enhances mystique and establishes for you a reputation that you can capitalise on during subsequent activities – and I realise it was necessary for this purpose to allow the person in question to wound you grievously with an axe and leave you for dead in order for you to make a successful getaway. This is a tried-and-trusted tactic. However, I felt it self-indulgent of you to leave the young lady alive *again* at the end of this second spree of yours, and indeed to give her an opportunity to let off a gun at you *three times*. Surely you need have 'played possum' only once. Rising from the floor after she had left you for dead *twice* smacks of masochism. I presume this female means a great deal to you – your text hints as much – and I grant you that, from the pictorial evidence, she *is* attractive, not least when terrified. I do think, however, that you are allowing sentiment to interfere with your art. It may be that you derive a particular thrill from persecuting the girl and encouraging her to test you to the limits of your mortality, and I acknowledge that there is pleasure to be had in inciting the object of one's obsession to penetrate one's body violently and repeatedly. This is not, however, a habit you should continue to cultivate, in my opinion, as it undermines the purity of your original concept and endangers the validity of your enterprise. You may want to think about ignoring the girl when next April 1st comes around, or eliminating her then, so as to indicate that you are beginning afresh, drawing a line under all that has gone before, starting with a clean slate.

That is something for you to consider, at any rate. My esteem for you remains undiminished, and you may be pleased to know that I have been assiduously recommending your work to those who share my specialised interest. Were you able to visit the Incisive Comments website, you would see that you have received an average visitor-review rating of five and four stars for, respectively, your previous and latest offerings. I am not the only one, it seems, who admires very much what you do.

Keep going!
X

***

Dear Fool-Killer,

Well, what can I say? In fairness, the hat-trick is very hard to pull off. I am only sorry that you felt you had to resort to gimmickry in order to try and make this year's offering more interesting. Hitherto a single picture of each subject has sufficed. Collage-composites made up from several Polaroid exposures … Well, not only is the idea hackneyed (and Hockneyed), but it also fails in practical terms, since it renders the images unclear and thus deprives them of much of their impact. The same goes for your attempt at a disjointed, oblique narrative. I have never been one for the Burroughs school of non-linear prose. Merely a disguise for an inability to write, if you ask me. Yes, it is very witty to have utilised a 'cut-up' style when describing laceration and dismemberment; it is also contrived and far from novel. What initially struck me as so strong about your work was its subtlety, its lack of overt artifice. You *are* clever, but you should leave that cleverness implicit. There is no need to show off about it.

On the plus side, I was glad to see that you followed my advice and got rid of that young lady. It was a bold move making her your first subject this year. I was fully expecting her to come second or third in the running order. Putting her at the top was a nice surprise, and the way in which you dispensed with her was nothing short of brilliant. You did not reveal before that her name was April. Knowing this, it makes wonderful felicitous sense that the deaths this year should commence with April first. Not only that, but the manner of her demise – liquefaction in an industrial meat-grinder – was a delicious linguistic/culinary *calembour*: you literally made an 'April fool' of her.

On the minus side – and the minuses significantly outweigh the pluses, I am afraid – I found the rest of the submission to be lacking in inspiration and inventiveness. The stabbing of the Israeli student with a swordfish was mildly amusing, making reference as it did to one of the putative origins of April Fool pranks, the Christian practice in the Middle Ages of attaching paper fish to the backs of Jews and other non-Christians. It also seemed like a tired retread of last year's death-by-frozen-trout, and typifies the general dearth of subtlety in your approach this time. Really, what with all the hackings and loppings

144

and slashings and slicings and skewerings and sunderings you undertook, I felt as though I were watching a Webster play, as directed by Ken Russell perhaps. Where you have hitherto displayed finesse, you now seem intent on wallowing in excess and crudity. Delivering death with sharp implements is, *per se*, not enough. Without wit, it becomes an exercise in mere butchery. Any infant can wield a sharp object and cause damage. Violence is child's play. What raises mass-murder to a level of maturity is a refinement, a guiding intelligence, an overall sensitivity to the loftier implications of the deed. The aptness of a choice of weapon, the poetic justice of a particular location, the ability to improvise using the materials to hand – these are the things that make homicide an entertainment, that transmute manslaughter into man's laughter. And these are the things in which your submission this year is almost wholly deficient. I suspect you knew this, and that is why you elected to dress up your text and pictures with fancy, 'difficult' stylings, using tricks of form to distract attention away from paucity of content. Remember: eggs and bacon is still eggs and bacon, no matter how many sprigs of parsley you put on the plate.

As I said in my opening paragraph, the hat-trick is very hard to pull off. Indeed, I cannot think of anyone, off the top of my head, who has started as strongly as you did and then kept the momentum up and the quality consistent through two subsequent outings. It was perhaps inevitable that you would lose your way at some point (although I must admit I had hopes that you would prove the exception to the rule). You have just under a year in which to devise your next spree, and also, of course, to recover from the shotgun wounds inflicted on you by your penultimate subject. (Incidentally, I can provide you with the telephone number of a surgeon if you want, a very discreet fellow whose speciality is facial reconstruction. It may be, of course, that you prefer disfigurement. Many of your kind do.) Might I suggest that you spend this period of retrenchment and recuperation wisely, using it as an opportunity to ask yourself why you are doing what you do and what you are really intending to achieve. Obviously, having left so many people dead, you are running short of subjects for whom you harbour a legitimate hatred, or even a mild grudge, and with this reduction in personal animosity towards your targets there may well come a concomitant decline in enthusiasm for your task. I have seen this many times before. The fire no longer burns in the belly. Now is the time, then, to address yourself to your work intellectually. Where heart and anger have so far carried you, the brain can continue to carry you. If you can make the transition from emotional to cerebral engagement, and make it successfully, there is no reason why you should not go on to have a long and fruitful career.

I wish you the best of luck,
X

***

Dear Fool-Killer,

Last year I suggested, did I not, that if you wished to re-attain the heights of you first two offerings, you needed to ponder deeply on the nature and purpose of your enterprise. Did you pay any heed? I would say, on the evidence before me, that you did not.

Where do I begin? This is, literally as well as metaphorically, hack work. Hack work of the lowest order. Dull, trudging, turgid, vapid, illuminated by not the slightest sparkle of wit, not the least glimmer of irony, not the tiniest flicker of anything approaching skill or proficiency or even competence. Were this an offering from a first-timer, I would make allowances for its inadequacies. I would give it credit for, if nothing else, existing. I would regard it with the indulgence commonly reserved for amateur efforts, commending it not for the way it was done but rather for the fact that it had been done at all. I can scarcely believe that the author of this submission is the same Fool-Killer who orchestrated two such superb nights of mayhem (and a third that was somewhat less enthralling but still had much to recommend it). It is almost as if a different person has donned your jester mask and gone around impersonating you, badly, perhaps in order to traduce your reputation and turn you into a figure of fun.

Where are the lethal tricks? What has become of the April Fool theme that was your calling card and, if I might be so bold, your *raison d'être?* What, for God's sake, has happened to the body-count? Half as many subjects means half as much fun. And all killed in the same way! One after another, meeting their Maker like pigs in an abattoir – repetitive, boring in the extreme, unimaginative, bland. Production-line termination. And the murder weapon? A cudgel with little tinkly bells on it. *What were you thinking?*

I am having trouble finding words to convey my contempt, and not just my contempt but my shame. I offered you, courtesy of my critic's expertise in this field, a reasonable proposition for hauling yourself out of the doldrums, and this is how you repay me, with an offering so shoddy, so entirely bereft of any redeeming feature, that it seems almost a deliberate insult, a slap in the face. A quick glance again at your Polaroids shows me a half-dozen corpses lying in various sprawled poses in hotel rooms. They could be bodies anywhere, subjects of anything from a poison-gas attack to a military coup in a Third World country. There is no sense that any of them deserved to die, that any of them in some way invited their own end. You say that they are all joke-shop proprietors, there at the hotel for a trade convention. *So what?* You say that their hand-buzzers and whoopee cushions and squirting buttonhole flowers and chilli-pepper chewing gum and exploding cigarettes were driving you crazy. *I do not believe you.* Annoyance is not an adequate motive for murder. If someone or something irritates us, we become peeved, we become angry, but not so intensely that we kill. There is righteous vengeance, and then there is petty, vindictive score-settling. I suspect you picked on joke-shop proprietors simply because their profession happens to have a vague connection with April Fools and all things prank-related. You may see this as expanding your range. I call it desperation.

Would that there were anything to praise in this latest effort of yours. The most I suppose I can do is remark favourably on the fact that you allowed one of your subjects to claw at your mask and pull it off, exposing the damaged face beneath. A scary moment, I imagine, for the fellow concerned, but frankly this kind of shock revelation is nothing new, and in my opinion cheapens what has gone before. Never removing your mask allows us, your observers, your audience, to project our own fears and illusions onto the unseen physiognomy of its wearer.

Remaining essentially faceless, or at any rate being identifiable only by the features of a factory-moulded face-mimicking piece of plastic, fixes and isolates you in our imaginations. You become powerfully, mysteriously, indelibly iconic. The moment we are permitted a glimpse behind the curtain, we see the little old man working the levers; we become the boy who perceived that the emperor was naked. All is lost in the realisation that you are just a human being, with eyes and nose and lips, and not some quasi-immortal manifestation of the id, an *ur*-monster that has crawled its way out of the swampy morass of our collective consciousness.

I am posting your new submission on the website not so that others might admire it – they will not – but so that it might serve as an instructive example, an object lesson in the misapplication of creativity. It is terrible to see a once-promising career descend into dismal, listless insipidity. If I were you, I would give serious consideration to whether it was worth my while carrying on. Sometimes it is nobler to admit that one's well has run dry than to keep dredging up mud from the bottom.

I wish you well in whatever endeavours you from here on pursue,
X

***

Dear Fool-Killer,

So you have at last joined the online community. Welcome to our little virtual enclave, our clandestine cyber-coterie of artists and aficionados.

And welcome *back*, Fool-Killer of old! Your fifth annual offering is a definite return to form, and I flatter myself that I am in part responsible for this renaissance. Your text certainly seems to indicate as much, citing my harsh review last time as the stimulus that prompted you into a sincere and thoroughgoing re-evaluation of yourself and your craft, your aims, your goals, with the result that you were artistically reinvigorated and attacked your work (and your subjects!) with a renewed zeal. Tributes such as this make the life of a humble critic worthwhile. If I am able, through my firm-but-fair judgments, to foment and foster creativity, then I have, in some small way, contributed to the cause of art, and there can be no greater satisfaction than that.

This year's submission is at once your most personal yet, and your most intricately structured. The multi-layered, self-reflexive aspects of it operate beautifully, better than other examples of this construction that I have seen in the past. Opening your text with a quotation from my last piece – 'It is almost as if a different person has donned your jester mask ...' – excellently sets us up for the sham revelation that it was *not* you running amok in that hotel last year after all but instead someone inspired by your previous works to put on an identical (and appropriately pellet-shredded) mask and go about slaughtering joke-shop proprietors in a kind of inelegant homage to the genuine Fool-Killer. Claiming that the impostor came across your work on a website not dissimilar to this one is a deftly tongue-in-cheek touch. Normally I am not a fan of postmodernism, but I cannot deny that in this instance I found the adoption of it effective and, all personal considerations aside, pleasing.

I was also pleased that, as well as managing by this means effectively to excise last year's submission from your canon, you have been able to link this year's offering directly back to your earlier works. Reintroducing April, or at least a girl remarkably similar to her in appearance, imbues the text and pictures with a sense of continuity and perhaps, dare I say it, of nostalgia. Not only that but it has allowed you to explore, with ferocious self-awareness and honesty, the traumatic event that impelled you in the first place to seek an outlet for your thoughts and feelings in the medium you have chosen. Your account of the childhood prank that left you physically and emotionally scarred is as affecting as any I have read. There is nothing worse than when a practical joke goes awry – in your case, when the school bullies slipped a powder into your orange juice believing it to be baking soda, whereas in fact it was caustic soda. Luckily for you, you swallowed only a sip, although of course that sip was enough to leave you, in your words, 'spitting blood for a week and shitting blood for a fortnight.' Unluckily for April, your friend at the time, she was the one who brought the drink to you, unaware that it had been doctored. This adds tremendous pathos to the fact that, for three years running, you terrorised her and her friends and family, when all along she was innocent of harming you. Using a look-alike to enable you to confront and acknowledge this self-damning truth was a masterstroke.

This year's deaths, too, are once more of a high standard, and because you have confined yourself to members of the gang of bullies, now adults, who inflicted the orange-juice prank on you all those years ago, you have rediscovered the inner logic and thematic unity missing from your previous two offerings. The climactic treatment of the erstwhile gang's ringleader is particularly rewarding, and your pictures of him literally vomiting his guts out are classic *grand guignol*, images of apposite retribution that neither Breughel nor, at the other end of the scale, Vincent Price would have been ashamed to be associated with.

If I have one niggling reservation, it is that you conclude your text with a description of one further killing, that of the moderator of the website where last year's 'fake' Fool-Killer discovered the work of the 'real' Fool-Killer. This struck me as a superfluous and over-obvious touch. I appreciate that this year's submission is all about playing games with reality, with the intention that by dismissing certain former truths as fiction you may arrive at a deeper artistic truth, or at any rate create the illusion of doing so. I think, however, that you can take deconstruction a step too far, especially when the facts – I, the real-life counterpart of your final subject, am still alive and writing this to you – contradict your textual claim.

That aside, I am delighted with this latest addition to your canon, so much so that I have, as you can see, not hesitated in delivering my verdict. Your submission arrived less than an hour ago, and here I am, having set down my thoughts on it already. Such is the swiftness of communication via modern technology that you can send your work to me almost as soon as it is finished and I can supply a commentary on it, if I so wish, straight away. A glance at my onscreen clock tells me it is not yet midnight. If I can wrap this up quickly, I may even be able to send it to you before April 1st is over. I am critiquing your work while the day on which it was created has still a few minutes left to run! I trust you are as amused by that notion as I am.

And now the front doorbell has rung. Who can it be at this hour?

Yours,
X

***

Thank you for accessing the **Incisive Comments** site.

Owing to unforeseen circumstances, activity at this site has now been permanently suspended.

One Copy Only
Ramsey Campbell

Call it fantasy. Call it addiction if you like. At least its effects are more benign than those that bring criminals before me. Take today's case, though it could have been any of a hundred where a denizen of the estate beyond the hill crossed town to rob a homeowner. The thief loaded his pockets with jewels but left his victim's first editions, merely flinging them off the shelves to make sure none of them was a storage box and using a few pages to demonstrate how he'd been trained as a child. As for his victim, the old dear may not even need crutches for the whole of what's left of her life. Her assailant was doing his best to appear incapable of causing so much damage: he was thinner than last time I'd had him in court, and wearing a new suit to compensate. He still watched you sidelong, showing as little of his face as he could, and kept feeling his chin for stubble as if to signify how much he missed the decoration. His social worker spoke up for him, and his lawyer applied himself to casting doubt on the victim and the police, so that barely enough of the jury found against the culprit to let him be sent to stay with many of his friends from the estate, though not for as long as I would have wished and of course not as long as I announced. If that leaves me more resigned than enraged, it's at least partly because I have to persuade myself yet again that Ken Gregory and I didn't do worse for less – not that I would expect anyone to understand who wasn't a privileged customer of Books Forever.

I've no idea how many there may be – it's one of several questions I wouldn't presume to ask. Quite a number of the customers are postal and have never seen the shop. I learned of it ten years ago, when the bookshop chains had begun to devote themselves to fewer and fatter titles, no doubt fattening their authors in the process. I still leafed through any books that seemed at all promising, but the best they had to offer were imitations of greatness: even Clarence Colman Hope had abandoned his visions of dark worlds illuminated by magic and heroism, having thought up a protagonist to my mind too criminal to be presented as a hero. I turned to spending my Saturday afternoons in the second-hand establishments, and in a Care For Children shop I was rewarded more than I immediately realised with a handful of issues of *Fantasy Magazine* the best part of 40 years old. Not only did they cost me under a fiver, but when I sat down after dinner to them and a brandy, I found stamped on each contents page the address of Books Forever.

Some of the tales told of challenges met and wrongs righted, and I thought there might be more where they came from. The next day I walked across the city to the hill. A November wind was sweeping the thoroughfares that swarmed with litter, and bearing stenches of the pinched streets of pygmy houses past the hill, the reek of charred garbage and of buildings set on fire to terrify the occupants or bring an end to them. The hill was the edge of that territory, and I found it hard to believe it could support a bookshop.

From the foot of the narrow potholed street I managed to distinguish part of a sign at the summit. Boo, it cried, a kind of glimpse I'd known to lead me only to a chemist's or a bookmaker's. Nevertheless I toiled up the uneven pavement crowded with parked cars, past sullen huddles of neglected houses, past cramped front gardens that doubled as play areas and rubbish tips, until I gained the height. Books Forever stood in the custody of a wine store and a Pakistani corner shop daubed with swastikas. Its meagre window was so grimy I was barely able to discern shelves packed with books. Sunday had left it closed and lightless, and its sometime painted door displayed no opening hours, but the presence of so many books and the possibility that some might store up wonders brought me back. Indeed, I returned the very next day, as soon as I was able to leave my chambers.

On the hill gangs of children stared as if I had mistaken my course, not they theirs. Several called out words and suggestions I should have hoped never to see admitted to print. Since they were too young for the law to apply, I could only soldier onward. The last of the sunset lingered on the hill, so that the window over the faded sign of Books Forever glowed as though the sun had found a haven above the stunted houses, while it was impossible to determine if the lower window was lit from within. When I applied my shoulder, the door stumbled inward under the unwelcoming clunk of the bell.

The man seated at the venerable desk on the far side of the dim room crammed with books on shelves and on the floor barely raised his face from the task of slipping photocopied catalogues into envelopes, and I couldn't tell for the sunset in his eyes whether he was gazing at me or beyond. He had a high wide frowning forehead, a long wedge of a face, a sprawl of grey hair that rested on the shoulders of his shabby leather jacket. 'Are you closing?' I felt bound to enquire.

He gazed at me as if hoping for better and fingered his forehead, adding more ink to its wrinkles. 'Depends what you're after.'

'A good book.'

'I don't buy any other kind.'

'I found your address in a magazine I bought in the Care For Children shop. Four issues from the '50s, the whole set.'

'*Fantasy Magazine*,' he said, as though answering a question almost too easy to be acknowledged. 'Should have brought them back here.'

'I will if you think I ought to.'

'Not you. The old fellow who bought them and then turned in his ticket, or his family should have looked where they came from, more like. They're your style, are they?'

'Anything that lets me see past the horizon.'

He seemed to focus on me at last. 'Look around,' he said. 'There's a light if you need it.'

The unstable brass switches were just inside the doorway, by a bookcase piled with volumes too tall or too crippled to stand. Three bare bulbs came alight above the cramped aisles. Perhaps shadows deepened the bookseller's frown, or perhaps he mistook for dislike my reaction to the spectacle of thousands of books arranged only by author. 'This is how bookshops used to be,' I hastened to remark.

'It's how you find what you didn't know you wanted,' he said, and turned back to his catalogues.

There was no lack of favourite names – Haggard, Hope, Malory, Tolkein – and nothing that I hadn't read by them. I looked into several novels that apparently promised to be fantastic, but the worlds they revealed were altogether too mundane. I was kneeling before the Vs when a fragile old man in a tweed overcoat and matching hat clambered down the stairs behind the desk. From the glances both he and the bookseller threw in my direction as the old man hurried empty-handed out of the shop, I took him as some kind of private customer. In case the proprietor wanted to close for the night I called 'Could you recommend something?'

'MacDonald,' he responded without looking up.

A book under that name boasted a knight in armour on its spine, while the cover had him on horseback, surrounded by goblins. He and the price were enough to send me with the book to the desk. 'If it's no good to you,' the bookseller said as he consigned the volume to a supermarket bag, 'bring it in.'

At least I was being invited to return. I picked my way downhill to the nearest car park and drove to my apartment, the higher floor of a detached Victorian town house. After dinner, which would have been either half of last night's casserole or the first half of that day's, I entrusted myself to the book. The armoured horseman proved to be not a knight but the old king; the hero was a miner's son who rescued him and married the princess. After their deaths, the city was destroyed by greedy mining of the gold beneath it. The novel was a children's book.

Rather than resent being thought childish, I appreciated the recommendation, not one any other bookseller I'd encountered would have been sufficiently imaginative to propose. It was my kind of tale, and would have been during my childhood if my parents hadn't confined me to improvingly prosaic fiction about the supposed deprivations of youngsters unluckier than the reader. At the end of a week of establishing at least a modicum of temporary protection for the public, I returned to Books Forever.

The bookseller looked ready to be disappointed as he said 'Had enough of it?'

'On the contrary, I've kept it to read again. Have you anything else as good?'

He fingered his inky forehead as if it contained a Braille message. 'White,' he said, and went back to securing a parcel with tape.

The name led me to a corner out of sight of his desk. I had barely touched the copy of *The Sword in the Stone* when he declared 'That's the early version, the best one.'

He was clearly pleased that I trusted his advice. 'We'll be seeing you again, shall we?' he asked as I paid for the book.

'I'll be in to see what's new or rather what's good.'

'I'll keep an eye open for you,' he said, and extended a hand of friendship. 'Ken Gregory.'

'Chris Miles,' I confided over a handshake that faintly inked my fingers, and left him when the ageing phone rang or more accurately rattled on the desk.

At home I discovered he had sold me another children's book. While parts of it were wry, it did sound the note of heroism. Next he introduced me to the tales of Alan Garner at the rate of one a week. The fourth concerned itself too much with the brand of teenage awkwardness the defenders of young miscreants try to offer as an excuse, and it was the only volume I returned to the shop. Gregory met it with wide-eyed surprise that aggravated his frown. 'Not your kind of myth?' he said.

'I'm more than happy reading adult books. Doesn't anybody write the sort of fantasy they used to?'

I remember my exact words and the way he gazed at me, as though attempting to peer deep into me or to decide if I had given him a password. After quite a pause he said 'Maybe you should have a session with my private stock.'

On two further occasions I'd seen customers descend the stairs. Each had bought a book from the public shelves; I assumed the price included payment for whatever they'd concealed about them. 'I didn't mean adult in that sense,' I said as neutrally as I could.

'Nor me either. Just trying to make your dreams come true.'

He seemed honestly disappointed, but the impression remained that the contents of the upper room were somehow illegitimate. I took it as my duty to investigate. 'Then I shouldn't turn you down,' I said, and stepped behind his desk.

'I ought to tell you I only keep reading copies upstairs.'

'By which you're implying …'

'If you find anything you like, you'll have to read it while you're there.'

I found this yet more suspect, and felt uncomfortably conspiratorial as I set foot on the lowest stair. Once I began to climb I felt insecure as well. The stairs were even steeper than they had appeared to be, and the wall seemed uncertain of its grip on the right-hand banister, while the left rail shifted as if all its crutches were about to prove inadequate. I had no doubt the bookseller could find himself in trouble for endangering his customers. By taking the stairs as a challenge I succeeded in reaching the top. Faced with a door that stood invitingly ajar, if only because it was unable quite to close, I pushed it wide.

The room beyond was smaller than I expected. Beneath a baggy ceiling webbed with cracks the stained walls were brown as aged pages. On either side of a burst armchair that squatted in front of the window a bookcase was less than full of books, none of which immediately looked objectionable. Through the dwarfish window, over the ridges of a few mean roofs, I could see the sky but no horizon. As I trod on the ragged carpet, to be greeted by a smell suggesting that the redolence of all the oldest books had gathered in the upper room, I glanced about for a switch but found none. 'Is there a light?' I called.

'There'll be enough.'

There was. Indeed, although the sun was nowhere to be seen, one book appeared to stand out from the rest as if a sunbeam had fallen on it, illuminating the words on the spine: *The Glorious Brethren* by Clarence Colman Hope. I had never heard of it, and yet it sounded unblessed with his recent cynicism. I read the opening pages and was hardly conscious of sitting down to read the entire book, in the armchair that contrived to be unobtrusively accommodating. The story told of a band of almost invincible and practically deathless knights who intervened on the side of the just when summoned by faith, and well short of the end I recognised it as Hope's finest work. Having lingered over the final scene, in which after the victory over Hitler the knights withdraw into the mists and are heard by a wounded soldier to vow

'Till the world has need of us again', I would gladly have reread the book from start to finish. I was making my way to the door when Gregory hurried upstairs. 'I'm guessing you found something to your taste,' his head remarked over the threshold.

'As you see. May I make you an offer? Whatever you think reasonable.'

'It's the only copy, sorry,' he said, staring up beneath his fiercest frown. 'Not for sale.'

I assumed he was waiting for its value to increase, even if that would be hindered by the absence of a jacket. As I reluctantly consigned the volume to a shelf, I was tempted to wish there were books whose nature might make him eager to appreciate my overlooking them, but I saw that the room hid nothing of the kind. 'If you want another read of it,' he said, 'you can always come back.'

I felt obliged to buy some item to express my gratitude. I bought a Tolkein omnibus, another edition of which I already owned, and bade Gregory adieu until next week. I was surprised to meet twilight outside the shop so soon after the brightness of the upper room, but my mind was still brimming like a chalice with the book I'd read.

Despite Gregory's offer, I was loath to take advantage of him, especially at the end of a Monday spent in preventing wrongdoers from doing so to the law. That evening I stayed in town to visit More 'n' Books. Beyond the posters for signings by chefs and footballers and television actresses, a few books had found space among a mob of snowmen in the window. I struggled through crowds of shoplifters or customers to the fantasy section, which was manned by a youth with a shaved pate at odds with his kaftan. 'Can I put you together with anything?' he said.

I'd had conversations with him before despairing of the present trend in fiction, and had found him to be knowledgeable. 'A book by Clarence Colman Hope,' I told him.

'We've got him signing his new one next month, but you said you don't like them that gritty.' He glanced around before murmuring 'Nor me either.'

'I'm looking for an early book. *The Glorious Brethren*.'

He raised a hand as if to feel for a recrudescence of hair. 'Would you know who by?'

'I just told you.'

'We've never had it. In fact I'm sure –' Instead of finishing his supposition he typed the title on a computer. 'There, I was certain I'd have heard of it,' he said. 'Never published and not forthcoming.'

'I assure you it has been published. I've not only seen it but read it.'

'If you can get more details we'll try and order it for you,' he said, though plainly more convinced by his machine than by me, and then gave in to asking 'What was it like?'

'Altogether his best.'

'If you're at the signing you'll have to tell him.'

'You think that might put him back on the right path.'

'Somebody should if they can.'

Who was better qualified than I? But I'd forgotten Christmas. I delayed visiting Books Forever until the weekend, only to find the shop locked for a week. As I trudged downhill past houses sparkling like constellations of stars so false they had fallen to earth, I could almost have imagined I had merely dreamed of mounting to the upper room, where a light appeared to have been left burning for the benefit of some solitary reader, unless it was the glow of the smudged sun.

Christmas resurrected memories of peace. At Midnight Mass in the church opposite my apartment I was able to believe for an hour that the children in the choir might never descend from the heights of mystery, even once their voices did. I spent the quiet week reaffirming the community I shared with a few friends, and in my hours alone read Tolkein in the edition I'd recently bought, though it was corrupted by misprints of which my old copy was innocent. All too soon a New Year as wicked as its predecessor was upon us, bringing revelry that turned into violence, some of the perpetrators of which it was my burden to judge. I wearied of their lies and excuses long before the week was done, and that Saturday I climbed the hill in something like despair. But the shutters had gone.

Gregory glanced up as though the clenching of his frown had raised his head, then nodded to me. 'May I go up?' I asked at once.

'There's nobody else.'

I took this for assent and hauled myself upstairs as swiftly as was safe. I was unsurprised to find the upper room offered more light than the sullen shady sky. I retrieved *The Glorious Brethren* from the shelf and examined the spine, then both sides of the title page, before taking the book to the threshold. 'Do you know who published this?'

'Wait there.' Gregory was already more than halfway up the stairs. 'Which is it?' he said, then didn't look. 'It'll be a proof copy. That's why they don't have jackets and some other bits and pieces, and why I can't sell them.'

'It's Clarence Colman Hope. They need to know the publisher at More 'n' Books so they can order it for me.'

Gregory shrugged as if attempting to dislodge an encumbrance that had landed on his shoulders. 'He's only ever had one publisher I know of,' he said, and watched until I replaced the volume on the shelf. None of its companions displayed a publisher's name. I lowered myself down the stairs to find Gregory awaiting me, his frown pressing his eyes narrow. 'What will you be telling them?' he said.

I couldn't see that he'd committed any offence, and so I tried to reassure him. 'I won't mention where I found it if you'd rather I didn't.'

'This was my father's shop. That was his room.'

'I understand,' I said, uncertain whether or not I did.

'He died up there. He said he wouldn't come down till he'd finished all the books he wanted to read.'

'I imagine I know how he felt.'

'He had the strongest mind I've ever come across. He didn't care about anything but books.'

For a moment I had the dismaying impression that the son proposed to cite childhood neglect to extenuate some crime. 'We all care about those,' I said, and left him.

Outside it was darker than seemed reasonable for the hour or after the illumination of the upper room. The twitching of obsolescent Christmas lights urged me downhill. The bogus snowmen that stood guard in the window of More 'n' Books showed no sign of melting. The aisles were clogged with clots of youngsters demonstrating in various ways their hostility to books. In the fantasy section several children were leafing through pornographic comics while their cronies contented themselves with disarraying the alphabet. I should have expected the assistant with the grey pate to intervene, but perhaps he was abashed by his kaftan. He limited himself to telling me 'I did a search for that title you asked after.'

'May I look forward to having it soon?'

'I'm afraid that's all you'll be able to do.' He took time to produce an apologetic smile before adding 'It must have been some dream.'

'Please make yourself clear.'

'The book doesn't exist.'

'You'll excuse me, but I've had a proof of it in my hands.'

'Did it have a publisher?'

'None was shown.'

'Then that's no proof.'

Though he'd let his smile drop, I couldn't judge if he was mocking me. I was close to betraying Gregory's confidence, but instead I suggested 'Perhaps you can trace another book for me.'

'If our computer can't nothing can.'

'*The Club of the Seven Dreamers* by H P Lovecraft.'

He tapped the keyboard and sent an arrow darting about the screen. After some minutes he said 'Never published.'

'Then *The House of the Worm* by the same author.'

It took him less time to decide to say 'No sign of that either.'

'Try *Last Dangerous Visions* by –'

'I know it,' he said, smiling as if someone had winked at him. 'You aren't going to say you've seen that too.'

Of course I had seen all of them in Gregory's upper room, but I'd heard enough to indicate that the assistant was as lacking in imagination as the computer. 'You mentioned you'd have Clarence Colman Hope here this month,' I said.

'I did.'

That sounded wary enough to be a question. 'When may we meet him?' I enquired.

'Next week.'

'More precisely, please.'

'Saturday,' the assistant was compelled to admit, and handed me from a stack on a counter a glossy sheet advertising Hope's appearance

161

and *The Third Book of Shagrat the Sly*. As I turned away he watched me, visibly regretting having given me the information, and I felt suspected of mischief. On the very few occasions when my parents had cause for that, they would fall silent enough to suggest I had done away with them – the first time for hours, the next for days, the last for nearly a week. I had learned not to plead and rage in my desperation to revive them, but now the injustice I was suffering and the sight of the children left unchecked among lewdness found the voice in which I pronounce sentence. 'Perhaps someone in authority will see fit to escort these boys somewhere more suitable,' I advocated, and as staff and loiterers gawped at me, went forth from the shop.

I might have sought solace in Books Forever, but my skull had begun to feel crushed, as it did when my parents' silence closed around it. For much of the rest of the weekend I lay on my bed, watched over by books that had been crowded out of the sitting-room. This was scarcely enough preparation for the succeeding week, throughout which the jury seemed bent on flaunting its distrust of the law. More than determination to hear Hope acknowledge his best work drove me when the week was executed to return to More 'n' Books.

The snowmen had been ousted from the window by posters of Hope's strongly angular square-bearded face and by piles of his books. A few seconds' survey confirmed that *The Glorious Brethren* was nowhere in evidence, and so I followed the throng to the performance area. This was a large upstairs room, bare except for a table heaped with *Shagrat the Sly* and confronted by perhaps a hundred sketchy chairs. Most were occupied, and I seated myself on the back row, eyed by the assistant with the scraped pate, who had donned a suit in deference to the celebrity. I saw him resolve to accost me, only to be prevented by the arrival several minutes late of Clarence Colman Hope.

I might not have recognised him. His beard had vanished, exposing his chin as weaker than he'd made it appear, and he was grown plump as a stuffed goose. He was at least a head shorter than any of his characters, and shorter still when measured against myself. He left no doubt that he was meant to be the centre of attention by flourishing his fists above his head and roaring 'Where's the applause?' Once that had subsided, and the assistant had stumbled through a redundant introduction during which his subject fed himself swigs of wine and mimed falling asleep, the author set to reading aloud passages from *Shagrat the Sly*, of which I struggled to believe he could ever be proud. Even worse than the way Shagrat stole and lied and cheated to defeat his opponents was the presentation of their magical skills as a pretext for his behaviour, as if envy can ever be an excuse. Worst of all were Hope's knowing glances at his audience beneath a cocked eyebrow that incited them to share his esteem for his creation. I could only clamp my lips together and wish at least some of the laughter to be merely dutiful. Eventually the ordeal was brought to an end, and the assistant was inviting questions when Hope interrupted him. 'I see some of you've got old books of mine. I'll sign them all so long as you buy the new one first.'

Two people with laps heaped with books laboured to their feet and tramped out shamefaced, and I wondered if they had been the only others of my mind. I was heartened when the first questioner to be chosen, a young woman with waist-length hair surmounted by an ornate silver comb, ventured to ask 'Will you be writing any more heroic fantasy?'

'Being a writer's heroic and all I write is fantasy.'

'I meant will you ever write any more like –'

'You mean you want me to regress.'

'No, just –'

'Just not letting anyone else get a word in, eh? I hope she quiets down when she's reading at least,' the author said with a leap of one eyebrow that advised his audience they were expected to laugh, which a few did. 'My turn for a question. How many of you would buy three hardcovers of it if I wrote some more old stuff?'

One girl's hand shot aloft, and two more wavered up elsewhere in the room. 'Well, you're my kind of readers. I'll be putting special messages in yours,' Hope told them. 'Only you aren't enough. I'd need everyone here and the rest of my fans to buy themselves a trio to keep my sales up where they ought to be. In case some of you are better at fantasy than sums, that means Midas tried reissuing my dusty stuff and only shifted a third of what Shagrat does for them.'

'Are you saying,' a man with a senile pony-tail suggested, 'you can't afford to write the kind of book you'd like to?'

Hope stared wordlessly at him for quite a pause, until the assistant mumbled red-faced 'Another question. Yes –'

'Let's have someone more my age,' Hope interrupted. 'Big lady at the back.'

'What can you tell us about *The Glorious Brethren*?'

'Give us a clue what you want to hear.'

'When you wrote it and when it's to be published.'

He looked as if he regretted having selected me. 'Not one of mine,' he declared. 'Doesn't sound like it ever would be, either.'

'I've seen it,' I assured him.

'Then you must be even better at fantasy than me,' Hope said, jerking up an eyebrow to ensure everyone else saw the joke.

I was about to inform him where the book was to be found until I realised that would put it at risk. Suppose it was indeed the only copy? I waved away any further dialogue, and the assistant was hastily choosing another questioner when someone in the middle of the room said 'I've seen it too.'

Before I'd finished willing that to have been elsewhere than Books Forever I recognised him as one of Gregory's privileged customers, a stooped shaggy greying man with an unnecessarily large head. 'I can show you if you like,' he said. 'It's here in town.'

'What is?' Hope demanded.

As I drew breath to head off the information, though I had little idea how, the crouched man said '*The Glorious Brethren*. It's got your name on it. It's in a shop.'

Hope gazed at him and then at me, and I made the worst mistake of my life: I glanced aside as though from guilt. 'You two can show me where once I've finished signing,' Hope said, no longer amused. 'We'll have a few more questions and then get to the books.'

I thought of approaching my fellow customer in case I could dissuade him from escorting Hope, but I feared that would only waste time. As I hurried out I saw the author glower at my leaving and the assistant look relieved. Entangled in my urgency was the unhelpful realisation that secretly I'd started to believe *The Glorious Brethren* existed for me alone. I dodged through the Saturday crowds and dashed up the hill, egged on by the lascivious comments of children and by the flickering of laggard Christmas lights. I hoped Books Forever would be locked, but one thrust of my shoulder threw the door wide.

Ken Gregory was pencilling prices in books on his desk. He met me with the commencement of a smile that quickly sank. 'Looks bad,' he said.

'I'm afraid it may be. I'm dreadfully sorry.'

'Long time since anyone's been that round here.'

If he had asked me what was wrong it might have required less effort to say 'Clarence Colman Hope's in town.'

'I heard. Have you met him?'

'Sadly.'

'A disappointment, was he? Writers can be. You're best off knowing just their books.'

I cleared my throat hard to dislodge words. 'I told him about *The Glorious Brethren*.'

To add to my discomfort, Gregory's lips considered grinning. 'How did he take it?'

'He's on his way here.'

Gregory opened the next book to enter the price. 'Can't blame him.'

He seemed not to be suggesting I was to be censured either, but it was shame that made me blurt 'Aren't you going to do anything?'

'Such as?' Gregory said with some weariness.

'Shouldn't you hide it at least?'

'There's nowhere any of those books can go except where they are. I found that out the hard way once.'

I was so distracted by his resignation that I might have asked him to elaborate if a car hadn't halted outside with a squall of brakes. It was black and slick as an eel, the Jaguar that disgorged Hope and his stooped admirer. The man barely had time to open the door for the author and sidle aside before Hope stalked in. As he saw me, his face grew puce and petulant, but he addressed the bookseller. 'I'm Clarence Colman Hope. I'm told you've got something you want people to believe is mine.'

'We usually have you in stock.'

Hope appeared to be taking that as a crafty insult when the stooped man strayed close to him. 'It's upstairs,' the man muttered, blushing with pride at having been of service, and indicated the route with a furtive thumb.

Hope strode to the gap beside the desk and planted his hands on his inflated hips. 'Are you letting me go up?' he demanded of Gregory.

'I don't see anybody in your way.'

The author advanced to the foot of the stairs and seized the banisters. As he set his weight on the first tread he looked suspicious of a trap. For the whole of his ascent the stairs performed a hoarse melody of protest. The stooped man was moving to follow when Gregory brandished an inky palm. 'Not you, and don't ever come back.'

The man averted his slumped face as he fled the shop, leaving the door ajar on the sight of a gang of children eyeing the Jaguar. I trudged in his wake, but Gregory called to me 'Just shut the door.'

I felt both pardoned and uneasy as I heard Hope plodding across the upper room. 'Where's some bloody light?' he was complaining. Perhaps his eyes adjusted to whatever gloom he found or brought with him, because his footsteps halted where I knew bookshelves to be. 'What's this?' he said in a voice subdued for him.

The silence endured longer than I was able to hold my breath. I glanced at Gregory, then away from his lack of an expression. At last Hope's footfalls thundered overhead, preceded to the doorway by his shout. 'I don't know who faked this, but I'll be making sure the lawyers find out, and by God when they do –'

By this time he had set about descending with one hand on the banister. I caught myself wishing for an instant that he had missed his footing, but that wasn't why his shout became a savage gasp. *The Glorious Brethren* had slipped from his clutch, because there was suddenly too little of it to hold. What fluttered through the air was nothing but dust and scraps no larger than postage stamps, which crumbled as they settled to the floor. He glared down at the ruin of the book in baffled rage, then lurched back into the upper room. 'All right then, I'll take something else,' he vowed. 'There's plenty here for the law to sort out.'

The bookseller stood so abruptly that a heap of books tumbled across the desk as his chair clattered against the wall. He flung himself at the stairs and scrambled up like a monkey. 'What else are you going to destroy that you can't do yourself?' he cried as he ran overhead. 'Here's *Edwin Drood* that Dickens finished after all. Here's *Arthur Gordon Pym* that Poe did. Or *The Castle of the Devil*, how about that? That's some Robert E Howard you won't find anywhere else. And look here, Malcolm Lowry did complete his last novel, and Scott Fitzgerald got around to finishing *The Last Tycoon*. Hang on though, maybe this is rarer, *The Night of the Eye* ...'

He named other books too, a flood of them. He must have meant Hope to be unable to choose from so many, but his voice fell like the final rumble of a storm. 'It's going to be Dickens, is it? You think there's already enough of him in the world.'

I heard Hope retreat from the shelves and saw him back out of the room, another book in his hand. I have no idea what I might have done, but by the time I darted past the desk it was too late. I never knew if they were only Gregory's feet that rushed across the upper room. I glimpsed the snatching of the book from Hope's grasp, but did I see him pushed? I know I saw him hurl himself thoughtlessly backwards as though to avoid some contact. His head was first to strike the floor, followed by his body at an angle that wrenched his mouth into an agonised grimace, unless it was the crunching of his neck that did. His heels dealt the leg of the desk a convulsive kick that threw several books on top of him, and then he was still.

As I dragged my gaze clear of Hope's distorted outraged face, Gregory leaned out of the upper room. His eyes weren't quite admitting to a question. Before I could acknowledge it and decide on my response, we heard a car draw up outside, and the window began to throb with light. The next moment a double slam of metal doors heralded the entrance of two policemen.

It was only later that I learned they had been summoned by a householder to deter children from breaking into Hope's car. I had to deal immediately with their presence. 'There's been an accident,' I told them. 'This chap lost his footing on the stairs not a minute ago. He'd been drinking. I'm a witness if you need one. I'm a judge.'

I may always remember the look of astonishment adjoining disbelief with which Gregory met that revelation. I waited until the ambulance had cleared Hope's remains away, and answered the few questions the police found it necessary to ask. Since then Gregory and I have never discussed the incident, but I know he understands how deeply I value his shop. Without the treasures of the upper room I might despair not just of my calling but of life itself. I never leave Books Forever without having made a purchase, but for years the purpose of my visits has been to reread a solitary volume: *The Return of the Brethren* by Clarence Colman Hope.

An Appropriate Pen
Dawn Knox

The old lady clawed at the sticky tape excitedly and removed the brown paper wrapping to reveal an antique wooden box. She caressed the smooth surface, wiping away the dust carefully with the back of her hand.

She hadn't received a present for years and she deliberately paused before opening the box, to savour the moment. Finally, curiosity drove her gnarled fingers to prise off the lid, and she gasped with pleasure and surprise at the beautiful silver pen nestling in folds of dusty, violet velvet.

There was a small card in the box, which she laid to one side, while she removed the ornate pen and held it in her claw-like grasp.

It felt just right. The right weight. The right fit.

In fact, perfect for all the writing that still had to be done.

She turned the box over, admiring the craftsmanship and the grain of the wood, although it surprised her that someone, with a blatant disregard for its beauty, had cut a series of v-shaped notches in the bottom edge.

Finally, she laid the pen back in the box and looked at the card.

'From a Well Wisher,' it said in beautiful copperplate writing.

It must have been from one of her neighbours, in appreciation of her many acts of kindness. She often received letters thanking her.

The Well Wisher could hardly have known what an appropriate gift he or she had sent, as the old lady spent much of her day secretly writing. Not silly, romantic novels or dreary diaries but important letters, whose contents were of the utmost significance.

She had heard that letters such as hers were known as 'poison pen' letters, but she preferred to think of them more as 'educational.' People needed to realise that all transgressions had to be paid for, and it was her job to make sure that all sinners suffered.

Her life's work was to mete out punishment to sinners by letter, and in order to do this successfully, she had developed three completely different styles of handwriting so that nothing could ever be traced back to her.

***

She had first realised that she had a calling when her brother, Thomas, had left the family home to get married. She hadn't liked her sister in law very much, but when Thomas had had a fling with his secretary, she had felt it only fair to write to Ruth, to inform her of her husband's infidelity. The ensuing divorce had been acrimonious to say the least, but that was part of the price that Thomas had had to pay – along with the large settlement that Ruth had demanded. There had been other occasions over the years when she had felt it necessary to chastise Thomas with anonymous letters, and when he moved to the next town and she no longer knew what he got up to, she wrote anyway, in the certainty that he was still transgressing.

After all, a leopard doesn't change its spots.

As she lost touch with Thomas, she began to look for sinners in her own village. And there were plenty of them. Some days, she carried four or five letters in her handbag, each addressed to a different transgressor, and travelled many miles, buying stamps in different post offices in various locations. The same post box was never used twice, and she even used latex gloves in case there was ever a question of tracing her fingerprints. Yes, she had thought of everything. There was no way that the educational letters could possibly be linked to her.

Who would suspect a tiny, jolly looking, old lady? Certainly not the neighbours, who dropped in occasionally and fed her little bits of gossip. She always waited for a while after receiving the information, before carefully composing her correspondence and arranging a 'Posting Day'.

One such neighbour was employed as a cleaner by the solicitors Snodgrass, Burton and Trellis, and the old lady had discovered over an afternoon cup of tea that Thomas was trying to get her removed from her house, on the grounds of senility or some other such nonsense. The neighbour had felt it her duty to inform the old lady and to denounce Thomas in very unladylike language. Such blasphemy was of course not to be ignored, and in due course the helpful neighbour had received a stern letter, although it had been so cleverly worded that there could be no possible link back to the old lady.

And as for Thomas … So he was about to evict her, was he?

Over her dead body.

***

Hers was the family home and Thomas had always loved the neatly laid out gardens and beautifully decorated rooms. She had spent a lot of money on having the place regularly redecorated and maintained. One day, it would go to her brother, as she had no other family, but he would have to wait for a while; she was definitely not going to be pushed out of her home to satisfy Thomas's selfish greed.

Her ungrateful sibling was overdue a letter.

She got out some notepaper, picked up the new silver pen and began to write.

> *It has come to the notice of an interested party that you are attempting to hound your poor, innocent sister from her home. You should be ashamed.*
> *Beware.*
> *I know your secret, you child molester and murderer! Where did you hide the bodies? Are they all in the house, or did you bury some in the garden?*
> *If your kind, considerate sister is removed from her*

house before she dies, I will go to the police with your
secret.
    Beware.

She reread the letter and smiled to herself. It was all lies, of course, but Thomas would not dare risk the police being called in to tear the house to pieces and to dig up the neat garden.

Then suddenly, she felt the urge to write more. The pen flew across the paper, leaving a trail of such malice that she could only wonder at her inventiveness. Gradually, she noticed that the colour of the ink had changed subtly from black to brownish red. It was as if the ink itself had become veritable venom, spawning words of pure poison. She had no idea that Thomas had been so evil, neither had she realised that she was capable of such hatred, but it was all there in front of her in the letter, so it must be true.

She was beginning to feel very slightly unreal, as if she were an observer, rather than the creator, and she decided that enough was enough. There were dark smudges at the edge of her vision. She was obviously getting tired. She would put the letter in an envelope right then and address it ready for a 'Posting Day' the next day, and then she would have a short nap. The frenzy of creativity had wearied her.

She placed the pen back in the box but found that she could not relax her grip. In bewilderment, she inspected her fingers. The skin seemed to have fused to the pen, and try as she might, she could not release it back in the box. Her hand began to throb, and as she watched, it started to swell until the usually flaccid, wrinkly skin became taut and shiny. A brownish-red tinge began steadily to creep from her hand up the veins in her arm, triggering such swelling that she thought her skin would surely burst. Black clouds seemed to billow around her, and to her horror, she saw the palm of her hand begin to split and crack and the pen finally fall from her grip with sections of flaky skin still attached. Surely the swelling would subside now that the pen – the focus of the infection that was permeating her body – was gone. But instinctively, she knew that this was not so. She could almost feel the insidious poison creeping through her, slowly penetrating the furthest reaches of her entire body. Her hand and arm were now crazed with fine cracks and fissures from which bloodstained lymph started to ooze, but worse than that was the sure feeling that her insides were slowly liquefying, like molten wax. She coughed and spat out a wad of bloody phlegm onto the table. She tried to scream, but no sound issued from her mouth, which was now contorted in a rictus of pain as her stomach was shredded within her. As she haemorrhaged internally and her life ebbed away, she became aware again of the billowing clouds in the room. There was a low chuckle and she felt a presence with her. Someone dark and misty, and with features that ebbed and flowed before her failing eyes. Struggling for breath, she saw a red-gloved hand pick up the pen, lovingly wipe it clean and then replace it carefully in the box. As life was leeched from her, she saw the glint of a small blade as the hand carved a neat notch in the bottom edge of the box. Her eyes dimmed completely, and the last thing she heard was the self-satisfied laughter once more.

***

Standing over the old lady's body, the Well Wisher laid a hand gently on her head, recognising that they had shared a mission, a calling. The figure then slipped a card into the wooden box and efficiently wrapped it in brown paper, securing it with sticky tape. It then diligently transcribed the name and address from the last of the old lady's letters onto the parcel. So poor beleaguered Thomas would be the next recipient. Shame, but those were the rules.

Puca Muc
Steve Lockley and Paul Lewis

The evening air was perfectly still and unbearably warm, like a clammy hand on her skin. Above the low hill, which stood sentinel over the village of Kraighten, tentative fingers of lightning scratched the sky. In the distance, storm clouds gathered into an obsidian bank against the impending darkness. Dear God, she thought. Let it rain tonight.

The wine glass on the table next to her was opaque with moisture. Eileen raised it to her lips, sipping an Australian Chardonnay that was like ice against her tongue. The relief was fleeting; no sooner had she swallowed than she felt the sticky heat renew its assault. She took another sip before putting the glass down, then shifted uncomfortably on the lounger, springs protesting as she moved. Her thin top was welded to her skin by perspiration, and she tugged at the offending garment irritably. It made no difference. As soon as she sat back, the cotton simply leeched itself to her again. Eileen swore, knowing she could not be overheard. Beyond the garden fence there was nothing but bleak and inhospitable countryside. It stretched on for miles to the rugged West coast, interrupted only by the occasional stone-scattered ruin. Eileen never felt nervous, living in such isolation. If anything, the remoteness comforted her. Most days she stayed in the nurses' home at the hospital. But when her rota weekend off or, like now, her leave came around, it was to the cottage she was raised in, and her parents left her, that she returned. The place sounded strangely incomplete without their voices echoing around, but she could never sell it. It was her home.

The heat was soporific, the wine even more so. Her eyes flickered and closed. Blood roared in her eyes. Her heart thumped, stopped, thumped again. Something was wrong. Eileen woke with a start, momentarily confused. The banging started anew, more vigorous this time, and she realised with a shudder of relief that someone was knocking at the cottage door. Eileen stood on legs that trembled ever so slightly and walked through the patio doors to the lounge. Indoors, the knocking seemed terribly loud, insistent enough to bring on a headache. 'All right, all right! I'm coming,' she called as she stepped into the hall. Her sweat-slicked fingers fumbled with the front door catch. Finally she had it, cursing under her breath as a fingernail caught. Eileen pulled the door open slightly and looked around the narrow gap. As used as she was to living alone, she knew you could never be too careful, even in a place like this.

'Oh, it's you,' she said, smiling at the little figure before her.

Patrick Tobin did not smile back. The boy's face was bright red, framed by a thick mop of black hair that was plastered to his skull. He held a grimy old Miami Dolphins baseball cap in his hands, which he kneaded and twisted over and over.

'Sorry to bother you, Miss O'Callaghan ...'

'Hey, haven't I told you a million times. Call me Eileen.'

'Yes, Miss Eileen.' He fell silent and looked down.

'And?' Eileen prompted softly. No response. 'Come on, darling. You must have had a reason for coming out here so late. All on your own as well.'

'It's me sister,' Patrick suddenly cried, voice cracking. 'She's sick, Miss Eileen. Don't know what's wrong with her. Da sent me. He wants you to help.'

Eileen's shoulders slumped. That was the trouble with being a nurse, living in a small village. Soon as anyone fell ill, it was she they turned to, even though she had told them time and time again that there was little she could do. That's what doctors were for, was the message she had tried to put over, but it was like talking to a brick wall. Still, she had a soft spot for Patrick. He was so unlike his father. And his sister. 'Step inside a minute while I get some shoes on,' she said, sighing as she held the door open wide.

Patrick trotted obediently behind her as she returned to the lounge, retrieving the glass from outside and draining it with a pang of regret. It had been a long, hard day and she was tired enough to drop where she stood. Ah well, lass. Too late now. Eileen found a pair of open-top sandals under the sofa and sat down while she slipped them on. 'When you say Brigit's sick, do you mean throwing up sick?' she asked.

'Nah,' Patrick said, shaking his head. 'She's getting pains. In her guts.'

'How bad?'

'Bad enough to make her scream.'

Could be anything from food poisoning to a heavy period. Of course it could just as easily be appendicitis. Either way, old man Tobin should have called for a doctor or an ambulance, not her.

'I'll take a look,' she said. 'But we may need to phone for help.'

'Tried,' said Patrick. 'Phones are all out. Da says it's the storm.'

Eileen frowned, reached for her own telephone. It was dead. The mobile in her bag was equally useless. Out here in the wild, the signal was non-existent. If it was appendicitis, they would have to drive the girl to the hospital in Ardrahan. But the town was 40 miles away, a little too far for comfort. 'Right,' she said, standing.

They hurried up the lane that separated her cottage from Kraighten. The village was little more than a scattering of old houses, a ramshackle bar and an equally tired shop, huddled around a small square. The pub's windows and door were wide open; rock music and raucous laughter drifted out. A man swore loudly and colourfully in Gaelic; some folk used old Irish even today. Another lane took them towards the Tobin farm. It was getting dark and Eileen reached out for Patrick's hand, smiling as she felt his fingers clutch hers. Poor little thing was only eight, and a really lovely kid with it. How the Tobins could have produced such a beautiful son and yet such a troublesome daughter was anyone's guess. Must be that Patrick took after his mother, God bless her soul, leaving Brigit to follow her pig of a dad. But that, she told herself, was by the by. Her own personal feelings were irrelevant. If the girl was sick, Eileen was duty bound to do whatever she could to help.

She heard the shouting when they were still some distance from the house. It sounded like two men, arguing vociferously. But their raised voices were swiftly drowned out as a girl, presumably Brigit, began to scream. Eileen felt Patrick tighten his grip on her hand, and she suppressed her own sense of unease for the child's sake. What in God's name was going on up there? She hurried on as fast as she dared, not wanting to stumble on the rocky path and equally aware that Patrick could not move as quickly as she. The screaming ended abruptly as they passed through an open gate and crunched up a gravel path to the house, every room of which was brightly lit. Its windows were like beacons, guiding the way. In what she guessed was the kitchen, Eileen could make out the squat figure of Brian Tobin. His back was to her and he faced a younger man whom Eileen did not recognise. There was no sign of Brigit.

Patrick ran ahead of her, suddenly bolder this close to home. He charged through the back door, yelling excitedly. Eileen could hear nothing in response. Her stomach fluttered nervously as she went in after the boy. She paused a moment, letting her eyes adjust to the brightness and giving herself a chance to take in the scene. If there was some kind of heated family dispute going on, and knowing this family like she did, she had no intention of letting herself get ensnared in it.

As it happened, she felt like she had blundered into a boxing ring, between rounds. Tobin was stood rigid to one side of the kitchen, fat, piggy face flushed and angry. Squaring up across from him, face equally thunderous, was the younger man Eileen had seen through the window. He had the air of a traveller about him, with his long, dark hair pulled back into a pony-tail and a gleaming gold hoop in one ear. His features were handsome and chiselled, his figure lean and muscled. Both men looked as if they had frozen at the very moment they were about to lunge at each other. They stared at her like two wicked schoolboys caught in an act of devilment. Eileen scarcely noticed. Her attention was instead drawn to the pale figure hunched in the opposite doorway. Patrick had been right; his sister *was* sick. Her skin was alabaster despite the heat, and her eyes looked as if they had collapsed into her skull. Beads of sweat clung to her forehead and her breathing was hoarse and laboured.

'Mother of God,' Eileen gasped. 'What happened to you?'

'Him,' Tobin said, voice thick with loathing. 'That dirty bastard.'

'Don't you fucking well start on me,' the other man answered, taking a step forward, hands curling into fists at his side. 'I told you before …'

'Shut up, the pair of you,' Eileen snapped. 'And watch your language.'

Tobin actually looked sheepish. 'Sorry.'

The younger man looked down, muttering something vaguely apologetic.

'I don't mean me,' Eileen said. 'I've heard worse. I meant the little one.' She crouched down to look Patrick in the eye. While the two men traded insults, he had huddled up against her.

'I think you'd better go on up to your room, darling, while I find out what's wrong with your sister. Then I'll come up and see you. Okay?'

'Okay,' Patrick said solemnly, walking past his sister into the hallway without another word. Eileen waited until he was out of earshot before fixing Tobin with her best no-nonsense look.

'Now. I want you to tell me exactly what is going on. Nice and quietly. With no cussing. And no threats either. Any nonsense and I walk out.'

'It's like I told you,' Tobin said, glaring at the other man. 'It's his fault.'

'For Christ's sake, Da, give it a rest!' The thin nightie Brigit wore was so big it appeared to drown her. It was only when, with a groan and painful grimace, the girl straightened that Eileen could see her distended stomach beneath the fabric. Little wonder Tobin was furious. It may be the 21st Century, but in this part of Ireland, a teenage girl who got herself pregnant was still nothing but a cheap, dirty whore.

'It wasn't Tommy,' Brigit said, eyes bright with tears. She was shaking violently, a look of such wide-eyed desperation on her face that Eileen suddenly knew there must be more to this than just another teenage pregnancy. 'I swear it wasn't.'

'Oh aye,' Tobin spat. 'Like I'm supposed to believe *that*?'

'How far gone would you say she is?' Tommy asked Eileen.

'She looks pretty much full term.'

'Exactly,' Tommy said. He jabbed a finger at Tobin. 'I've only been here since the start of the summer. Six weeks at most. How d'you explain that, eh?'

Tobin seemed momentarily lost for words. Then he turned his baleful gaze on his daughter. 'You'll tell me who the father is, you little slut, or I'll ...'

'That's enough!' Eileen said, fury rising within her as she saw Brigit flinch at her father's words. 'I warned you, Tobin. Any more of that and you'll be sorting all this out without any help from me.' It was a bluff, of course, though Tobin had no way of knowing that. Sure, the girl had the devil in her, yet right now she looked so pitiful and fragile that Eileen could not help but sympathise. Brigit was hardly the first unmarried girl to get herself pregnant and she would not be the last, but that would not help her feel any less frightened or any less alone.

'Try not to worry,' Eileen told her gently. 'You'll be fine. Only we need to get you to the hospital.'

'No,' Brigit said through gritted teeth. She looked ready to collapse.

'It's the best place for you.'

'I meant no time. I think it's on its way.'

'Sweet Jesus,' Eileen heard one of the men murmur behind her. She ignored the voice, along with the one in her head, the one that insisted she was so far out of her depth she was close to drowning. *You're not up to this, girl. The last time you did midwifery it was part of your training. That would be nearly 20 years ago now, wouldn't it?* Eileen shook her head, silencing the voice. Sure, it had been a long time, but she remembered what she had learned back then and, besides, had kept up to date with her studies. She could handle this. Brigit was young and strong. Chances were there would be no complications. The only possibility was toxaemia. For sure the girl had piled on the weight in a very short time; Eileen had seen her only a few weeks earlier and there had been no obvious sign of pregnancy. Then again, maybe Brigit had merely been good at hiding her condition. Ah well, she would cross that bridge when, or rather if, she came to it. No point worrying about something that might never happen.

'Right,' she said, clapping her hands together. 'Brigit, go on up to your room and wait for me. I'll just be a minute.' The girl nodded and turned away. As she did, Eileen caught a look of panic on her face, as if she could not bear the prospect of being alone, even for a moment. 'Don't panic, love. I know what I'm doing, I'm a nurse, remember?'

Her attempt at levity was wasted. Eileen stared morosely at the girl's hunched, retreating figure for a few seconds, then turned to face the two men. 'I'm going to need plenty of hot water. And a fresh bar of soap. Some disinfectant, too.'

She could hardly believe what she was saying. It was like a corny TV show.

'What can I do?' Tobin asked her. He seemed subdued now.

'Nothing just yet. I'll call you when I need you.'

'But I'm her father!'

'You could always go and get help,' Tommy said. He looked apologetically at Eileen. 'No offence, lady, but I don't see any harm in calling an ambulance.'

'Lines are down,' said Eileen. 'And my mobile doesn't work out here.'

'So why not use the phone box in the village?'

Eileen saw her own confusion echoed in Tobin's face. 'I don't get you.'

'Land lines,' Tommy said slowly, as if addressing backward children. 'The phone box lines are underground, not overhead. Storm won't have touched them.'

Of course! Eileen almost slapped her own head, she felt so stupid. There may not be time to get Brigit to hospital, but having the paramedics bring out a midwife, even if they arrived halfway through, would make a world of difference.

'Good idea,' she said, smiling at Tommy to mask her foolishness. 'Do you mind going? Tell them my name. They all know me there. And ask them to get a midwife out here as well.'

'Sure,' the younger man said. 'Anything to help.'

'I'll be the one who goes,' Tobin insisted. 'Like I said, I'm her father.'

'Why don't you both go?' said Eileen. 'I won't need you for a while. Brigit is not going to have her baby *just* yet. And maybe you can sort your differences out along the way. Oh, and take Patrick with you.

Poor little thing hasn't a clue what's going on.'

She stood to one side while Tobin called his son downstairs and, with obvious ill grace, left the house, Tommy right after him. 'Don't worry about a thing,' she assured both men as they departed in sullen silence. 'Brigit's in good hands.'

When the door closed behind them, she let out a long sigh of relief. She had known exactly what she was doing, contriving to get them all out of the house like that. The only way she would get to talk to Brigit in peace was by ensuring there could be no interruptions. Her shoulders sagged as tension eased within her. Eileen now felt more relaxed than she had any right to be. She collected the towels and unwrapped the bar of soap Tobin had laid out ready, before making her way upstairs. The bulb that lit the stairs was dim, and this, coupled with the insulating properties of the farmhouse's old stone walls, mitigated the worst effects of the heat. It was slightly stuffier on the first floor, but a small window on the landing admitted a refreshingly cool breeze, which she guessed was a vanguard of the impending storm. Through an open door ahead of her she could see Brigit prone on a single bed, body convulsing in what Eileen assumed to be the grip of accelerated contractions, until she heard the sobbing.

'Hey now,' she said softly as she entered the room. 'I'm here to help.'

Brigit turned to face her, features contorted. Tears had left glistening tracks down her cheeks. 'If you want to help, get this bastard thing out of me and kill it.'

'Your baby is going to be just fine,' Eileen assured her, moving towards the bed. 'And so are you. Just try to keep calm. We'll get through this together.'

'I don't *want* to get through this!' Eileen wailed. 'I just want it out of me!'

Eileen closed her eyes, trying to gather her thoughts. She recalled what Jenny Tonnison, her midwifery tutor back in her training days, used to tell her. That the biggest part of a midwife's job was keeping the mother relaxed; that and dealing with the pain. Well, she had nothing to take the physical pain out of this particular delivery, and it seemed Brigit was going to be a hard nut to crack in terms of inspiring calm.

She sat on the edge of the bed, placed a hand on the girl's trembling shoulder.

'I know you're afraid,' Eileen said. ' I understand why. It's only natural when …'

'Natural?' Brigit snapped back, voice hoarse. '*Natural?* There's nothing natural about this. I'm telling you, it's not a baby inside me. It's a fucking *demon.*'

'We can worry about that later,' Eileen answered. It was an effort to stay calm in the face of the girl's hostility, but somehow she managed it.

'Listen,' Brigit said. She took Eileen's hand in her own, squeezed it with frightening strength. 'When I tell you I got a demon inside me I don't mean that 'cos I'm having a bastard baby. I mean, what's in my belly isn't human, all right? Wasn't Tommy or no other man put it in me. It was the *Puca Muc.*'

'*Puca muc?*' Eileen suppressed a sudden urge to laugh. *Pig ghost.* Kraighten's version of the bogeyman. Half human, half swine, the *Puca Muc* haunted the woods that surrounded the village. Or at least it did in the minds of generations of children who, having being told in graphic detail by their parents the horrible fate awaiting any child caught by the *Puca Muc*, would never stray too far from home and always returned safely before dark. 'There's no such thing, love. It's just a story.'

Brigit released Eileen's hand, rolled her eyes to the ceiling.

'How can it be just a story?' she asked in an eerie monotone. 'With me only three weeks gone?'

Eileen was confused. 'You mean you only found out three weeks ago?'

'No,' Brigit answered in that same flat voice. It was as if the fear and the anger, any emotion at all in fact, had been suddenly drained from her. 'I meant what I said. I'm only three weeks gone. Twenty-three days, to be precise. Since it happened.'

'Since what happened?'

'The night I arranged to meet Tommy.'

'Tommy? But I thought you said he …'

'Oh, he's not the father,' Brigit said with a harsh, bitter laugh, then instantly grimaced as a contraction took hold and a wave of pain rippled through her. 'God, I wish he had been. I love him, you know. But he could never love me, not after this.'

'How long have you known him?' Eileen whispered, keen to maintain the conversation if that was what it took to keep Brigit relaxed.

'Tommy? Oh, not long. Month at best. I was in Billy's Bar one night with my mates, having a couple of lagers, when in he came. He'd been working in the fields all day and he had such a colour on him. The minute I saw him, I knew …'

***

Brigit saw him and immediately knew he was the one. Jesus, if he wasn't as tall, dark and handsome as the hero in those Mills and Boon books Ma used to read. He looked fit and strong, the muscles in his arms bunching impressively when he raised his beer glass to his lips, and his skin was browned by the sun. He was leaning against the bar, chatting to a couple of farmers, and she guessed he was one of the gypsy boys who came to work the fields each year, though she was certain she had not seen him before. If she had, she would have remembered him for sure. A hard finger poked her in the small of her back and a teasing voice whispered in her ear, 'Stop your staring, you randy little cow.'

'I wasn't staring,' she said shortly, though she could not help smiling as she heard Joyce Connolly giggle behind her. 'And you can buy me a drink for your cheek.'

'My shout anyway,' Joyce said, pushing past to get to the bar. Brigit stole a glance at the stranger and, as she did, his eyes met hers. He winked, raised his glass in a brief salute, before carrying on with his conversation. She felt her cheeks burn hotly and quickly turned away, trying to look as if she were merely checking out who was in the bar. Luckily some of the girls she and Joyce hung out with were already there. They had taken over one of the large tables, transformed it into a forest of glasses shrouded in smoke. She made her way over to them and sat with her back to the rest of the room so as to avoid having to look at the stranger again; if he caught her staring, she would just die.

Joyce arrived with their lagers, the first of many drinks that night. It was a Friday and most of the girls had just been paid, while Brigit's purse held several notes that she had sweet-talked Da into parting with. A couple of hours later and she was well and truly pissed, so drunk she felt not the slightest embarrassment when she tripped on her way to the toilet and felt a strong arm grip her elbow, holding her steady.

'Ta,' she said, and, looking up into a lean, tanned face, saw for the first time who it was she had stumbled into. 'Oh, it's you. Mills and Boon.' Her voice was slurred.

'Actually, it's Tommy.'

'Well, Tommy, it's nice to meet you.' Despite her drunken state, Brigit was amazed at her nerve. Not long before, she had been too afraid to look at him. Now she was having what almost amounted to a proper conversation! 'You gonna buy me a drink?'

He laughed loudly. 'Not backward in coming forward, are you?'

'Mine's a pint of lager.' Brigit paused, frowning. Too much more and she'd not be able to talk sense at all. Making a fool of herself now was the last thing she wanted. 'Come to think of it, make that half a lager. I'll be back in a couple of ticks.'

The rest of the night passed in a blur. They talked and Brigit managed a few more drinks, but by now she had actually started to feel sober. Maybe it was excitement, or the sheer disbelief she felt at being so close to this man, listening to his wild tales of his life on the road. His voice was deep and confident, and he punctuated his tall stories with bursts of laughter. Jesus God Almighty, he was perfect, Brigit thought. It was with no small self-satisfaction that she caught the jealous glances the other girls threw her way.

Soon old Joe was ringing the bell to sound last orders, and Brigit and Tommy picked up their glasses and stepped away from the bar to make room for the rush of folk desperate for one more drink. As they did, Tommy took her free hand in his and asked if he could see her again. 'Nothing too grand,' he said in that disarmingly wicked way of his. 'Maybe a couple of drinks here one night. I may even throw in a bag of nuts.'

'That'd be great,' Brigit said. It still felt like a dream. 'How about tomorrow?'

184

'Then tomorrow it is,' said Tommy. 'Want me to call for you?'

She shook her head. Da would be down on her like a ton of bricks if he even suspected she was seeing someone, let alone someone as old as Tommy. He was, Brigit knew, nearly 30, even if he looked a lot younger than that. 'I'll meet you.'

'Where? Here?'

Brigit almost said yes, but then had second thoughts. It would be nice to spend a little time alone with him before they came to the bar. There was no privacy here, and she really did want to get to know him better. The woods were quiet, riddled with secret places where they would be immune from prying eyes. 'Do you know the old orchard?'

'You mean in the woods? By some old ruins?'

'That's it,' said Brigit. 'See you there at – seven-thirty?'

'Seven-thirty it is,' Tommy said. He kissed her on the cheek. 'Can't wait.'

Which is why, come eight o'clock the following evening and Brigit was still alone in the orchard, fed up with waiting, she finally had to admit that Tommy was nothing but a lying bastard and she had been a gullible fool. She sighed loudly and shifted on the cool grass, her back against the remains of an ancient wall. The orchard had been abandoned generations ago, and now there was nothing left of the house that had once stood in the grounds apart from a few rocks and the vague outline of the foundations. No doubt everything else had been stolen to help build some of the outlying farmhouses. Brigit had been drawn here day after day as a child. Partly because she was not supposed to, it being so close to that weird chasm where a waterfall broke from sheer rock, and partly because of the *Puca Muc*, which the kids would scare each other with stories about.

A cloud passed across the sky, suddenly casting the orchard into shadow. Brigit shivered as the breeze picked up, making the trees creak and groan, their leaves sounding like the sweeping of a thousand brooms. Then everything fell silent again so that she was able to hear soft movement through the undergrowth of the deep woods to her right. She peered into the gloom, caught a flash of motion. 'Tommy? Is that you?'

Nothing. Not even the sound of a bird. The world had turned mute. Goosebumps rippled her skin. The sun was slowly sinking towards the horizon. Before long, her shorts and T-shirt would not be enough to keep her warm. 'Stop messing around, will you?'

Still he refused to make himself known. Perhaps Brigit had imagined it. Or it had been just an animal. A cat, maybe, or a fox. Her heart leapt as something moved again, something she knew had been crouching in the bushes, watching her. Then it stood, a shadowy figure that rose with menacing slowness, giving out a low grunt.

'Come on, Tommy. Stop fucking about.'

The *Puca Muc*. Is that what he was pretending to be? Brigit remembered the tale her Nan had told about the pig ghost that had been seen around even when the old woman was young. The story was that a boy had fallen over the edge of the cliff into the waterfall. It had taken him all night to climb back to the top, trying time after time to complete the ascent only to fall back each time before finally reaching safety. But his efforts were in vain. When he was found in the morning, exposure had got the better of him, and he was dead. He was dirty and naked, his clothes torn away by the torrent of water, and his hands and feet were shredded to bloody ribbons. The man who found the body mistook it at first for that of a pig. Not long after that, someone had seen what they had called a ghost, swine-like but standing upright on two legs, screaming a hellish squeal. The story had not scared her then, not much anyway, and there was no reason for her to be afraid of it now. Yet how could Tommy have known about the *Puca Muc*? He had not been in the area long enough. Someone must have told him.

'Very funny,' she called out. 'Now do you plan to stay in the bushes playing with yourself all day or wouldn't you rather come and play with me?'

The cloud completed its journey across the sun, suddenly making the orchard lighter, and Brigit saw that it was not Tommy. Even though she could not make out his features clearly through the dense trees, whoever was standing in the undergrowth was much bigger than him. Nervous now, Brigit looked around for the way back towards the road, but she had lost all sense of direction. The thumping of her heart masked all other sounds, save her ragged breathing, which seemed to be growing louder and more erratic. With a deep chill of fear, she realised that it was not her own breathing she could hear.

Blind panic gripped her and she started to run, out of the orchard and into the trees, away from whoever was watching her, praying she had guessed right and was heading back towards the road. At least from there she would have the chance of being seen by someone else; a chance of being safe. From behind, she could hear the figure suddenly begin to give chase. Brigit could almost feel the sudden burst of raw power as it set off in pursuit. Almost weeping with terror, she increased her pace, gulping down great lungfuls of air until she felt as though her chest would burst. Branches clawed at her face, and she raised a hand to protect her eyes and to swipe at the tears that blurred her vision. The ground underfoot was uneven where roots had spread and tangled, but she dared not look down. More than once she almost tripped; only luck coupled with sheer willpower kept her going. From over her shoulder came the sound of relentless pursuit. *Don't look back, don't look back*, she kept telling herself, but she could not resist taking a backwards glance to see if she was outrunning her pursuer, and immediately wished she hadn't. Whoever it was seemed to be gaining on her, swatting aside the sturdiest of branches as if they did not exist. Again the light was too poor for Brigit to make out his face, but he was hunched over as he ran, seeming more animal than human. *Puca Muc*, she thought, and in sheer desperation accepted the word of the calm voice that answered her back, *There's no such thing*.

As she turned to look ahead again, a branch whipped across her face, tearing the flesh. Burning pain flared. Brigit stumbled and fell as she lost her footing in a tangle of brambles and couch grass. Knowing how close the thing was behind her, she rolled away from where she had fallen, cowering in the undergrowth, desperately holding back her sobs of pain and fear. When she touched her face, cautiously, biting her tongue against the stinging pain, her fingers came away bloody. She lay as still as she could, heart like a trip-hammer in her chest, hoping against hope that she would remain unnoticed.

The grunting grew louder then stopped, only to be replaced by a more bestial, a more primal sound – sniffs and snuffles, like an animal tracing the path of its prey, alternating as they grew louder and closer, until Brigit could see nearby trees move as they were pushed against or brushed aside. A few yards away from her, a single column of fading yellow light had pierced the canopy overhead, despite the sun being so low in the sky, but when she looked from it and back into the gloom, she could see nothing. Then there was movement again, and the shape lumbered into the light.

It was hard to control the sudden horrified intake of breath as she saw the creature that had been in pursuit. Even though its back was to her at first, she could see it was no ordinary man. Its broad and too-heavily-muscled shoulders and arms, all covered in a grey leathery skin, flexed as the creature looked up to the sun, seemingly entranced by the light. Slowly, it turned around on the spot, searching its surroundings. Then it looked straight at her with small eyes set in an overlarge head with tusks protruding up and down from drooling lips. Her mind now accepted what her heart already knew. It was the *Puca Muc*.

The creature grunted again and continued to turn.

It hasn't seen me, she thought. Maybe, just maybe, if she could stay still long enough, it would leave and let her get away. But then it sniffed again and took a step forwards, then another, until it was charging straight at her. No longer even attempting to choke back her screams, Brigit scrambled to her feet, only for her ankle to become caught in a length of bramble, sending her headlong into deep bracken.

Then the creature was upon her. She fought to break free, swinging both fists against flesh that felt like thick rubber, but the beast was too strong. Two-fingered hands clawed at her clothes as the thing sat astride her, ripping and shredding her flimsy T-shirt. Instinctively, Brigit tried to cover her breasts with her hands, but brute force prevailed, and in an instant her shorts and underwear had been torn from her. Its eyes gleamed with malevolent intelligence, boring into her own until they held captive her soul. Brigit lay there, unable to move, unable to give voice to the agony that wracked her body when the *Puca Muc* forced its way inside her. It felt like she was being split in two.

The last thing she heard before she slipped into something near unconsciousness was the creature's piercing screech of triumph. When she came to she was alone. The sounds of birds had returned to the trees and the first stars had begun to emerge in the evening sky. Brigit felt a momentary relief, convinced it had all been a nightmare, but then the pain roared back into life and she knew beyond doubt her violation had been no dream. The creature's seed was in her womb; she swore she could feel it. Vomit rose in her throat and she spewed long and hard. When she had finished, she reached for what was left of her clothes and, with trembling hands, pulled them on, panicking when she found the blood on her thighs amid the cuts and scratches. By now the woods were well and truly dark, but somehow she managed to find her way back to the road. Later she would not remember the journey home, only her relief at finding the house empty. She climbed the stairs to the bathroom, each step a lesson in agony, and started to run a bath. While she waited for it to fill, she hugged herself to prevent the chills that coursed through her from ripping her apart. Then she stepped into the scalding water and scrubbed with soap and a coarse flannel until the water had turned red and her skin was livid. But she could do nothing about the filthiness she felt inside her body and her mind, nothing except cry.

And cry, and cry and cry.

The next morning she felt sick again.

Within two days her stomach had started to swell.

***

The air in the room was rank with sweat; the heat had not abated even though the storm had broken and the rain that attacked the window sounded like claws scraping the glass. The rest of Brigit's story emerged in fits and starts as she fought to tell it against the agony of her contractions. Most of it washed over Eileen, who was intent on helping the girl to breathe correctly and to deal with the worst of the pain. The stifling atmosphere made concentrating on the task at hand almost impossible. Even so, she heard enough of what Brigit was saying to gather that Tommy had phoned the next day, making sure the old man had left the house first, to explain he hadn't stood her up, he swore. He'd been delayed at work, that was all. Brigit, though, could hardly bring herself to answer, so deep was her shame and her misery, and refused point blank to see him. Finally, tonight, having called and been refused maybe a dozen times, he had turned up on her doorstep just as she was about to give birth to whatever festered inside her.

Now Tommy was waiting outside the bedroom door, along with Brian Tobin, waiting for Eileen to summon them. Deeming Patrick too young to observe his sister's discomfort, Eileen had ordered him sent to a neighbour.

'Won't be long now,' she whispered, wincing as the girl's hand squeezed hers with devastating strength in reaction to another juddering spasm. *Poor thing. She's having to go through this without so much as a whiff of entonox to numb her senses.*

'Just get it out of me!' Brigit screamed again.

Eileen examined the girl again, could see she was fully dilated now. At the same time, she had a clear glimpse of the fresh scar tissue that scored the flesh at the top of her inner thighs. There could be little doubt that the poor thing had been attacked. Surely this much damage could never be inflicted between two consenting adults. Yet neither could Eileen give any credence to the girl's story about the pig ghost. It didn't exist. Not even in rural Ireland. *People think we're behind the rest of the world out here in the wild,* she thought. *And maybe we are. But not* that *far behind.* Maybe it was easier for Brigit to deal with it this way. She had been attacked, possibly by Tommy, the traveller she seemed so taken up with. It could be that she had made up the tale about the *Puca Muc*, had convinced herself it was true, rather than face up to a more mundane but equally horrifying reality. If she loved Tommy, as she said, she would probably say anything rather than lose him. But then why would she feel this way about his baby?

'I can see it,' Eileen called excitedly as a small pink dome topped with hair began to extrude. *Got to remember, got to remember*, she thought. The girl was relying on her to get her through this, and even if she did not want the child, she would still need tending to. 'Push now!' Eileen called, and with the next contraction the baby's head emerged. 'And another.' In a matter of minutes she had managed to turn the infant, its flesh slick against her fingers, so that its shoulders followed swiftly by its tiny body emerged bloody but unharmed from the womb. As if allergic to the outside world, it began to bawl lustily.

'Got a good pair of lungs on him,' Eileen said, tying and cutting the umbilical cord before wrapping the infant in a towel. Her hands shook so badly that for one terrifying moment she thought she would drop the precious bundle. Despite her dismissal of Brigit's story, in the seconds before the child had been born she had actually believed that it could be true after all, that the thing she was bringing into the world would burst out, all heavy shoulders and chattering jaws. She silently mocked her lapse into superstitious dread, for the lad – it was indeed a boy – was just about perfect. 'Will you hold him?'

Brigit shook her head violently. 'I don't even want to *see* the fucking thing.'

'Darling, he's fine. You've got a beautiful baby boy.'

'I still don't want it!'

'I'll take him,' said Tobin, who had entered the room silently and remained a discreet distance away. 'Doesn't matter who the father is. He's still my grandson.'

His size belied the gentleness with which he took the child from Eileen's arms. He held the baby close to his chest and bent to kiss its forehead. Eileen, amazed at the transformation in the man, was touched to see tears spill from his eyes. He looked up at her, obviously troubled. 'Is it normal for him to cry like this?' he asked.

'Poor mite is probably starving,' she answered. That was the one problem she had not figured out in advance, as obvious as it was. There was no chance of finding any formula milk in the house, and Brigit was hardly likely to accept the child at her breast, not in her current state of mind. With luck, the ambulance would be there soon and the midwife would have some of the powdered milk with her; bottles and teats, too. If not, she'd have to send Tommy into the village to knock up Peggy in the general store. Meanwhile, Eileen thought it would be an idea to get the child cleaned up as best as she could. With the blood and mucus cleared away, maybe Brigit would see through her own twisted fantasy long enough to accept it as the beautiful little thing that it was.

'Pass him over,' she said, mustering up a cheerfulness that she did not feel. 'Your daughter needs her father now. I'll get this one into the bathroom and cleaned up.'

But before she left the room, Brigit stared up at her, eyes wide. 'It's not over,' she moaned. 'There's something else inside me. I can feel it pushing out.'

'Nothing to worry about,' Eileen assured her. 'It's just the placenta. The afterbirth. It won't harm you, so just go with the contractions. Won't take long.'

'I'm here, my girl,' Tobin said tenderly, sitting on the bed and holding his daughter with both hands as Eileen left the bedroom. The atmosphere on the landing was blessedly cool in comparison. She paused there a moment, eyes closed, the infant's cries almost fading into the distance as cold air embraced and lulled her senses. Then she became aware of Tommy at her elbow, a look of helpless confusion on his face.

'Is it over?' he asked, eyes in constant motion, darting between Eileen, the bedroom door and the baby. 'I mean, do you think they'd mind if I went in now?'

'I should think that would be fine,' she said, smiling at him. 'Even that miserable old sod seems to have mellowed since this little darling dropped into the world.'

'I'll go see them, then,' he said with touching hesitancy, and moved towards the door. Eileen stepped across the hall and into the bathroom, crouching to place the baby, still in its towel, on the floor while she ran warm water into the sink. Taking a flannel, she knelt at the infant's side and gently unwrapped the cloth. It came away red. She frowned. There seemed to be an awful lot of blood on its body. As softly as she could, Eileen wiped at it with the flannel and saw there was something wrong with the child's skin, some kind of blemish that twisted the flesh into small, blue-and-scarlet lumps. She used the cloth again, more urgently now, only vaguely registering Brigit's screams. Her mind spun and gorge rose from her stomach as each swipe of the flannel cleared away more mucus and blood until she could see how the baby had been bitten over and over by whatever filthy, half-human creature it had shared Brigit's womb with.

From the room behind she could hear the two men join the girl's screams of terror. *Twins*, she thought numbly. *Something else I should have thought of.* And rising above the clamour came a high-pitched hellish squeal.

An Old Passion
Storm Constantine

Well, of course she threw a garden party as soon as the place was decent. She had to show it off, and who could blame her? I went with Cathy, because Ted wouldn't go with me. 'She was unbearable when she was only slightly rich,' he said. 'Now, we're talking about torture, an afternoon in Hell.'

'I'm sure it won't be that bad,' I said, but privately I agreed with him. I'm not sure what made me go, really. I knew my skin would be crawling with annoyance by the end of the afternoon, but I suppose I was just curious. My friend had acquired a stately home. She was living in it. I had to go and see.

Helen had gone to school with Cathy and me, and because we all still lived in the area around the village where we'd grown up, we'd kept in touch. Cathy and I had married the sons of farmers, as our parents had expected, while Helen had gone off to college and run wild for a while. She had come back to the village now and again throughout her teens and early twenties, adopting every city fad that was going, showing off to us, her provincial sisters, stuck out in the sticks. I don't think we ever really liked her. You can't actually *like* a person like Helen, so familiar yet so distant, but we were always curious, always entertained.

Something went wrong when she hit her quarter century, although she never confided in us about it. She came home, skulked dramatically round the village for a few weeks in dark glasses, looked tragic and wore wide hats like a film star. Then it was forgotten, whatever *it* was, and she was her usual bragging self again. Still, she stuck around after that, wheedled her way in with the new money, who drank in the pubs on the edge of the village.

While Cathy and I met our husbands and duly began to produce families, Helen secured jobs from her new friends, drove around in a new car, bought a cottage, did it up (quite well, too), and kept on partying. Sometimes, she'd visit us and gently scorn what she called our 'giving in to tradition'. Of course I envied her; who wouldn't? She was graceful and wild and witty, and had *fun*.

'Where did we go wrong?' Cathy asked one day, after a morning get-together, as we watched the dust of Helen's car disappearing down Cathy's driveway. 'God, I hate her, the bitch! Where *did* we go wrong?'

Then we laughed together, went back inside, and had another gin. Our lives weren't that bad, really.

***

Helen was 32 when she met Roland Marchant. He was the one she'd been waiting for, the son of an industrialist, busy being propelled up the ladder of affluence by Daddy, oozing wealth and smarm. Helen met him at some do or other she'd gone to with friends and, with an unerring huntress's sense for a prime kill, set her sights and brought the prey down. Shall we say it was a short engagement? City bred, he was interested in village life, in country life, and I suspect it was more at his insistence than Helen's that she brought him visiting. He thought the farms were quaint and wanted to try driving a tractor. Ted, and Cathy's husband, Rupert, were strained but polite. Fortunately, the tractor lark never got beyond the evening of Scotch and Roland's loud voice. Well, no-one reminded him about it.

'I don't know what's worse,' Cathy said. 'A rich boor who's pompous and condescending or a rich boor who's devoted to being everybody's best buddy.'

Still, we accepted the antique brandies, and such like, and were always coolly friendly.

Deermount House came on the market because the Pargeters couldn't keep the place up. Sons and daughter had moved away and had no interest in the family pile; the roof was caving in. Roland fought

off developers, hoteliers, theme park entrepreneurs, conference centre
planners and outbid the lot. He acquired Deermount House lock, stock
and barrel. The Pargeters took very little away with them, other than
an unspeakably large stash and a sense of financial relief. Roland and
Helen would live there. They would be neighbours. Oh, wonderful.

When Helen came to tell me the news, I couldn't stop myself saying,
'Isn't it a bit big for just you and Roland?'

Helen laughed. 'Don't be absurd, Anna! It's a fucking mansion.
How can a mansion be "too big"? You simply have to live bigger.'

I could almost hear her knuckles cracking at the prospect.

***

The garden party recreated some idyllic post-war age as Helen imagined
it. It was all bunting and vicars with megaphones, that sort of thing.
The gardens were a mess, actually, utterly run to seed, but Roland had
had the lawns rotor scythed, so it didn't look too bad. The first thing
Cathy and I noticed about the house was the new roof. It looked rather
peculiar, so clean and regular, atop the sagging façade of the house.
Rather like an old woman wearing a teenager's hat. We presumed the
rest of the building would soon succumb to cosmetic surgery, its
wrinkles nipped and tucked, so that it matched the roof.

It appeared that everyone from the village and surrounding farms
had come to be nosy. Children shrieked, piped band music stuttered,
vicars cajoled. The river, caressed by ancient willows, oozed slowly
through the gardens, like an ancient snake that knew its own territory.
There were swans, of course. Summer as it had once been, perhaps.

Then Helen came gliding up the lawns towards us from the river,
backlit by gleaming water. She looked divine in a flowered sundress,
required large hat, silken blonde hair and ready red smile. 'Darlings!
So glad you came!' she screamed. God, it was embarrassing. Yes, we
were jealous.

'You *must* see the house!' Helen insisted, and we had to follow her
inside. Once there, the spirit of the place claimed us and envy and
irritation gave way to awe.

'Helen, you've done wonders!' Cathy exclaimed, craning her neck to try and take in the appallingly massive vista of the stuccoed ceiling in the main hall.

'Oh, it wasn't me,' Helen said, almost apologetically. 'Roland got designers in, architects, the lot. I just sat around waiting for them to finish. Didn't have a word in it.'

Did she mind about that? I wondered, mentally filing the thought to repeat to Cathy later.

'But you simply have to see my new man,' Helen said, her eyes shining. Cathy and I exchanged a glance, and Cathy shrugged. New man? Our minds were open.

Helen led us upstairs to a long, well-lit gallery that overlooked the gardens. All the paintings have been restored, she told us. 'I found him only a few days ago. He's divine.' She had paused before a painting, and was gesturing at it with some reverence.

'Who is it?' I asked.

'Rufus Aston,' Helen said grandly. We were clearly supposed to know who that was.

'A Pargeter ancestor?' Cathy suggested.

'Oh no!' Helen answered. 'He was a poet. Haven't you heard of him?'

No, we hadn't. Had anyone? He was beautiful, I suppose, although the chins of long dead people always seem too weak for my taste. Perhaps that is the fault of long dead painters rather than their models. The poet's hair was a resplendent red, his eyes dark and limpid, the mouth a little too generous, although not that wide. I estimated, with my untutored eye, he had lived in the 19th Century. Helen confirmed this. 'Yes, I've been researching.'

'Did he live here?' Cathy asked, politely. I dared not look at her for fear of grinning.

'No,' Helen explained, 'but he stayed here quite often over a period of several years. Best of all, he died here!'

Best of all?

'Oh,' said Cathy and I together.

'Isn't it romantic?' Helen enthused. 'I'm reading up about him like mad, though it's hard to find things out.'

Well, Rufus Aston was obviously the latest fad. Helen's enthusiasm would be poured into him, and continue to be so, until it overflowed and her attention surged elsewhere.

***

We didn't see much of her for a few weeks after the garden party. We were busy with the harvest, and Helen, presumably, with renovating Deermount House and its grounds. Roland had asked Ted about buying horses, hiring grooms. Cathy's aunt, Mags, had been taken on as a cook. From her came the gossip. She felt that Roland and Helen were not like real people. They never seemed to argue, and spoke to one another as if they were acting in a play about domestic bliss. Such sunshine, such idyll. Is it any surprise, then, that they were threatened by thunderstorms? The weather always has to change.

Helen came calling three weeks after the garden party. She sat at my kitchen table, while I washed the breakfast things at the sink. I thought she seemed a little on edge, which was unusual for her. 'Everything all right?' I enquired.

Helen scowled at my youngest, who was hanging on to my skirts and attempting to disrupt our conversation. She, of course, would never want children.

'Fine,' she said. 'Everything's fine. I'm a bit exhausted, naturally. The job's never ending! Still, Rolly and I wouldn't have missed taking the place for the world. We love it.' She lit a cigarette. Her nails were immaculate. I doubted she ever applied hand to paint stripper herself. 'Do you know, I think I must be the luckiest woman alive.'

I winced, and smiled at her in what I hoped was a convincing fashion.

'Roland is buying me a mare,' she said.

I took a few moments to consider the wonder of a woman who had married the most incredibly rich man and was actually in love with him. It seemed that way. Her eyes went moist when she mentioned his name.

'You were never much into riding,' I said.

'I have the time now.' Helen leaned down and produced a bottle of gin from her large bag. 'Oh, for God's sake, Anna, come and sit down.

Leave the washing-up. Have a drink.'

I obeyed her, instinctively sensing she wanted to talk. I even shooed the boy out into the garden. 'Well?' I said, sipping gin.

Helen laughed. 'Well, what?' She leaned back in her chair, struck a pose with the cigarette.

'What is it you want to say?'

Helen leaned forward and squeezed my arm where it lay on the table. 'Oh darling, you country women are just so intuitive!'

That was the sort of remark I was used to putting up with. I declined to respond.

'The thing is, I've discovered some magic, some real magic.'

'Oh? Witchcraft in the old grounds, then?'

'No, nothing like that.' She adopted an earnest expression, lowered her voice. 'I think Rufus is trying to contact me.'

'Rufus?' I had forgotten about the poet, and imagined this must be an old flame.

'Don't you remember the painting I showed you?

'Oh yes.' I paused. 'Hel, are we talking ghosts, here?'

'Nothing so banal,' she answered. 'A ghost is just a picture, a memory. Rufus is stronger than that. I'm sure I've seen him.'

'Oh Helen! Where?' I am not a sceptic, but not for one moment could I imagine a worldly woman like Helen being in tune with something spiritual.

'In the gardens,' she replied. 'Anna, I couldn't tell anyone else about this. Rolly would think I'd gone mad and start to worry, and Cathy would just laugh.'

'You'd better tell me about it,' I said.

I was, as usual, curious. Helen was always interesting. She had caught sight of a man, whom she now presumed to be Rufus Aston, in one of the more tangled corners of the gardens. Every morning, she walked her new Labrador puppies in the grounds, and it was always then that she saw him. Never at night, never at dusk, but in clear morning sunlight. He would be standing amid the shoulder-high grasses, as still as a stone, but with an air of absolute alertness. 'He doesn't look like a ghost; he's completely solid,' she said. 'And he watches me. The thing is, it doesn't scare me.'

'Are you sure it's not just some young man who's taken a shine to you?' I asked. 'Why do you think it's Rufus?'

'Because it looks like him, silly. The clothes, the hair, the face. It's him.' She took a drink, swallowed. 'I know it is. But what does he want from me?' Only then did her brow cloud, but it wasn't with fear.

We talked about further research. Even I became a little infected with her enthusiasm. Helen didn't know where the poet was buried, or even how he'd died. Only that his last moments had been spent at Deermount House, although whether he had expired within the walls or out in the grounds, she didn't know. I believed her utterly. There was no question of it.

'Perhaps I should hold a séance,' she said.

I frowned. 'Oh, I don't think … I think that's asking for trouble. No, don't do that.'

'I trust your instincts, darling,' she said, standing up. 'Well, I must be off. Keep the gin. I'll let you know what I find out.'

I tell Cathy everything, but I didn't tell her about Helen's visit. Probably because I believed Helen and, as she had correctly pointed out, Cathy would laugh about it. I didn't tell anyone, not even Ted, who would genuinely have been interested. Perhaps I should have done.

We held a Halloween party for the children at Cathy and Rupert's. While the kids screamed round us in garish costumes, Cathy and I sipped port in the flickering light of pumpkin lamps. Our men had sloped off down the pub. I felt warm, at one with myself. The pagan new year.

'Have you seen much of Helen?' Cathy asked.

'No,' I answered. In fact, I hadn't seen her since the morning she'd told me about her apparition. 'You?'

'Nothing. Mags thinks she's out of sorts. Perhaps we should visit.'

'Out of sorts? What's wrong with her?' Just for a moment, my blissful mood froze.

'Oh, nothing serious, I don't think. Mags says she's distracted. Apparently, she's got a new set of friends, though where she dredged them up from, heaven knows. Mags thinks they're weird. The place is crawling with them. They're ghost hunters, or something like that. Helen actually held a séance up there, you know.'

'No! Cath, why didn't you tell me?'

Cathy looked surprised at my outburst. 'I only found out today. Why? What do you know?'

'As much as you do. Remember the painting she showed us, the new man?'

'You think she's trying to call his ghost up?' Cathy, predictably, cackled.

'It could be dangerous, Cath. I think Helen's fragile, for all her panache. Deermount House is such a big old place, and she's rattling round in it, on her own with dear Rolly, who's about as sensitive as a plank. Perhaps she's becoming too imaginative. You know how easily impressed she is. What if these new friends of hers are a bit, well, shady?'

'Yeah, you're right. Shall we call on the off-chance tomorrow?'

I nodded. 'Yes, but keep a zip on it, Cath. Don't ridicule her.'

Cathy gave me a studying look. 'Why is it we care about her, Annie? What keeps us there for her?'

I shrugged. 'Don't know. Old bonds, I suppose.'

'She shuts us out when she's having crises though. Remember when she first came back?'

'I remember. As I said, I think she's fragile. And, for all her ways, she's always been generous.'

'Yes, generous.' Cathy took a slug of port. 'I hope I don't want something awful to happen to her.'

'Course you don't,' I said.

***

Halloween, Samhain, the pagan new year, the time when the veil is thin between the worlds. If we should have visited Helen, perhaps it should have been the night before, the time when the dead come back to commune with the living. We were unprepared for the maelstrom of energy that greeted us at Deermount House.

Helen came like a hurricane into the drawing room where her

housekeeper had installed us. She seemed almost hysterically delighted to see us. She hugged us, and her skin felt feverish, hot, against our own. 'My dears, my dears!' she said.

'Hi,' Cathy said. 'We wondered how you were. Haven't seen you for ages.'

'I'm fine,' Helen answered. 'Brilliantly fine.' She looked at me, and a secretive cast came into her expression. Forget the offer of tea, or anything stronger: she launched straight into her new obsession. 'Anna, I've been continuing with my research.'

'Come up with anything?' I asked.

She rolled her eyes. 'Have I just? I'm on a quest, now.'

Quest? Cathy and I sat down, while Helen leaned against the mantelpiece to light a cigarette. Her fever had cooled. She seemed quite businesslike.

'Psychic questing,' Helen said. 'A lot of people are doing it.' I noticed she did not look at Cathy as she spoke, although her voice was firm and confident, as if challenging Cathy to poke fun. 'I wrote to some people who are into it, and they've been helping me. It's a science, you know.'

How far had she gone that she could speak this way in front of Cathy? Her reserve had vanished, which to me spoke of a replacement mania.

'Are you questing about Rufus Aston?' I asked.

She nodded. 'Absolutely. There's more to it than meets the eye. He was involved in something, Anna, something from the past that can still affect the present.'

'Oh really!' exclaimed Cathy, unable to contain herself.

Helen gave her a hard look, the hardest look I'd ever seen her give anyone. 'You can scoff, Cath,' she said in a cool voice, 'but I know what I've seen and experienced. I was sceptical once, too. If you can listen to me with an open mind, I'll tell you about it.'

Why had I thought she was fragile? She wasn't. If anything, her experiences, whatever they were, had strengthened her. There was a new steel to Helen Marchant, almost as if she'd somehow become anchored to the earth, had slowed down, become part of real life. Absurd. But that's how it felt. And from the way she spoke, it was impossible to laugh at her, even for Cathy.

With the help of her new friends, who were thorough researchers and had recourse to documents that Helen would not even have thought about, she had discovered that Rufus Aston had been found dead in the grounds of the house, during a visit in the summer of 1883. He had been 22 years old. The cause of death was given as an overdose of laudanum. Well, they were all into it, then, weren't they? Poets and artists, the bohemians. The incumbent of the House at the time, Richard Pargeter, had been a patron of the arts, and much else besides, it seems. The glitterati of artistic society had regularly gathered at the estate, or so Helen said, but I must admit I'd not heard of any of the names she cited as evidence. 'They had a society,' Helen said. 'A secret society. There's no documentation about it, but Steve – he's my psychic aide – picked it all up at the … well …' She looked guiltily at me. 'We had a little session here a few days ago. I know you think it's dangerous to meddle with, Anna, but honestly, it's quite safe with people like Steve around, who know what they're doing. Pargeter was head of the society, like a kind of High Priest, I suppose. They were seeking immortality.'

'Well, at least poor old Rufus never grew old!' Cathy observed.

'Quite,' Helen agreed. 'Things got a bit out of hand, apparently. The strange thing is, there are so few records about what went on. Strangest of all, Richard Pargeter just sort of fades from history not long after Rufus's death. There's no mention, other than that his brother took over the estate. We can only presume something was effectively hushed up.'

'But this is all conjecture,' Cathy said. 'The facts are, a man died, in not very suspicious circumstances, really, and then Richard Pargeter stepped down. Probably to avoid a scandal, or something. This other stuff, about secret societies and immortality, was only dreamed up at your séance.'

'I realise it appears that way,' Helen said. 'But if you'd been involved, you'd feel the same way I do. I was there. I heard him speak. Through Steve.'

'Heard who speak? Rufus Aston?'

She shook her head. 'No, no. Pargeter. He took over Steve's body. It was outrageous!'

'His ghost came?' I said, as an exclamation rather than a question, but Helen answered me.

'Of course not! Pargeter's not dead. But he is very powerful.'

'Er … what does Roland think about all this?' I enquired, quite gobsmacked by her revelation. Neither Cathy nor I could bring ourselves to question Helen about it.

'He thinks it's just a quaint little interest of mine. Poor Rolly, he's not very spiritual!' She laughed.

Cathy wound the visit up very quickly after that, and we left. On the way back, Cathy broke a silence between us to say, 'She's off her head, Annie, and there's nothing we can do about it.'

Was there anything I, or anyone else, could do? Perhaps we had no right. Helen did not seem ill, or even particularly disturbed. She was excited, yes, but who wouldn't be, in her shoes? Cathy didn't believe the stuff about the séance and the psychic questers. She thought they had to be charlatans. I, for whatever reason, call it instinct or gut reaction, was not convinced about that. Still, I wasn't going to admit that to Cathy. I told Ted about it though, because he has a casual interest in strange phenomena. He was waiting to find his first crop circle, in fact, although his aim would be to disprove more than prove the evidence. In Helen's case, he thought the danger of applying that much concentration, or will power, to a search, was that you tended to find whatever you were looking for, be it a demon from ages past or a pound coin on the pavement.

'It can lead to a kind of group hysteria,' he said. 'Then you'll believe, in fact, see, anything. And is that reality or not? It's marshy ground, I think. We don't know enough about it.' Ted reads up on that kind of thing. I asked him to find me the article he'd seen about it. I wanted to read it too.

'I'd be wary of getting involved,' Ted said, but he trusted me not to.

Helen phoned me two days later. Her voice was low, so she must have had company somewhere in the house. 'Anna, this is a secret, but I have to let you in on it. We're going to quest for his tomb!'

'Excuse me? Whose?' I'd lost track of who she believed was dead and who not.

'Aston's! He's buried around here somewhere, but no-one knows where. There's no record, but we're going to find it. Steve is absolutely quivering with vibrations.'

'Lucky Steve,' I said, and then added carefully, 'You will take care, won't you, Hel.'

'It's all in good hands, Anna, don't worry. I'll let you know about it.' The phone went down. Just that. I was left looking at my own receiver, wondering if I should do anything, and if so, what. In the event, I did nothing.

***

I expected to hear something from Helen pretty soon, but then we had a crisis with our eldest, who had a messy accident with a broken limb, and blood and screams. So I was preoccupied with running backwards and forwards to the hospital in the nearest town for a while. I forgot about Helen's quest. She phoned me a couple of times to ask how we were, but didn't mention much about her new interest. I had the impression things had faded out a little. Perhaps, as they hadn't found the tomb, Helen's enthusiasm was dying.

The next news came from Cathy, via Mags. 'You won't believe this,' Cathy said, breezing into my kitchen one morning. 'Helen's buying a church!'

'What? You're joking!'

'No. Do you suppose she's found religion now?'

'What's been going on?' I hadn't heard from Helen for weeks, so had assumed Rufus Aston had gone the way of all her previous crazes. This must be a new one.

'Well, the ghost hunters are out,' Cathy said gleefully. 'Mags thinks a disagreement happened, or perhaps Roland got sick of them. Anyway, Helen has done up a room in the house like an Egyptian temple or something. No-one's allowed in there, but Mags had a peek when the designers were in. She says the house absolutely reeks of incense some mornings when she goes in. Can you believe it? Has dear Helen become a sorceress now?'

'God, I dread to think! But where does the church come into this?'

'Mags doesn't know exactly. All she does know is that it's an abandoned church – practically a ruin – near Loxcombe, and that Roland is buying it for Helen. She only found out about it because Roland was bragging in front of his friends when she was serving sherry to them last Sunday. He thinks Helen's into conservation. Thinks it's a great idea. There was talk of opening a craft centre in it. Agh! It's too much! Can you imagine it? Helen in High Priestess robes, selling joss sticks and corn dollies?' She fell back in her chair, laughing helplessly.

I joined in with the hilarity, although inside I felt a little disturbed, and absurdly, somehow disloyal to Helen for laughing.

I called her in the afternoon. 'So, what's all this, stranger?' I said in a jokey manner. 'Where have you been, what have you been up to, and why are you buying a church?' I expected the usual breezy answer, but Helen was reticent.

'How do you know about that?'

'Little bird told me,' I replied glibly. 'Is it true?'

She didn't want to answer me, I know she didn't, but eventually she said, with utmost reluctance, 'Well, yes.'

'Why?'

I heard her sigh down the line. 'Anna, I found the tomb.'

It didn't take a genius to work out where it was. I wanted to see her. I don't know why, but the impulse could not be ignored. 'Can you come over?'

She hesitated. 'All right. Give me an hour.'

In the event, she didn't arrive when she'd promised, and I had to drive to the school around three o'clock to pick up the middle child, with my youngest in the back of the Discovery, making havoc, as usual. Eldest son was prolonging his convalescence at Ted's parents' for a few days.

I waited outside the school for my daughter, tapping my fingernails against the steering wheel, wondering why Helen had stood me up, and desperate to get back in case I missed her. Then coincidence spilled beans from the mouth of my lovely daughter, as she threw her bag in through the passenger door and climbed up beside me. 'Mum, there's witches at Deermount House!'

'What, darling?'

'Ben said so. His brother saw them in the grounds, wearing robes and everything. There was a fire. Is Aunty Helen a witch?'

I laughed, in a brittle fashion. 'Probably just one of her parties. You know what she's like.' Already, my daughter did. Must be that country woman intuition Helen spoke about.

Helen was waiting for us when we got home, leaning against her shiny black car, which looked like a big cat, and actually was, in another, brand name sense. She was wearing a big coat and dark glasses, her glossy hair covered by a scarf. 'Don't you dare mention witches!' I hissed at my daughter as she tumbled out of the Discovery.

Daughter despatched to friends nearby for pony activities, with the firm directive, despite complaints, to take younger brother with her, I settled Helen in the parlour. I considered making tea, and then poured her a glass of wine instead. She took off her dark glasses, and yes, she looked haggard. Make-up could not conceal the dark puffiness below her eyes. Worse, her nails were lacquerless and bitten. It was too much, almost as if she'd designed herself to look like the archetype of a troubled woman. The biggest shock was when she took off her scarf and shook out her hair. She'd cut it to shoulder length and dyed it red.

'That's a change,' I remarked, almost choking.

'Mmm.' Helen rubbed her forehead.

'You look terrible,' I said, 'although I suppose you know that.'

Helen managed to avoid my eyes by reaching down to delve in her bag for cigarettes and lighter. 'I haven't been sleeping well, actually.'

'What's going on?' I demanded.

She lit up, blew smoke at me, or rather a smoke screen in front of herself. 'It's nothing bad, Anna, honestly. Just tiring.' A monumental lie.

'Is it anything to do with the tomb you found, or the secret temple in the house?'

Helen smiled wanly. 'God, you just can't get the staff nowadays, can you? I presume your information comes from the fount of all rumour, Mags Whitely?'

'I never betray my informants,' I answered, 'but what I heard concerns me, Hel. And look at you! What are you doing to yourself? What's the temple for?'

'I find comfort in it,' Helen said. 'I feel safe there.'

I shook my head slowly. 'Even my daughter talks of witches in the gardens at Deermount. Just what is going on?'

Helen considered for a moment, and then relented. 'All right. I don't want this going back to Cathy, but, well, I would appreciate a chat.'

I gave her my promise, and I meant it. She spoke at length about how much she'd found out about the secret society of Deermount House, circa 1883. The Bearers of the Old Light, they called themselves. All of the information had been channelled through Steve during psychic sittings. (The so-called witches in the garden, incidentally, had been an outdoor séance.) The Bearers of the Old Light had consisted of ten members, three of them women, all of them artistic or creative, but for Richard Pargeter, who called the shots. Helen said that he was a vampire for the creative energy of the others, but that he also replenished them, whatever that meant. They sought immortality, through magical artefacts, which failed, and then through ritual. 'It's not magic as we know it,' Helen said, 'but a form of parascience. It's trying to make contact with a more evolved form of yourself, who of course knows all the answers.'

And Rufus? His death, Helen said, was not accidental.

'Exactly *what* it was is difficult to establish. Steve never made contact with Rufus. He thought that Pargeter was blocking him.'

'Ah, yes,' I ventured, 'I remember you saying something outrageous like Richard Pargeter wasn't dead ...'

Helen nodded. 'I know it sounds crazy, I know it does. I don't want to believe it myself, but Steve was convinced. And now, I feel him myself, around the house, in the back of my head, everywhere.'

I shivered, thinking of cruel eyes beyond the window, where the afternoon was darkening. 'I hate to say this, but how ... how *genuine* do you think this Steve is?'

Helen flicked me a crystalline glance. 'No-one could act that well,' she said shortly.

'So you're saying Pargeter actually found immortality?' I risked a smile. 'I'm sorry, but I find that very hard to believe. What has he been doing for the past hundred years? Do his family know about him? And how on earth did he manage to live so long? Come on, Hel, you must agree it's pretty far-fetched!'

'It's not just far fetched, it's insane,' Helen said. 'But I also believe it to be true.' She leaned towards me. 'He's making his presence felt to me, Anna, he really is.' She shuddered, and looked around herself, as if a malevolent draught had suddenly chilled her.

My spine prickled in sympathy. 'Do you think you're in danger?' I asked her gently.

She gave me a naked, wild look that made me jump. For a second, something else seemed to look from the face of my friend. I remember saying her name in shock. Then she shook her head, hiding her face with that new, red hair.

'I don't know, but I feel I have to … I need Rufus's help. I'm sure he'd be able to tell me what to do.' She rubbed her face wearily with her hands. 'God, Anna, why did I get into this? Why? Now, it's too late. I'm in it!'

Sitting there, in my cosy parlour, it was hard to believe this other world existed; a world of magicians, secret societies, voices from beyond, psychic quests, supernatural threat. And yet, there was Helen before me, a ragged, haunted Helen who'd uttered the first regrets I'd ever heard from her, the first truly honest words concerning herself. I realised, with some awe, it was also the first time she had truly confided in me. No bravado, no wit, no barrier; just a frightened woman.

'I'll help you,' I said impulsively. 'Whatever I can do …'

She reached to squeeze my hands. 'Darling, thank you, but I don't know what you can do, other than listen to my ravings! Steve and the others have gone now. I'm afraid I threw them out. Stupid of me! I realise I need them, and yet I don't want to be part of their world.'

'Why did you throw them out?'

She sighed. 'Two reasons. First, I haven't seen Rufus in the gardens since they came, or since Richard Pargeter made his presence felt. I believed Rufus would come back once they'd gone, but he hasn't. And second, I thought this nightmare would end if Steve and the others left. But it hasn't. I feel *he's* there with me all the time, Anna, watching me, waiting for a weak moment. He hates me.'

'Pargeter?'

She nodded miserably. 'Sometimes I tell myself it's only my imagination. I tell myself not to be so silly, to throw off these ridiculous fears. Then I'm in bed at night, terrified, and whatever I do, however I scream, and hit out, I can't wake Rolly up, and I'm alone with this ...' She struggled for colourful enough words. 'With this ... *evil*, cold mind. All around me. My little temple offers some respite, but not for much longer, I'm sure.'

'Perhaps you should contact Steve and his friends again,' I suggested lamely.

She shook her head vehemently. 'No. Then it would just go on and on. They love this kind of stuff. It's like a drug to them. They'd only make it worse, I'm sure.'

'Then someone else. There must be other people who deal with this kind of thing? A priest even.'

She nodded, a little distantly. 'Yes ... you're right.' Then she flicked her attention back to me. 'But I know Rufus can help me. I nearly have him now, Anna, what's left of him.'

'No, Hel, no!' I insisted. 'Go home, get your spooky journals, or whatever it is you have, and ring some people. Get someone to help you. Leave it alone until then. Have you told Roland about it?'

She laughed coldly. 'Don't be ridiculous! He'd have me committed.'

'Surely not; he loves you.'

'Yes, I think he does. But he's afraid of madness, of anything he can't see and touch and control. If he could say to people, "Oh, we have a ghost, you know," he'd love it, but not this, not something real and dreadful.' She took a breath and dropped her cigarettes and lighter back into her bag. 'Anyway, I must be going. Hate to sound dramatic, but I don't like being out alone after dark.'

I stood up with her, and we embraced awkwardly. 'Helen, this is vile!'

She smiled tightly and put on her coat.

'Will you call me tomorrow, after you've contacted some other psychics or something?'

'Yes, I will.'

As I watched her Jag glide off towards the road, I was afraid that I'd never see her again. I wish, in some ways, that had been true.

***

That evening, as we shared a nightcap in the parlour, I told Ted everything. I watched his eyes and I could see his feelings shifting from belief to disbelief and back again. Like me, he didn't want to believe it, for believing in it meant it had to be dealt with, and how do you deal with a thing like that? Far better to ignore it, to scoff, to cling stubbornly to the mundane world, where only what you can see and touch are real, and there are no hidden powers. Perhaps it is worse for a man, because men are brought up to think they have to be in control, otherwise they're sunk. We, as women, are somewhat more attuned to the unseen, the tides of our blood and instincts. We accept the unacceptable more readily.

'Those weirdoes have put these crazy ideas into her head,' my husband declared, taking a stand. 'You must see that, Annie. They've scared her to death. She lives in a huge, echoing, empty house, and she's afraid of it. You know yourself she's gullible. Now every echo is a disembodied voice, and every shadow a spook. She's conjuring things up from her own mind. You must see that I'm right.'

I looked at him steadily. He *could* be right. The explanation was rational and reasonable.

'If you want to help her,' Ted said, 'you should make her believe what I've just said. Then her phantoms will disappear, I'm sure of it.' He smiled and adopted an eerie tone. 'Whether they're real or not.'

I laughed. 'Ted!'

He shrugged. 'It's just a question of belief.'

'You're quite a little mystic in your own way, aren't you,' I said. 'So you won't mind driving out with me to Helen's church tomorrow.'

He pulled a comical face that was halfway to a frown. 'What for?'

'I just want to see, and I'd rather be with you than with Helen. I'd feel safer with your rationality around. It would be like a shield, if there is anything nasty there.'

Ted rolled his eyes. 'I can't believe we're having this conversation, but okay, if that's what you want …'

I knew it. He was hooked.

Kids off-loaded to grandparents once more, we drove out to Loxcombe in the morning. It was a Saturday, a bright, cold day. There were two churches in Loxcombe, but it didn't take us long to locate the semi-ruin that would soon belong to the Marchants. It was a dull little place, neglected and feeling sorry for itself. Ted and I nosed around the graveyard, and squinted at the plain, weathered stones, but there was no sign of Rufus Aston.

'Surely, if his grave was here,' Ted said, 'it would be well known. He was a kind of personality, after all.'

'I don't think he was that well known,' I said. 'As far as I'm aware, there are no books in existence of his poetry.'

Ted pulled an exasperated face. 'What the hell are we doing here?' he asked the sky, throwing up his hands.

The door to the church was locked, but we found a smaller door round the back, which was open a few inches but stuck. Ted applied brawn to the wood, and eventually there was enough room for us to wriggle inside. The interior smelled musty and damp, the pews had been ripped to pieces, and the uninspiring stained-glass windows broken. Still there was one wonder left. It was Ted who found it, and the awe in his voice when he said 'Annie, come and look at this!' alerted me immediately; the tomb of the poet.

There was no legend to tell us that inside lay the remains of the poet, but I recognised him immediately. There lay the stone effigy of Rufus Aston. The tomb was enormous, fit for a king. My first thought was that Rufus had been dearly loved by someone: a someone who could have afforded to pay for this monument, even if they had neglected to leave a reminder for the world concerning exactly who lay within it. The carving of the effigy was exquisite.

But for the colour of the stone – a strange, shiny black – he could have been a youth lying there asleep. The long hair was not stiffly stylised, but reproduced as flowing over the stone, down the sides of the sarcophagus. One long-fingered hand lay lightly on his breast, the other at his side. His shirt was open at the collar, revealing a slender throat, with the wonderful hollow that invites a finger to trace its depths. I touched him, with reverence, while Ted looked on. Neither of us said a word. If anything of Rufus *was* still there, he was certainly at peace. Even though the building was vandalised, the tranquillity seemed to flow from the tomb of the poet in waves. Helen should not, must not, violate this. Her problem was not Rufus, not now. She must not drag what was left him, essence or spirit, back into whatever filthy enterprise Richard Pargeter, alive or dead, represented. If an image of Rufus had ever haunted Helen's garden, it must simply have been a memory, a captured moment in time replaying throughout history, not an essence, or a soul. I was entirely sure about these thoughts; so sure, it was like a telepathic message. Perhaps Rufus's guardian angel was still around, keeping an eye out for him. I took a step back, and saw the inscription on the side of the tomb. Although there was no name to the words, I knew they had once been penned by the exquisite hand mimicked in stone above them:

Let me resist this old passion, let it pass over me.
For the flower of this love is death, which I have picked with my own hands
Pressed my own face into the flesh of it, taken the scent within.
'Strange they should put that on the tomb,' Ted murmured.
I glanced at him. 'Not strange to whoever chose it.'
What could I say to Helen? How could I dissuade her from trying to disturb the eternal rest of Rufus Aston? Back home, I called her immediately, but her housekeeper answered the phone. Mrs Marchant was ill, she wasn't taking calls. 'This is important,' I told her. 'Very important.'
'I'm sorry, Mrs Brown. She won't come to the phone. She's in bed. Can I take a message?'
'What's wrong with her?' I demanded.

'The flu,' answered the housekeeper. 'Is there any message?'

'Just say I called.' I slammed down the phone, thwarted. Was Helen's illness feigned so she did not have to speak to me? I was getting paranoid. Still, I phoned Cathy straight away.

'Cath, will you call Mags at Deermount for me?'

'Why?' Cathy's voice showed she sensed intrigue.

'Ask her if Helen is ill, and if so, with what? I've been trying to get in touch with her, but the housekeeper isn't being very helpful.'

Cathy phoned back about 15 minutes later. 'Madam has the flu,' she reported.

I slumped in relief. Flu might keep Helen away from Loxcombe for a while.

'However,' Cathy continued. 'Mags has news. Since the psychics were kicked out, Madam and Sir have been arguing. Apparently, Helen looks a right wreck at the moment. She's not eating, she's chain-smoking, and she leaves all the lights on in the house at night. Must be costing them a fortune in electricity, given the size of the place! And that's not all. The feudal slaves, bless them, are starting to get spooked as well. The girl who looks after the horses won't go near the stables at night now, and the housekeeper saw something nasty on the stairs. She thought it was a big stain on the stair carpet, like oil, but when she went indignantly to investigate, scrubbing brush in hand, no doubt, the stain reared up and flew off like smoke. Poor woman nearly fell down stairs.'

'Cathy,' I said. 'You don't believe any of that, do you?'

'Well, it was probably a cat, or a bird, or something,' she said, 'but what a good tale, eh?'

'Has Mags told you how Roland's taking all this?'

'Spending time in the city, of course! What do you expect?'

'What's Helen doing about it, the funny goings on, I mean?'

'She has the phone with her in bed, and several tons of *Psychics' Monthly* beside her. Soon the old pile will be crawling with fat women in long dresses and beads, and cadaverous men who've never had girlfriends. Ghosts, beware!'

'Cath, you're enjoying this, aren't you!'

She laughed. 'It's the best of her obsessions yet!'

I wanted to slam down the phone, angry with Cathy for the first time in years. Helen hadn't mentioned her arguments with Roland, or the staff's experiences. She hadn't confided in me that deeply then. And I was right: she *was* avoiding speaking to me.

***

I phoned Helen every day, and after four attempts, she deigned to speak. I had resolved not be too pushy. 'How are you?' I began.

She did sound very snuffly. 'Oh, I'm over the worst. And you?'

Once the pleasantries were over, I asked her how she was getting on with locating a suitable psychic.

'Some have been here already,' she said. 'I'm surprised Mags hasn't told Cathy.' The rebuke did not go unregistered, but I ignored it.

'Any success?'

'It's too early to tell.'

I took a deep breath. 'And the church at Loxcombe? Have you been there yet?'

'Of course. Ages ago. Did you think I'd buy it without seeing it?'

'You've seen the tomb, then?'

'What do you think?'

'What's it like?'

'Just a tomb,' Helen answered. Her voice was positively waspish. 'What did you expect?'

'A gravestone in a graveyard?'

'That's exactly what it is.'

The lie outraged me. So much so I did a stupid thing and blurted out. 'Helen, that's bullshit! I've been there! I've seen it!'

There was a silence and then Helen said in a slow, chilling voice, 'How dare you!'

'You don't own it yet,' I said. 'Helen, I've got to speak to you about this. You mustn't go charging in there, desecrating Aston's tomb! Rufus is at rest. You must have been able to feel it! It would be wrong, so terribly wrong to …'

I realised I was speaking to a dead line. My friend Helen had put the phone down on me, probably right after she'd asked me how I dared.

***

There was silence for days. Cathy reported the comings and goings of the psychics, with one or two amusing anecdotes concerning their appearance and behaviour, but other than that, nothing. I must have picked up the phone a dozen times with the intention of calling Helen, but pride stopped me. If she wanted me, she knew where I was.

Then Roland called us in the middle of the night. Ted got out of bed to answer the phone and I followed him down, sensing trouble.

'It's all right,' I heard him say, soothingly. 'Now think, Roland, where would she go?'

Helen had disappeared. Of course, we offered to help Roland look for her. We couldn't leave the kids alone, so Ted drove up to Deermount. Later he told me Roland was in a terrible state, out of his mind with worry. He confessed his wife hadn't been right for weeks, perhaps months. He blamed himself. He should have done something, got her to see someone, anything.

They found her at Loxcombe. Ted thought it was the obvious place. 'She was lying on top of him, on top of the tomb,' Ted said to me. 'It was …' He shook his head. 'God, Annie, she's out of her mind. You should have seen her. Writhing over that effigy in her dressing gown with nothing on beneath, mud up to her knees, her face scratched. Her face. It was like something out of Bedlam! Hardly human. God, that poor man. Poor Roland.'

They'd carried her home and called the doctor. Scant hours later, an ambulance had come and Helen had been taken away. Roland, in a rare moment of eloquence, said dazedly to Ted, as they watched the ambulance disappear down the drive, 'It's as if she's no longer with us. That person, it's not Helen, it's not her.'

***

Ted brought Roland back to the farm. He stayed with us for over a week. That was the end of it, really. The rest was simply having the details filled in. Helen's breakdown was acute. She was going to be away for a long time. Ted, Cathy, Rupert and I did what we could to comfort Roland. He isn't really a bad sort, and he was so bewildered and lost after the event, it was pathetic. I spent some time blaming myself, thinking I could have done something, told someone, but what good would that do now? I did take some action though. First, I found the psychic Steve's number and called him. My intention was to bawl him out over what had happened to Helen, but when I began telling him, he seemed genuinely appalled and asked if he could come to talk to me. Rather surprised, I agreed.

He arrived with his girlfriend, Rachel, the same evening. They were young, earnest types, and not at all what I expected. Very down to earth, in fact.

'Helen had a problem before we got there,' Steve told me. 'She was obviously suffering from some past trauma, and whatever was being repressed ignited the presence in the house. When she asked us to leave, I knew I shouldn't just let it go at that. I wish I hadn't now. I could have done something.'

'We've all been blaming ourselves,' I said, kindly. 'You're not alone in that.'

I told him about the tomb at Loxcombe and expressed my concern for Rufus Aston. We agreed to drive out there together at the weekend, to see if Steve could pick anything up. I was amazed at myself. Only weeks before, I had been scoffing at the boy, now I spoke to him as intimately as to an old friend.

So, Ted and I and Steve and Rachel followed the lanes to the church on another bright, cold Saturday. I was nervous of what I might feel, and dreaded seeing some relic of Helen's dementia on the tomb, but there was nothing. Steve seemed to light up like a candle as he nosed energetically around the building. His hands skimmed the contours of Rufus's effigy. He nodded vigorously to himself.

'They hid him here,' he said. There was a weird light inside him, invisible yet entirely brilliant, that turned him into something quite beautiful.

'They?' I prompted.

'Rufus's friends. Away from Pargeter. He escaped, you see. I've always thought that. What Rufus must have realised was that true immortality means relinquishing the flesh. Therefore, we are all immortal already. Anything else is just a travesty against nature. Rufus's death was his statement to Pargeter. An escape and a denial.'

'Oh …' I traced the words on the side of the tomb. 'Were Pargeter and Aston lovers, do you think?'

'It's not unlikely,' Steve said, 'but I feel that's Rufus's business, don't you?'

I felt strangely chastened.

'But anyway, Rufus's friends must have thought it was important to hide his remains from Pargeter. There's some strong cloaking around this place. The church is almost invisible, an unattractive dump, and yet,' he gestured at the tomb, 'here it is. A hidden masterpiece.'

'Why did Helen come here?' I asked. 'Was she trying to reach Rufus's spirit?'

Steve frowned. 'I don't think Helen was quite herself by then,' he remarked, but that was all.

'Will she ever be?' Ted enquired. We were both deferring to this intense youth.

Steve shrugged. 'I can't say.' He looked back at the tomb, let his hand hover over the breast of the effigy. 'But I can reassure you that whatever Helen tried to do, our friend here didn't bat an eyelid. The love and protection around him are too strong. He can't be reached by something like that.'

Relieved, we walked back into the harsh sunlight. I felt buoyant, melancholy, but sadly happy, if that's possible.

***

I went to visit Helen in hospital, and I wish I hadn't. Roland was right. The Helen we knew had gone. Perhaps she was only hiding, and could be coaxed back into that limp, listless form, but I doubt it. A year has passed, and she's still there, in that hospital, sitting in the same chair, looking out of the same window, seeing nothing. I hope she's not suffering inside. Perhaps, like Rufus, she's spurned the flesh, and what lives in her body is something else, something that's trapped there now. That would be justice, I think.

***

Two postscripts. The first was that Roland's attempt to buy the church at Loxcombe fell through. He had no real idea what had been going on in Helen's life and mind, and entertained the wistful notion that he could buy the place and do it up as a craft shop for Helen, for when she got out of hospital, if ever. Something blocked him though, and he was very puzzled about it, because his money usually meant he got everything he wanted. I suspected Rufus still had friends around who made sure the Marchants couldn't get near him. Strangely enough, a couple of months later, the church was sold, and renovated, but who had bought it and what they wanted it for, no one knew. Workmen came and went, a high fence was put up around it, and a caretaker came to live in a caravan in the graveyard. To this day, the church is still barricaded against the world, more invisible now than it ever was. Weird.

The second postscript results from a visit from Helen's mother. She had never had much time for Cathy and me. We thought she'd considered us common and unsuitable friends for her glittering daughter. Now, she wanted to talk to me. I realised I had seen a lot more of Helen over the past year than she had. She was devastated by what had happened, naturally. Her dream girl had disappeared, as dreams do when you wake up to reality. Rumours had filtered back to her concerning hauntings and possession, and she needed reassurance. I told her the rumours were exaggerated. 'Helen was ill,' I said. 'There were no ghosts, not really.'

Helen's mother nodded at that. Then she told me the truth about something, which was sadly pertinent to the whole tragic drama. The reason Helen had returned to the village when she was 25 was that she'd had a breakdown in the city. She had, in fact, been in hospital for a month before she came home. Apparently, she'd got mixed up with some very dodgy characters, who were into a peculiar sort of cult, which involved a lot of drugs and sex and sheer debauchery. Helen must have been attracted to it because most of the devotees were very rich. She had (perhaps inevitably, given his bank balance), fallen for the guru of the outfit, and he'd used her in every conceivable way. She'd put up with this, until she'd discovered her Great Man was also abusing, in similar ways, most of the other members of the group, both male and female. There were complications by then, and Helen's mind caved in. Speaking as if her mouth was full of bile, Helen's mother spat out almost indecipherable words about pregnancy and unmentionable diseases. Poor Helen. No-one had realised she was in such a mess. If only we'd known about her past, we might have been more alert for trouble in the present.

Afterwards, I thought about the superficial parallels between Helen and Rufus Aston.

In some ways, it had been like a replay, but it wasn't finished. There had been no solution, no true denouement. Roland still lives at Deermount, waiting for his wife to return to the world. But it's a bad place now. You can feel it sometimes, up there at the house, so I don't go there often. Something waiting, like a nerve end, to be touched.

Walking Wounded
Michael Marshall Smith

When after two days the discomfort in his side had not lessened, merely mutated, Richard began to get mildly concerned. It didn't hurt as often as it had at first, and he could make a wider range of movements without triggering discomfort; but when the pain did come it was somehow deeper, as if settled into the bone.

Christine's answer to the problem was straightforward in its logic, and strident in delivery. He should go to casualty, or at the very least to the doctor's surgery just opposite their new flat in Kingsley Road. Richard's view, though unspoken, was just as definite: bollocks to that. There were more than enough dull, post-move tasks to be endured without traipsing up to the Royal Free and sitting with stoic old women and bleeding youths in a purgatory of peeling linoleum. As they were now condemned to living on a different branch of the Northern line to Hampstead, it would require two dogleg trips down to Camden and back out again – together with a potentially limitless spell on a waiting room bench – and burn up a whole afternoon. Even less appealing, for some reason, was the prospect of going across the road and explaining in front of an audience of whey-faced locals that he had been living somewhere else, now lived just across the road, and wished both to register with the surgery and to have the doctor's doubtless apathetic opinion on a rather unspecific pain in Richard's side. And that he was very sorry for being middle-class and would they please not beat him up. He couldn't be bothered, in other words, and instead decided to dedicate Monday to taking a variety of objects out of cardboard boxes and trying to work out where they could be least unattractively placed.

Christine had returned to work, at least, which meant she couldn't see his winces or hear the swearing that greeted every new object for which there simply wasn't room.

The weekend had been hell, and not just because Richard hadn't wanted to move in the first place. He had, in one way; he'd believed they *should* move, instead of actually wanting to. It had come to him one night while lying in bed in the flat in Belsize Park, listening to the even cadence of Chris's breathing and wondering at what point in the last couple of months they had stopped falling asleep together. At first they'd drifted off simultaneously, facing each other, four hands clasped into a declaration, determined not to leave each other even for the hours they spent in another realm. Richard half-remembered a poem by someone long dead – Herrick, possibly? – the gist of which had been that though we all inhabit the same place during the day, at night each one is hurled into a separate world. Well, it hadn't been that way with them, not at first. Yet after nine months there he was, lying awake, happy to be in the same bed as Chris but wondering where she was.

Eventually he'd got up and wandered through into the sitting room. In the half-light, it looked the same as it always had. You couldn't see which pictures had been taken down, which objects had been removed from shelves and hidden in boxes at the bottom of cupboards. You couldn't tell that for three years he had lived there with someone else.

But Richard knew he had, and so did Christine.

As he gazed out over the garden in which Susan's attempts at horticulture still struggled for life in the face of their joint indifference, Richard finally realised that they should move. Understood, suddenly and with cold guilt, that Chris probably didn't like living there. It was a lovely flat, with huge rooms and high ceilings. It was on Belsize Avenue, which meant not only was it within three minutes walk of Haverstock Hill, with its cafés, stores and tube station, but also that Belsize 'village' was just around the corner. A small enclave of shops specifically designed to cater to the needs of the local well-heeled, the village was so comprehensively stocked with pâtés, wine, videos and magazines that you hardly ever actually needed to go up to Hampstead, itself only a pleasant ten minutes' stroll away. The view from the front of the flat itself was onto the Avenue, wide and spaced with ancient trees. The back was onto a garden neatly bordered by an old brick wall, and although only a few plants grew with any real enthusiasm, the general effect was still pleasing.

But the view through Christine's eyes was probably different. She perhaps saw the local pubs and restaurants in which Richard and Susan had spent years of happy evenings. She maybe felt the tightness with which her predecessor had held Richard's hand as they walked down to the village, past the gnarled Mulberry tree that was the sole survivor of the garden of a country house that had originally stood there. She certainly wondered which particular patches of carpet within the flat had provided arenas for cheerful, drunken sex. This had come out one night after they'd come back rather drunk and irritable from an unsuccessful dinner party at one of Chris's friends. Richard had been bored enough by the evening to respond angrily to the question, and the matter had been dropped.

Standing there in the middle of the night, staring around a room stripped of its familiarity by darkness, he remembered the conversation, the nearest thing they'd yet had to a full-blown row. For a moment he saw the flat as she probably did, and almost believed he could hear the rustling of gifts from another woman, condemned to storage but stirring in their boxes, remembering the places where they had once stood.

The next morning, over cappuccinos on Haverstock Hill, he'd suggested they move. At the eagerness of her response, he felt a band loosen in his chest that he hadn't even realised was there, and the rest of the day was wonderful.

***

Not so the move. Three years' worth of flotsam, 50 boxes full of stuff. Possessions and belongings he'd believed were individual objects metamorphosed into generic crap that had to be manhandled and sorted through. The flat they'd finally found to move into was tiny. Well, not tiny; the living room and kitchen were big enough, and there was a roof garden. But a good deal smaller than Belsize Avenue, and nearly 20 boxes of Richard's stuff had to go into storage. Books that he seldom looked at, but would have preferred to have around; videos that he didn't want to watch next week, but might in a couple of months; old clothes that he never wore but had too much sentimental value to be thrown away. And, of course, the Susan collection.

Objects in boxes, rounded up and buried deeper by putting in further boxes, then sent off to be hidden in some warehouse in Kings Cross. At a cost of 15 pounds a week, this was going to make living in the new flat even more expensive than the old one – despite the fact it was in Kentish Town and you couldn't buy chicken liver and hazelnut pâté locally for love nor money.

On Friday night, the two of them huddled baffled and alone in the huge living room in Belsize Avenue, surrounded by mountains of cardboard. They drank cups of coffee and tried to watch television, but the flat had already taken its leave of them. When they went to bed, it was if they were lying on a cold hillside in a country where their visa had expired.

The next morning, two affable Australians arrived with a van the size of Denmark, and Richard watched, vicariously exhausted, as they trotted up and down the stairs, taking his life away. Chris bristled with female cleaning know-how in the kitchen, periodically sweeping past him with a damp cloth in her hand, humming to herself. As the final pieces of furniture were dragged away, Richard tried to say goodbye to the flat, but the walls stared back at him with vacant indifference, and offered nothing more than dust in corners that had previously been hidden. Dust, some particles of which were probably Susan's skin – and his and Chris's, of course. He left to the sound of a Hoover, and followed the van to their new home. Where, it transpired, his main bookcase could not be taken up the stairs. The two Australians, by now rather bedraggled and hot, struggled gamely in the dying light but eventually had to confess themselves beaten. Richard, rather depressed, allowed them to put the bookcase back in the van, to be taken off with the other storage items. Much later, he held out a tenner to each of them, watched the van squeeze off down the narrow road, and then turned and walked into his new home.

Chris was still at Belsize Avenue, putting the finishing touches to the cleaning and negotiating with the old twonk who owned the place. While he waited for her to arrive, Richard moved a few boxes around, not wanting to do anything significant before Chris was there to share it with him, but too tired simply to sit still. The lower hallway was almost completely impassable, and he resolved to carry a couple of boxes up to the living room. It was while he was struggling up the stairs with one of them that he hurt himself.

He was about halfway up, panting under a box that seemed to weigh more than the house itself, when he slipped on a cushion lying on the stairs. Muscles that he hadn't used since his athletic glory days at school kicked into action, and he managed to avoid falling, but collided heavily with the wall instead. The corner of the box he was carrying crunched solidly into his ribs. For a moment the pain was truly startling, and a small voice in his head said, 'Well, that's done it'.

He let the box slide to the floor and stood panting for a while, fingers tentatively feeling for what he was sure must be at least one broken rib. He half expected it to be protruding from his chest. He couldn't find anything that gave more than usual, however, and after a recuperative cigarette, he carefully pushed the box the remainder of the journey up the stairs.

Half an hour later, Chris arrived, happily cross about their previous landlord's attempts to whittle money off their deposit, and set to work on the kitchen. They fell asleep together that night, three of their hands together; one of Richard's unconsciously guarding his side.

***

The next morning it hurt like hell, but as a fully-fledged male human, Richard knew exactly how to deal with this: he ignored it. After four days of looking at the cardboard boxes cheerfully emblazoned with the logo of the removal firm, he had begun to hate the sight of them, and concentrated first on unpacking everything so he could be rid of them. In the morning he worked in the living room, listening to the sound of Chris whistling in the kitchen and bathroom. He discovered that two of the boxes shouldn't even have been there at all, but were supposed to have been taken with the others and put in storage. One was full of computer manuals for software he either never used or knew back to front; the other was a box of Susan Objects. As he opened it, Richard realised why it had hurt quite so much when making contact with his ribs: it contained, amongst other things, a heavy and angular bronze that she had made and presented to him. He was lucky it hadn't impaled him to the wall.

As it wasn't worth calling the removal men out to collect the boxes, they both ended up in his microscopic study, squatting on top of the filing cabinet. More precious space taken up by stuff that shouldn't even be there; either in the flat or in his life.

The rest of the weekend disappeared into a blur of tidal movement and pizza. Objects migrated from room to room, in smaller and slower circles, until they finally found their new resting places. Chris efficiently unpacked all the clothes and put them in the fitted wardrobes, cooing over the increase in hanging space. Richard tried to organise his books into his *decreased* shelving space, eventually having to lay many of them on their side and pile them up vertically. He set his desk and computer up, and checked his e-mail, obscurely irritated to find that no-one had tried to contact him in the couple of days he'd been off-line.

***

By Monday most of it was done, and Richard spent the morning trying to make his study habitable by clearing the few remaining boxes. At 11.00, Chris called from work, cheerful and full of vim, and he was glad to sense that the move had made her happy. As they were chatting, he realised that he must at some point have scraped his left hand, because there were a series of shallow scratches, like paper cuts, over the palm and underside of the fingers. They hardly seemed significant against the pain in his side, and aside from washing his hands when the conversation was over, he ignored them.

In the afternoon, he took a break and walked down to the local corner store for some cigarettes. It was only his second visit, but he knew he'd already seen all it had to offer. The equivalent store in Belsize Village had stocked American magazines, fresh-baked bread and three different types of pesto. Next door had been the delicatessen with home-made duck's liver and port pâté to die for. 'Raj's EZShop' sold none of these things, instead concentrating single-mindedly on the pot noodle and toilet roll end of the market.

When he left the shop, Richard went and peered dispiritedly at the grubby menu hanging in the window of the restaurant opposite. Eritrean food, whatever the hell that was. One of the dishes was described as 'three pieces of cooked meat,' which seemed both strangely specific and discomfortingly vague. Huddling into his jacket against the cold, he turned and walked for home, feeling – he imagined – rather like a deposed Russian aristocrat, allowed to live after the revolution but condemned to lack everything he had once held dear. The sight of a small, white dog scuttling by seemed only to underline his isolation.

When Chris returned at 6.00 she couldn't understand his quietness, and he didn't have the heart to try to explain it to her.

'What's that?'

The answer, Richard saw, appeared to be that it was a scratch. About four inches long, it ran across his chest directly over his heart. He hadn't noticed it before, but it seemed to have healed and thus must have been there for a day or two.

'Another souvenir from the move,' he guessed. It was after midnight and they were lying in bed, having just abandoned an attempt to make love. It wasn't that there was any lack of enthusiasm – far from it – simply that the pain in Richard's ribs was a little too bracing to ignore. He was fine so long as he kept his chest facing directly forwards, but any twisting and it felt as if someone was stoving in his rib cage with a well-aimed boot. 'And no, I'm not going to the doctor about it.'

Chris smiled, started to tickle him, and then realised she shouldn't. Instead she sighed theatrically and kissed him on the nose before turning to lie on her side.

'You'd better get well soon,' she said, 'or I'm going to have to buy a do-it-yourself book.'

'You'll go blind,' he said, turning off the bedside light, and she giggled quietly in the dark.

He rolled gingerly so that he was snuggled into her back, and lightly stroked her shoulder, waiting for sleep. After a moment, he noticed a wetness under his hand, and stopped, pulling his hand out from under the duvet. In the threadbare moonlight he confirmed what he'd already suspected. Earlier in the evening he'd noticed that the little cuts seemed to be exuding tiny amounts of blood. It was still happening. Constantly being reopened when he lugged boxes around, presumably.

'S'nice,' Chris murmured sleepily. 'Don't stop.'

Richard slid his hand back under the duvet and moved it gently against her shoulder again, using the backs of his fingers and cupping his palm away from her.

***

The bathroom was tiny, but very adequately equipped with mirrors. Richard couldn't help noticing the change as soon as he took off his dressing gown the next morning. There was still no sign of bruising over his ribs, which worried him. Something that hurt as much as that ought to have an external manifestation, he believed, unless it indicated internal damage. The pain was a little different that morning, less like a kicking, more as if two of the ribs were moving tightly against each other. A kind of cartilaginous twisting.

There were also a number of new scratches.

Mostly short, they were primarily congregated over his stomach and chest. It looked as though a cat with its claws out had run over him in the night. As they didn't have a cat, this seemed unlikely, and Richard frowned as he regarded himself in the mirror.

Also odd was the mark on his chest. Perhaps it was just seeing it in proper light, but this morning it looked like more than just a scratch. By spreading his fingers out on either side, he found he could pull the cut slightly apart, and that it was a millimetre or so deep. When he allowed it to close again, it did so with a faint liquidity, the sides tacky with lymph. It wasn't healing properly. In fact – and Richard held up his left hand to confirm this – it was doing the same as the cuts on his palm. They too seemed as fresh as the day before – if not a little fresher. Glad that Chris had left the house before he'd made it out of bed, Richard quickly showered, patting himself dry around the cuts, and covered them with clothes.

By lunchtime, the flat was finally in order, and Richard had to admit parts of it looked pretty good. The kitchen was the one room that was bigger than he'd been used to, and with the late morning light slanting into it was very attractive. The table was a little larger than would have been ideal, but at least you could get at the fridge without performing contortions. The living room upstairs also looked pretty bijou, if you ignored the way in which his books were crammed into the bookcases. Chris had already established a nest on the larger of the two sofas; her book, ashtray and an empty coffee mug placed within easy reach. Richard perched on the other sofa for a while, eyes vaguely running over his books and realising he ought to make an effort to colonise a corner of the room for his own.

Human, All Too Human. The title brought Richard out of his reverie. A second-hand volume of Nietzsche, bought for him as a joke by Susan. It shouldn't have been on the shelf, but in one of the storage boxes. Chris didn't know it had been a present from Susan, but then it hadn't been Chris who'd insisted he take the other stuff down. It had simply seemed to be the right thing to do, and Richard had methodically worked around the old flat hiding things the day before Chris moved in. Hiding them from whom, he hadn't been sure. It had been six months since he and Susan had split up, and she wasn't even seeing the man she'd left him for any more. To have the old mementos still out didn't cause him any pain, and he'd thought he'd put them away purely out of consideration for Chris.

But as he looked over the bookcase, he realised how much the book of Nietzsche stood out in their new flat. It smelled of Susan. Some tiny part of her, a speck of skin or smear of oil, must surely still be on it somewhere. If he could sense that, then surely Chris could too.

He walked across the room, took the book from the shelf, and walked downstairs to put it in the box on top of his filing cabinet in the study.

On the way, he diverted into the bathroom. As he absently opened his fly, he noticed an unexpected sensation at his fingertips. He brushed them around inside his trousers again, trying to work out what he'd felt. Then he slowly removed them, and held his hand up.

His fingers were spotted with blood.

Richard stared coldly at them for a while, and then calmly undid the button of his trousers. Carefully he lowered them, and then pushed down his boxer shorts.

More cuts. A long red line ran from the middle of his right thigh around to within a couple of inches of his testicles. A similar one lay across the very bottom of his stomach. A much shorter but slightly deeper slit lay across the base of his penis, and it was from this that the majority of the blood was flowing. It wasn't a bad cut, and hardly put one in mind of *The Texas Chainsaw Massacre*, but Richard would have much preferred it not to have been there.

Looking up at the mirror above the toilet, he reached up and undid the buttons on his shirt. The scratches on his stomach now looked more like cuts, and a small, thin line of blood rolled down from the cut on his chest.

***

Like many people, Richard wasn't fond of doctors. It wasn't the sepulchral gloom of waiting rooms he minded, or the grim pleasure their receptionists took in patronising you. It was the boredom and the sense of potential catastrophe, combined with a knowledge that there wasn't a great deal they could do. If you had something really bad, they sent you to a hospital. If it was trivial, it would go away of its own accord.

It was partly for these reasons that Richard simply did his shirt and trousers back up again, after patting at some of the cuts with pieces of toilet paper. It was partly also because he was afraid. He didn't know where the scratches were coming from, but the fact that far from healing, they seemed to be getting worse, was worrying. With his vague semi-understanding of such things, he wondered if it meant his blood had stopped clotting, and if so, what that meant. He didn't think you could suddenly develop haemophilia. It didn't seem very likely. But what then? Perhaps he was tired, run-down after the move, and that was making a difference.

In the end, he resolved to just go on ignoring it a little longer, like a mole that keeps growing but you don't wish to believe might be malignant. He spent the afternoon sitting carefully at his desk, trying to work and resisting the urge to peek at parts of his body. It was almost certainly his imagination, he believed, that made it feel as if a warm, plump drop of blood had sweated from the cut on his chest and rolled slowly down beneath his shirt; and the dampness he felt around his crotch was the result of his having turned the heating up high. Absolutely.

He took care to shower well before Chris was due home. The cuts were still there, and had been joined by another on his upper arm. When he was dry, he took some surgical dressings and micropore tape from the bathroom cabinet and covered the ones that were bleeding most. He then chose his darkest shirt from the wardrobe and sat in the kitchen, waiting for Chris to come home. He would have gone upstairs, but didn't really feel comfortable up there by himself yet. Although most of the objects in the room were his, Chris had arranged them, and the room seemed a little forlorn without her to fill in their underlying structure.

***

That evening, they went out to a pub in Soho, a birthday drink for one of Chris's mates. Chris had several different groups of friends, Richard had discovered. He had also discovered that the ones she regarded as her closest were the ones he loathed the most. It wasn't because of anything intrinsically unpleasant about them, more their insufferable air of having known each other since before the dawn of time, like some heroic group, the Knights of the Pine Table. Unless you could remember the hilarious occasion when they all went down to the Dangling Cock in Mulchester and good old 'Kipper' Philips sang 'Bohemian Rhapsody' straight through while lying on the bar with a pint on his head before going on to amusingly prang his father's car on the steps of the village church, you were clearly no more than one of life's spear carriers – even after you'd been going out with one of them for nearly a year. In their terms, God was a bit of a Johnny-come-lately, and the Devil, had he turned up with a card and a present, would have been treated with the cloying indulgence reserved for friends' younger siblings.

Luckily that evening they were seeing a different and more recent group, some of whom were certified human beings. Richard stood at the bar affably enough, slowly downing a long series of Kronenbourgs while Chris alternately went to talk to people or brought them to talk to him. One of the latter, a doctor whom Richard believed to be called Kate, peered hard at him as soon as she hove into view.

'What's that?' she asked, bluntly.

Richard was about to tell her that what he was holding was called a cigarette, that it consisted of the dried and rolled leaves of the tobacco plant, and that he had every intention – regardless of any objections she or anyone else might have – of sticking it in his mouth and lighting it, when he realised she was looking at his left hand. Too late, he tried to slip it into his pocket, but she reached out and snatched it up.

'Been in a fight, have you?' she asked. Behind her Chris turned from the man she was talking to and looked over Kate's shoulder at Richard's hand.

'No,' he said. 'Just a bizarre flat relocation accident.'

'Hmm,' Kate said, her mouth pursed into a small moue of consideration. 'Looks like someone's come at you with a knife, if you ask me.'

Chris looked up at Richard, eyes wide, and he groaned inwardly.

'Well, things between Chris and me haven't been so good lately …' he tried, and got a laugh from both of them. Kate wasn't to be deflected, however.

'I'm serious,' she said, holding up her own hand to demonstrate. 'Someone tries to kill you with a knife, what do you do? You hold your hands up. And what happens is often the blade will nick the defending hands a couple of times before the knife gets through. See it all the time in casualty. Little cuts, just like those.'

Richard pretended to examine the cuts on his hand, and shrugged.

'Maybe Kate could look at your ribs,' Chris said.

'I'm sure there's nothing she'd like better,' he said. 'After a hard day at the coal face, there's probably nothing she'd like more than to look at another piece of fossilised wood.'

'What's wrong with your ribs?' Kate asked, squinting at him closely.

'Nothing,' he said. 'Just banged them.'

'Does this hurt?' she asked, and suddenly cuffed him around the back of the head.

'No,' he said, laughing.

'Then you're probably all right,' she winked, and disappeared to get a drink. Chris frowned for a moment, caught between irritation at not having got to the bottom of his rib problem and happiness at seeing him get on with one of her friends. Just then, a fresh influx of people arrived at the door and Richard was saved from having to watch her choose which emotion to go with.

Mid-evening, he went to the gents and shut himself into one of the cubicles. He changed the dressings on his penis and chest, and noted that some of the cuts on his stomach were now slick with blood. He didn't have enough micropore to dress them, and realised he would just have to hope that they stayed manageable until he got home. The cuts on his hands didn't seem to be getting any deeper.

Obviously they were just nicks. Almost, as Kate had said, as if someone had come at him with a knife.

They got home well after midnight. Chris was more drunk than Richard, but he didn't mind. She was one of those rare people who got even cuter when she was plastered, instead of maudlin or argumentative. Chris staggered straight into the bathroom, to do whatever the hell it was she spent hours in there doing. Richard made his way into the study to check the answerphone, banging into walls whose positions he still hadn't really internalised.

One message. Sitting heavily down on his chair, Richard pressed the play button. Without noticing he was doing it, he reached forward and turned down the volume so only he would hear what was on the tape. A habit born of the first weeks of his relationship with Chris, when Susan was still calling fairly regularly. Her messages, though generally short and uncontroversial, were not things he wanted Chris to hear. Again, a programme of protection, now no longer needed. Feeling self-righteous, and burping gently, Richard turned the volume back up. He almost jumped out of his skin when he realised the message actually was from Susan, and quickly turned the volume back down.

She said hello, in the diffident way she had, and went on to observe that they hadn't seen each other that year yet. There was no reproach, simply a statement of fact. She asked him to call her soon, to arrange a drink.

The message had just finished when Chris caroomed out of the bathroom smelling of toothpaste and moisturiser.

''ny messages?'

'Just a wrong number,' he said.

She shook her head slightly, apparently to clear it, rather than in negation. 'Coming to bed then?' she asked, slyly. Waggling her eyebrows, she performed a slow grind with her pelvis, managing both not to fall over and not to look silly, which was a hell of a trick. Richard made his 'Sex life in ancient Rome' face, inspired by a book he'd read many years before.

'Too right,' he said. 'Be there in a minute.'

But he stayed in the study for a quarter of an hour, long enough to ensure that Chris would have fallen asleep. Wearing pyjamas for the first time in ten years, he slipped quietly in beside her and waited for the morning.

The bedroom seemed very small as he lay there, and whereas in Belsize Park the moonlight had sliced in, casting attractive shadows on the wall, in Kingsley Road the only visitors in the night were the curdled orange of a streetlight outside and the sound of a siren in the distance.

***

As soon as Chris had dragged herself groaning out of the house, Richard got up and went through to the bathroom. He knew before he took his night clothes off what he was going to find. He could feel parts of the pyjama top sticking to areas on his chest and stomach, and his crotch felt warm and wet. The marks on his stomach now looked like proper cuts, and the gash on his chest had opened still further. His penis was covered in dark blood, and the gashes around it were nasty. He looked as if he had collided with a threshing machine. His ribs still hurt a great deal, though the pain seemed to be constricting, concentrating around a specific point rather than applying to the whole of his side.

He stood there for ten minutes, staring at himself in the mirror. So much damage. As he watched, he saw a faint line slowly draw itself down three inches of his forearm; a thin, raised scab. He knew that by the end of the day it would have reverted into a cut.

Mid morning, he called Susan at her office number. As always, he was surprised by how official she sounded when he spoke to her there. She had always been languid of voice, in complete contrast to her physical and emotional vivacity – but when you talked to her at work, she sounded like a headmistress. Her tone mellowed when she realised who it was. She tried to pin him down to a date for a drink, but he avoided the issue. They'd seen each other twice since she'd left him for John Ayer; once while he'd been living with Chris. Chris had been very relaxed about the meetings, but Richard hadn't. On both occasions, he and Susan had spent a good deal of time talking about Ayer; the first time focusing on why Susan had left Richard for him, the second on how unhappy she was about the fact that Ayer had in turn left her without even saying goodbye. Either she hadn't realised how much the conversations would hurt Richard, or she hadn't even thought about it. Most likely she had just taken comfort from talking to him in the way she always had.

'You're avoiding it, aren't you,' Susan said, eventually.

'What?'

'Naming a day. Why?'

'I'm not,' he protested, feebly. 'Just busy, you know. I don't want to say a date and then have to cancel.'

'I really want to see you,' she said. 'I miss you.'

Don't say that, thought Richard miserably. Please don't say that.

'And there's something else,' she added. 'It was a year today when …'

'When what?' Richard asked, confused. They'd split up about 18 months earlier.

'The last time I saw John,' she said, and finally Richard understood.

That afternoon he took a walk to kill time, trolling up and down the surrounding streets, trying to find something to like. He discovered another corner store nearby, but it didn't stock Parma ham either. Little dusty bags of fuses hung behind the counter, and the plastic strips of the cold cabinet were completely opaque. A little further afield he found a local video store, but he'd seen every thriller they had, most of them more than once. The storekeeper seemed to stare at him as he left, as if wondering what he was doing there.

After a while, he simply walked, not looking for anything. Slab-faced women clumped by, screaming at children already getting into method for their five minutes of fame on *CrimeWatch UK*. Pipe-cleaner men stalked the streets in brown trousers and zip-up jackets, heads fizzing with racing results. The pavements seemed unnaturally grey, as if waiting for a second coat of reality, and hard green leaves spiralled down to join brown ashes already fallen.

And yet, as he started to head back towards Kingsley Road, he noticed a small dog standing on a corner, different from the one he'd seen before. White with a black head and lolling tongue, the dog stood still and looked at him, big brown eyes rolling with good humour. It didn't bark, but merely panted, ready to play some game he didn't know.

Richard stared at the dog, suddenly sensing that some other life was possible here, that he was occluding something from himself. The dog skittered on the spot slightly, keeping his eyes on Richard, and then abruptly sat down. Ready to wait. Ready to still be there.

Richard looked at him a little longer and then set off for the tube station. He used the public phone there to leave a message at Kingsley Road, telling Chris he'd gone out unexpectedly and might be back late.

At 11.00, he left the George and walked down Belsize Avenue. He didn't know how important the precise time was, and he couldn't actually remember it, but it felt right. Earlier in the evening, he had walked past the old flat, establishing that the 'For Let' sign was still outside. Probably the landlord had jacked the rent up so high he couldn't find any takers.

During the hours he had spent in the pub, he had checked the cuts only twice. Then he had ignored them, his only concession being to roll the sleeve of his shirt down to hide what was now a deep gash on his forearm. When he looked at himself in the mirror of the gents, his face seemed pale; whether from the lighting or blood loss he didn't know. As he could now push his fingers deep enough into the slash on his chest to feel his sternum, he suspected it was probably the latter. When he used the toilet, he did so with his eyes closed. He didn't want to know what it looked like down there: the sensation of his fingers on ragged and sliced flesh was more than enough. The pain in his side had continued to condense, and was now restricted to a rough circle four inches in diameter. It was time to go.

He slowed as he approached the flat, trying to time it so that he drew outside when there was no-one else in sight. As he waited, he marvelled quietly at how different the sounds were from those in Kentish Town. There was no shouting, no roar of maniac traffic or young bloods looking for damage. All you could hear was distant laughter, the sound of people having dinner, braving the cold and sitting outside Café Pasta or the Pizza Express. This area was different, and it wasn't his home any more. As he realised that, it was with relief. It was time to say goodbye.

When the street was empty, he walked quietly along the side of the building to the wall. Only about six feet tall, it held a gate through to the garden. Both sets of keys had been yielded, but Richard knew from experience that he could climb over. More than once he or Susan had forgotten their keys on the way out to get drunk and he'd had to let them back in this way.

He jumped up, arms extended, and grabbed the top of the wall. His side tore at him, but he ignored it and scrabbled up. Without pausing, he slid over the top and dropped silently onto the other side, leaving a few slithers of blood behind. The window to the kitchen was there in the wall, dark and cold. Chris had left a dishcloth neatly folded over the tap in the sink. Other than that, the room looked as if it had been moulded in an alien's mind. Richard turned away and walked out into the garden.

He limped towards the centre, trying to recall how it had gone. In some ways he could remember everything; in others it was as if it had never happened to him, was just a second-hand tale told by someone else. A phone call to an office number he'd copied from Susan's filofax before she left. An agreement to meet for a drink, on a night Richard knew she'd be out of town. Two men, meeting to sort things out in a gentlemanly fashion.

The stalks of Susan's abandoned plants nodded suddenly in a faint breeze, and an eddy of leaves chased each other slowly around the walls. Richard glanced towards the living room window. Inside it was empty, a couple of pieces of furniture stark against walls painted with dark, triangular shadows. It was too dark to see, and he was too far away, but he knew the dust was gone. Even that little part had been sucked up and buried away.

He felt a strange sensation on his forearm, and looked down in time to see the gash there disappearing, from bottom to top, from finish to start. It went quickly, as quickly as it had been made. He turned to look at the verdant patch of grass, expecting to see it move, but it was still. Then he felt a warm sensation in his crotch, and realised it too would soon be whole. He had hacked at him there long after he knew Ayer was dead; hacked symbolically and pointlessly until the penis that had rooted and snuffled into Susan had been reduced to a scrap of offal.

The leaves moved again, faster, and the garden grew darker as if some huge cloud had moved into position overhead. It was now difficult to see as far as the end wall of the garden, and when he heard the distant sounds from there, Richard realised the ground was not going to open up. No, first the wound in his chest, the fatal wound, would disappear. Then the cuts on his stomach, and the nicks on his hands from where Ayer had resisted, trying to be angry but so scared he had pissed his designer jeans.

Finally the pain in his side would go; the first pain, the pain caused by Richard's initial vicious kick after he had pushed his drunken rival over. A spasm of hate, flashes of violence, wipe pans of memory.

Then they would be back to that moment, or a moment before. Something would come towards him, out of the dry, rasping shadows, and they would talk again. How it would go, Richard didn't know, but he knew he could win, that he could walk away back to Chris and never come back here again. It was time. Time to go.

Time to play a different game.

Blackfriars
David J Howe

From: 'Sue' <rich-bitch@hotmail.com>
To: 'Keith' <kbarber@lineone.net>
Subject: Lunch
Sent: Fri, 31 May 2002 19:19:25 +0100

Hi Keithy

Love to do lunch tomorrow. You know I miss you loads when I'm not
with you. Last week was just fab … you know what I'm talking about.
    See you at 12. Usual place.

Sue
xxx

From: 'Sue' <rich-bitch@hotmail.com>
To: 'Mike' <antique.kid@yahoo.com>
Subject: You *are* dumped
Sent: Fri, 31 May 2002 19:23:45 +0100

Mike

I don't know how many times I'm going to have to tell you, but I really
don't want to see or hear from you again.

Please stop calling my mobile, and stop hanging round my flat. Seriously. If you bother me again I'll be contacting the police.

Sue

Mobile Phone Transcript:

Call Made: Sat, 1 Jun 2002 11:50:43

Sue: Hi honey

Tony: Hi there. Where are you?

Sue: Just out shopping. Listen. I'm going to be a little late back this afternoon. Got to pick up some stuff.

Tony: Okay.

Sue: Just didn't want you to worry, babe.

Tony: See you later then.

Sue: Okay. Byee. Kiss kiss.

Tony: Love you. Bye.

CALL ENDS

***

The restaurant was, as usual, packed. Waiters circulated attentively with bottles of wine and water, the swing door to the kitchen was overworked, as a constant stream of mouth-watering dishes emerged while plates piled with detritus and cutlery returned.

At her usual corner table, Sue surveyed the organised chaos around her. It was a wonder that all these people managed to get through their lives intact. She picked up the slim stem of her champagne flute and sipped at the ice cold liquid. Her plate of *moules meurnieres* sat finished in front of her, while opposite, Keith sat holding her free hand gently, and gazing into her eyes intently.

She gently placed the wine glass back on the table. Keith was older than her – all the men in her life were – but only by about ten years. He was handsome in a rugged kind of way, but had the most beautiful hands. He was also pretty good in bed, which, quite frankly, was a great bonus. So many of her men were just too old, portly, and past it to manage anything more than a quick fumble before dropping off to sleep. But with Keith … Well, he had some staying power, and was handy with his tongue as well.

Her attention switched back to Keith as he raised his eyebrows at her in anticipation of her response. She smiled. Not just any smile, but her special, patented, make-any-man-in-the-room-look-at-me smile.

'So that's a yes then?' asked Keith, his own face breaking into a grin.

Sue nodded. 'Just as soon as you have the paperwork ready, then I'll be happy to sign.'

'That's brilliant,' said Keith, raising her hand to his lips to kiss it gently. 'And as we agreed, you'd be starting with me as a partner, with, of course, the salary you wanted. I had to pull quite a few strings to get this through with Harry, but he can see the sense in having a younger head joining us.'

'I'm sure it will all go swimmingly,' said Sue with another grin. She picked up her champagne once more. 'To us.'

'To us,' echoed Keith, clinking his glass against hers.

'There is just one thing,' said Keith. He leaned closer to her. 'It is okay for us to be seen together now, is it? It's just that, with Tony running a rival firm and all that …'

Sue laughed and, shifting in her seat, gently ran her foot up the side of Keith's leg. 'It's fine,' she insisted. 'In any case, I'm about to dump the loser.' Putting down her glass, she picked up Keith's hand and gently sucked on his thumb. 'You are so much more my type than he is,' she muttered, raising her eyes to look directly into Keith's.

Keith smiled dreamily. 'I'll see you later on, then …?'

'You bet, lover.'

A waiter swooped on their table and spirited away the plates. Their glasses were refilled, and, at a gesture from Keith, the bill was presented.

At that moment, Sue's mobile phone rang. She let go of Keith and dived for her bag to get it. Removing the phone, she checked the caller, put it to her ear and started out of the restaurant, looking back at Keith with a 'see you outside' glance.

Keith nodded and watched her go, as did most of the male clientele of the restaurant.

***

Sue was gorgeous. She was radiant. Today her fine blonde hair was brushed, conditioned, and shining down to the middle of her back. She was wearing a smart pair of pinstripe trousers, with a low cut white T-shirt and stylish jacket. Her face was elfin and perfectly proportioned. Plucked eyebrows, alabaster skin, and just a touch of lipstick and powder completed a look that turned most men into babbling idiots the moment they saw her.

Keith really could not understand why she was still with Tony, partner in a rival antiques firm and some 30 years her senior, when Tony's company seemed to be in such a shambles. No wonder that when Sue had first met him at a trade fair some three months back, she had joined him for dinner, and then for sex – both on the same day. Keith shrugged. Tony's loss …

He picked up the bill and grimaced at the cost – over two thirds was the bottle of champagne that Sue had chosen to celebrate her new job. Shaking his head, he added his MasterCard to the bill and gestured for a waiter. At least he would get his just rewards later in the week, when Sue was due to visit for their now-regular sessions of sex and debauchery. He smiled. There was nothing that fazed that girl. Endlessly imaginative, energetic and sensual … what a catch.

***

Mobile Phone Transcript:

Call Made: Sat, 1 Jun 2002 13:26:32

Sue: Hi Tony!

Tony: Just wanted to see how late you were going to be? Did you get what you wanted?

Sue: Oh yes. Not too late.

Tony: You know I love you.

Sue: I know. I love you too.

Tony: Did you eat yet?

Sue: I picked up a quick sandwich on my way. I'm fine.

Tony: Well tonight I've something special planned for us. Some good news.

Sue: That's excellent. Listen, I'm going to have to dash. I'll see you about four. Okay?

Tony: Okay. Don't be late. See you then. Love you.

Sue: Love you too. Bye.

CALL ENDS

***

Keith walked out of the restaurant to see Sue just putting her mobile into the Gucci bag she carried. Stepping up behind her, he held her round the waist. She turned and looked into his grey eyes.

'All done?' she asked.

'Paid and ready to go.'

Sue slid her hand up around the back of Keith's head and pulled his face towards her. Her tongue snaked out and tickled around his lips before moving closer. Keith's hands cupped her perfect buttocks as she kissed him passionately. When he came up for air, she stepped backwards, smiling that million watt smile once more.

'So ... see you tomorrow, then,' she said.

Keith looked confused. 'Tomorrow?'

'To discuss the paperwork. Needs a lot of discussion does paperwork ...'

Keith smiled. 'I see. What time should I expect you at the shop?'

Sue looked at him. 'Who said anything about the shop? The paperwork I want to discuss is in your bedroom. I'll be at your flat at 11.30 for a pre-lunch discussion.'

'11.30 ...' Keith remembered that he was supposed to be meeting Henry for lunch the next day. However, Sue was at that moment adjusting her bra strap, giving him a glimpse of more of the perfect pair of breasts struggling to break free from her T-shirt. 'That's fine. See you then.'

Sue suddenly looked worried. 'Oh, sorry, Keith, could you lend me 20 ... I'm a little short at the moment.'

'Sure, no problem.' Keith extracted a note from his wallet and passed it over.

Sue took it and grinned. 'You know ... when this deal has gone through and I'm partner in your company ... I promise you the night of your life.'

With a leery wink and a final peck on Keith's lips, Sue turned and walked off down the street, Keith's eyes watching her long legs and perfect shape as she retreated from him. He suddenly realised he was standing there on a busy street with his wallet and mouth open. He shut both, and returned the wallet to his jacket pocket.

Sue Cavendish. What a babe!

***

An hour or so later, as Sue turned the corner into the street where Tony's flat was, she became aware of a figure hovering behind her. She stopped and turned, hand instinctively going for the small attack spray she always carried with her.

'Oh – it's you.'

The figure was that of Mike, ex-boyfriend, ex-antiques dealer, ex-member of the human race.

'Sue … I … I …'

'Didn't you get my e-mail?' Sue looked him up and down. Mike was unshaven, and looked as if this had been the case for at least a week. His shirt was stained and rumpled, two buttons were missing, and the shirt-tails were pulled from his grubby jeans at one side. His eyes were red and slightly unfocused, and he swayed a little.

'No … no … I don't suppose you did.' She muttered to herself. 'What do you want? I told you it was over.'

Mike started crying. 'Sue …' he blurted. 'Sue … I'm ruined. The money … the business … all gone. Stolen.'

Sue looked worried for a moment. 'But that's all your fault, Mike,' she stated. 'No-one asked you to make those investments. No-one told you how to spend your money.'

'But I thought … I thought you loved me. I loved you – I love you, Sue – Come back to me, and we can sort it all out.'

Sue shook her head. 'Whatever did I see in you, Mike? – except for your money, of course. Thanks for the car, the holidays – oh, and the bag, of course.' She lifted the £1,000 Gucci object before him. 'The rest I just took. Silly of you to leave passbooks lying around, of course – such a temptation for a girl.'

Mike's eyes widened. 'But Sue …'

She turned on her heel and started walking away from him. Mike had to shuffle along beside her to keep up.

'*But Sue … But Sue …* Is that all you can say? You really were useless. Useless in business and useless in bed. But I got what I wanted. Thought I was just a pretty face, eh? Thought I'd be just some arm candy for those important meetings. Well I got what I wanted. I got your money. I got your business. I got your life.'

Sue stopped walking and turned to Mike. 'You see, Mike, you never realised that I was using you all along. You were so blinded by the fucking, that you never saw the rest of me coming. Oh, and you *never* made me come, either, just in case you thought you did.'

Sue smiled as she saw the impact of her words hit home. 'So, Mikey, *darling*, there's nothing you can do. If you lay one finger on me, then I'll have you in court on a harassment charge. If you try and tell anyone about this discussion, then I'll deny it – who would believe a hopeless, washed up, drunken old lech anyway. That's even if you had the money to afford the legal bills, because ... oh yes ... in case you forgot – you're bankrupt. You're a jealous fool, Mike. Maybe next time – if there is a next time – you won't let your pathetic cock make your decisions for you.'

Sue turned and stalked off down the street, leaving Mike crying in the gutter. He fell to his knees and wept. Not just for his business, his ex-wife whom he left and divorced for Sue or his bankruptcy when he finally discovered that all the money had mysteriously vanished, leaving bills unpaid and angry creditors at his door. He cried because Sue was right, and he knew she was right. He had fallen for the worst bitch in the world, and she had taken everything.

Sue meanwhile was quietly smiling to herself. Things a girl has to do to get on these days ...

She strutted on down the street, and as she approached Tony's flat, she suddenly had the sense that someone was watching her. She spun round. There was no-one to be seen. Even that miserable prick Mike had gone. She walked on down the street, slower now, and as she reached the entrance to the flat, she looked around again. Standing opposite her on the other side of the road was a figure wearing a black monk's habit. She looked at the figure, but could not see his face, as it was in darkness inside the cowl. A car passed by, and, in the blink of an eye, the figure was gone. Sue looked up and down the street, but there was no sign of the figure. She narrowed her eyes. Maybe another ex-boyfriend out to cause her trouble – well, just let him try. She smiled to herself and let herself into Tony's flat.

***

The first thing she saw was a massive bunch of flowers on the dining table. The spray was of red and white carnations, her favourites, and she smiled when she saw the note attached to them: 'To Sue. Missing you. Tony.'

'Surprise?'

Sue span round to see Tony standing in the doorway to the kitchen. She squealed with pleasure and leaped at him, almost knocking him over. Planting little kisses all over his balding pate, she hugged him tight.

'Oh, Tony, they're wonderful. Thanks so much. I'm just popping upstairs to freshen up. Could you put them in water for me? Thanks hon.'

She hurried out of the room and up to the bathroom, leaving Tony smiling happily to himself. He could not really believe his luck. That a 54 year old ex-bank manager, running his own antiques company, could have landed one of the hottest girls he had ever laid eyes on, was amazing. He rubbed his hand over his head, smoothing down the grey hair at the back. He picked up the bunch of flowers and headed for the kitchen. As he prepared the bouquet, he heard the shower go on, and smiled again at the thought of Sue under the water. She liked to make love in the most unusual places, and the shower was one of her favourites. Even though he sometimes slipped – being on the wrong side of 50 certainly slowed down your reactions – she never seemed too disappointed.

By the time Sue reappeared about 45 minutes later, the flowers were proudly displayed on the table. Tony looked appreciatively at Sue, who had changed into a figure-hugging pair of velvet tracksuit bottoms and a crop top, her damp blonde hair held back in a ponytail. He poured her a glass of wine, and she idly flicked through a newspaper as he fussed in the kitchen, creating a meal of crusty bread and fresh pâté, baked salmon and lemon with asparagus and rice, and a rich chocolate mousse for dessert. His ex-wife may have hated his passion for food (to which his expanding waistline bore testament) but Sue seemed not to mind, and she also loved being looked after. From the moment he had first set eyes on her, two years ago in the local auction rooms, Tony had known she was all he wanted. She had flirted with him outrageously, and it wasn't long before she had been taking him to her bed on a weekly, then daily basis. He had left his wife, sold the house and moved in with Sue, whose knowledge of antiques promised to reap dividends for his company. Before long, she had been all but running the business with him, taking care of all the paperwork – a task for which Tony had never had much aptitude. His two partners in the company seemed uncertain, but Tony had faith in Sue, and was good at arguing his case.

After the courses had been dished up, and Tony had been vaguely disappointed that Sue had only picked at her food, he decided to share his big news.

'We've agreed a bonus for the work so far,' he explained. 'I had to talk them round, but I think you'll be well pleased with the amount. Five thousand.'

'Five thousand!' Sue looked aghast at Tony. She had been expecting ten thousand at least, although, as she hastily checked herself, with the money she had been quietly extracting from Tony's business, maybe they couldn't afford more. 'That's brilliant,' she concluded after a pause.

Tony looked apologetic. 'It would have been more,' he explained hastily, 'but cash flow is a problem – we're really looking to you to start to turn things around.'

Sue nodded. She was turning things around all right. Right around into her bank account. One of the things about looking good, she reflected, was that people seemed to trust you. And also they underestimated what you knew. Sue knew her antiques. She had read and studied hard until she could tell the difference between the real thing and a fake at ten paces. She knew what to buy and when, and also where to go for the best bargains, and the best profits. However, for the most part she let this knowledge out a little at a time. Gaining the trust of others, and a reputation for being a good money-maker. And this was certainly true. At only 24 years old, she currently had a personal wealth of far more than the firms who paid her. This was mainly because, for every item she sold for her various bosses, strangely, another two would not appear on inventories, only to surface some weeks later in certain private sales, netting an impressive amount of money from the right buyers.

Now, thanks to her liaison with Tony, she knew that his company was very nearly bankrupt. Bad investments and poor sales would be nominally to blame, and no-one would ever think to look to Tony's mistress and lover as the root cause of the problem. She had made sure that she was entirely blameless in all dealings, and the money she ended up with directly from the company was mainly through payments for her work and, of course, gifts from Tony.

She realised that Tony was still speaking to her, and tuned in to catch the tail end of his sentence: '… belonged to an old lady. Should be some nice stuff there, and we've got in first this time.'

'Sorry, where's that?'

'Tomorrow … I just explained …' Tony smiled his long-suffering smile. 'We're going to clear a house tomorrow, up Blackfriars way. An ancient pile by all accounts. Belonged to an old lady who died a month or so back. Untouched since.' He grinned and laid his hands over his ample belly. 'We might strike lucky.'

Sue smiled back, deep in her own thoughts. 'We might indeed. We might indeed.'

***

From: 'Sue' <rich-bitch@hotmail.com>
To: 'Keith' <kbarber@lineone.net>
Subject: Our meeting today
Sent: Sun, 2 June 2002 08:18:54 +0100

Hi Keithy

Sorry babe. Something's come up. Have to miss our chat at lunch. I'll make it up to you next time.

Love

Sue
xxx

***

To say that the house was untouched was an understatement. Tony blew gently at the mantelpiece and a cloud of dust and dead insects took flight. He flapped his hand and shook his head.

Sue rubbed a finger experimentally across a table, leaving a deep groove in the dust. She rubbed her fingers together in a vain attempt to clean them.

'This place is a pit,' she said with a sniff. 'How could anyone live in these conditions?'

Tony nodded. 'Incredible,' he agreed. 'But just look at some of this stuff.' He removed a mounted plate from the wall, muttering to himself, Shame about the clips, they've chipped the edges a little. Still – not often you see one of those.' He made a note on the clipboard he was carrying and moved off around the room.

Sue checked that Tony was occupied and gently eased open a drawer on the cabinet she was standing by. Inside was a drift of papers: bills, receipts, letters, demands – the detritus of a life. She idly plucked one out. It bore a 1965 date – had this old lady never thrown anything away? She closed the drawer and opened the next one along. Her eyes widened imperceptibly as a velvet case was revealed. She gently extracted the case from the drawer and opened it. Diamonds sparkled. Sue smiled to herself and, with a glance to see that Tony was occupied with a selection of canes and walking sticks in an elephant's foot by the door, slipped the velvet case into her bag to join the other items hidden there.

She checked that there was nothing else in the drawer.

'Just off to check another room,' she called. Tony mumbled something, absorbed in trying to date a silver cane top.

Sue ducked out of the room and headed to the stairs. Her passing raised eddies of dust along the edges of the floor carpet, which was filthy and matted, and in places slightly tacky. Sue climbed the stairs without touching the banister rail, which looked like it had been coated with some sort of jam.

Upstairs, she pushed gently at the first door, and entered the dark room beyond. It was a bedroom, the curtains pulled tight shut. She moved to the window and tentatively grasped one of the curtains. Giving it a quick shake, she pulled it open in a cloud of dust. A large, grey cobweb held the curtains closed, but Sue tugged harder and the cobweb finally tore free and the cloth parted, revealing a grimy window matted with more cobwebs, dust and dead insects. A few small spiders scurried for safety, and a colony of woodlice tumbled progressively from a hole in the rotten wood of the window frame.

Sue dusted her hands off and turned to survey the room now that there was some light. Her eye was caught by an ancient tallboy in the corner, stacked with trinkets, crockery and figurines. She moved closer and her expert eyes scanned the contents. A small Victorian pill box and a set of Lalique glasswork figurines found their way into her bag before her eye was caught by something right at the back of the tallboy.

Masked by a swathe of cobweb was a chalice. Not a normal drinking cup, but a dull metal chalice inset with coppery swirls and the glint of gemstones. Sue moved some of the other worthless junk to one side and brushed away the cobweb so she could see the thing better. Certainly something unique. She grasped its stem and drew it from the back of the shelf. It was filthy dirty and encrusted with muck, as though it had been found in a riverbed and never cleaned. She rubbed her thumb across the rim to reveal several green and red gems. They certainly looked like genuine emeralds and rubies, and the object had a good heft, suggesting it was made from pewter or bronze. Sue pondered as she looked at the object, turning it in her hand.

'Sue? You up there?'

Tony's call snapped her back to reality, and she hastily added the chalice to the other objects in her bag, moving back the trinkets on the shelf to obscure the fact that something was missing from the tallboy.

'Yup!' she called.

'Anything?' Tony asked, coming into the room.

'A few bits and pieces. She gestured to the tallboy, and Tony moved across with his clipboard and pen poised to record anything that might be of value. Sue wandered out of the room and back downstairs. Outside the front door, she took a deep breath to clear her lungs of the dust and grime from within the house. She patted her bag and smiled. Not a bad day's work.

***

Shrouded By Darkness

From: 'Sue Cavendish' <antiquelady@hotmail.com>
To: 'Jacob' <jweigler@warwick.ac.uk>
Subject: Chalice identification
Sent: Sun, 2 June 2002 13:43:23 +0100

Hi Jacob

I wonder if you might be able to help with some identification.

Attached is a pic of an object I came across today. I've been checking on various internet sites for information on this chalice but so far have come up blank. The usual sources are also vague on the subject.

As this is one of your favourite subjects, I wonder if you have any other clues as to its origin, history and so on.

Sorry I've not been in touch of late. Work's keeping me in London. I promise I'll get up to Warwick soon for one of our special sessions. You know I can't keep away for too long.

Meantime I look forward to hearing what you can dig up about this object.

Love

Sue
xxx

From: 'Jacob' <jweigler@warwick.ac.uk>
To: 'Sue Cavendish' <antiquelady@hotmail.com>
Subject: re: Chalice identification
Sent: Sun, 2 June 2002 14:05:43 +0100

Hi there antiquelady,

You're a naughty girl! I don't hear from you for months and then you want my help ... However on the promise of seeing you again ... :->

The reason you probably can't find any information about your chalice is that it isn't a chalice at all. It's a goblet (and I could go into

252

all the differences, but I'm sure at this stage you're not that bothered).

Check out the papers held at the Institute site at www.c-tec.gov.org (I didn't tell you any of this by the way – kind of classified information as this is a government site). The entry code changes each day, and so today click on the words 'unauthorised' and 'special' in turn. They're in the historical artifacts section, and you'll need a login id and password to access them. Use 'Warwick' as the ID, and JacoBA34526 as the password (it's case dependent as well). I think the one you're looking for is in case file L57935/C – but there are several there, and maybe you can figure out which one you have.

If this is what you're after, then look after the object. It seems to be quite rare and maybe if you clean it up a little, it might be more obvious what you have.

You owe me big time for this (as usual :->) so try and get up to Warwick as soon as you can to pay your debts.

Yours

Jacob Weigler
Art History Department
Warwick University Campus

***

Sue read Jacob's note with growing pleasure. Looking at the filthy chalice – correction, goblet – it was hard to imagine that it could have any real worth. But then Jacob was rarely wrong on these things, and was a useful person to know. She made a mental note to try and get to Warwick soon, if only to ensure that Jacob remained faithful to her as a source of knowledge. She smiled – amazing what you can get with the occasional blow job and flash of your boobs.

She opened up an internet browser and entered in the web address that Jacob had given her. Almost immediately a 'Cannot find server' page appeared. Sue looked at it blankly and followed Jacob's instructions as to which words to click. Suddenly the page changed and she was presented with a sign in/password screen. She shook her head. Strange. Entering the details Jacob had supplied, she found herself faced with an impressive library search function.

Everything seemed to be here. What an incredible resource, and trust Jacob to know all about it. Before long, she had located the catalogue and was comparing images of goblets with the one on the table in front of her. The one Jacob had suggested was pretty close, but on comparison, Sue decided that it wasn't the one. Shame, as Jacob's choice was a one-of-a-kind piece from the 13th Century, missing for more than 500 years and worth pretty much whatever the buyer wanted to charge. Several world-renowned institutes, including the Getty in America and the British Museum in England, were offering substantial prices for information as to its whereabouts.

Several pages later on in the online catalogue of lost treasures, Sue came across an ink sketch of something that looked far more promising. She looked at the simple sketch, and then across at the goblet sitting on her desk. The gemstones seemed to be in the same places. The patterns of the copper etching were very similar indeed, and overall the shape of the fluting on the stem, the base and the rim seemed to match her find.

'The Goblet of the Black Friars,' she read, 'was lost around the early 1700s during a publicly-suppressed spate of witch hunts in central London. It was rumoured to be at the centre of rites carried out by the Black Friars, based on the banks of the Thames close to the site of what is now Blackfriars Station. The Goblet is still worshipped by several underground cults as being the basis of power, and many of their rites revolve around the quest to locate the object. The vessel is rumoured to grant the heart's desire to the owner, although quite how the rite to achieve this is performed has been lost. This sketch was found amongst the possessions of an ex-cultist when he died in the late 1800s, and its accuracy cannot be verified.'

Sue sat back in her chair and read the text through a couple of times. She thoughtfully picked up the goblet and studied it closely.

'Heart's desire, eh – didn't do much for the old lady though, did you.' Looking closer at the side of the cup, Sue thought she could make out some additional inscriptions under the muck. She rubbed at it with her thumb, and revealed what looked like the rough shape of the Thames. She rubbed harder, revealing more finely etched lines surrounding the line of the river. As she ran her thumb over the cleared space, she suddenly felt a sharp pain. A bead of blood emerged and smeared over the surface of the goblet. The blood seemed to darken as it touched the metal, and a cloud moved over the sun outside, plunging the room into a gloomy darkness.

Sue looked up. 'Shit. All I want is more money than I know what to do with, and a fucking cut thumb and tetanus isn't going to help with that.'

The cloud moved on and the room was lightened once more. Blood continued to run from Sue's thumb and started to drip onto her desk.

'Bugger.' Sue leaped up and carried the goblet into the kitchen area, where she ran her thumb under the cold tap for a moment before studying the damage. A thin slit in the flesh gaped as she squeezed it, and more blood beaded up within. She reached for the antiseptic and liberally doused her thumb, wincing as the stinging started and then faded off. A plaster completed the exercise before she returned to the goblet and, after a moment's hesitation, held it under the tap. One of the key concerns when restoring old and tarnished objects was to take time and to do the research before anything else. Otherwise one always ran the risk of irreparably damaging the item. As the water washed over the goblet, so the muck and grime started to clear and Sue could see that it was etched with sigils and designs. The map section she had revealed resolved into an impressively detailed, if tiny, map of London, showing the bends in the Thames, and a pointer line leading to a location close to Blackfriars Station.

Sue rubbed her sore thumb thoughtfully with her fingers, and gently set the goblet onto the draining board. Returning to Tony's office, she printed out the information on the goblet, and then grabbed the London *A-Z* book from the reference shelf. Opening it to the overall map of London, she returned to the goblet and started to compare the maps.

Maybe, just maybe, after all this time the marked location might still be there.

***

Mobile Phone Transcript:

Call Made: Sun, 2 Jun 2002 15:07:35

Tony: Hi.

Geoff: Hi Tony, Geoff here.

Tony: Hi Geoff. Everything okay?

Geoff: Well … no, not really.

Tony: What's up?

Geoff: Well, I'm here with Francine looking through the accounts, and … well … we're in a bad shape.

Tony: What? What do you mean?

Geoff: Basically, unless things turn around very soon, we're looking at having to close or sell the business.

Tony: Wha –

Geoff: I know it's a shock. I couldn't believe it either, but Francine has checked and double checked and basically whatever money we had here has gone. All seems legitimate expenses, but the bottom line is that there's nothing left.

Tony: But I –

Geoff: So the first thing we have to do is to try and cut back. Did you tell Sue about the appointment yet?

Tony: Well … yes.

Geoff: That's a shame. We can't do it, Tony. We can't afford to pay her anything. You'll have to explain –

Tony: What do you mean?

Geoff: It's as I say, we don't have any funds. Sue will have to be dropped, and whatever we owe her will have to be paid later – if at all – in instalments.

Tony: But I don't –

Geoff: Sorry, mate, but that's the situation. We need to get together tomorrow to talk about this, so I'm contacting Alan. I wanted to check the situation with Sue so you can let her know that we won't be needing her. Sorry you've already told her. There's also some problem with the savings accounts – but we can go over that tomorrow as well.

Tony: Okay.

Geoff: Sorry to be the bearer of sad news, Tony. Hopefully we can sort something out, but it really doesn't look good.

Tony: Tomorrow then.

Geoff: Sure. Sorry.

CALL ENDS

***

Sue left Blackfriars Station and headed to the Bridge, as she felt that this was perhaps the best place to get her bearings. The Blackfriars area of London, just to the north of the Thames by Blackfriars Bridge, is a maze of small alleys and passages, intersected by the newer main thoroughfares of the bridge crossing and the main arterial routes of Embankment and Upper Thames Street alongside the river. From

Blackfriars Bridge, Sue looked up and down the Thames, seeing the frontage of the various buildings ranged along the raised river bank. She pulled her *A-Z* from her bag and opened it to the page marked with a sheet of paper. On the paper was a crayon rubbing of the map from the side of the goblet, and she double checked that against the *A-Z* before looking up and setting off towards the end of the bridge.

The newer roads were of course not shown on the goblet map, but these had to some extent taken the paths of earlier roads, and Sue followed a series of turnings until she arrived at a small alley leading off Carter Court, which in turn led to an unmarked passageway between two sets of ancient buildings. There was a strong stench of river sewage here, and Sue edged her way down the passage gingerly, her flat shoes crunching over broken glass. She stuffed the *A-Z* back into her bag and surveyed the passage carefully. This was as close as she could get to the location marked on the goblet. The finely intricate etchings and lines created an impressively accurate view of the location. As she moved further down the passage, Sue's feet scuffed at the ground, and she kicked a small stone along. It span and danced, and then fell with a glassy chink to one side. Intrigued by the sound, Sue crouched down and saw that, half hidden at the base of the wall, was a small window into the building. The pathway had obviously been laid after the building had been completed, as there was a small lip of about a foot between the path and the level of the window's lower sill.

Sue glanced up and down the passage, but all was silent. No-one ever came this way – there was no normal London rubbish cluttering the passage: none of the old newspapers, coke cans, bottles, or even the more modern refuse found in such places: used needles and spent condoms. She returned her attention to the window and pushed against the glass. It creaked gently and gave a little.

Sue stood and looked around the passage. A little way up, she found what she was looking for: an old house brick, caked with bird droppings and half buried in the path. She wrenched it up, being careful not to damage her nails, and carried it to the half-buried window. Then she placed it on the ground before her, and with a final check to ensure that no-one was around, kicked the brick through the window. The glass didn't so much shatter as crumble, and with a few more well-aimed kicks with the flat of her foot, Sue had cleared the window frame of glass fragments.

A musty, dead smell greeted her as she peered into the blackness. From her bag she fetched a small penlight torch, and shone it into the darkness. There was nothing to see except some vague shapes shifting in the gloom and dust. She sniffed, and, looking around her once again, sat down on the floor and fed her legs through the window. Like a child going down stairs she shifted her bottom from the path and down to the sill so her legs were dangling into the building. Then, ducking her head, she braced herself on her arms and let herself drop into the gloom.

It was only about three or four feet to the floor, and she landed with a gentle crunch of broken glass. She shone the torch around her. It seemed to be an empty room. The dust disturbed by her arrival swirled around her, and the torchlight caught constant glimpses of movement as she walked through the room. Her feet were obscured by the murk that swirled around her legs.

To one side she found a black opening with steps leading down, while further along was a hatchway in the wall, securely closed and, it seemed, boarded shut. The only other exit was the shape of a doorway, but instead of a door, it boasted a bricked-up façade, the mortar crumbling with age and spilling out from the uppermost levels, showing that the door had been bricked up from the other side and the masons had been unable to keep the mortar neat towards the top.

She returned to the steps leading down, and, swinging the torch from side to side, started to descend. More than once she had to brush trailing cobwebs from her face, as the steps curled down. The walls to either side were ancient and covered with moss and mildew. The air became damp, and the steps a little slippery underfoot.

Sue's breathing became a little laboured and, she noticed, her breath started to steam a little in the chill air. After a few moments, she reached the bottom of the steps and was faced with a closed metal door, rusted at the bottom. She shrugged and pushed at it, not really expecting much, but the ancient hinges abruptly snapped with a clang, and the door fell backwards away from her, crashing to the ground with an echoing bang, which reverberated around her in the confined stairwell. She shone her torch through the opening, and, as the dust slowly settled, she found herself faced with another door, but this time of wood. Ancient timbers tied together with cross braces, and enormous hinges made from some sort of metal – not iron this time, it seemed, as there was no rust or corrosion visible. The door also featured an inset carving. Sue smiled to see that the carving was of her goblet. Unmistakable.

She moved closer to the door, and in the dusty silence examined the handle. There did not seem to be a lock, but the handle was bonded to the door with a clay or pottery seal. There were markings there similar to some of those on the goblet, as well as several lines of cuneiform script.

'Abandon hope all ye who enter here,' muttered Sue under her breath, somewhat sarcastically. Holding the torch in her teeth, she examined the seal with her hands. It seemed brittle. She removed one of her shoes, and with a smart tap, broke the seal in two. Replacing her shoe, she pulled the two halves of the seal away from the door with her hands, and placed them to one side. Then, with a deep breath, she twisted the handle on the door and pushed.

Nothing. The door did not budge an inch. Somewhat cross, she put her shoulder to it and pushed hard. Not a thing. She released the handle and stood back, shining the torch around the edges of the door and then again at the handle. Then, with realisation, she grasped the handle once more and pulled. With an echoing wooden creak, it swung towards her, releasing a wave of dust and cobwebs from behind it. The stench was like nothing she had smelt before. Dust and damp and rotting food and ordure. She coughed and held her breath, blinking her eyes to clear them of the dust.

Holding the torch before her, she stepped through the doorway and into the room beyond. She was surprised to find that the floor was dry, and seemed to be of loose earth. Her feet sank into it a little as she stepped in, leaving clear footprints in her wake. The room was fully enclosed, with only the large wooden door she had opened as a means of entry and exit. It was perhaps ten feet across, and circular, the bricked walls soaring up until they were lost in darkness above. So what was the point of this?, she thought.

Sue leaned against the wall at one side and idly swung her flashlight around. A sealed room. No other entrance. So a storeroom, perhaps. But why was there nothing in it? It had been cleared out. But why then go to all the bother of sealing the outer door in such an elaborate fashion? It didn't make sense. She scuffed her foot against the ground.

And why was the floor of loose earth? Perhaps because something was buried here ...

Sue crouched down and started to move the earth with her hand. The soil was icy cold and clammy. Suddenly her torch caught a glint of gold, and Sue dug a little deeper to reveal a gold coin. Brushing it off, she looked at it closely. It seemed to be a perfect example of a Roman coin, the sort of thing she would not hesitate to add to her bag should she come across it in her work. She dug a little more and found five more similar coins. It seemed that untold wealth was hers. She pocketed the coins and stood, brushing down her jeans.

Sue smiled to herself. A little excavation work, and who knew what riches she would find? With a spring in her step, she left the room and clattered up the ancient staircase beyond.

The lower storeroom descended into pitch darkness for a moment as the echoes of Sue's departure faded, and then a faint glimmer of greenish light sprung into existence, apparently coming from the fabric of the walls themselves. The damp brickwork was outlined in green, and the light spilled across the rough dirt floor in waves. The earth started to heave. Gently at first in one place, and then in several others. Small white objects burst from the ground and waved gently in the stale air, before pushing up and out of the earth. Skeletal, almost mummified hands attached to decaying arm bones, still with shreds of muscle, skin and fibre attached, waved from the floor as three figures started to clamber out of the ground. Their heads were in shadow, and their bodies clad in rotting and mildewed black robes, tattered and fraying around their emaciated feet. The robes were held together with rope belts, and from the belts hung several rusting and greenly glinting objects. Knives and spikes, stained with ancient blood and dirt.

For a moment the three figures stood silently in the chamber, unmoving. Then there came the hiss of a voice, as unfamiliar air was forced across taut vocal chords, and frayed lips and tongue struggled to form words. 'We are summoned. We must now wait and fulfil the curse.'

With a single movement, the Black Friars stepped back towards the greenly-glowing walls, which faded to darkness, leaving only faint rustling sounds, and the echoes of Sue clambering back out of the upper room onto the pathway.

***

Having finished her shower, Sue returned downstairs to find Tony there looking extremely sheepish.

'Hi,' he mumbled. 'Sue ... we've got to talk.'

Sue breezed past him. 'About what?'

Tony followed her into the living room and stood by the door as she poured herself a glass of gin, adding a splash of soda from the siphon.

'Well ... you know I said yesterday about the bonus and the job ...?'

Sue looked at him and nodded, a faint smile playing around her lips. She was enjoying watching Tony squirm.

'Well,' Tony started to wring his hands. Sue could not believe that anyone would actually do that. 'Well,' he started again. 'I was wrong.'

Sue looked at him in the ensuing silence. 'You were wrong.' She repeated flatly.

Tony nodded. 'Wrong about that, and wrong about lots of other things, it seems.'

'So my bonus ...'

'... is not going to happen,' finished Tony. 'I had a call – Geoff – he says there simply isn't the money to justify it. I tried to talk him out of it – I tried – but he wouldn't listen. There's a meeting tomorrow and –'

'No bonus,' said Sue in a voice like ice. 'After all the work I've put in ...' She took a deep breath.

'Don't worry,' mumbled Tony. 'It'll all work itself out. It'll all be fine. We've still got each other. I ...'

Sue laughed at this. Out loud. It was time. She loved these times. When the men she used floundered on the end of her hook, flapping and gasping for one final kind word, for a last fuck, for sympathy.

'Why are you laughing?' asked Tony. 'I can't see what's so funny.'

Sue shook her head. 'That's it, Tony. It's the end. After all I've done. I can't stay with you now.'

'Can't stay? But why? I love you!'

Sue gestured at him, her velvet dressing gown gaping to reveal her slim and shapely legs. 'Look at you! Just look! You've no money. No looks. And very soon no job. What on earth would I want to stay for?'

Tony frowned. 'What do you mean, "no job"? Who have you been talking to?'

'No-one, my darling Tony. It's obvious. Despite my best efforts on your behalf, the money's just not been coming in, has it? This is why you're trying to fob me off now, isn't it? Well I've had enough. I saw this coming.'

'What?' Tony's mouth gaped open. 'What do you mean?'

'This time next week,' said Sue sweetly, 'I'll be co-partner in Keith Barber's company – remember Keith? Your rival? Well we're the best of friends. More than friends, really. I can see a hostile take-over coming up for your failure of an antiques company.'

Tony staggered in the doorway as the impact of her words hit him. He stumbled to the table and sat down on one of the chairs, his face red and his breath heaving. 'You … you …'

'What's that Tony?' Sue asked sweetly, brushing past him again to the door.

'But I love you – you love me – you said!'

'Oh, I say lots of things, darling. Doesn't mean I mean them.' Sue turned to leave the room. 'And I never loved you,' she fired back. 'Off to pack now. Don't try and stop me.'

And with that she swept from the room, leaving Tony sitting at the table staring into space. His hands trembled as he re-ran the last few minutes through his mind again and again. A tear emerged from his right eye and tumbled down his cheek, where it rested.

***

Shrouded By Darkness

From: 'Sue' <rich-bitch@hotmail.com>
To: 'Keith' <kbarber@lineone.net>
Subject: Tomorrow
Sent: Sun, 2 June 2002 18:30:12 +0100

Keith

Hi darling. Just to say that I'm free tomorrow to chat about the deal.
See you usual time and place. And bring a bottle – I feel like celebrating.

Love

Sue
xxx

***

Having hurriedly dumped most of her things in her bags – whatever remained she could collect later on – Sue dropped them off at her own flat before getting changed once more for her evening's entertainment. She slipped into a pair of black jeans and an old black T-shirt, pulling back her hair and tucking it under a black cap. A camouflage jacket completed the ensemble. She hauled an old canvas bag from storage, and included with it a hurricane lamp, trowel and a small folding shovel – relics from when she had had a brief flirtation with archaeology at university before deciding that much better pickings could be had from places where you didn't have to dig them up yourself.

The sun was just setting as she arrived at Blackfriars Station and retraced her steps back to the alleyway and down into the eerily silent and deserted building. The hurricane lamp threw everything into stark relief as she made her way down the damp curving stairs and into the icy lower room, her breath fogging in front of her face from the chill.

She quickly unpacked her tools and returned to where she had found the coins.

'Nothing ventured …' she muttered to herself as she started to dig and sift the earth with the trowel. As a gold coin came into view, she smiled to herself.

***

Tony had sought solace from the day's events in the only way he knew. His friend the bottle. Aside from Sue, from whom it was impossible to keep secrets, no-one knew that Tony liked his tipple a little too much. That the visits to the supermarkets became more frequent as the stress increased. That the number of trips to the bottle bank likewise increased.

Staring into his glass, Tony reflected again on what could possibly have gone wrong here. He knew Sue loved him. She had told him so enough times. And the sex – the sex was amazing. Well, when he wasn't too drunk to perform it was amazing. What on earth could she be worried about there? And all that stuff about him losing his money and job – well that had to be a bluff, didn't it? Had to be.

He pushed himself to his feet and staggered over to the drinks cabinet to refresh his glass for the umpteenth time since Sue had walked out. As he did so, his eye caught an unusual shape on the drainer in the kitchen area. He frowned and wandered out to have a closer look. It was a goblet or a chalice or something. Obviously Sue had been cleaning it and had left it to dry. But where had it come from?

Tony grasped it by the stem and carried it back into the living area. Slumping back down in his chair, whiskey in one hand and the goblet in the other, he studied the piece. Fairly good looking really, gemstones, some metal filigree inlaid into it, and meticulously etched.

As he studied the goblet, Tony did not notice that the lights in the room seemed to dim, and in their place a faint green glow appeared, seeping from the very fabric of the building.

Without warning, Tony's whiskey glass shattered in his hand.

'Fuck and damn!' he exclaimed, swapping the goblet from his good hand to his cut one as he rummaged in his pocket for the handkerchief that he knew was there. The blood from his hand spread over the surface of the goblet, and seemed to sink into it. Giving up the search for the hankie, Tony started to cry. First his job, then Sue, now this. He'd never wanted any of this. All he'd ever wanted was to be with Sue forever and ever …

The temperature in the room abruptly dropped several degrees, and Tony looked up through tear-blurred eyes as the darkness pressed in all around. There was a faint whispering sound, as though material was being brushed against material. Seated in his chair, Tony realised that he was not alone. From out of the darkness on either side of him, two silent figures in black robes materialised. He was certain they appeared from nowhere, but how could that be possible?

In front of him, backlit by a faint green glow, a third figure seemed to congeal from the motes of dust floating in the air. It took a step towards him, metal instruments clinking gently at its waist. Tony sat staring at the figure. His heart was beating nineteen to the dozen, and, despite the chill air, sweat broke out on his pate and started to run down his temples.

'You have the goblet.'

The voice was like rusty knives gently sliding against each other. A susurrant, whispering, sexless cadence that set Tony's nerves jumping. He looked at his bleeding hand, which was clenched tight around the goblet.

'You have a heart's desire. You have the goblet. Choose. Destroy the goblet and set us free.'

The whispering voice was without threat. The words were clear.

Tony, looking at the goblet, hitched in his breath. 'Will … will I be with Sue if I do?' he asked, saying the first thing that came to mind at that time.

The spectral Friar standing in the gloom before him said nothing. The cowl covering its face slid back to reveal a face of bone, sinew and desiccated flesh. The blank eye sockets gave nothing away, but with a gentle clicking of bone on bone, the creature shook its head.

Tony stared wide-eyed at the Friar. No. The creature said he would not keep Sue if he destroyed the goblet. This fact echoed in his mind for a moment. Then, with an effort of will, Tony lifted the bloody goblet and placed it on the table. 'Then I will not destroy the goblet. Sue is more important.'

The Friar did not respond, but its grinning face turned towards the goblet on the table. 'So be it,' the rasping voice whispered. 'Your choice. Now you will get your heart's desire – but there is a price …'

***

After about an hour's digging, Sue was filthy dirty, but had a growing hoard in her canvas sack. After the coins, she had found some jewellery. Some work with the spade had revealed a couple of small chests, rusted shut but reassuringly heavy. More coins had followed.

She worked her way around the small chamber, trying to excavate methodically, and trying not to miss an inch. She leaned back on her haunches and wiped her face. Was it getting even colder in here? Her breath suddenly steamed in front of her, and when the fog cleared, she was looking at the legs of someone dressed in a long black cloak or robe.

With a squeal, she pushed backwards, straight into the legs of a second figure standing behind her. She slowly rose to her feet, brushing her hands together.

'Um – look – I can explain … Is this your stuff?'

The figures silently regarded her, and Sue noticed that their clothes were frayed and mouldy. The hurricane lamp cast their faces in deep shadow, their hoods covering whatever features they might have.

She stepped back, and checked where the entrance to the chamber was positioned.

'Well, if it's all the same to you, I'd better be on my way.' She turned to leave, only to find the doorway now blocked by a third figure, one that had not been there a second earlier. Her blood turned to ice, and she looked around frantically. What had she stumbled into here? Who were these people?

'Look,' she began in her best conciliatory voice. 'Can we just talk about this for a moment?'

'You have the goblet.'

The rusty voice echoed around the confined space, and Sue realised that the creature in the doorway had spoken. 'Goblet – yes – I have the goblet. But it's not here. I'd have to get it for you. Valuable, is it?'

'Immeasurably. You have a heart's desire. You have the goblet. Choose. Destroy the goblet and set us free.'

'Destroy …' Sue was suddenly alert for the money. 'But you said it was immeasurably valuable. How valuable is that, then?'

There was silence. All Sue could hear was the thudding of her heart and the sound of her own breathing.

'So why should I destroy it, then? If it's so valuable. I think perhaps you'd better let me go, and I can bring you the goblet later on? Yes?'

'So be it,' hissed the Friar, and stepped to one side.

Sue took her chance and bolted for the door. Without looking back, she raced up the steps in pitch darkness, and all but threw herself through the window opening and out into the comparatively fresh night air of London.

***

Sue's hand trembled as she tried to get the key to Tony's flat in the lock. Finally she managed it, and tumbled exhausted through the door. She slammed it behind her and fixed the safety lock. Taking two big gulps of air, she headed off to the kitchen, where she had left the goblet after washing and drying it. When she got to the drainer, however, the goblet was gone. She span round and recoiled in horror as Tony lurched from out of the darkness in the living area and stood in the doorway before her. His face and hair were covered with blood, and blood had also saturated his clothes, which hung loosely on his frame. He swayed a little, forward and backward, until his eyes, wide and shockingly white against the red blood, fixed on her face.

His mouth opened and a thin stream of blood trickled out. 'Sue – I did it …' he whispered. 'I got what I wanted. But the price … the price …' He breathed in, a hollow rattling sound, and Sue skittered away around the kitchen area, searching for an exit that wasn't there. She noticed a pool of blood slowly spreading across the tiled floor towards her.

Tony blinked at her, and his mouth spread in an insane rictus grin. 'See how much I love you, Sue. See how much!' Tony's body swayed once more, and then he fell face-first to the floor. Sue crammed her fists to her mouth in an attempt to stop herself from screaming.

Tony's body had been cleanly eviscerated from behind. His back had been neatly cut open and most of his organs removed. The same procedure had been carried out to the back of his head, his arms and legs. His clothing had been hanging to the front of his body while the whole of his rear had been expertly flayed and dissected while Tony still lived. Blood leaked from exposed veins and muscle, and Sue could see the remains of his heart pumping still in the otherwise empty cavity of his chest. He should have been dead, but was miraculously still alive. His head turned to grin at her.

Sue became aware of a movement in the room behind him, and looked up to see the three Friars standing there, one holding Tony's guts, another cradling part of his brain in its hands, while the third held the flayed strips of Tony's skin casually by its side. At this she screamed. Long and hard. And after the first scream came sobbing cries of disbelief, as she slowly sank down against the kitchen cupboards, her feet resting in the still-spreading pool of Tony's blood.

One of the Friars stepped forward – it may have been the same one as before, but to Sue all three looked alike. 'Why?' she blurted between hitching gasps for breath. 'Why have you done this?'

'Greed.' The whispering voice cut through Sue's tears.

'Simple greed. We were cursed by our greed to deliver the heart's desire of those who summon us, with an unthinkable price to be paid. We want peace. If you destroy the goblet, we will be free, but you will get nothing.'

Nothing. She would get nothing. The concept horrified her more than the Friars, and she shook her head. 'I … I can't.'

'Your choice,' whispered the Friar with a note of sadness. 'Now you will get your heart's desire – but there is a price …'

***

Anyone walking through the back streets of Blackfriars might wonder, as they pass a certain alley at a certain time, why they can hear faint crying. Few would investigate further – such sounds can be commonplace in London, and anyway, it's always someone else's problem.

Down the alley and through the shattered window, now boarded over from inside. Into the pitch blackness. Down the chill steps and past the now closed and bolted iron door to the sealed and warded wooden door. And beyond the door, in the circular chamber ...

***

Sue raises her eyes to the flickering green light that plays around the ceiling of the chamber. Her tears are bright. Around her are riches of all kinds: gold and silver ingots; coins from every realm on earth; banknotes and fine jewellery; caskets overflowing with baubles and riches beyond belief. She sniffs and reaches out tentatively to touch her wealth, to handle her riches, but her arms end in ragged stumps, crudely sewn up with black thread, and weeping blood and pus. Seeing her arms, Sue starts crying. She is hopeless with grief.

There is a sound behind her, and she turns her head, eyes wide as she sees a humanoid shape in the room behind her. It is Tony. His skin is sallow and peeling from his bones. What remains of his clothes is hanging in tatters. His back glistens wetly in the emerald light. He cannot walk well, and so collapses to the earthy floor behind Sue and takes her gently in his bloody half-arms.

'Shh,' he consoles her. 'Shh. I got my heart's desire too. Now we'll never, ever, be parted.'

Sue's scream can barely be heard in the street above.

***

From: 'Keith' <kbarber@lineone.net>
To: 'Sue' <rich-bitch@hotmail.com>
Subject: Where were you

Sue

Just hoping you're OK. I waited for an hour but you didn't show. No

answer from the mobile as well. Hope all's well. Call me when you
can.

Love

Keith

Date: Mon, 3 Jun 2002 13:40:21 +0100
From: 'Postmaster' <postmaster@lineone.net>
Sender: <postmaster@lineone.net>
To: < kbarber@lineone.net >
Subject: Undeliverable Mail

Unknown user: rich-bitch@hotmail.com

The Heart Of New Orleans
Poppy Z Brite

A bar where I sometimes drink has New Orleans street scenes painted on the walls. Not cliché tourist shit like Carnival parades and jazz funerals, but regular people's views of the city: a dilapidated old shotgun house, a snowball stand, the kind of Mid-City corner grocery out of which I'd expect to see the grocer being rolled on a gurney, shot dead in a robbery that netted $26. I guess most people wouldn't imagine the dead grocer, but I see him or some equally sad variation several times a month.

I don't go to this bar too often, because I'll just be wanting to relax and drink my bourbon, and I'll catch myself making up stories about the people in the murals. That wouldn't be so bad except that the stories inevitably end in their deaths. I've always been able to look death straight in the eye, but I prefer not to do so during my off-hours. To be kicking back with a shot of Wild Turkey, to gaze at a painting of a nice old man playing dominoes and suddenly find myself imagining him in cardiac arrest – it makes me feel like I am riding on a bum trip, as people used to say and probably still do somewhere.

I have always prided myself on fulfilling my position as coroner of New Orleans with no trace of morbidity. I may never live up to my predecessor, who played a mean jazz trumpet, but I am a bit of a bon vivant in my own quiet way. I enjoy the bourbon, though seldom to excess. Fine restaurants are an important part of my life. I try to keep up with the local literary scene, once even speaking in a very general way about some of my odder cases to a group of mystery writers at the

Tennessee Williams Festival. In short, I like to think that I'm not particularly death-obsessed as coroners go, nor cursed with an overactive imagination.

So I keep telling myself that the case of the Stubbs boy was just an anomaly, one of the many inexplicable but ultimately mundane things that any medical worker will encounter in the course of a long career. I tell myself that even as I slide another fragment of his heart under the microscope, and I try to stay away from the bar with the street scenes on the walls, and occasionally I have an extra drink before turning in at night.

Children's deaths are terribly hard on everyone who must deal with them, even a childless and relatively heartless bastard like me. A little body on the slab looks less natural, somehow, than the body of an adult. You know they never contemplated their mortality, never pondered when and how it would come, never went through all the maundering about life and death and the cosmos that adults think separates them from their simian brothers. Perhaps that should make the sight more bearable, but instead it only accentuates their terrible vulnerability: they never even knew it was coming, yet here they lie.

As dead children go, five-year-old Matthew Stubbs was less heartrending than many I have seen. He was not beaten to death by a parent or stepparent; he was not left to freeze in an unheated apartment while his guardians smoked crack next door; he was not shot in his mother's arms. He was simply the victim of a stupid accident far too common in south Louisiana: left alone for a few minutes while his mother checked on dinner, he let himself into a neighbour's yard, fell face-first into a wading pool, and drowned in a few inches of tepid water. That was what the officers on the scene had surmised, anyway. My job was to disprove or confirm this dreary little scenario.

Matthew was a handsome little boy with dark curly hair and long eyelashes that lay damply against his livid cheeks. Aside from some whitish purge in his mouth and nostrils – a mixture of water and mucus whipped into a froth by his struggling lungs – I found no external signs of trauma on him, nothing to suggest he had been dumped in the pool rather than fallen. His blood had the bright cherry-red colour characteristic of oxygen deprivation. His lungs were full of more white

273

froth, and his stomach contained only water and a few fragments of the cold spaghetti he'd reportedly had for lunch that day. This was a straightforward drowning; I saw scores of them every summer. People fell out of boats or went swimming in the Mississippi and often didn't surface until days later. For the sake of his parents, I was glad this boy hadn't been in the water long enough to show any disfigurement.

Nothing seemed strange about the case until I examined the heart. I excised it from its moorings and cupped it in my gloved hand, preparing to weigh it, when something caught my eye. I held the little organ up to the light and tilted it this way and that, trying to understand what I saw. Internal organs are as distinctive as hands or facial features, with infinite subtleties of colour, shape, venation. But I'd never seen a pattern like the one that covered the entire surface of this child's heart. Hundreds and hundreds of tiny lines were somehow etched upon the muscle, spiralling from the aorta and vena cava all the way down to the tips of the ventricles. When I dissected the heart and washed out the blood that had clotted there, I saw similar marks covering its inner chambers. Bringing a piece of the tissue close to my eyes, I thought I could make out loops and spikes, as if the lines were made up of words far too small to read.

Of course that couldn't be; it was simply a strange pattern of striation in the muscle fibres. The fact that I'd never seen anything like it was of no consequence – I'd never seen a teratoma, either, until the day I found a mass of undifferentiated tissue with two baby teeth embedded in a man's left kidney. The man had lived with this inside him for 57 years, dying of a wholly unrelated aneurysm. There had been no need to inform his family of the absorbed twin's existence, which was why it now floated in a jar on my desk instead of being cremated with him.

At least I had heard of teratomas, though, had read about them and seen pictures. I'd never heard of anyone whose heart looked as if someone had taken an engraving tool to it. This condition had nothing to do with Matthew Stubbs' death, though, so it concerned me only as a curiosity. I noted it into the small microphone clipped to my lapel, then preserved the organ in a container of formalin. Though it didn't relate to the cause of death, it was certainly notable enough to save. Perhaps I'd show it to my former assistant, Jeffrey, who always appreciated an anomaly. He was in medical school at Tulane now, but he had always been among the most trusted of my staff and sometimes dropped by the morgue to see how I was doing. I got the feeling he worried about me since my separation from my husband. Seymour had never formally announced that he was leaving me – he'd just gone up to New York to visit his family and kept extending the 'vacation.' He'd been up there for seven months now. *Typical passive-aggressive poet*, I thought when I let it enter my mind at all.

I had six other posts that day, seven the next. In the flow of gunshot wounds, car accident injuries, and heart attacks, nothing happened to remind me of one drowned little boy. I didn't think of Matthew Stubbs again until his parents showed up two days later to invite me to his funeral.

This isn't as rare as you might think. Some families would like to pretend that I and my office don't exist; never mind thinking about what we do here. But some perceive that their loved ones have shared a final, intimate relationship with me, and they want me along for one more step. I almost always find a way of gracefully declining. I would have done so in this case if Leonetta Stubbs hadn't bulldozed right over me.

For one thing, they usually call rather than dropping by. When I heard that Mr and Mrs Stubbs were at the morgue's front desk, I expected a lawsuit at worst, an hysterical outburst at best. I made sure there was no blood on my lab coat before going up front to see what they wanted, but I couldn't protect them from the bleak appearance or antiseptically rotten smell of the place. I never ask decedents' family members to come here if I can avoid it. To me it is part work, part home, but to many it is the material of nightmares.

Henry Stubbs was a tall honest-faced man with a dazed look in his dark eyes. Despite the Irish surname, his olive complexion and thick shock of black hair made me suspect a Sicilian mother or grandmother. Though he shook my hand and spoke politely to me, I could tell he had turned most of his grief inward, and that his wife was the driving force here. Even in mourning, Leonetta Stubbs was something of a vision. Though she couldn't have been much older than 35, her black shirtwaist dress, little pillbox hat, and deep red lipstick were like things an old lady would wear. The self-conscious hipsters who have begun to take over the Bywater and Lower Ninth Ward in recent years sometimes dress similarly, but unlike them, Leonetta didn't remind me of a child playing dress-up; something about the ensemble told me she knew of no other way to present herself. I imagined a closet full of severe dresses and outdated hats, possibly even inherited from her mother.

'Dr Brite,' she said, and clasped my hand in both of her own. Until I actually looked down and saw them with my own eyes, I couldn't quite fathom that she was wearing gloves – white cotton ones that in no way went with the rest of her outfit. Outside of the newspaper's Carnival pages, I wasn't sure I had ever seen a woman wearing gloves before.

'I have been waiting on tenterhooks to speak to you,' she told me.

Though the family lived in a lower-middle-class neighbourhood off Elysian Fields, her voice was rich with Uptown accents. Something running along the surface of it made me know she hadn't been raised Uptown, but had worked hard to cultivate that voice.

'Thank you for taking the time to talk to us,' said her husband. He had a regular gritty, yatty New Orleans accent, and those were just about the only words he said to me.

'Of course,' I said. 'I'm so sorry about your son. Is there something I can do for you?'

'Might we chat in your office?' Leonetta asked.

I pictured my desk covered with autopsy reports, bulletin boards full of glossy crime-scene photos, shelves crammed with models of internal organs and things in jars. 'There's really no room to sit down in my office. If you'll take a chair over here, perhaps I can help you.'

We settled in the hard plastic chairs common to all official waiting rooms, as if such places must provide as little comfort as possible. I gazed at Leonetta, concerned about the purpose of her visit but also frankly curious by now.

'You must think me such a dreadful mother,' she said.

It wasn't what I had expected, but I'd heard it before. 'Not at all. It's true that people don't realise how fast a child can get into trouble, but some accidents are unavoidable.'

'Bosh,' she said. 'Bosh, bother, and bullshit.' The expletive startled me coming out of her mouth, but no more so than the previous two words had done. Just as I'd never met anyone wearing white gloves, I had never heard anyone say 'bosh' before. 'Of course I should have been watching him more closely. He was my only child, you know. I only left him in the yard because I was trying to cook that wretched red gravy, and I'm not used to it. You see, I don't cook. Henry's mother thinks I should cook more. In fact, she gave me the recipe.'

I couldn't help glancing at Henry, who only looked more miserable.

'I didn't know if it would boil over, or burn, or what it might do. I was only trying to prove that I could do something the rest of the family takes for granted. They're all wonderful cooks, to hear his mother tell it. Not me, though, not silly Leonetta with her airs and pretensions. I couldn't even make spaghetti sauce without letting the baby drown, could I, Henry?'

Henry Stubbs rose from the uncomfortable chair. 'I'll wait in the car,' he said, and disappeared through the exit door with one anguished glance back at me and his wife.

'They're not people of quality,' she said with the air of one imparting a dirty secret. 'I thought Henry would amount to something when I married him. He talked about going to law school, but that was only meant to impress me. Now he works in that damn candy factory with his father, and he'll never do anything more than that.'

'Mrs Stubbs, I hardly think –'

She went on as if I had not spoken. 'My son was an exceptional child. I'm sure you could tell, even … in his condition. Doubtless there are biological differences between normal people and geniuses.'

Of course I thought then of the strange patterns I had observed in the tissue of the little boy's heart, but I said nothing, wanting to neither feed nor destroy whatever delusions sustained her.

'His playschool teacher said he was gifted. His IQ couldn't even be measured with the regular tests.'

'Mrs Stubbs …'

'Oh, I know what you're going to say. Or would say if you weren't too polite. He was only five. It was too early to tell about these things. That's exactly what his father said. "What you talking about, Leonetta? He's just a baby. He ain't no Einstein."'

I was struck by the bitterness that came into her voice when she mentioned her husband, and also by her skill at mimicking his homely accent.

'He *was* a genius, though. Not an Einstein – his talents didn't lie in the direction of math, science, all that nonsense.' With a flip of her gloved hand she dismissed entire fields of scholarly pursuit. 'My son would have written great books someday. I know, because he told me so.'

'He told you …?'

'Of course he could already read. He couldn't write yet, not really, but he could give dictation. He'd tell little stories and I would write them down. One day we stapled them all together in a kind of book, and he said to me, "Momma, I'm going to write a real book someday."

'"You are?" I asked him. "What are you going to write about?"

'"About the true heart of New Orleans," he told me.'

My face must have expressed the scepticism I felt, for Leonetta said to me, 'I know how it sounds, doctor. Not like something a five-year-old would say. He did, though. My son was truly exceptional.'

She turned wide cornflower-blue eyes upon me. While I sympathised with her loss, I had thought her a rude and arrogant woman. She'd come here looking for absolution, or at least trying to justify the carelessness that had killed her son. She had humiliated her grieving husband in front of me. Looking into her eyes, though, I saw the vulnerability she didn't mean to reveal, and I found myself identifying with it to a dangerous degree. In those eyes I thought I saw the universal futility of life, the futility we are forever trying to deny because accepting it would obviate our reasons for continuing to live. You risk your soul trying to snatch a man from death's grasp, and two years later he dies of cancer at age 40. You let a husband see parts of yourself no-one else knows, and he turns his back and leaves you. You put all your love and hope into a beautiful little boy who drowns in a few inches of water. I saw terrible things in Leonetta Stubbs' eyes, but I could not look away.

'Doctor,' she said, 'that book will never be written. But I thank you for taking care of Matthew. Would you do one more thing for him? Would you come to his funeral?'

In that moment there was very little I could have refused her. She gave me the name of the funeral home and the time of the Mass the next day, and as I ushered her out the door, I wondered what force of nature had just rolled over me.

When I finished work late that evening, I couldn't bear the thought of my empty house. I went to the bar with the street scenes on the walls, drank two shots of bourbon, contemplated a third but knew how the media would salivate if I were pulled over for drunk driving. The crowd in the bar seemed younger than usual, and their vigour depressed me. I drove home, drank another bourbon at my kitchen table, went to bed. I thought I'd never sleep. Then, abruptly, I found myself back in the bar. An unknown but familiar-looking young man had joined me at my table. His dark hair was clipped short, his features unremarkably handsome. It was his eyes that arrested me: they were as intense as Leonetta's, but nearly black.

'It's pretty embarrassing,' he said. 'I mean, what a stupid way to go, in a damn wading pool. Being five years old is no excuse for stupidity.'

'What happened? Why did you fall in?'

'It was just one of those things. Just one of those crazy flings. I just wanted to go wading, but somehow I tripped getting in. I remember thinking, *Oh, no big deal, I'll get up in a second, it'll be easy.* And then I tried, and … I just didn't have my body any more. Do you know what I mean? It just wasn't *there.*'

'Probably you inhaled reflexively and lost consciousness. The shock can paralyse the vagus nerve –'

'No offence, doctor, but I don't really care about the vagus nerve, or the Las Vegas nerve, or whatever you want to call it. None of it makes any difference to me.'

'Is this the future? Am I seeing the life you would have lived?'

He smiled thinly. 'Future? It doesn't mean anything to me. I'm five, I'm 26, I'm 82. I know it all.' I thought I saw a look of fear cross his face, but it was gone in an instant. 'There's no distinction for me, no concept of time. Nothing but an infinity of killed possibilities.'

'Did you ever write that book?'

'What book?'

'Your mother said you intended to write a book. A book about the true heart of New Orleans.'

'My mother says a lot of things. But the heart of New Orleans? You can see it in the face of that lady right there.' He gestured toward one of the murals, at the painted figure of a white woman standing on the porch of a tiny Victorian shotgun house. Her hands were planted on her hips; a garishly patterned wrap concealed most of her ample figure. 'Can you hear her? She's hollering for her kids to come in the house before it starts raining. She's saying, "Darla! Tom-MY! Get in here before I come knock you upside da head with one a'dem bricks!" Hear her?'

His normal speaking voice wasn't as self-consciously cultured as Leonetta's, but it was a long way from downtown. When he imitated the woman calling her children, though, he seemed to *become* her for a moment, or nearly so. I could hear 20 years of cigarettes in her voice, could feel the weariness in her swollen ankles, could smell the chicory coffee, garlic, and mildew odours that permeated the little house. Apparently he hadn't just inherited his mother's talent for mimicry; he had surpassed it.

He would have surpassed it, I reminded myself, *if he had lived*. He had not lived. I had autopsied him myself, had touched his strange heart. Matthew Stubbs was laid out in a child-sized casket somewhere in the city, ready to be buried the next day, and this was only a dream.

Even so, it was better than the stories I had often found myself making up about the murals. He hadn't killed off the woman as I would have been compelled to do. Rather, with a few deft strokes, he had made me imagine her whole life. I began to wonder if his mother was right. Perhaps he was an exceptional child; perhaps he would grow up to write a great book about New Orleans.

Had been an exceptional child. *Would have written* a great book. Sitting here beside him, watching him sip a tall glass of beer, it was hard to remember that he would never do any of these things.

'You're right,' I told him. 'That is the heart of New Orleans. One of them, anyway.'

'It's all written down,' he said, touching the back of my hand. 'Keep it safe for me, will you?'

Suddenly I was awake in a lonely bed, the cats curled near my feet more an annoyance than a comfort. A faint taste of bourbon lingered in my mouth … but of course it would; I'd had two shots at the bar and another before retiring. Pale dawn light had begun to fill the room. Knowing I would not sleep again, I rose to make coffee. Seymour had always brought me coffee in bed fixed just the way I liked it, and I could never get it quite right. Every morning as I spooned the grounds into the filter, I thought I heard Sarah Vaughan singing, 'Once you told me I'd awaken with the sun – and order orange juice for one …' Too true, Sarah, but at least you could sing like God's own cello. What could I do except cut into cold flesh to offer the living cold comfort?

Not wanting to make conversation with anyone, I intended to arrive just in time for the Mass, but the visitation was still going on when I entered the funeral home on Elysian Fields Avenue. Funerals of small children tend to be sparsely attended – the children themselves haven't had time to form a large social group, and the parents' friends, who usually have kids of their own, don't like confronting the ephemerality of these young lives. But the lobby and viewing room were packed with people. From the St Joseph prayer cards stacked on a side table, I assumed the Stubbses were Catholic, so perhaps they were an unusually large family.

I approached the casket. At least they hadn't dressed him in a suit – there are few sights more pathetically creepy than a dead child wearing a tiny suit and tie. Matthew wore children's clothes, a blue shirt and a pair of yellow overalls with Cookie Monster embroidered on the breast pocket. A white rosary twined around the fingers of one small hand. His face looked much worse than it had when I'd autopsied him, cheeks unnaturally pink from too much arterial fluid, lips sewn tightly shut, long eyelashes poking from the swollen flesh like a shrunken head's. As I turned away, I thought a sarcastic voice spoke softly in my ear: 'Why do the sweetest flowers wither and fall from the stem?' But no-one was there.

The Mass was dreadful, tweedling organ music and platitudes about how God's will benefits us even when we cannot understand it. I wondered how Henry and Leonetta Stubbs were supposed to have benefited from their small son's death. The mourners were required to rise and sit back down seemingly hundreds of times, and since I wasn't raised Catholic, I was always a beat behind. Several rows ahead, a handsome young man seemed to be having as much trouble as I. He looked familiar, and eventually I recognised him as a young chef who had won a James Beard award a few years earlier. I am ashamed to admit that I spent the remainder of the Mass entertaining myself with memories of his fresh sardines in Galliano-laced sweet and sour sauce.

I was on my way out when Leonetta Stubbs approached me. 'Dr Brite, thank you so much for coming.'

'Not at all,' I said awkwardly.

'I hoped you would. I wanted to give you this – for taking care of Matthew.'

She pressed a piece of folded manila paper into my hand. I unfolded it and saw a child's crayon drawing. It was crude, but I could make out the figure of a woman in front of a house and some children nearby. Below it, in an adult's handwriting, were written the words: 'Darla! Tommy! Get in here before I knock you upside the head!'

'He told me what to write,' said Leonetta, 'and I wrote it for him. I suppose you could call it a cartoon, couldn't you?'

'Yes indeed,' I said as gooseflesh rippled up my arms. 'What does it mean?'

'Well, I told you that my husband doesn't make a great deal of money, and I'm afraid we live in a rather … *low-quality* neighbourhood. One day the woman next door was screaming at her children to come in before it started to rain. For some reason this struck Matthew as hilarious – I suppose he liked the idea of her being so concerned for their welfare that she'd threaten them with a beating. For such a young child, he had a very well-developed sense of irony.'

'I can see that.' I folded the drawing and slipped it into my pocket. 'Thank you, Mrs Stubbs. Take care of yourself.'

As I climbed into my car, I began to talk out loud. 'Yes, absolutely, a very well-developed sense of irony. Leaving your story in a place where no-one can find it until you're dead and autopsied. Or maybe you couldn't help it; maybe you were just made that way. But you must have done many drawings. What caused your mother to give me that particular one? Did you make her do it? And what am I supposed to do with your damn story anyway? What did you mean, keep it safe for you? Am I supposed to transcribe it? Publish it? Burn it? What? Why do I have to be responsible for everything?'

If Seymour were here, I could have asked him whether I might be going mad, but he was gone. I had no sense of perspective any more, nothing to measure myself against. I turned off Esplanade onto Broad Street and headed for the morgue, where a small boy's heart lay dreaming in formalin. I wondered if I would be able to read it.

Mannequins
Mark Samuels

Your eyes did see my unformed substance.
– From Psalm 139

The office tower had long fascinated me. The building dominated the skyline in the Euston area of London and consisted of 27 floors with an exterior of green, dark glass. I would gaze at this structure from the window of Barlow and Barlow Associates, the architectural firm at which I had been employed for the past five years. During this period of time, I had observed a process of gradual abandonment taking place, in which company after company deserted the edifice. Commercial success seemed to elude any business located there. An increasing number of its windows stayed dark at night. From what information I could gather, those working within its confines complained of a general malaise and progressive worsening of staff morale. I learnt that various health and safety checks were made in order to try and determine the nature of the problem, but that these proved inconclusive. There were rumours about the air-conditioning carrying some form of Legionnaires' disease, but extensive tests showed no trace of its presence. Blame was officially attached to a psychosomatic tendency that indiscriminately affected all those who worked in the tower. This conclusion satisfied no-one and was not favoured as the reason for the nebulous degeneration amongst the staff and management, with both sides preferring to cling tenaciously to their own theories as to the true cause of the problem.

Finally, I saw that the last of the companies had seemingly relocated and the single floor that had been lit during the hours of darkness now possessed windows as black and as much a part of the night as the others. In my mind's eye I saw the building's abandoned and silent spaces, empty offices and labyrinth of chill corridors. The vacancy of the tower stood in stark contrast to the teeming metropolis surrounding it, whose streets were filled with men who swarmed like a colony of insects.

I came to believe that the structure had a profound effect upon my work. My past architectural designs, created on behalf of the firm, brought me little satisfaction. My realised projects had consisted only of nondescript homes, public utilities and an unremarkable bus depot in the north of the country. I longed for the opportunity to work on a larger scale, on some construct that could be seen for miles around; my own pinnacle amongst the others scattered across the city. It was my ambition to be the designer of another tower that might have the same stark prominence: rising high above the teeming hordes, framed only by the sky and whose very existence provoked awe. In idle moments, I would draw plans of my own proposals, and invariably their lineaments carried some recollection of the structure that was in my view for most of the day.

I told myself that it was solely for the purposes of my pet architectural project that I so badly wished to wander freely around inside the office tower. Yet perhaps it was also my desire for isolation that drew me to it.

Certainly I was conscious of its appeal becoming stronger as more and more of the windows were unlit at evening. Thus, now completely abandoned, it seemed to me a consummation of terrible beauty amidst the maddening whirl of asinine human activity. I viewed it as a vertical desert, closed off from the outside world, a region without any distractions. Whenever I thought of finally examining its interior, the prospect was combined with a sense of my being in an abandoned structure, without the trappings of human occupancy. It would be like entering a desolate cathedral and paying homage to a cryptically absent god.

A few days after the lights on that last occupied floor were extinguished I tried to gain entry to the deserted edifice. I had done my work for the day at the architects firm and tramped through the series of streets that lay between my place of employment and my destination. Even though I knew that my expedition was likely to end in failure, I felt that an attempt to gain entrance to the office tower had to be made. If I encountered a night watchman patrolling outside, I hoped that I might even be able to bribe him into allowing me access to the interior of the building.

As I drew near to that gigantic monolith, it gradually blotted out much of the night sky. Up close, I was forced to accept the fact that gaining entry was next to impossible. The foyer had been boarded over and padlocked and the first two floors were protected by corrugated iron sheets. Looking up again at the darkened windows beyond these iron sheets, I fancied that I saw briefly a pale white face at one of them. But the sight was momentary and I told myself that it must have been only an illusion. The whole building was almost certainly deserted, and there was no reason for anyone to be in there.

For a time, I wandered aimlessly around the building's perimeter and across the abandoned square of concrete loggias and unused parking facilities in which it stood. In the end, however, I gave up on my hopeless task and made my way home to my apartment on the other side of the city.

For weeks thereafter, I would think of the edifice during the day, while at night I would dream of treading those lost corridors and empty offices, canteens, stairways, storage rooms and bathrooms. During my lunch hours at the company where I worked, I would make studies of the tower, charting its angles and lines in great detail. My fascination with it made my colleagues curious, and some of them even asked to view the structure through my field glasses. These I had purchased so that I could examine it in more detail from a distance. I felt resentment at any interest my fellow workers displayed, and believed that only I alone could truly appreciate the splendid starkness of its design and the desolation that it housed within.

Doubtless this behaviour added to my already strange reputation.

Those who knew me had long regarded me with a certain suspicion. This attitude seemed to stem primarily from knowledge of the amnesia that had afflicted me five years earlier.

***

They found me wandering aimlessly in the streets of the city, unable to tell anyone who I was or whence I came. Personal memories of my past life did not return and my new identity was constructed piecemeal from then on. Consequently, I felt like a character that disappeared after the first act of a play, only to re-emerge in the second act of an entirely different play. For the first year after my amnesia, I was an object of unwelcome attention by the police, for it was obvious that my features had been radically changed. Evidence of plastic surgery was apparent from the scars I bore. However, my blank fingerprints denied the authorities the means of linking me to any criminal or suspect whose details they had on file. DNA tests were maddeningly inconsistent. It appeared that I had been a victim of some assault or accident, for both my hair and teeth were absent and I was forced to resort to artificial substitutes. Even dental records were useless in helping to establish my former identity.

Eventually the police had to concede that there were insufficient grounds for keeping me under surveillance. It was then that I began to try and start my life all over again. Every job vacancy for which I had applied had been with firms of architects, and I felt an unaccountable compulsion to take up this type of employment. After months of fruitless interviews, Barlow and Barlow Associates agreed to take me on as a trainee for a trial period, on a very low rate of pay. However, it was soon apparent that I was already familiar with the requirements of the position. Indeed, as I worked, a feeling of déjà vu was my almost constant companion, and specialised knowledge that I was not aware of possessing came back to me. Consequently, I rose through the firm's ranks with great rapidity and was soon entrusted with senior projects, though their very limited scope gave me no real sense of satisfaction. Barlow and Barlow realised that they had gained an employee whose abilities were of a high order and yet who was without the usual architectural qualifications that accompany them.

***

One afternoon, whilst I was making my way back from a café where I had purchased a sandwich for my lunch, I was handed a flyer. I had just turned a busy corner close to the local underground station, and from amongst the crowd of people an individual had stepped forward and thrust a piece of paper into my hand. I had taken it automatically. But when I glanced at it, I was astonished to find that it was an advertising leaflet with the name 'Eleazer Golmi' printed in bold letters across the top. It was a name of great interest to me, no less than the name of a man I considered a genius. I looked back over my shoulder to try and locate the man who was handing out these flyers, but he was lost in the crowd.

I turned back towards the direction from which I'd just come, pushing past the people in my way, until I was at the spot where the flyer had been handed to me, just outside the station. I could see no-one handing out leaflets. There was a homeless man wrapped in a blanket asking for spare change, a woman giving away free lifestyle magazines, but no sign of my quarry. Then, out of the corner of my eye, I caught sight of a stiff-backed person walking awkwardly towards the ticket barriers in the station, and he half-turned to regard me from behind dark glasses. Our gazes met and, though I could make out nothing of his shielded eyes, I was struck by the strangeness of his skin, which possessed an almost plastic sheen.

Once I was back in my office, I examined the flyer more closely. It was an invitation to an art installation that, it suggested, had long been housed on the uppermost floors of the tower, and whose existence I had not suspected. This installation, conceived by the artist Eleazer Golmi, had apparently been exhibited there for an indefinite period. It was entitled *Mannequins in Aspects of Terror*, and the leaflet claimed that the participant would enjoy an audio and visual art-experience of 'infinite claustrophobia.' Golmi's output was well known to me, though not in the context of the art world. He had also been the architect that had been responsible for the very building in which this installation was housed.

Due to my interest in his structure, I had tried on several occasions to track down Golmi and express my appreciation for his designs, but had been advised that he no longer worked in the profession and had, effectively, 'gone underground' after a severe personal crisis ten years earlier. Those persons I spoke to regarding Golmi had said that some sort of nervous breakdown was to blame for his disappearance. But now it seemed that he had returned and completely reinvented himself as a conceptual artist.

The flyer told me that the installation had been temporarily closed for new additions to be incorporated into the work, but that it was due to reopen on the last day of the following week. Admission was on the door, with no prior booking required.

***

When I arrived at the office tower on the designated night, I found that the padlocks had been removed, the boards covering its windows had been taken away and the foyer had been opened. The installation was advertised by means of a hastily erected poster on a small hoarding next to the entrance. This poster had a gaudy, yellow background and black lettering in a gothic script. At its centre was a grainy photograph of Golmi. He was in his fifties, with Brylcreemed grey hair. He possessed a high forehead and dark eyes. One of them, the right, seemed considerably larger than the other, giving him a strange, almost lop-sided appearance. Even aside from this outlandish feature, the face in the photograph was bizarre. Its expression had that rigid look that was common in Daguerreotypes from the mid 19th Century, where the subject had to be perfectly still for four or five minutes due to the time the camera shutter had to be open for the exposure.

I again gazed up at the monolith whose presence signified the vacancy in which I longed to immerse myself. The fact that Golmi had designed the very building that he had chosen as the backdrop to his art installation offered the possibility that he, too, had realised the spectral potential of the tower. Perhaps he was also one of those who relished desolate spaces in the teeming metropolis. Might this not be indicated by the fact that he had kept his installation intact as the edifice became utterly deserted? I wondered if it were the case that some dim intimation had come to him during his architect days as to the final destiny of his project: to house his own personal nightmare, to create a zone where human beings could not live. Could the blueprint of elaborate angles and lines that went to make up the structure have been designed to cause the very malaise from which those that worked there had suffered? Might not the mannequins in his latest project, the art installation, be metaphors for those assimilated within the interior vacuum of the building? I thought of plastic imitations of the human body: unthinking, blank; form without content, eyes that stare but do not see, hands that reach but do not grasp, mouths shaped for noise but unable to speak.

I entered the foyer and made my way to an unmanned desk with a sign declaring that the installation began on floor 25 and that payment was to be made after the 'art-experience.' Next to the sign was a list of entry times. I saw by my watch that the next vacant slot was in some 20 minutes. The last visitor had signed the register five minutes earlier and marked the entry time clearly. It seemed that admittance was staggered to ensure that each visitor was sufficiently isolated.

At the time allocated, I accordingly signed in my name in the register, then wandered over to one of several lifts. A sign indicated that this only was to be used in order to visit the art installation, the others being out of order. I watched the numbers on the indicator board above the entrance flash from 25 downwards as the lift descended. While I waited, I looked over at the blank spaces where once there had been brass plaques advertising the companies that had traded in the tower.

When the lift arrived, I opened the outer door and then pulled back the inner trellis door that separated me from the panelled wooden cage within. The interior was not large, having a capacity for a maximum of four persons. The back wall was comprised of a full-length mirror. Gazing into it, I was somewhat startled by my anxious-looking appearance. My eyes seemed to stare wildly from behind my glasses and my cheeks were pale and drawn with tension. The business suit that I was obliged to wear to work seemed apt, as did the briefcase I carried, since I had come directly from my office and had not had the opportunity to change my clothes.

I still harboured unease at the idea of the sterility and emptiness of the edifice being compromised by its now housing an art installation. I hoped that my only consolation would not lie simply in the fact that it alone would provide the access that I craved to the building itself. At worst, I thought that I might be able to bypass the installation and explore those regions unaffected by it. Doubtless it was this internal conflict that had given rise to the feeling of tension that welled up inside me.

The cage rumbled upward through the lift shaft, and floor after floor passed me by before I reached the twenty-fifth, where the installation began. I pulled back the trellis door, opened the outer one and entered a long, deserted corridor that was dimly lit and silent. The floor was covered in tiled green linoleum. It curled upwards with old age where it met the walls. In certain places it had come away altogether, revealing the stained concrete underneath. I also saw holes in the false ceiling, where panels of polystyrene had fallen down. Teeming cables and wires spilled out of these gaps. There was an opening to my left and, impelled by sheer curiosity, I went through it into an abandoned bathroom that was thick with dust. The cubicle doors hung ajar and the toilet bowls were broken, with fragments of porcelain scattered everywhere. I left and went back to the corridor, where I saw a notice, indicating the direction I was to follow. I turned right. Up until this point, I could discern no evidence of the art installation, for this new corridor seemed to be nearly identical to the first one. I was, however, beginning to feel a sense of emptiness creep over me, deadening my spirits, and replacing the tension I'd previously felt. The isolation was complete. I felt utterly alone, and as I walked through the confines of this artificial void, its atmosphere of neglect and decay steadily numbed my mind.

And then, as if from a great distance, I believed that I heard a sound, much like the white noise found on frequencies between radio stations. It grew no louder as I proceeded, and I could not detect its source, though I suspected that it must have been piped through concealed speakers. Looking through the windows to my left, I saw the vast panorama of the city below, its glittering sodium-orange lights appearing to be so very far removed from this enclave of desolation. Within the building, it was eternal twilight, grey and shadowy.

There was a large office to my right and I entered into it. The room was completely empty and there were marks on the thin carpet where tables, chairs and filing cabinets must have once stood. I moved on. By now, it was only through a conscious effort that I could detect the continuous hiss of background static, familiarity having rendered it subliminal. But when I made the effort, I realised that it served as no distraction, but was like whispering in a void, unintelligible yet charged with an awful significance, some cryptic nothingness behind surface reality. I saw another notice as I passed along the next corridor. It was a ragged thing, with letters scrawled as if in a child's handwriting, and made of cardboard. Written upon it were the words: *Mannequins in Aspects of Terror.*

Then I encountered the first of the mannequins. In the twilight of that corridor, and from a distance, I initially thought that it was an attendant, but the object's perfect stillness suggested otherwise.

As I drew nearer to the mannequin, I noticed that the background hiss contained a new element. This change in its nature alerted me again to its presence. There were definite words amongst the static, though broken and garbled, like speech distorted by poor radio reception. I could not make out the words, but the voice seemed to speak as if in terrible pain, as if it were incoherent with that pain. I thought that one of the words might be 'alive' croaked out over and over again, but could not be sure. I had drawn close enough to see the face of the mannequin. The artist had indeed wrought a thing of terror. Its face was rigid and frozen in stark panic, as if it was confronted by an unbearably horrific sight. The arms were raised, warding off some approaching menace. As I stared at the dummy, I felt contaminated by its aspect, and could not help imagining that my own features were mimicking its expression. And I thought of that gaping, lifeless mouth actually forming the broken words that mingled with the low, background noise of the static, driving my mind towards the infinite moment of fear in which the mannequin itself had been frozen.

This noise began to fade as I continued to walk along the length of the corridor, and was gradually replaced by another sound, like that of people muttering lowly to each other whilst engaged in office work in some part of the building very close by. The voices were just audible, and I could not shake off the feeling that those speaking were conscious of my presence and even discussing my imminent arrival, even though the idea was patently absurd.

I even began to mutter to myself involuntarily, and the sound of my own voice offered no comfort, for its low and enfeebled tone only mimicked that of those ahead.

At the next turning was a room that appeared, at first glance, to be still in use, for it was brightly lit, unlike the rest of the twenty-fifth floor. I paused for a moment, taken in by the illusion, until I perceived that the figures therein were absolutely motionless. I entered and had the unsettling idea that they had stopped their activities once I had first caught sight of them. I told myself that a hidden motion sensor had detected me and must have simply turned off a tape recording that was part of the installation, but the irrational part of my mind still insisted that I was being observed and, even worse, possibly *controlled* in some indefinable fashion.

Four mannequins occupied this office, all of which, except one, were hunched in front of dead computer screens. Their hands were at the keyboards, as if they had just been interrupted in the act of typing. The dummies were dressed in pinstriped business suits that showed signs of old age and wear. The elbows and cuffs of their jackets were frayed, with patches of ugly discoloration in the fabric. The mannequins seemed to be smiling. But as I drew closer for a better look at them, I saw that those smiles were not pleasant, but were crafted so as to resemble the grins of lunatics, without humour or warmth.

The only dummy standing had been clad in one of the same shoddy suits as the others, but its expression was entirely different. The thing's eyes bulged and its mouth was open in a grimace of agony much wider than any possible in a mouth of flesh and bone, a grimace that reached literally across the whole width of its plastic face. Its body was twisted over to one side as if in contorted agony. This thing of profound deformity seemed to have been designed wholly in order to convey repellence to its observer.

When I had left the place and carried on walking along the corridor outside, the sounds of activity started up again behind me, furtively at first, but with increasing boldness as each step that I took drew me further away from the source. I could not help looking back as I moved away, for I had an irrational dread that the standing mannequin would start into spasmodic life and come after me. I could not rid my mind of the image.

***

This whole experience had not been quite what I had anticipated. The mannequins did not seem to symbolise the void that I had imagined. They seemed rather to stand for some greater abyss that lay beyond it, a wasteland, not where thoughts die away, but where they are endlessly repeated, where madness is continuous and without cessation.

I had by this time reached the stairwell up to the next floor, and a notice indicated that I was to ascend. The walls here were in a state of advanced decay, being riddled with cracks and spaces where the sepia paint had flaked off. A draught of air coming from above bore with it the unmistakable odour of mould. The noise of movement ahead became louder, and I could hardly bring myself to make the climb up the stairwell. The echoes filtered through a door directly at the top, and now that the sound was clearer, I detected what I thought were more voices. These were not like the low mutterings that I had heard previously. They were much clearer and made no attempt at concealment. They filled me with dread. These voices possessed a breathless and hollow quality, as if the unintelligible words they uttered were formed by some imperfect replica of the human model, speaking in accents that betrayed their attempt at imitation. I thought of lips not designed for speech, croaking out anguished words, trying, vainly, to communicate but hampered by their own rigidity.

I stood there on the stairwell for what seemed like hours. Whether it was the awful atmosphere that worked on my brain or whether the sound was real I couldn't tell, but I heard from the floor below awkward footsteps coming closer. Whatever it was seemed to stagger forward, dragging its limbs awkwardly like a drunk. The sound made me panic, and I raced towards the door ahead, bolting through it, with no other thought save flight.

When I was through the door, the sound of the broken voices ceased. I stood shaking with my back to it, listening for signs of movement. There was none. And I wondered, if I dared open the door again, would I find a form slumped on the stairs, a form horribly familiar, now again inanimate, or would a dummy be standing there with a look of triumph, its impossibly wide mouth framed in a grimace that reached from ear to ear and with arms outstretched as if to clutch me in a deathly embrace? Yet I heard nothing further and so I pressed on, knowing that I could not bear to retrace my steps.

Although all was now quiet, the smell of the mould was overpowering. It grew everywhere in this new corridor. There were great patches of it on bare walls and even underfoot on the worn linoleum. A notice told me to bear left, and doing so I found myself in another abandoned office. On a table were several duplicate sheets of paper, filled with handwritten words. The strip lighting here was as poor as elsewhere in the building, and this, coupled with the awkward script, made the writing difficult to decipher. But I carried the papers to the dusty window, where the faint illumination from outside made reading a little easier. The manuscript was some sort of manifesto, or statement, written by the artist Golmi:

Mannequins in Aspects of Terror: An Art Installation by Eleazer Golmi

Many have ruminated on the attraction of horror in art and in literature, and have drawn erroneous conclusions. The art of false horror seeks not to engender actual fear, but to distance those experiencing it and allow them a pleasurable frisson – the sensation that one might approach without arrival. But this art installation is an immersion into terror. It is designed to generate a situation in which the individual is subject to that terror and participates directly in it. In this installation, one does not play a character, as does an actor in a play: one *is* that character. Nor must the artist himself be exempt from this necessary immersion. In order for the work of art to be authentic, he also must become a component of it. He must feel the terror that he creates.

Remember that there is always an end to suffering in life: pain, disease and madness lead either to recovery or to extinction, but such is not necessarily the case in art. In art, a moment of suffering may be fixed for all eternity.

Imagine, if you will, simulacra whose existence is such a state. This is the purpose of my installation. The desolate spaces are my own enclosed universe of terror. And the mannequins are my children, playing in the wilderness of torment, in the misery of one moment of supreme terror. And I, too, play with them; having been allowed this privilege by deciphering the secret of the alphabet of the 221 gates.

The greatest fear of which I can conceive is not that of murder or torture or any of the outrages that man inflicts upon his fellow man. The greatest fear is the prolongation of life indefinitely, to a point where all thoughts are endlessly revisited, where every memory loses its meaning by repetition, where concepts finally blend into one: consciousness doomed to immortality – a mind filled with the nightmare of its own being, a mind that is dying in perpetuity without final release.

Our flesh and blood perish, and with them perishes the mind. But imagine a mind in a body that cannot die: a body of plastic and paint carefully crafted in an aspect of pain, terror, disease, madness or decay. The form mirrors the inner torment. And then further imagine what it might be like to be a mind imprisoned forever within that artificial body. What distinction is there between mind and matter? Imprisoned within a mannequin in an aspect of terror, the two become one.

The mind, now riddled with the continuous agony of its new body, built expressly for suffering, believes it to be the only existence it has ever known. Plastic and paint seem more real than flesh and blood. Who then is to say which of them is artificial? And should these new bodies start into motion, should those glass eyes turn in their sockets, who then would deny their occupants the right to welcome visitors to this cryptic universe of terror I have wrought? To welcome them in the only way they know how, so that the same visitors might also participate in their haunted cavalcade throughout all eternity? Let me then conclude by thanking you for choosing to experience my installation, for choosing to contribute to my pretty little vision, where henceforth you will see only through my eyes.

YHVH Elohim Met.

As I finished reading those words, I was overwhelmed by the sensation that I was trapped in another man's nightmare. I felt as if I no longer possessed an independent existence and that, like the dummies I had encountered, I was some mental construction wrought by Eleazer Golmi. The idea was ridiculous of course. I had not been dreamed into existence. And yet in this 'enclosed universe of terror' as he termed it, the identity I had forged over the past five years seemed under assault. What was I, after all, but a man with no past, an amnesiac whose own life had been partially obliterated by an unknown accident?

I left the room feeling shaken and drained and made my way again along the grimy corridor covered with mould. All the doors that I passed were locked, although many had glass panels beyond which I could see more of the mannequins. Some had their faces turned to the walls and were set in crouching positions, whilst others were curled up in a ball on the concrete floor, surrounded by debris. There was one dummy, however, that had been positioned in front of one of the windows in the doors. It was more horrifying than any I had seen thus far.

The dummy's face, if such a corroded and incomplete thing could be called a face, was close to the glass panel. Its head was thrown back and the eyes had been rolled up in their sockets. All that remained of its artificial hair were a few charred strands hanging from a mutilated scalp. The paint covering that terrifying visage had been clawed away and the plastic beneath was scarred and pitted as if burnt by acid. Yet in what remained of its features, still it was possible to recognise a hint of awareness of the creative destruction that the artist had exercised upon it. This awareness, frozen in time, was that it had been shaped to suffer and that it existed for no other purpose. That I knew this to be the case was not simply a matter of seeing. It was more a chilling feeling of *kinship* with the object. The longer I was in its presence, the more this feeling gained upon me. And a horrible idea came to me that my own flesh was merely a temporary reprieve, an interlude between escape and recapture.

I finally turned away in dismay. But I had come far and reasoned that I had almost reached the end of this 'art installation'. I turned left into a further corridor. At the far end there was a handwritten sign reading 'Exit'.

There was no way to go but forward in order to end the experience. As I began to walk towards a set of double doors where the passageway terminated, I felt stiffness in my limbs, like the onset of cramp, and my movements became awkward. I told myself that it was only exhaustion that slowed me down, that the horrible sensations I was experiencing were a consequence of shock. At the same time, I was aware that the command I had over my movements seemed to slip away, as if I were a mere automaton. Even my gaze seemed to be controlled by another will.

By the time I reached the end of the corridor, the pain I suffered in my limbs was unbearable. I pushed open the doors, drawn forward as if by invisible strings, and beyond found a large room that had once served as a canteen. The tables and plastic chairs were still there, though some were broken and others had been tipped over. Rubbish, mostly polystyrene cups and empty cartons, was strewn all around the canteen's linoleum floor, and the tiled walls were smeared with grease. Scattered amongst all this debris were dozens and dozens of mannequin parts. There were no doors leading off this room, only windows letting in a sickly sodium glow cast by the city lights outside.

The dummies here had been torn to pieces. There were heads, torsos and limbs scattered around. It seemed that someone had crafted these things and then deliberately wrecked them. My own agony was so awful that I could hardly register the enormity of the scene before me. Despite having no control over my motion, or gaze, I was still directed to walk amongst those last horrors.

The closest mannequin to me had the appearance of the victim of a car crash. Its face and trunk had been smashed in and one of its arms was ripped away. Only the eyes were whole, the glass eyes, and peering into them I knew, with awful clarity, that consciousness was present in what remained. There was a mind imprisoned in this broken form that was experiencing an agony that no living thing could bear, that flesh and blood could not possibly tolerate. The artist, the maker of these mannequins, had reached beyond the boundaries of pain and terror in his work, had taken them to an extreme that no human form was designed to experience. The very word agony could not begin to describe their state: to be endlessly dying and never to be released.

But I moved on, screaming soundlessly in my mind, as my stiff limbs were willed into motion by another mind, each step being the action of that which was not made to move. And all around me were those dismembered dummies in their eternal death throes, each separate part riddled with pain. As my legs jerked forwards, one of my feet caught the arm of a mannequin, sending it clattering across the floor.

My eyes involuntarily rolled back in their sockets. I saw the reflected lights shifting and changing on the ceiling as my knees buckled under me, and with a clatter my body slumped forward to the floor amongst the mounds of mutilated plastic remains.

I heard the sound of footsteps approaching and then felt myself being turned over onto my back. Looming above me was a man whose skin seemed more like plastic than flesh. His right eye was much larger than his left, and this gave his features a lop-sided appearance. He made a low, grinding noise like broken machine gears, trying to gain control of a mouth that should not be able to utter sounds. Although the words were indistinct, he seemed to be saying, '*Good to have you back.*'

He delved into a leather tool-bag that he carried with him, drew out a blowtorch and ignited the hissing gas flow. The blue jet of flame glittered in his dead, cold eyes. And I knew that the agony that I had experienced up to now was only a foretaste of that eternal agony to come once the artist Golmi set to work on my helpless, immobile body.

Jewels In The Dust
Peter Crowther

Dear, beauteous death! the jewel of the just,
Shining nowhere but in the dark;
What mysteries do lie beyond thy dust,
Could man outlook that mark!
– From *Silex Scintillans: 'They are all gone'*
Henry Vaughan (1622-1695)

Abigail Rutherford swept into the room in a blaze of maroon cotton
and a myriad wafts of silk scarves whose designs dwarfed even the
ambitious creations of Jackson Pollock – comparatively pedestrian
efforts as far as Abigail would have it – and whose colours would have
rivalled even Joseph's fabled coat.

'Today's the day!' she announced with a bravura wave of an arm
that was skinny and wattled, the fingers of the hand at the end slender
enough to pick locks, pushing the sweet scent of lavender before her
like a summer tide.

Tommy looked up from the comic book spread out between his
elbows on the floor, the gaudily-coloured pages a mystery of shape
and form and secret actions in night-time cities, strangely-garbed and
muscular heroes braving death – and worse! – as they swung between
concrete towers and over the glittering streets far, far below. 'Really?'
he asked, pulling himself to a kneeling position.

'Really!' Abigail confirmed.

'Yay!' said Tommy.

He leapt to his feet and did a little skip and jump around the comic book.

'Careful,' Marianne Rutherford cautioned her son, with a big smile. 'You'll be wanting another copy of that magazine if you scuff the pages.'

She turned to her mother-in-law and tilted her head to one side as she always did when she was offering a change of mind. 'Are you sure, Abby? I mean, *really* sure that today's the day? It's just Saturday – a fine May Saturday I grant you, but just another Saturday.'

Abigail did a twirl and burst into a fit of coughing, which soon spread into laughter.

'As sure. As I'll. Ever be,' she said, pausing for breath between each point. She leaned against the wall, smiling at her grandson with thin lips that carried a swipe of lipstick, cheeks that bore the trace of hastily-applied, pink-coloured powder, and eyes that carried the sky in them, complete with cotton-candy clouds.

'And it's not. Just another. Saturday. It's Derby Day.'

'Derby Day?'

'Derby Day!' young Tommy exclaimed, his face a glade of smiles.

'That's right,' Abigail said, her voice not quite able to match the volume of her grandson's. 'So, scoot. Young fella,' she added, ignoring the quizzical look on her daughter-in-law's face. She clapped her hands as though shooing errant cats busy chewing the plants in her beloved garden, the three rings – engagement, wedding and eternity – giving out the faintest *clink* before settling once more.

'Make haste!' she urged.

'Bring sodas. Bring potato chips,' she advised.

'Run and jump. And greet the day!' she instructed.

Tommy disappeared in a flash, the swinging to and fro of the room door on a steadily decreasing fulcrum the only sign that he had ever been there at all. That and the sound of small feet pounding up the stairs and a small voice calling out to the gods of childhood and eternal summer.

Marianne looked across at the window. It was still early outside – early in big-wide-world terms, where activities among the wind-blown fields and hedgerows commenced long before they did inside the house. Everything was new out there, as though each thing – every glimmering ray of sunlight and every tiny drop of dew – were a one-off, a never-to-be-repeated, infinitesimally small theatrical performance. New and only ever *now*.

Inside the house, it was different. Here, within the labyrinth of walls and windows that was the home they all shared, everything was familiar: radio news shows that forever reminded listeners of the time and told them what the weather was going to be like, and the sound of bacon frying and Mister Coffee percolating, each mingling with calls for missing neckties, socks and comic books, and all of them forever underpinned by the soft, susurrant hum put out by the old amalgam of wooden joists and nailed-on clapboard stretching itself to meet the onslaught of another day. Every one of them a repeat performance. Like scenes on the VCR, rewound and re-played forever without deviation.

Time stolen rather than spent.

Time waiting to die.

***

To Marianne Rutherford, the world outside looked momentarily immense, unpredictable and somehow achingly wonderful, its sound signatures harder to place, complex rhythms and discordant refrains.

A haven.

A release.

An escape.

Marianne turned around and mentally shook off the feeling of cramp unfolding in her stomach as she took in the full creative excess of Abigail's outfit.

'That's quite a combination,' she said, a mischievous grin on her face as she stood up and planted a kiss on her mother-in-law's cheek. 'One thing's for sure: we're not likely to lose you.' She took hold of Abigail's shoulders and held her at arms' length. 'My oh my, don't you look the bee's knees!'

Abigail shuddered, her breath coming hoarse and sounding

wheezing, deep down inside her body.

'The bees' knees. And the cat's PJs.' She returned the smile and affected a small slap on Marianne's arm. 'Got to. Look my. Best. On Derby Day,' she said between gulps of air. 'For Jack.'

Marianne fought off the frown that threatened to engulf her face. 'Right,' she said. 'For Jack. On Derby Day.'

Marianne felt Abigail's bony shoulders stiffen as she turned her back around again, immediately cursing herself when she saw Abby wince and try to cover it up.

In truth, the dress hung awkwardly from Abigail's scrawny frame. It fell all the way to her ankles – ankles puffed up with water from the steroids. Marianne recalled those previous occasions when the dress had come out – 'Red letter days,' was how Abby referred to them, by virtue of the fact that the dress had been the last present from her beloved Jack – and how, in those suddenly seemingly distant days of another life, the dress had extended only to just below Abigail's knees. Then the garment itself had seemed to be alive and proud, like a peacock unfurling its tail-feathers: now it looked equally as tired and spent as its owner.

'Well,' she said, backing Abby gently to a chair, 'I think you look wonderful, and I'm sure Bill is going to think so, too.'

Bill came into the room with a big grin on his face. To a degree, it managed to cover the darkness below his eyes. 'You gonna make some sandwiches, honey? It's the Big Day.'

Marianne gave her husband a mock salute. 'Yeah, Mom already told us. Derby Day,' she said, with just the slightest of upwards movements of her eyebrows.

***

There had been so many Big Days this past seven or eight months, as the weeks had fallen from the calendar at almost the same rate as the pounds had fallen from Abigail Rutherford's once-ample frame.

Thanksgiving had been the first one, when Abigail had spent the full day out in the garden, taking in the fall air as she waited to be called to join her beloved Jack. But that night, as they'd all sat down to one of Marianne's turkey dinners, the table resplendent with sweet potatoes and corn cobs, sausages rolled in strips of bacon, bowls of peas with knobs of butter melting over them like flower-heads, Abigail had announced that she didn't think today was going to be the Big Day after all. Patting her son's arm, she'd said, 'But I'm guessing it'll be soon,' her sentences full and flowing, before the tumour had eventually taken away her breath.

Christmas Eve and Christmas Day had followed, with New Year's Eve and New Year's Day hot behind them. And January had seen Martin Luther King's birthday and even Martin Luther King Junior Day … but still Abigail had made it through to midnight, her carefully-chosen clothes returned to the wardrobe in the small room she occupied in her son's house.

Groundhog Day had come and gone, and then Lincoln's Birthday and Valentine's Day – a particularly fitting occasion for her and Jack to be reunited, Abigail had thought. By then, the chemo had taken a toll, and she was increasingly tired. Then Presidents' Day, and Washington's Birthday – 'All of them great men,' Abigail had proclaimed to Bill, 'just like your father. And I reckon that today. Will definitely be. The day he calls for me to join him.'

But it hadn't been. Nor had the day that Daylight Savings began – 'That's because. We lost an hour,' Abigail had explained as Bill and Marianne had tucked her up in her bed, the shadows playing around the walls like mischievous elves. 'Your dad … he needs. The full 24 hours. To get me.'

And snuggling down beneath the sheets, she'd added, 'But it'll be. Soon. Secretaries Day. I was a secretary when your dad met me.' And she'd closed her eyes and smiled at the memory. 'My, but he was handsome. Still is, for that matter.'

By that point, the cancer had spread throughout her body. It was just a matter of time. But Secretaries Day had turned out not to be the Big Day, though it had been the day that the breathing apparatus was delivered to the house. Taking her first swig from the oxygen tank, Abigail had winked knowingly at Bill and Marianne. 'See, I told you it was going to be a big day today,' she'd confided in them. 'Just not *the*

Big Day. But it'll be soon. You mark my words. Maybe it'll be Mother's Day.'

***

Today, the first Saturday in May, Mother's Day was still more than a week away. But Abigail seemed convinced. Convinced because it was Derby Day.

'Sandwiches coming right up,' Marianne said, affecting a stiff-handed salute as she opened the icebox. She stared at the shelves of packages and jars, cold cuts, butter cartons and fruit juice bottles, individually wrapped cheeses from the deli on Sycamore, tubs of yoghurt, taramasalata and hummus, small hillocks of salad greens, cucumber and tomatoes. 'What'll it be, oh great one?'

'Everything!' Bill said. 'What say you, Mom?'

Abigail chuckled appreciatively. 'Sure ... let's have everything. Let's have –' She took a deep breath and shuddered. 'Let's have sandwiches fit ... for a king and his queen,' she said, her words laboured, her hand clenched but for the index finger pointing upwards and circling.

'Fit for placing. Before. A visiting. Dignitary. From far-off. Alpha Centauri. Come here to spend. The afternoon.' She chuckled and added, 'And maybe get a little tan.'

Marianne laughed appreciatively.

'Can we have peanut butter?' Tommy asked in a nasal whine as he reappeared laden with more examples of four-colour comic book wonder. 'And that tart jelly stuff?'

'Tart jelly stuff?' Abigail said, screwing up her face. 'Sounds yucky!'

'He means the boysenberry,' Marianne said as she transferred more of the icebox onto the breakfast counter. 'He likes it spread with peanut butter and slices of banana.'

'Ugh! Gross!' Abigail said, rolling her eyes around and around at Tommy. 'Who'd be. Nine years old!'

Bill loaded water into the kettle and placed it on the electric hob. 'Let's have coffee, too. Real stuff, not the instant.'

'And make it leaded,' Abigail added. 'None of that decaf. Not today. If I pee myself. Then at least. It'll keep me cool.'

'Mom!' Marianne said in time with Tommy's sniggers. She was cutting through cheese-topped breadcakes, setting them all out across the counter, tops next to bottoms. 'I can see where we're heading with this,' she said. 'It's Decadent Day.'

Tommy frowned as he watched his mother work. 'I thought it was Derby Day,' he said, to no-one in particular.

'It sure is, son,' Bill said, and he ruffled his son's hair. 'What your mom means is that it's both of them. Two days all rolled up in one.'

'So what's a deck-a-dent day?'

'Dec-a-dent day.' Abigail said before spelling it out and then repeating it as though it were a mantra. She slumped tiredly onto a stool and took a deep breath. 'It's a day when. We don't let anything matter, Tommy. A day when. None of the normal rules. Apply.'

'I'm not sure that's a good idea, Mom: we have to have –'

Abigail nodded. 'Your father's right, Tommy. We have to have. Rules. Or the world … well. It just wouldn't. Hang together.' She smiled gently at Tommy's father and then quickly looked away. 'Everything would just fly off. In confusion. Like … *whooosh*!' She swept her arms up in the air to either side, and then collapsed forward coughing.

As his father took hold of her and gently patted her back, Tommy said, 'You mean like gravity?'

'That's right,' Bill said softly between *shh* and *there* and *okay now* sounds as he continued to pat and rub. 'Like gravity.' Eventually the coughing subsided.

'You okay, Gran?' Tommy had thought about it before even asking. Maybe if she *wasn't* okay they wouldn't even leave the house. And he so wanted to go out and picnic, feel the grass springing up beneath his sneakers, trying to get right inside with his toes. It had been such a long time since they'd done anything at all, what with Gran's constant coughing and that gizmo tank of air she sucked on while she was watching the game shows on TV.

As he watched her, waiting for a reply, Tommy suddenly noticed – just for the most fleeting of seconds – how thin she'd gotten; like she could get through doors when they were still closed. It looked to him as though Gran could do with a whole heap of peanut butter, banana slices and boys-and-berry jam sandwiches to build her up again, and maybe a couple of chocolate spread ones and a carton of vanilla yoghurt or strawberry and caramel mousse from the Safeway store.

'I'm as fine as wine. And as frisky. As whiskey,' came the reply, though it was a little wheezy and not altogether convincing, the memory of a voice rather than the voice itself.

Tommy hoped his father hadn't noticed. He looked around at his mother and saw she was watching him as she loaded cold meats onto buttered bread and spread that gungy brown stuff that had a fancy boy's name – Hugh Muss – and looked like his poops when he was sick and they were all runny. He saw her smile at him, a strange smile, kind of sad and yet not sad.

Marianne watched her son watching her. For just a second she thought of herself back at nine years old, tried to imagine what the world looked like through those young eyes. 'You all ready?' she said, breaking the eye lock and placing a cheesy top on a mound of lettuce, sliced ham and pickle. 'I'm gonna be done here in a few minutes and we don't want to be waiting while you get things together.'

Tommy shrugged and held out the confusion of comic books. 'I got things to read,' he said triumphantly.

'And you've brushed your teeth?'

Tommy thought for a second. What the heck did brushing his teeth matter? They were going out to eat, weren't they? He certainly didn't want all the sandwiches to taste of peppermint. Boy, parents could be a little wacky sometimes.

He nodded. 'Before,' he added with a jerk of his head. 'When I got washed up.'

'Clean shorts?'

He looked down at his shorts, saw the dangling figure of Spiderman hanging from his belt, and then noticed the stain on his left leg just below the pocket and the bulge of his Bart Simpson handkerchief. He shifted his leg slightly and lowered the comic books to cover it. It wasn't a big stain. 'Can we take the frisbee?' he said, changing the subject, and he skilfully shifted the need for an answer from his mother to his father who seemed to have stopped patting and rubbing.

'Can we, Dad?'

'Sure. We can do anything today.'

''Cos it's a deck-a-dent day, right?'

Everyone seemed to find this amusing, and all thoughts of clean shorts went off on the wind.

***

Abigail sat up front alongside Tommy's father, a place usually reserved for his mom. The fact was that Gran was the only one Tommy's dad would let up there, like she was the President's wife visiting for the day. There was a lot of huffing and puffing as Bill and Marianne helped Abigail into the seat and fastened the belt across her. There were a couple of *Sorry, Mom*s followed each time by *That's okay, son* or *That's okay, Marianne, it's just me sitting awkward*, and then she was in place, wheezing like a train or the air-conditioning pump before Bill had fixed it last spring.

Tommy slid into the back of the old Chevrolet, the familiar smell of creased and worn leather drifting up to meet him. He slid his comic books onto the shelf behind the seat, tossed the frisbee on top and pulled his cap on tight. 'We taking the roof off, Dad?'

Bill Rutherford plopped into the driver's seat and looked across at Abigail. 'How about it, Mom? You up for a little fresh air?'

Tommy's grandmother patted her son's knee. 'Let's go. The whole way. Let's take off the sides. While we're at it –' She glanced around at Tommy and did that spinning movement with her eyes. '– And let's. Let's take off the hood. And the trunk lid. Let's just strip ourselves. Strip ourselves down. To the bare essentials. What say you, Tommy?'

Tommy chuckled. 'Sounds good to me, Gran,' he said.

Marianne slid in next to Tommy and put an arm around him. 'You think we should, honey?' she said, aiming the question at Tommy's father. 'Mom's gonna get cold.'

Tommy saw his father look into the rear view mirror. It was a strange look, aimed at Tommy's mom. It said, this look, that nothing mattered today. Today, nobody was going to get cold. Today, nobody was going to get *any*thing bad.

'Sure,' Tommy's mom said, responding to that wordless glance as

309

she pulled her son close, squeezing him under his armpit, sending him into paroxysms of wonderful agony. 'We're gonna be fine and dandy back here, curled up like a couple of hibernating bears. *Woo-woo-woo!*' She squeezed him some more.

'Mom – MOM – don't – *Please* don't.'

She stopped, and Tommy immediately wished she would do it again, but Dad had started the engine and the roof was starting back on its pulley system. The early summer sky revealed itself in thin slices as the canvas roof whined backwards.

Clouds rolled.

Blue shone everywhere.

Birds flew and the air was thick with a million zillion microscopic bugs and gnats, each of them bound for distant lands – lands such as the trashcans over by the back porch, or the drainhole beneath the fall-pipes at each corner of the house. Those things must smell like chocolate syrup to those tiny things, Tommy thought, and just for a moment, he regretted the odd occasion when he had joined in with the other guys in the schoolyard, removing wings and legs from creatures that wanted nothing more than to be able to languish on a nice turd or deep into the potato peelings and coffee grounds inside a bag of garbage.

The roof reached its destination and gave out a thick grumble. Bill got out, walked to the back of the car and leaned on the canvas, first at one side and then at the other. At Tommy's mother's side, Bill leaned over and gave Marianne a kiss on the cheek. Tommy watched for a second and then looked away. He had seen something in that small affection – he had seen tears in his father's eyes. It made him feel a little anxious – the way he did when Miss Gradzsky announced a surprise math quiz and the only homework he'd done had been to catch up on what the Avengers were doing in this month's issue. The comic books!

He turned around to the back shelf and saw it was now securely covered by the folded roof. Oh well, he wouldn't need them until they got to where they were going. Which was –

'Where we going anyway?' he asked as his father fastened the seat belt and slipped the gear lever into reverse.

'Oh, that's a mighty fine point,' Bill said over his shoulder as the car drifted back out of the drive and onto the road along the front of the house. 'Where'd you think, honey?'

Marianne didn't answer right away. Tommy turned to look up at her, and he saw that she too had those same tears in her eyes. 'Well, it's got to be Mom's choice,' she said. 'It's her day, after all.'

Tommy leaned forward and stood up behind Abigail's seat. 'Where we going, Gran?'

Abigail looked across at her son and, in a soft voice, said, 'All the way. We're going. All the way. Today.'

Bill smiled and swallowed hard.

Tommy leaned forward. '*Where* we going, Gran?'

Abigail slapped her knees and breathed in deeply. 'Well, I reckon we should go down to Morgan's Meadow, down by the stream.' She shifted around so she could see Tommy's face. 'But before it gets too wide so's you can't go paddling.'

'Neat!'

Abigail closed her eyes and laughed. 'Yes, neat!'

Tommy knelt up on the seat and leaned on the folded roof as they backed out onto the road. Then, with a slight clunk of gears meshing, they were on their way. He watched the road dovetail onto itself, cars parked at the roadside shifting by and coming together as they moved further away from the house.

***

'Honey?'

'Yeah?'

'Is she asleep?'

Bill looked to his side at the crumpled-up figure. 'Yeah, I think so.'

'So's Tommy.' Marianne stroked a lick of hair from her son's forehead. 'She okay, d'you think?'

Bill shrugged. 'Right now, all we can say is she's here.'

He signalled right and turned out of town, passing the junkyard and heading for Walton Flats. 'You know,' he said, settling his arms on the steering wheel, 'I got to thinking this morning.'

'Sounds ominous.'

'No, nothing too … nothing too morbid.'

'This while you were still in bed? I woke up one time and could feel you were awake.'

'How could you feel I was awake?'

'I don't know,' Marianne said, suddenly wondering how it was that she *did* know, but totally convinced that she did. 'Your breathing changes when you're awake.'

Bill was silent for a minute and then said, 'No, it was while I was shaving.'

'Mmm. And what were you thinking?'

He made a sound that was part laugh and part apology for what he was about to say. 'I was thinking about now – the absolute now that we have right at this very instant.'

'While you were shaving, you were thinking about us in the car?'

'No, I was thinking about the now that I had *then*.'

Marianne glanced down at Tommy and shifted her arm. Tommy grunted and moved closer to her.

'I was thinking about *all* the nows, every single nanosecond of time that we kind of close our eyes to because we're thinking about what's coming along, either looking forward to it or …' His voice trailed off.

Marianne reached out a hand and rubbed her husband's neck.

'I was thinking about how, when we have everything we could possibly want in the world and we're with the people we so dearly want to be with, about how … oh, it sounds silly.'

'No, it doesn't. Go ahead. Tell me what you were thinking.'

'Well, I was thinking, wouldn't it be great if we could just freeze that frame. If we could just stop everything from moving on and changing.'

'You mean …' Marianne glanced at the back of Abigail's head and heard a soft snore. 'You mean Mom?'

'Yes, but more than that. Everything.'

'What else is there? What else is bothering you, honey?'

'That's just it. Nothing was bothering me. And then …' He nodded sideways at Abigail. 'Then we had the visit to the doctor, then to the hospital, and then the operation, and the radiotherapy, and then – now

– the shortness of breath, another visit to the doctor, the x-ray – and here we are. Waiting.'

They had been told that Abigail had three to six months, though the likelihood was that it would be closer to three. Then, as the breathing worsened, even that prognosis seemed to be a little overly optimistic. They were looking at weeks, the doctor had told them, Abigail nodding, a small smile of acceptance on her lips.

'I'm not sure I'm foll ...'

'Well, it was all that – *all* that – that kind of started me thinking about how brief it all is. The time we have, you know? But how, if we added every single fraction of time together and truly appreciated it, life would be almost endless.' He slowed to make a left turn.

'But it still wouldn't *be* endless,' Marianne said. 'Mom, and *my* mom and dad – they wouldn't always be with us. And Tommy would still grow older and he'd still find his own life and his own adventures.'

'Yes, I guess that's it.'

'What's it?'

'What you said – about adventures. That's what life is, just one big adventure.'

'Oh, honey,' Marianne said, her voice soft and low. 'It'll all work out okay.'

The car slowed down and Bill prepared to make a left onto the strip leading onto the meadows. Tommy sat up quickly, his head narrowly missing Marianne's chin, and said, 'We here yet?'

Bill turned the wheel and moved through a gap in the traffic, the car juddering as it moved onto the rough track. 'Almost,' he said. 'Couple more minutes.'

***

She could feel him in the car right next to her; smell his cologne and the grease he used to put on his hair. But she knew that if she opened her eyes, he wouldn't be there. There would only be the car, and her son and Marianne and Tommy, and outside the window it would be a world where her husband no longer existed.

Oh, Jack, she thought, squeezing her eyes tight, *I'm causing them such sadness.*

They love you, Abby. The wind whispering through her hearing aid sounded just like his voice. Sounded just the way he always spoke to her. *Be happy with that. Your time will come. And it won't be …*

She felt small hands on her shoulder, rubbing it gently. 'Gran? You awake?' She lifted her head to make out she'd just woken up and hadn't heard the conversation her son and Marianne had been having, but the truth of the matter was she didn't sleep too well now, and her dreams – such as they were – were filled with images of the cancer turning itself over and over inside her.

'You bet. I'm awake,' she said. She turned to look across the meadows and, just for a second, she thought she could see horses, lots of horses, being led in a procession by men so small they could have been boys. But it must have been the sunlight through the trees and refracting through the window glass, because there were no horses and no men.

'You gonna park down by the river, honey?' Marianne asked.

Bill didn't speak.

'Honey?'

'Oh, yeah, sorry. I was just thinking how deserted it is.'

'And on Derby Day, too!' Tommy added. 'Maybe everyone's gone someplace else.'

It was true. Since they had pulled onto the dirt track leading through the meadows, they had not seen another car nor even kids out walking or sitting listening to their radio, or playing with balls.

'It's nice. It's not …' Abigail ventured stiltedly, '… too crowded.'

But there *were* people there, weren't there? She could see them – there behind the trees and just around back of the bushes – could see their striped jackets and their boaters, the occasional flash of pink parasol. She squinted her eyes and concentrated, but the meadows were empty.

Bill pulled the old Chevrolet up onto the grass alongside a thin pathway that wound its way down to the riverside. The air was filled with the sounds of summer, of sunshine and of water burbling its way over the ancient stones of the riverbed. Bill got out and pulled the seat forward for Marianne before going around to let Abigail out. Tommy ran his feet on the carpet like a train, his hand clasped on the bright yellow frisbee and his lungs greedily gulping in the outside air.

'Just hold your horses there a minute, Scout, while we get your Gran out,' Bill chided.

Marianne went around to the trunk and got out the hamper, setting it down beside her on the grass. Then she lifted out a pile of old sheets and rugs.

Tommy pushed the now vacant seat forward and made to slide out, but the sight of his father holding onto his Gran stopped him in his tracks.

Bill held onto Abigail tightly, and Tommy could see her thin arms dithering from side to side, like a butterfly not sure whether it wanted to settle on this flower or maybe this one, and her hair blowing in thin wisps in the gentle breeze.

'You okay, Mom?'

'I'm fine, son,' came the reply. 'Just as fine as wine.'

'Not too cold?'

Now with a firm hold on the Chevvie's door, Abigail straightened up and smoothed out Tommy's dad's collar. The smile she gave him was a secret smile, knowing and sad. Tommy frowned, and though he hadn't made so much as even the tiniest noise, both of them turned to look at him. 'We're just fine,' she answered, with that big grin and a hunch-up of her shoulders that suggested being a part – along with her grandson – of some great and exciting plan. 'Aren't we, Tommy?'

'We sure are,' Tommy agreed, and just to prove it, he lofted the frisbee high into the sky, tracing its path with his hand over his eyes as though he were saluting it.

'Tommy,' Marianne shouted, 'will you come and take some things, please? Let's get this picnic on the road!'

***

Jack came to see his wife after they had eaten.

Bill had gone down to the riverside with Tommy, and Marianne – who had started out with such fine intentions to read the daily newspaper

– had succumbed to the after-effects of the food and the sunshine, her eyelids drooping slowly until they had closed completely. Abigail watched her son and grandson while she listened to their distant voices, mingled in with the sound of her own breathing and Marianne's soft snores. It was as though they were in a different world, the two men – a world that Abigail was able to look into and hear but could not actually visit.

He's a fine boy, Jack said hunkering down beside her.

'Land sakes!' Abigail said, the words coming out as a hiss, her hand up to the collar on her sweater, fingers trembling over the chain he had bought her those many long years before.

Shh! he whispered, glancing at Marianne.

'You gave. Me a start,' Abigail said.

He shifted around so that he was in front of her and smiled. *You look as handsome as ever, Abby ... Mighty handsome, if you don't mind my saying*. His eyes travelled up and down her form, and Abby felt a blush starting in her cheeks. *You're wearing my dress*, he said.

'Of course!'

You look ... beautiful.

Abigail shook her head and made to reach out to him. But Jack pulled away. *Uh uh*, he said. *That's not in the rules.*

'Can't I. Touch you?'

He made a tight-lipped mouth and shook his head, his eyes mischievous as ever. *Not yet, anyways.*

'But I thought –' She lowered her voice when Marianne shuffled onto her side. 'I thought. You'd come. For me. I thought. Today. Was the day. The special day.'

All days are special, Abby. What's so different about this one?

'Well, I figured. You'd come for me. Today.' She hung her head down and said, 'I'm sick, Jack. Terrible sick.'

I know that, Abby.

'I'm going. To die.'

Yes, you are.

'And soon.'

Right again. Soon. But not today.

Abigail looked up at her husband and, just for a second, he looked

17 years old again, and then he was thirty-something. Then in his fifties. Then he was a young buck of 22. Seemed like he couldn't stay put for more than a minute at a time.

'So when –' she asked, '– exactly?'

Jack shrugged. The sound of laughter drifted over from the river, and Jack and Abigail turned to look. Tommy was doubled up in hysterics pointing at his father. Bill was standing pulling up his trousers – even from here they could see that Bill had somehow gotten into the water.

They're going to come back, Jack said, turning back to face her. *I have to go.*

'But you didn't. You didn't. Answer me, Jack. When?'

I don't rightly know, Abby. But someday soon. Maybe tomorrow; maybe next week ... He shrugged again. *Like I say, soon. But it might not be a day that has anything written beneath it on the calendar. There'll be nothing special about it.* He looked back at Bill and Tommy, slowly making their way up the embankment towards them. *And certainly nothing special about it for them.*

With Jack's attention momentarily distracted from her, Abigail wondered if she could shoot out her hand and take a hold of her husband's wrist – if doing so – her living skin joining up with the her husband's ghost's – might mean she would die right there and then. But the laughter drifted up to her and into her head like the fizzy bubbles from a bottle of 7 Up, and she turned, her hand halfway out in front of her but stopped short of its target. Bill waved to her and she raised her hand and waved back, feeling suddenly weak but somehow strong as well.

'They can't see you,' she said as she looked back at him.

Jack nodded. *But I'm gonna have to go anyways.*

'Do you. Do you have to?'

He nodded again, this time with a deep sadness etched into his face – his 78-year-old face, the one she had watched those years ago, lying so still on her pillow as he drifted away from her, his hand locked in hers as he fought to stay another few minutes.

Like I said, Abby, all days are special. And, right now, these last days you're spending with Bill and his lovely wife and that fine boy –

these days are special to them. These days are like small gems – like jewels in the dust. Make them count. Every single one of them.

And then he reached out and touched her cheek.

Fire and ice.

Soft and hard.

Dark and light.

A thousand sensations shot through Abigail Rutherford's face and coursed up and down her body, setting her fingers to tingle and her toes to curl.

I was never real good with rules, he said.

'I love you so much, Jack,' she said, her words coming out in a stream without any pauses for breath.

I love you too, Abby. I always will. And then he was gone.

***

Tommy was the first one to appear, the sound of his pounding feet waking Marianne in a fluster.

'What's the matter? What's happened?'

'Dad –' Tommy could hardly speak from a mixture of exertion and laughter. 'Dad fell in the river!'

'I didn't fall in the ...'

Marianne got to her feet. 'Bill? Are you okay, honey?'

'I'm fine.' He flapped his trousers at her and gave a weak smile. 'Slipped off the stepping stones, that's all.'

'You should've seen him, Mom! Gran, you should have –'

Abigail nodded and made a mock-scowl. 'He was never. Real good. On his feet. Your father,' she said. She pulled the blanket from around her shoulders and threw it over towards her son. 'You make sure. They're dry. You'll get. Rheumatics.'

Tommy frowned. 'Room attics?'

'Hush now, Tommy. Let's get your father dried up and back home.'

Drying his feet while Marianne and Tommy loaded the picnic things into the trunk, Bill sensed he was being watched. He shook his head. 'Could've happened to anyone, Mom,' he said.

'I know. But it was. Always you. It happened to.'

He wiped out his shoes and, pulling a face, slipped them onto his feet.

'You had a nice time?'

She nodded emphatically. 'I've had a wonderful time.'

'How you feeling?'

She lifted a hand to her cheek and rubbed the spot where Jack had touched it. It felt warm. Special.

'I'm feeling. Just fine,' she said. 'It's been. A great day.'

Bill nodded and, just for a second, he frowned.

She reached out then and took her son's hand. 'A special day.'

***

For the rest of her life – a rich, happy and fulfilled life – and one that turned out to be a little longer than she had once hoped – Abigail Rutherford treated *every* day as a special day, savouring every minute and every hour as though it truly was her last.

Which, of course, is what we all should do.

20-20 Vision
Debbie Bennett

www.omegahousingproject.com
Housing for the 2020s

DO YOU KNOW
How people lived just 100 years ago?
Click here for a great game! See if *you* could survive on post-war rations!

Available soon!
20-20 VISION
5000 BRAND NEW, fully-automated, computer-controlled condos
Be the FIRST to participate in the new North West Social Housing Experiment!
Self-aware houses ANTICIPATE your EVERY need!
Click here for a virtual tour

Omega Housing solves the population crisis
Omega Housing – from beginning to end

www.omegahousingproject.com

***

3rd March

There was a message on the vidscreen when she got back from work. Katy knew it was from the Social Trust – it had the familiar eye-in-the-sky logo that she'd seen most days since she and Rico had moved into the small and squalid room. That was the problem with Trust-sponsored accommodation; constant brainwashing by slogan quite literally came with the territory as there were vidscreens everywhere, bombarding you with adverts for a better standard of living. And while Katy wasn't exactly happy with the standard of living she had right now, it was infinitely preferable to the one she'd had before.

She tossed her bag onto the bed and eased her feet out of the high heels she always wore. Rico was nowhere to be seen. *Out drinking again? Why do I bother?* Part of her knew she'd only got together with him to jump a few rungs of the housing ladder – two people together were cheaper and easier to house than if they lived apart. But it pissed her off that he couldn't hold down a job for more than a week, and if she'd known what a lazy slob he was *before* they'd got together, the relationship would never have got past first base.

Down the hallway, she headed for the bathroom and one of the dozen shower cubicles. No baths – they cost too much in terms of space and water. Besides, who would want to lie in a bath separated from the communal room by nothing more than a thin polycarb screen? The one advantage of working late, Katy had discovered, was that the bathrooms were generally empty – most people had been in and gone out again for the evening by the time she got back from work.

So when do I tell him? She soaped herself quickly and wondered when to break the news to Rico that she'd lost her job. It wasn't just her – her whole department was being made redundant the next month. Computers were cheaper to employ than people. And with both of them out of work, they wouldn't even qualify for this dump. The Trust contributions she made through her salary enabled them to live here – that and the recent *lebensraum* legislation that entitled them to a precise size of accommodation. It was a complex calculation, designed so that nobody but the authorities could understand it. All she knew was that they'd have to leave there soon – and there wasn't anywhere else to go.

Katy dried herself and wrapped the towel around her body. There were cobwebs around the chrome hooks and she wondered when anybody had last bothered to clean. She didn't like spiders. God, she'd kill for her own place – not that she was the tidiest of people, but at least it would be her own mess and not somebody else's. She was as sociable as the next person, but sometimes longed for just a bit of solitude – the chance to spend some time just being, rather than constantly jostling and queuing for life. But the bathroom was still quiet, and she tucked the towel in and pulled back the polycarb screen – to find that she wasn't alone any more. Leaning against one of the washbasins stood Rico's best mate, Harley.

'What do *you* want?' She really wasn't in the mood for this. She'd never liked the man; he was charmless and arrogant, and never seemed to dress in anything other than a white T-shirt and black leather bike jacket. He had nothing in common with Rico. Or maybe he did.

'Nice tits.'

God, did men *never* grow up? 'I'm glad you approve.'

'You're wasted on Rico, y'know?'

Believe me, I know. 'Go away, Harley. I'm not interested. How hard can it be to understand?'

'As hard as you want it, hon.'

Are you for real? she wanted to ask him. Did he study 1950s films in his spare time? She wondered if she wrote *dickhead* back to front with a thick black pen on his forehead, how many times he'd have to look in the mirror before he got the message.

'So when's it to be?'

'What?' She packed up her toiletries, careful not to let the towel drop.

'You and me.' He pushed himself off the washbasin and stood between Katy and the door.

'Listen to me, Harley.' Wash bag close to her chest, she stared him straight in the eye. 'There will never be a you and me. I wouldn't touch you if you were the last man on the planet. Got that? Now get out of my way.'

Harley didn't move for a moment. Then he smiled. 'You'll change your mind,' he said softly. Reaching out with one nicotine-stained finger, he drew it gently down one of her cheeks, then touched it to his own lips.

Katy shivered, but Harley stepped out the way and she bolted back to the safety of her room.

***

4th March

The message was still on the vidscreen when she came back from breakfast. It was flashing at her now. She was surprised Rico hadn't already opened it, but he'd been drunk by the time she'd found him last night and was still comatose in bed.

She reached for the remote and hit the *Message* button. Tinny classical music curled in wisps from invisible speakers like smoke, taking a few seconds to blend together and reveal itself as the Social Trust's jingle.

There's a surprise. The Trust sent out ad messages two or three times a week and you had no choice but to open them. Left alone, the message would be beeping by tomorrow; and the day after, they'd be called to the Trust's local office and shown the small print in their contract. *So I have to open it – I don't have to read it*, Katy reminded herself as she poked her toes underneath the bed to find her work shoes.

She hated the mornings the most. Queuing for the washbasins with whatever low-lives the Trust were dumping in there that week; queuing for the inclusive breakfast, which consisted of nothing more than warm, faintly-scorched bread and chicory coffee; queuing for the bus to work; and queuing to clock on with the stupid plastic chip card that ruled her life.

'Omega Housing Project present to you … 20-20 Vision.'

Katy found her shoes and pulled a brush through her hair.

'Please watch the screen for the opportunity of a lifetime.'

The bland intersex voice hit just the right pitch to make tuning it out impossible.

More tinny music and Katy couldn't help but watch. She heard a groan next to her, and out of the corner of her eye saw Rico roll over, grab a pillow and put it over his head. She wondered what would happen if she sat on it.

'Do *you* want to escape Trust housing? Yes, *you*. Are you tired of your life? Would you like to take part in a new social experiment?'

Now you're talking. Katy put the hairbrush down. This was unlike the normal rubbish they churned out. True, the usual ads were meant to inspire them to work hard and escape the Trust's obligations to assist them, but they were generally upbeat and positive, telling people that they'd never had it so good.

'Congratulations! You have been selected to be one of 5000 couples to participate in this experiment. Live the life you've dreamed of ...'

Damn. Couples only. She'd have to keep Rico sweet, then. Still, it might cushion the blow of her redundancy. She nudged the lump under the blankets with one elbow. 'Rico – watch this.'

'Mmm?' A head emerged from under the pillow, thin-faced with dark hair. Katy liked to think he bore more than a passing resemblance to her screen hero Keanu Reeves – or at least how Keanu had looked 20 years earlier in the classic *Matrix* films, before he'd become middle-aged and boring. She loved the films of her parents' generation; they were so much more exciting that the modern stuff. *Imagine – a whole world inside a computer! A whole life!* But the vidscreen had paused.

'Insert your chip-id card for a personal appointment to view one of these 5000 brand new, fully-automated, computer-controlled condos.'

'What?' Rico now, scratching his chin sleepily. 'Cool.'

Katy fished her chip card from her bag and pushed it into the vidscreen slot, then stuck her right thumb on the keypad sensor. Both of them jumped as the tinny music increased in volume.

'Kathryn Farrell, you are guaranteed a place on the 20-20 Vision Scheme. Your appointment is 09.15 on 6th March. Please arrive on time.' A website flashed up across the bottom of the screen.

'Go on, then. Have a look. I'm awake now.' Rico broke wind loudly, and Katy rolled her eyes and stood up.

'Can't. I'll be late for work. I'll check it out at lunchtime, or you can while I'm out. And Rico – we'd stand more chance of winning this if you got down to the Trust Employment Centre today.'

'You heard the voice. A guaranteed place.'

Yes – guaranteed for me. Who said anything about you? But it had also said couples. Did that mean she had to take a partner or would they provide one for her? Which was the better devil – known or unknown? God forbid, she could end up with someone like Harley.

'If we did get a place, we'd need money for furnishings.' She tried another approach. 'You could have your own pod-station.'

He made a face. 'All right. I get the message.'

She grabbed her bag. 'Should be back around seven. Want to eat out?'

'Can we afford it?' he asked pointedly.

She grinned. 'See you in the Slammer.'

***

6th March

From the outside, the block looked all shiny glass and steel. The old canal ran alongside one wall, but the sluggish water was now contained within a sleek metal channel. It looked impressive, but Katy could see grilles in the building wall below the waterline and cloudy waste churning out into the current. Hi-tech luxury dumping its toxins to be carried away and treated in the less salubrious parts of town.

The entrance was over the canal bridge. She remembered seeing old photographs of Manchester at the turn of the millennium, when they were only just beginning to regenerate the city and make the urban decay blossom into new, modern life. *More like growing fungus on rotten wood.* In older photos still, there were sepia canal people on the bridges, people who both lived and made their living on the waterways, ferrying coal and salt around the country. It was happening again in some cities, where traffic flow was so slow by road, it was actually quicker on the water. Katy wondered if she'd be able to get a boat to work one day, if they lived here.

On the other side of the bridge, a large vidscreen was inset into the building wall, proclaiming Omega Housing's new project. Even Rico was impressed – she could tell by the way he'd stopped talking and the tilt of his head as he looked up at the block. Outside the entrance, a security camera watched them as Katy pressed her thumb on the sensor. Black glass doors slid silently apart and they hesitated for a moment.

'Who've you been sleeping with, Kats?'

'Excuse me?'

Rico grinned. 'Opportunities don't just fall into your lap. You must have done something to deserve this.' He waved his arms expansively. 'So who was it? Your boss?'

He was joking, she knew he was – but he had a point. Real life didn't work this way. Suddenly nervous, she grabbed his hand as they stepped over the threshold and the doors slid shut behind them.

There was nobody in the foyer to greet them. Three large yucca plants stood in chrome pots in front of a black window. Outside, darkened through the glass, she could see a deck area, with jasmine climbing up a wooden trellis and raised planting. Island clumps of hebes and what looked like escalonia were dotted around in a sea of bark chippings. The deck too was deserted.

'Look.' Rico dragged her attention back inside. He was pointing at a panel by the elevator doors, where there was a series of thumb sensors next to a list of numbers and small plaques with names. Two-thirds of the way up, at number 63, the plaque said Kathryn Farrell.

'Have we moved in already?' It was spookily quiet, with not even a hum of air-conditioning.

But Rico was impatient. 'Do you think we're meant to go up, then?'

'In a minute.' She wanted to explore down there first. There were a couple of doors leading off the foyer; one was obviously the exit to the decking and garden, but the other was next to the elevator, and led into the bowels of the building.

She opened it cautiously. *Come into my parlour, said the spider* ... But there were no spiders here and this door led down to a sports hall or swimming pool, judging by the whiff of chlorine and the faint sound of voices. 'There are people down here,' she said, wanting Rico to come with her and seek out company.

'Well, we can go and meet them later on, when we know if we'll be neighbours.' He pursed his lips. 'Come on, Kats. The message said to be on time.'

True. She'd checked out the website at work and found a message for her, confirming the appointment time and giving an address. Reluctantly, she let the door close and allowed the sensor pad on the elevator control panel to read her identity. The doors opened as silently as the front doors had and they stepped inside; before they had time to study the control panel, the lift was moving swiftly, and Katy could feel her breakfast trying to stay grounded.

A few seconds later and the doors opened again to reveal a short corridor with aluminium floor tiles – except they weren't, she discovered, as she took a few paces. They were actually some kind of linoleum, designed to absorb sound and dirt but look distinctly 21st Century. The walls were similar, with hidden lighting and no windows.

'So where now?' she asked, not really needing an answer but wanting to hear how the sound echoed; she wasn't surprised when it didn't, the walls and floor swallowing the words as if they hadn't eaten in months.

Rico didn't seem to notice. 'Down here.' There were numbers by each door – nothing odd about that. At number 63 was yet another sensor pad next to a plain steel door with a spy-hole in the centre. There was no mailbox, and yet Katy didn't recall having seen any in the foyer. *So where does the post go, then?* Maybe there was another entrance to the building.

There was no handle either, but the door clicked open to her thumbprint. Inside, a small internal hallway opened out into a magnificent living area with bare brick walls, wooden flooring and a full height picture window. Katy hadn't realised what floor they were on, but they must have been eight or nine storeys up, and the view across the city was spectacular, so much so that to start with neither of them saw the person sitting on the Philippe Starck-inspired stool at the breakfast bar.

The movement out of the corner of her eye made her jump. *Are spiders scared of heights?* But it was only a man, a sales rep in a smart suit with slicked-back hair and an eye-in-the-sky pin badge in his lapel.

'Hello, Kathryn. Welcome to your new home.'

Neither Katy nor Rico spoke as the door swung smoothly closed behind them. For a moment, Katy had an impulse to turn and run, but why should she be scared? *This is mine?* She stared around the room;

everything was shiny new, with that plasticky packaging smell that suggested the furniture was straight out of the warehouse. It was a showroom apartment, untouched and unlived-in.

'Overwhelming, isn't it?' The man laughed, though not unkindly. He turned to Rico. 'And you are?'

'The boyfriend.' Rico was giving nothing away and Katy had to jump in.

'Rico. We've been together two years now.'

'A permanent contract?'

'Not yet.' She felt almost ashamed that they hadn't signed a life-contract yet, hadn't even discussed how long it might be for. She could do a lot worse than Rico, for all his faults.

The man frowned. 'We'd prefer you to have a minimum of a five year contract.' He looked apologetic. 'I don't mean to be personal, but …'

'We'll sort it.' Katy knew she'd sign up to a lifetime, if it meant she could live in Heaven.

The man made a note on his palm PC and smiled again. 'So let me give you the guided tour, Kathryn and … Rico. As you'll have seen from the vidmail, these condos are the ultimate in 21st Century living. This home is completely self-aware and controlled by the building's master computer in the basement. It knows where you are, what you're doing and what you want – even before you know yourself! Imagine the luxury of a long, hot bath where you don't even have to turn on a tap. Think about being able to call home at lunchtime and then return to find the meal you've chosen is ready to eat.'

Think about the luxury of not having to share this with anyone!

'Here's the kitchen,' the salesman continued, taking them further into the apartment. 'Everything in here is computer-controlled. You decide what food you want in the fridge, program it in, and when supplies are low, they'll be ordered and delivered to maintenance on floor 1, where someone will be assigned to restock.'

'So someone else will be in here?' Rico was quick to pick up on these things, but the man didn't seem upset.

'At a convenient time, of course. You tell us when.'

'And who pays for all this?'

'Rico!' Katy wanted to kick him for being so negative. She didn't care who paid. She'd sell her body to live here.

'No, no – he's right to ask,' replied the salesman. 'There's an annual maintenance charge that covers these things. The Trust will pay the first year for you – not for the food, of course – but after that it's up to you. You do have a job?' He looked worried for a moment.

If only you knew. But he didn't and neither did Rico. If they did, the man would usher them straight out of this piece of heaven and they'd be living in the hell on the streets within a month. So she swallowed the lump in her throat and nodded, relieved that her soon-to-be-ex-employer was a privately-owned company and would be unlikely to report back to the Trust. With luck, she'd find another job in a month or so, and she had just enough savings to feed herself until she did. Rico was another matter, though – he really would have to make an effort and find work.

The man showed them the lighting. There were no curtains at the huge windows, but they darkened to near-opacity automatically, according to the light level outside. Of course, he explained, they could override it at any time; to demonstrate, he touched a sensor pad on the wall, and the glass slowly coloured to the black of the windows they'd seen in the foyer downstairs. The entire apartment was sound-proofed too, and security was computer-controlled and linked to Katy's own thumb-print; they could arrange for Rico's to be added after they moved in.

An hour later and she was signing the paperwork and stamping her thumb on the special oil-receptive coating underneath. Even Rico had lost most of his reservations and scrawled his signature in the co-habitee box. The salesman was full of congratulations and said that Katy's chip card had been credited with enough money for them to celebrate with a meal and a drink.

'Spread the word,' he said as they were leaving. 'This is the future of Social Housing. 20-20 Vision want to encourage you young people to own a part of your future.'

'Yeah, yeah,' muttered Rico as they took the elevator back down to the foyer. 'Is he real? Where's the catch?'

Katy had to agree with him as they walked down the canal towpath back to their housing block. And yet, she couldn't help comparing their one-room flea-pit with the apartment and she knew that she couldn't turn it down, not when she finally had a chance to make something of her life.

They went for lunch at the Slammer, the old Strangeways Prison converted into yet more housing, but it did have a peculiarly atmospheric bar and restaurant. That was one of the reasons she'd agreed to move in with Rico, as there was no way she could ever have lived in a former prison cell, the size of which happened to be the exact amount of *lebensraum* allocated to a single person of her age and status. As a child, she'd wondered what had happened to all the prisoners, until her parents had told her about their holidays in the Isle of Man and how nobody could go there any more. It was a good idea, but hadn't really solved the population crisis for more than a couple of years.

'So,' said Rico, after he'd let her pay for both lunch and drinks, 'what did you make of all that?'

Rico, I've lost my job. No, she couldn't tell him just yet. What if he told Omega Housing and they lost the apartment? 'Fantastic,' she said brightly, instead. 'I'd move in tomorrow, if we could.' The place was filling up and she had to shout to make herself heard.

'He said a week. Don't know why – it looked ready to move into now.'

'It's an odd place.' Katy couldn't quite put her finger on it. 'So quiet. Too quiet.' *Bliss! Nowhere can be too quiet. Not after Trust housing.* There'd been people in the pool though – she'd heard them down the corridor. It would have been nice to check it out.

'It'll be fine.' Rico looked beyond her. 'There's Harley.'

How to kill the day stone dead. Katy shook her head and ate her lunch.

***

13th March

It was depressing. The entire sum of her life to date and she could fit it into two large cases. The room didn't even look any different after they'd packed. All the furniture, bedding and even the clock on the wall were owned by the Trust. The room was supposed to be cleaned weekly, but Katy had never seen any evidence of it – there were still crumbs on the floor by the chest that she remembered dropping when they'd first moved in. And yet more cobwebs on the ceiling, though she'd never noticed them before now.

She was surprised Rico had managed to fill even one case – how could a few pairs of jeans and half a dozen T-shirts take up so much room? But they were done and ready and standing in the doorway taking one last look. Already there was another couple waiting down the hall, ready to take over their room; Katy wondered if they'd even bother to change the bedding.

Harley had found a car for them. What with fuel prices and carbon-emissions tax, there was nobody they knew who could afford to run a car. But Harley had contacts and he drove it himself, sliding his hand onto Katy's knee when Rico wasn't looking. Katy resisted the urge to slap him – it was too far to walk with three suitcases – so she had to settle for a cold look, and watch him smirk as he stopped at the traffic lights.

Up in the apartment, even Harley was impressed enough to forget the sexual innuendos for a moment and stare out of the window at the view. Spring sunshine flooded the room with light, and Katy noticed a couple of pots on the tiny balcony, filled with dwarf daffodils.

She dragged her cases through into the bedroom. There was an en-suite bathroom, and the thought of a real bath, without having to wander public hallways first, was enough to make her want to strip off there and then. *And that'd really give Harley a hard-on.* No – best wait 'til they were alone and she could relax properly. So she unpacked instead, hanging her clothes in the small but perfectly-formed walk-in closet. The fridge and larder contained the bare necessities – enough for a day or so. She'd been given a tick-list the day before and selected just a few items, authorising them to debit her chip card. Katy knew she'd have to be careful – she'd never catered for herself before, and things could easily get out of control – and she'd decided to get food in herself to begin with, just until she knew how much it was all going to cost. But at least they could have a meal together that night, in their own place, and finally start a new life. She and Rico had even got the preliminary paperwork for a life-contract, although they hadn't yet discussed the terms or length. *Maybe tonight.*

Harley was at the front door and about to leave. 'How do I get out of here, then?' he called. 'There's no knob.'

'You don't need a –' Katy broke off, realising how he'd interpret the comment.

He raised his eyebrows. 'D'you know?' he suggested, 'I'm beginning to think that maybe *you* don't.'

Katy gritted her teeth. 'Give it a rest.' She pressed her thumb on the pad by the door. '*That's* how you get out.'

The door clicked and Harley pushed it gently. 'Right, I'll leave you two lovebirds to settle in and christen the place, then. See you in the Slammer later?'

Not if I see you first. But he *had* driven them here, and it wasn't his fault he was a complete moron. 'Thanks for the lift.'

'I'll give you a ride any time, hon.'

'Harley, get out.' She was not going to let him intimidate her any more – not in her own apartment.

Her own apartment. It sounded good and she kicked her shoes off and let them clatter across the wooden floor. It was just her and Rico now, and maybe they could make a go of it, now that they had enough space to actually live, rather than just survive.

***

14th March

Katy woke up early and stretched. The room was so quiet she could hear Rico breathing next to her. It was Sunday, and she'd made sure there were croissants and coffee in the kitchen – all she needed now was a newspaper and she'd feel like a real grown-up, an adult at last in her own house with her own possessions, and leading her own life.

She dressed and crept out of the apartment to avoid waking Rico. Outside, the air seemed fresh and clear and she sat on the decking for ten minutes, admiring the forsythia that was just starting to flower along the perimeter of the garden. She wondered who did the gardening and if they'd let her help occasionally. Her grandfather had had a garden, and she remembered many childhood days spent following him around as he'd pointed out the plants to her. If only her grandfather could see her now. Which reminded her that her parents were coming the following weekend to see the new place, and she'd have to see if the sofa in the lounge really did convert into a spare bed as the salesman had promised it would.

Katy found a newsagents and bought a paper, then returned to the apartment. By the elevator doors, she opened the other door again and could hear faint sounds of laughter. *What time do people get up in this place?* Maybe after they'd had breakfast, she and Rico could come back down here and explore, or even have a swim?

Rico was quite happy to do whatever she wanted when he finally got out of bed some hours later, maybe realising he was onto a good thing here. But as Katy was all too aware, she was just as dependent on him, as without a partner, she wouldn't be eligible for this place. And she still hadn't told him about her impending redundancy. She wondered if it would matter if Rico had a job instead of her – if Omega Housing were bothered which one of them was earning, as long as they had some income between them.

Katy had finished her breakfast long ago and was curled up on the sofa in the lounge, reading the paper. As usual, the main news concerned the population crisis and the latest proposals the Government had for dealing with it. Compulsory sterilisation was one option, but no politician had dared go too far down that road yet – they were still at the stage of paying people not to have children. *Or not to have sex?* she wondered. It'd be kind of difficult to police. *The sex police?*

She giggled and Rico looked up from his toast. He wasn't a croissant person – definitely a tea-and-toast man. *News of the World* to her *Mail on Sunday*.

'What?' He took a slurp of tea.

'Nothing. Just this article about the population explosion. What will they do, do you think, when there are just too many people?'

'Like there are now, you mean?'

'No, really too many people.' *When you can't move for people.*

Can't breathe any more, as there's no room left to grow plants to provide oxygen ... Actually, it was quite scary. But it would never get to that stage.

Rico shrugged. He didn't worry about things the way she did, was content just to let the future happen in its own time. Maybe he was right. Why worry, when she couldn't do anything about it?

Neither of them had any swimming costumes, as there were few public pools these days. But Katy had a top-and-briefs set that she thought might do – at least it wasn't see-through when wet – and Rico found a pair of boxer shorts with miniature Union Jacks all over them. Two towels later and they were back in the foyer and looking forward to meeting some of the other residents. Rico was concerned that the sensors still weren't accepting his thumb-print; Katy made a mental note to vidmail the Omega Housing people the next day and query it – if she was out at work all day, Rico would be a prisoner in the apartment if he couldn't activate the sensors himself.

Katy pushed open the door that led down to where they'd heard people on several occasions now. There was a long corridor ahead of them and it was strangely quiet.

'Maybe it's closed today?' she wondered out loud, but Rico didn't agree.

'On a Sunday? Should be the busiest day.'

Katy pursed her lips. It was too quiet. At a bend in the corridor, she was fully expecting to see a deserted swimming pool – or at least a door with a closed sign and a notice with opening times on it – but there was nothing. Instead, the corridor just ended in a store-room behind the elevator shaft. She frowned. Metal shelving covered one wall, filled with dusty bits of junk. There was a smell of aerosol polish and an old Hoover slumped in one corner. In the other stood several large plastic containers. Katy crouched down and read the label.

'Well that's where the chlorine smell came from,' she said, standing up. 'But the noise?' She *knew* she'd heard people earlier. Rico prodded some of the packaging on the shelves. There were old rolls of carpet and a box of electrical bits and pieces.

'There were people down here,' Katy insisted. 'I heard them. You did too, when we first came here – remember?' She wasn't going mad, was she? Had they imagined it, ready to believe anything in this amazing building?

Rico nodded. 'I remember.'

'So where– ?'

'I don't *know*, Kats.' He seemed impatient. 'But we were obviously wrong, weren't we? Come on, let's go. I don't think we're supposed to be in here.'

***

15th March

Katy didn't want to go to work. Today was the day she'd find out how long she had left at the company and get her formal notification of redundancy. Today she'd have to accept it as reality, and know that if she didn't find another job soon, they might have to leave this apartment. Today, she'd have to tell Rico, before someone else did.

Today, Rico can go and look for a job himself. Why should it be she doing everything anyway? If he wanted that new pod-station he'd been eyeing up in the window of the store in town, he could go out and earn the money himself.

Katy scrambled out of bed, remembered that Harley had stayed over the previous night and hurriedly pulled a bathrobe on, tying it tightly. After the disappointment with the swimming pool that wasn't, they'd gone out and met him in the Slammer, and then the three of them had spent the afternoon watching a series of old 2D films on the television, before drinking themselves silly on cheap beer and getting a takeaway.

But even Harley couldn't spoil the luxury of her having her own bathroom. She thought about having a long, hot shower, but decided to wait until they'd got rid of their guest, so she padded through to the kitchen to make coffee instead. The stench of the previous night's food hit her; she made a face and threw all the cartons down the waste disposal. For some reason the tap didn't work, so she poured the last of the milk into a glass and took it back into the bedroom, preferring Rico's company to Harley's in the lounge.

She went to clean her teeth, but the bathroom taps weren't working either. She had a number somewhere for building maintenance and assumed it was one of the teething problems of a new building – that or some outside workman had put a spade through a pipe. There'd been water shortages before in Trust housing – they'd been unable to shower for two days once – but she hoped that wasn't the case here, that she was beyond all that now she had a place of her own.

Katy wasn't sure if she wanted to go to work without having had a shower or cleaned her teeth, but she got dressed anyway; an extra spray of deodorant would have to do. Back in the kitchen, there was no food in the fridge or cupboards, as she'd forgotten to buy any – not used to self-catering. Maybe having the kitchen re-stocked automatically wasn't such a bad idea, after all? But they'd only been here two nights and it was all still new. She could grab a muffin from the canteen at work easily enough.

The fridge light had broken – another job to report to building maintenance. Katy wondered if she should start making a list. Finding her shoes, she went to wake Rico before she left for work. The bedroom was light and sunny, and Rico groaned and closed his eyes.

'Jesus, Kats. Shut the curtains.'

'There aren't any.'

'You know what I mean. Press the friggin' button, or whatever. My head's thumping.'

And whose fault is that? He'd drunk far more than she had last night, but then he didn't have to get up for work, did he? And as far as Katy knew, Harley didn't work, though he always seemed to have money to burn.

She found the window button, but the glass didn't darken automatically, like the salesman had shown them, and they'd discovered for themselves, endlessly fiddling the day before. Had they broken it? Fused the electrics or something? That might explain why the fridge light wasn't working either. She couldn't check the main lights as there weren't any switches; they worked off photoelectric sensors and came on automatically when it got dark and there was someone in the room. The man had told them how energy-efficient the system was – sensing body heat and switching off when the room was empty. All they had was an override panel on the wall by the bed, to switch the lights off when they wanted to sleep. There was no way of overriding the system to switch them on. What else would use electricity? The kettle. But that was dead as well, and Katy realised that the electrics were off as well as the water. Some palace this was turning out to be.

In the lounge, she kicked the lump under the duvet on the sofa.

'Get up, Harley. Some of us have jobs to go to.'

'Then piss off, why don't you?' came a muffled reply.

What does *Rico see in this guy?* Katy thought about pulling the duvet off, but reasoned that he'd take that as an open invitation. 'Either you leave with me now, or you'll be stuck in here all day,' she said instead, realising that the same applied to Rico too, and there was no food in the apartment. Even if she vidmailed Omega Housing first thing, she'd probably still have to come back at lunchtime.

'How d'you work that one out, then?' Harley sat up, bare-chested, and Katy was glad she hadn't ripped back the covers.

'No keys,' she explained. 'And this place only recognises me right now. Without me, you're locked in.'

He grinned and winked at her. 'Sounds like heaven to me.'

Get a life! She wandered back to the kitchen area. There was still no water. She'd have to buy some bottles later; keep some under the sink if this was likely to happen frequently. Still, they'd hardly be promoting the apartments if there were serious problems – it had to be just a one-off incident.

'Kats? There's no power!' Rico frowned as he came out of the bedroom, wearing nothing but a pair of stripy shorts. Harley wolf-whistled and Katy turned her back on the pair of them, not wanting to know if Harley was similarly-attired – or, God forbid, naked.

'I know.' She found a carton of juice in the fridge. 'It's juice or juice, I'm afraid. You can come out with me in a minute, go down to Omega Housing's offices and sort this mess out. Get them to register your thumbprint as well while you're there.'

'Why don't you go see if any of your neighbours are having

problems?' suggested Harley, taking a glass of orange juice. 'Maybe it's just in here.'

It was hardly the best way to meet the people next door, but it was a good idea, nonetheless – even if it wasn't yet eight o'clock. They really should have gone round the day before, invited people back for drinks. Wasn't that what you did when you finally got your own place?, Katy thought as she stuck her thumb on the door sensor.

Nothing happened.

Oh, God – power's off. Of course! Everything was electronic, computer-controlled, and with no electricity, there'd be no computer. But surely they'd have a back-up system in the building – a generator or even a battery to keep things ticking over until the power was restored, or the failsafe system kicked in? Even the vidscreen was dead and wouldn't react to her chip card. They'd just have to wait.

'We can't get out,' she said in a small voice, feeling suddenly, stupidly vulnerable.

'Don't be silly.' Rico stabbed the sensor himself. But if it hadn't recognised him the day before, it wasn't going to then, even if it was working. And there wasn't even a comforting beep or a red warning LED; there was nothing, and they were trapped.

Harley jumped out of the makeshift bed, and Katy was relieved to see he wasn't naked. Pulling on his jeans, he opened the kitchen drawer and found a vegetable knife. Levering it underneath the edge of the door sensor, he had the plastic cover off in seconds.

'Harley! You'll –'

'Break it?' He raised his eyebrows. 'In case you hadn't noticed, hon – it's already fucked.' He stuck a finger on the circuit board underneath. 'Dead as Charlie, that is.'

'So what now?' Rico downed the juice she'd given him. 'We're stuck here 'til the power's back up? Looks like you're skipping work today, then, Kats.'

She shrugged. 'I'm leaving anyway.' What did it matter if she missed a day, under the circumstances? She had leave owing.

'What?'

Now was as good a time as any. 'They made me redundant at the beginning of the month. I've only got a few weeks left.'

'Then how … ?'

'I know, I know.' She stared out of the window. It was so clear outside, she could see the Pennines in the distance. 'So we'll be eating beans for a while. Or you could get a job yourself, you know.'

'Will we lose this place?'

Harley snorted from across the room. 'How will they kick you out if you can't open the door?'

'Good point. Perhaps we should lock ourselves in.'

With no food or water? Katy shook her head and took off her sweater. It was warm in the apartment, but of course the air-conditioning was off as well.

***

16th March

'There never was a swimming pool, was there?'

'No, I don't think so.' Rico was licking his finger and sticking it in the empty bread bag, collecting crumbs like diamonds.

'What pool?' Harley in his underpants was no longer a disturbing sight. In fact, Katy herself was down to a bra and lacy boxers, despite the comments she'd got initially. She was past caring what the man thought or said. It was just too hot and stuffy.

'The pool we thought was downstairs.' *The pool they* wanted *us to think was downstairs.* Another rose-tinted view of paradise, she thought as she leaned over and sucked Rico's finger. Well, the glasses were well and truly off now. So much for 2020 Vision – the only true vision was hindsight.

'Sounds like fun,' said Harley tonelessly. 'Are we out of water now?'

Without thinking, Rico had used the toilet, forgetting that they couldn't flush it. And by mid-afternoon, Katy was seriously considering drinking the contents of the bowl anyway – either that or levering off the bathroom panels and hunting for the cistern. The milk and orange were long gone.

They'd barely slept the previous night. The room was dark, but the city lights twinkled invitingly in the distance – evidence that life still went on elsewhere. And in the morning, the rush-hour traffic queued its way past the building and Katy swore she could see people down there looking up at her. She waved and shouted, but the glass was too thick and they were too far up. There was no sign of any workmen come to repair burst water mains or faulty electrics.

Katy and Rico made love. Harley didn't even comment.

***

17th March

Between the three of them, they dragged the sofa across to the window. All at one end, Harley counted to three and they shoved hard. The sofa scraped the wood noisily but merely made a dull thunk against the glass. Katy sat down and leaned against the wall; she would have cried if her body could have spared the moisture.

Rico picked up the designer breakfast-bar stool and ran at the window with it. There was a splintering sound and Katy thought she could see a crack, but it was only a streak of rain washing the window. One of the legs was bent on the stool and Rico tossed it across the room; the vidscreen on the wall by the door shattered in slow-motion and fell to the floor in tiny shards.

Harley took the electronic door sensor apart and wired it up to a torch battery. Rico broke the leg off the bar stool and tried to lever the door open by sheer brute force. Katy wondered why someone at work hadn't called round to check on her. She'd given them her new address the previous week. Surely somebody would miss her?

That night, all three of them lay together in the bed, cold for the first time.

***

18th March

'Could you fit down the waste disposal, Kats?'

'Don't be stupid. The man said there's an incinerator in the basement.'

'The man said a lot of things.'

***

19th March

The chute wasn't much more than a hole in the wall in the kitchen. She sat on the edge, face up against the wall, and let her bare legs dangle down the tube. The salesman had said it led to the basement where the rubbish was incinerated, but presumably the incinerator needed electricity to operate, like everything else in this hell-hole. With Rico holding her wrists, she let herself drop over the edge. But the angle was too sharp to wriggle around and she couldn't make her bones fit in the space available. Even the grease in the chute didn't help, and the smell made her gag as she caught her hair under one shoulder and felt some of it rip away.

Rico pulled her back up, but he couldn't meet her eyes, and it was Harley who gave her a brief hug and told her it didn't matter, that the power would be on in a matter of hours and they could all go out and get drunk at the Slammer.

***

20th March

'Weren't your folks coming this weekend, Kats?'

Is it a week already? 'They won't be able to get in. And the doorbell doesn't work.'

'But they know the address, don't they? They'll check up.'

'What address?' *Does this building have a name on it? Did I give them directions?* 'I can't remember.'

'What about you, Harl? Did you tell anyone where we were?'

'Harl?'

***

24th March

'Rico?'

Silence.

She pushed him with her foot but he didn't respond. Harley had gone days ago and she could see his legs in the bedroom doorway. He was starting to smell.

'Rico?' She tried again, and this time managed to sit up and touch his arm. It was cold and stiff. She shivered, scared of being alone more than anything else.

***

25th March

Cobwebs in the corner of the window frame.

Spiders. Spider-man.

Come into my parlour ...

***

26th March

From her position lying on her side, with her head on one arm and looking out of the window at the rain, Katy found that if she twisted slightly she could see the Sunday papers under a chair. She crawled across the floor, stopping half way to get her breath, and reached underneath with one thin and bony hand. In the colour supplement was the article on the population explosion. Next to it was a half-page advert.

Omega Housing solves the population crisis
Omega Housing – from beginning to end

www.omegahousingproject.com

Red

Richard Christian Matheson

He kept walking.

The day was hot and miserable and he wiped his forehead. Up another 20 feet, he could make out more. Thank God. Maybe he'd find it all. He picked up the pace and his breathing got thick. He struggled on, remembering his vow to himself to go through with this, not to stop until he was done. Maybe it had been a mistake to ask this favour. But it was the only way he could think of to work it out. Still, maybe it had been a mistake.

He felt an edge to his stomach as he stopped and leaned down to what was at his feet. He grimaced, lifted it into the large canvas bag he carried, wiped his hands and moved on. The added weight in the bag promised more and he somehow felt better. He had found most of what he was looking for in the first mile. Only a half mile more to go, to convince himself; to be sure. To not go insane.

It was a nightmare for him to realise how far he'd gone that morning with no suspicion, no clue. He held the bag more tightly and walked on. Ahead, the forms who waited got bigger; closer. They stood with arms crossed, people gathered and complaining behind them. They would have to wait.

He saw something a few yards up, swallowed and walked closer. It was everywhere, and he shut his eyes, trying not to see how it must have been. But he saw it all. Heard it in his head. The sounds were horrible and he couldn't make them go away. Nothing would go away until he had everything, he was certain of that. Then, his mind would at last have some chance to find a place of comfort. To go on.

He bent down and picked up what he could, then walked on, scanning ahead. The sun was beating down and he felt his shirt soaking with sweat under the arms and on his back. He was nearing the forms who waited when he stopped, seeing something halfway between himself and them. It had lost its shape, but he knew what it was and couldn't step any closer. He placed the bag down and slowly sat cross-legged on the baking ground, staring. His body began to shake.

A sombre-looking man walked to him and carefully picked up the object, placing it in the canvas bag and cinching the top. He gently coaxed the weeping man to stand and the man nodded through tears. Together, they walked toward the others, who were glancing at watches and losing patience.

'But I'm not finished,' the man cried.

His voice broke and his eyes grew hot and puffy.

'Please … I'll go crazy … Just a little longer?'

The sombre-looking man hated what was happening. He made the decision.

'I'm sorry, sir. Headquarters said I could give you only the half hour you asked for. That's all I can do. It's a very busy road.'

The man tried to struggle away, but was held more tightly. He began to scream and plead. Two middle-aged women who were waiting watched uncomfortably.

'Whoever allowed this should be reported,' said one, shaking her head critically.

'The poor man is ready to have a nervous breakdown. It's cruel.'

The other said she'd heard they felt awful for the man, whose little girl had grabbed on to the back bumper of his car when he'd left for work that morning. The girl had gotten caught and he'd never known.

They watched an officer approaching with the crying man, whom he helped into the hot squad car. Then, the officer grabbed the canvas bag and, as it began to drip red onto the blacktop, he gently placed it into the trunk beside the mangled tricycle. The backed up traffic began to honk and traffic was waved on as the man was driven away.

Seven Feet
Christopher Fowler

Cleethorpes was a crap mouser. She would hide underneath the sink if a rodent, a squirrel or a neighbour's cat even came near the open back door. Clearly, sleeping 16 hours a day drained her reserves of nervous energy, and she was forced to play dead if her territory was threatened. She was good at a couple of things: batting moths about until they expired with their wings in dusty tatters, and staring at a spot on the wall three feet above the top of Edward's head. What could cats see, he wondered, that humans couldn't.

Cleethorpes was his only companion now Sam was dead and Gill had gone. He'd bought her because everyone else had bought one. That was the month the price of cats skyrocketed. Hell, every cats' home in the country sold out in days, and pretty soon the mangiest strays were changing hands for incredible prices. It was the weirdest form of panic buying that Edward had ever seen.

He'd lived in Camden Town for years, and had been thinking of getting out even before he met Gill; the area was being compared to Moscow and Johannesburg after eight murders on its streets in as many weeks earned the area a new nickname, *Murder Mile*. There were 700 police operating in the borough, which badly needed over a thousand. It was strange, then, to think that the real threat to their lives eventually came not from muggers, but from fast-food outlets.

Edward lived in a flat in Eversholt Street, one of the most peculiar roads in the neighbourhood. In one stretch of a few hundred yards there was a Roman Catholic church, a sports centre, a legendary rock pub, council flats, a bingo hall, a juvenile detention centre, an Italian café, a Victorian men's hostel for transients and an audacious green-glass development of million pound loft apartments. Edward was on the ground floor of the council block, a bad place to be as it turned out. The Regent's Canal ran nearby, and most of the road's drains emptied into it. The Council eventually riveted steel grilles over the pipe covers, but by then it was too late.

***

Edward glanced over at Gill's photograph, pinned on the cork noticeboard beside the cooker. Once, her eyes had been the colour of cyanothus blossom, her hair saturated in sunlight, but now the picture appeared to be fading, as if it was determined to remove her from the world. He missed Gill more than he missed Sam, because nothing he could do would ever bring Sam back, but Gill was still around, living in Hackney with her two brothers. He knew he was unlikely ever to see her again. He missed her to the point where he would say her name aloud at odd moments for no reason at all. In those last days after Sam's death, she had grown so thin and pale that it seemed she was being erased from her surroundings. He watched helplessly as her bones appeared beneath her flesh, her clothes began hanging loosely on her thin arms. Gill's jaw-length blonde hair draped forward over her face as she endlessly scoured and bleached the kitchen counters. She stopped voicing her thoughts, becoming barely more visible than the water stains on the walls behind her. She would hush him with a raised finger, straining to listen for the scurrying scratch of claws in the walls, under the cupboards, across the rafters.

Rats. Some people's worst nightmare, but the thought of them no longer troubled him. What had happened to their family had happened to people all over the city. 'Rats!' thought Edward as he welded the back door shut, 'They fought the dogs and killed the cats, and bit the babies in the cradles …' He couldn't remember the rest of Robert Browning's poem. It hadn't been quite like that, because Camden Town was hardly Hamelin, but London could have done with a pied piper.

Instead, all they'd got was a distracted mayor and his dithering officials, hopelessly failing to cope with a crisis.

He pulled the goggles to the top of his head and examined his handiwork. The steel plates only ran across to the middle of the door, but were better than nothing. Now he could sort out the chewed gap underneath. It wasn't more than two inches deep, but a cat-sized rat was capable of folding its ribs flat enough to slide through with ease. He remembered watching thousands of them one evening as they'd rippled in a brown tapestry through the back gardens. There had been nights when he'd sat in the darkened lounge with his feet lifted off the floor and a cricket bat across his knees, listening to the scampering conspiracy passing over the roofs, feet pattering in the kitchen, under the beds, under his chair. He'd watched as one plump brown rat with eyes like drops of black resin had fidgeted its way between books on a shelf, daring him into a display of pitifully slow reactions.

The best solution would be to rivet a steel bar across the space under the door, but the only one he had left was too short. He thought about risking a trip to the shops, but most of the ones in the high street had closed for good, and all the hardware stores had sold out of stock weeks ago. It was hard to imagine how much a city of eight million people could change in just four months. So many had left. The Tubes were a no-go zone, of course, and it was dangerous to move around in the open at night. The rats were no longer frightened by people.

He was still deciding what to do when his mobile buzzed its way across the work counter.

'Is that Edward?' asked a cultured, unfamiliar voice.

'Yeah, who's that?'

'I don't suppose you'll remember me. We only met once, at a party. I'm Damon, Gillian's brother.'

The line fell warily silent. Damon, sanctimonious religious nut, Gill's older brother. What was the name of the other one? Matthew. Fuck. *Fuck.*

'Are you still there?'

'Yeah, sorry, you caught me a bit by surprise.'

'I guess it's a bit of a bolt from the blue. Are you still living in Camden?'

'One of the last to leave the epicentre. The streets are pretty quiet around here now.'

'I saw it on the news, didn't recognise the place. Not that I ever really knew it to begin with. Our family's from Hampshire, but I expect you remember that.'

Stop being so damned chatty and tell me what the hell you want, thought Edward. His next thought hit hard: *Gill's condition has deteriorated; she's made him call me.*

'It's about Gillian, isn't it?'

'I'm afraid – she's been a lot worse lately. We've had a tough time looking after her. She had the problem, you know, with dirt and germs –'

Spermophobia, thought Edward. *Mysophobia.* A lot of people had developed such phobias since the rats came.

'Now there are other things. She's become terrified of disease.'

Nephophobia, Pathophobia. Once arcane medical terms, now almost everyday parlance. They were closely connected; not so surprising when you remembered what she'd been through.

'It's been making life very difficult for us.'

'I can imagine.' Everything had to be cleaned over and over again. Floors scrubbed, handles and counters sprayed with disinfectant, the air kept refrigerated. All her foodstuffs had to be washed and vacuum-sealed in plastic before she would consider eating them. Edward had watched the roots of fear digging deeper within her day by day, until she could barely function and he could no longer cope.

'She's lost so much weight. She's become frightened of the bacteria in her own body. She was living on the top floor of the house, refused to take any visitors except us, and now she's gone missing.'

'What do you mean?'

'It doesn't seem possible, but it's true. We thought you should know.'

'Do you have any idea where she might have gone?'

'She couldn't have gone anywhere; that's the incredible part of it. We very badly need your help. Can you come over tonight?'

This is a turnaround, Edward thought. *Her family spent a year trying to get me to clear off, and now they need me.*

'I suppose I can come. Both of you are still okay?'

'We're fine. We take a lot of precautions.'

'Has the family been vaccinated?'

'No. Matthew and our father feel that the Lord protects us. Do you remember the address?'

'Of course. I can be there in around an hour.'

Edward was surprised they had found the nerve to call at all. The brothers had him pegged as a man of science, a member of the tribe that had helped to bring about the present crisis. People like him had warmed the planet and genetically modified its harvests, bringing abundance and pestilence. Their religion sought to exclude, and their faith was vindictive. Men who sought to accuse were men to be avoided. But he owed it to Gill to go to them.

He used the short steel bar to block the gap in the door, and covered the shortfall by welding a biscuit-tin lid over it. Not an ideal solution, but one that would have to do for now. The sun would soon be setting. The red neon sign above the Kentucky Fried Chicken outlet opposite had flickered on. It was the only part of the store that was still intact. Rioters had smashed up most of the junk-food joints in the area, looking for someone to blame.

Pest-controllers had put the massive rise in the number of rats down to three causes. The wetter, warmer winters caused flooding that lengthened the rat's breeding periods and drove them above ground. Councils reduced their spending on street cleaning. Most disastrously of all, takeaway litter left the street-bins overflowing with chicken bones and burger buns. The rat population rose by 30 percent in a single year. They thrived in London's Victorian drainage system, in the sewers and canal outlets, in the Tube lines and railway cuttings. Beneath the city was a maze of interconnected pipework, with openings into almost every street. They moved into the gardens and then the houses, colonising and spreading as each property became vacant.

One much-cited statistic suggested that a single pair of rats could spawn a maximum number of nearly a hundred billion rats in just five years. It was a sign of the burgeoning rodent population that they began to be spotted during the day; starvation drove them out into the light, and into densely populated areas. They no longer knew fear. Worse, they sensed that others were afraid of them.

Edward had always known about the dangers of disease. As a young biology student he had been required to study pathogenic microbes. London had not seen a case of plague in almost a century. The Black Death of the Middle Ages had wiped out a third of the European population. The bacterium *Yersinia pestis* had finally been eradicated by fire in London in 1666. Plague had returned to consume 10 million Indians early in the 20th Century, and had killed 200 as recently as 1994. Now it was back in a virulent new strain, and rampant. It had arrived via infected rat fleas, in a ship's container from the East, or perhaps from a poorly fumigated cargo plane, no-one was sure, and everyone was anxious to assign blame. Rats brought leptospirosis, hantavirus and rat-bite fever, and they were only the fatal diseases.

***

Edward drove through the empty streets of King's Cross with the windows of the Peugeot tightly closed and the air-conditioning set to an icy temperature. Lying in the road outside McDonald's, a bloated, blackened corpse had been partially covered by a cardboard standee for Caramel McFlurries. The gesture, presumably intended to provide some privacy in death, had only created further indignity. It was the first time he'd seen a body on the street, and the sight shocked him. It was a sign that the services could no longer cope, or that people were starting not to care. Most of the infected crept away into private corners to die, even though there were no red crosses to keep them in their houses this time.

The plague bacillus had evolved in terms of lethality. It no longer swelled the lymph glands of the neck, armpits and groin. It went straight to the lungs and caused catastrophic internal haemorrhaging. Death came fast as the lungs filled with septicaemic pus and fluid. There was a preventative vaccine, but it proved useless once the outbreak began. Tetracycline and streptomycin, once seen as effective antibiotics against plague, also failed against the emerging drug-resistant strains. All you could do was burn and disinfect; the city air stank of both, but it was preferable to the smell of death. It had been a hot summer, and the still afternoons were filled with the stench of rotting flesh.

Edward had been vaccinated at the college. Gill had blamed him for failing to vaccinate their son in time. Sam had been four months old when he died. His cradle had been left near an open window. They could only assume that a rat had entered the room foraging for food, and had come close enough for its fleas to jump to fresh breeding grounds. The child's pale skin had blackened with necrosis before the overworked doctors of University College Hospital could get around to seeing him. Gill quickly developed a phobic reaction to germs, and was collected by her brothers a few weeks after.

Edward dropped out of college. In theory, it would have been a good time to stay, because students were being drafted into the race to find more powerful weapons against the disease, but he couldn't bear to immerse himself in the subject, having so recently watched his child die in the very same building. He wondered why he hadn't fled to the countryside like so many others. It was safer there, but no-one was entirely immune. He found it hard to consider leaving the city where he had been born, and was fascinated by this slow decanting of the population. An eerie calm had descended on even the most populous districts. There were no tourists; nobody wanted to fly into Britain. People had become terrified of human contact, and kept their outside journeys to a minimum. *Mad cow disease was a comparative picnic*, he thought, with a grim chuckle.

The little car bounced across the end of Upper Street, heading toward Shoreditch. The shadows were long on the gold-sheened tarmac. A blizzard of newspapers rolled across the City Road, adding to the sense of desolation. Edward spun the wheel, watching for pedestrians. He had started to think of them as survivors. There were hardly any cars on the road, although he was surprised to pass a bus in service. At the junction of Old Street and Pitfield Street, a shifting amoeba-shape fluctuated around the doorway of a closed supermarket. The glossy black rats scattered in every direction as he drove past. You could never drive over them, however fast you went. There were now more rats than humans, approximately three for every man, woman and child, and the odds kept growing in their favour. They grew bolder each day, and had become quite brazen about their battle for occupancy. It had been said that in a city as crowded as London, you were never more than 15 feet away from a rat. Scientists warned that when the distance between rodent and human lowered to just seven feet, conditions would be perfect for the return of the plague. The flea, *Xenopsylla cheopis,* sucked up diseased rat blood and transported it to humans with shocking efficiency.

A great black patch shimmered across the road like a boiling oil slick, splitting and vanishing between the buildings. Without realising it, he found himself gripping the sweat-slick wheel so tightly that his nails were digging into his palms. *Rattus rattus.* No-one knew where the black rat had originated, so their Latin name was suitably unrevealing. The brown ones – the English ones, *Rattus norvegicus* – lived in burrows and came from China. They grew to nearly a foot and a half, and ate anything at all. They could chew their way through brick and concrete; they had to keep chewing to stop their incisors from growing back into their skulls. The black ones were smaller, with larger ears, and lived off the ground in round nests. Edward had woken in the middle of the night two weeks earlier and found a dozen of them in his kitchen, feeding from a waste bin. He had run at them with a broom, but they had simply skittered up the curtains and through a hole they had made in the ceiling to the drainpipes outside. The black ones were acrobats; they loved heights. Although they were less aggressive, they seemed to be outnumbering their brown cousins. At least, he saw more of them each day.

He fumigated the furniture and carpets for ticks and fleas, but still developed clusters of painful red welts on his ankles, his arms, his back. He was glad that Gill was no longer here, but missed her terribly. She had slipped away from him, her mind distracted by a future she could not imagine or tolerate.

***

Damon and Matthew lived with their father above offices in Hoxton, having bought the building at the height of the area's property boom. These had once been the homes of well-to-do Edwardian families, but more than half a century of neglect had followed, until the district had been rediscovered by newly wealthy artists. That bubble had burst too, and now the houses were in fast decline as thousands of rats scampered into the basements.

As Edward climbed the steps, spotlights clicked on. He could hear movement all around him. He looked up and saw the old man through the haze of white light. Gill's father was silently watching him from an open upstairs window.

There was no bell. Edward slapped his hand against the front door glass and waited. Matthew answered the door. What was it about the over-religious that made them keep their hair so neat? Matthew's blond fringe formed a perfect wave about his smooth, scrubbed face. He smiled and shook Edward's hand.

'I'm glad you could make it,' he said, as though he'd invited Edward to dinner. 'We don't get many visitors.'

He led the way upstairs, then along a bare white hall into an undecorated space that served as their living quarters. There were no personal effects of any kind on display. A stripped-oak table and four chairs stood in the centre of the bright room. Damon rose to shake his hand. Edward had forgotten how alike the brothers were. They had the eyes of zealots, bright and black and dead. They spoke with great intensity, weighing their words, watching him as they spoke.

'Tell me what happened,' Edward instructed, seating himself. He didn't want to be there any longer than was strictly necessary.

'Father can't get around anymore, so we moved him from his quarters at the top of the house and cleaned it out for Gillian. We thought if we couldn't cure her, we should at least make her feel secure, so we put her up there. But the black rats ...'

'They're good climbers.'

'That's right. They came up the drainpipes and burrowed in through the attic, so we had to move her. The only place we could think where she'd be safe was within our congregation.'

Ah yes, thought Edward, *the Church of Latter-Day Nutters. I remember all too well.* Gill had fallen out with her father over religion. He had raised his sons in a far-right Christian offshoot that came with more rules than the Highway Code. Quite how he had fetched up in this biblical backwater was a mystery, but Gill was having none of it. Her brothers had proven more susceptible, and when the plague rats had moved in, the two of them had adopted an insufferably smug attitude that drove the children further apart. Matthew was the father of three immaculately coiffed children whom Edward had christened 'the Midwich Cuckoos.' Damon's wife was the whitest woman Edward had ever met, someone who encouraged knitting as stress therapy at Christian coffee mornings. He didn't like them, their politics or their religion, but was forced to admit that they had at least been helpful to his wife. He doubted their motives, however, suspecting that they were more concerned with restoring the family to a complete unit and turning Gill back into a surrogate mother.

'We took her to our church,' Matthew explained. 'It was built in 1860. The walls are three feet thick. There are no electrical cables, no drainpipes, nothing the smallest rat could wriggle its way into. The vestry doors are wooden, and some of the stained-glass windows are shaky, but it's always been a place of safety.'

Edward had to admit that it was a smart idea. Gill's condition was untreatable without access to a psychiatrist and medication, and right now the hospitals were nightmarish no-go areas where rats went to feast on the helpless sick.

Matthew seated himself opposite. 'Gillian settled into the church, and we hoped she was starting to find some comfort in the protection of the Lord. Then some members of our congregation started spending their nights there, and she began to worry that they were bringing the plague fleas, even though we fumigated them before entering. We couldn't bear to see her suffer, so we built her a special room, right there in the middle of the apse –'

'– We made her as comfortable as we could,' Damon interrupted. 'Ten feet by 12. Four walls, a ceiling, a floor, a lockable door and a ventilation grille constructed from a strong, fine mesh.'

He looked as sheepish as a schoolboy describing a woodwork project.

'Father directed the operation, because he'd had some experience in carpentry. We moved her bed in there, and her books, and she was finally able to get some sleep. She even stopped taking the sleeping pills you used to give her.'

The pills to which she had become addicted when we lived together,

thought Edward bitterly. *The habit I was blamed for creating.*
'I don't understand,' Edward said aloud. 'What happened?'
'I think we'd better go over to the church,' said Matthew gently.

***

It wasn't far from the house, smaller than he'd imagined, slim and plain, without buttresses or arches, very little tracery. The former Welsh presbytery was sandwiched between two taller glass buildings, commerce dominating religion, darkening the streets with the inevitability of London rain. Outside its single door sat a barrel-chested black man who would have passed for a nightclub bouncer if it weren't for the cricket pads strapped on his legs. He lumbered aside as Damon and Matthew approached. The small church was afire with the light of a thousand coloured candles looted from luxury stores. Many were shaped like popular cartoon characters: Batman, Pokémon figures and Daffy Duck burned irreverently along the altar and apse. The pews had been removed and stacked against a wall. In the centre of the aisle stood an oblong wooden box bolted into the stone floor and propped with planks, like the back of a film set. A small door was inset in a wall of the cube, and that was guarded by an elderly woman who sat reading in a high-backed armchair. In the nave, a dozen family friends were talking quietly on orange plastic chairs that surrounded a low oak table. They fell silent with suspicion as Edward passed them. Matthew withdrew a key from his jacket and unlocked the door of the box, pushing it open and clicking on the light.

'We rigged a bulb to a car battery, because she wouldn't sleep in the dark,' Damon explained, waving a manicured hand at the room, which was bare but for an unfurled white futon, an Indian rug and a stack of dog-eared religious books. The box smelled of fresh paint and incense.

'You built it of wood,' said Edward, thumping the thin wall with his fist. 'That makes no sense, Damon. A rat would be through this in a minute.'

'What else could we do? It made her feel safer, and that was all that counted. We wanted to take away her pain. Can you imagine what it is

355

like to see someone in your own family suffer so much? Our father worshipped her.'

Edward detected an undercurrent of resentment in Damon's voice. He and Gill had not chosen to marry. In the eyes of her brothers, it was a sin that prevented Edward from ever being treated as a member of the family.

'You're not telling me she disappeared from inside?' he asked. 'How could she have got out?'

'That's what we thought you might be able to explain to us,' snapped Matthew. 'Why do you think we asked you here?'

'I don't understand. You locked her in each night?'

'We did it for her own good.'

'How could it be good to lock a frightened woman inside a room?'

'She'd been getting panic attacks – growing confused, running into the street. Her aunt Alice has been sitting outside every night since this thing began. Anything Gillian's needed, she's always been given.'

'When did she go missing?'

'The night before last. We thought she'd come back.'

'You didn't see her leave?' Edward asked the old lady.

'No,' replied Alice, daring him to defy her. 'I was here all night.'

'And she didn't pass you. Are you sure you never left your chair?'

'Not once. And I didn't fall asleep, either. I don't sleep at night with those things crawling all over the roof.'

'Did you let anyone else into the room?'

'Of course not,' Alice said indignantly. 'Only family and regular worshippers are allowed into the church. We don't want other people in here.' *Of course not,* thought Edward. *What's the point of organised religion if you can't exclude unbelievers?*

'And no-one except Gillian used the room,' Damon added.

'That was the point. That was why we asked you to come.'

Edward studied the two brothers. He could just about understand Damon, squeaky-clean and neatly groomed in a blazer and a pressed white shirt that provided him with an aura of faith made visible, but Matthew seemed in a state of perpetual anger, a church warrior who had no patience with the unconverted. He remained a mystery.

'Why me?' Edward asked. 'What made you call me?'

Momentarily stumped, the brothers looked at each other awkwardly.

'Well – you slept with her.' Presumably they thought he must know her better for having done so.

'I knew her until our son died, but then – well, when someone changes that much, it becomes impossible to understand how they think anymore.'

Edward hoped they would appreciate his point of view. He wanted to make contact with them just once.

'Let me take a look around. I'll see what I can do.'

The brothers stepped back, cognisant of their ineffectiveness, their hands awkwardly at their sides. Behind them, the church door opened and the congregation slowly streamed in. The men and women who arranged themselves at the rear of the church looked grey and beaten. Faith was all they had left.

'I'm sorry, it's time for our evening service to begin,' Damon explained.

'Do what you have to do,' Edward said, accepting the red plastic torch that Matthew was offering him. 'I'll call you if I find anything.'

***

A series of narrow alleys ran beside the church. If Gill had managed to slip past the old lady, she would have had to enter them. Edward looked up at the dimming blue strip of evening sky. Along the gutters sat fat nests constructed of branches and bin bags, the black plastic shredded into malleable strips. As he watched, one bulged and disgorged a family of coal-eyed rats. They clung to the drainpipes, staring into his torch beam, before suddenly spiralling down at him. He moved hastily aside as they scurried over his shoes and down the corridor of dirt-encrusted brick.

The end of the alley opened out into a small, litter-strewn square. He hardly knew where to begin his search. If the family had failed to find her, how would he succeed? On the steps of a boarded-up block of flats sat an elderly man swathed in a dirty green sleeping bag. The man stared wildly at him, as if he had just awoken from a nightmare.

'All right?' asked Edward, nodding curtly. The old man beckoned him. Edward tried to stay beyond range of his pungent stale aroma, but was summoned nearer.

'What is it?' he asked, wondering how anyone dared to sleep rough in the city now. The old man pulled back the top of his sleeping bag as if shyly revealing a treasure, and allowed him to look in on the hundred or so hairless baby rats that wriggled over his bare stomach like maggots, pink and blind.

Perhaps that was the only way you could survive on the streets now, thought Edward, riven with disgust: you had to take their side. He wondered if, as a host for their offspring, the old man had been made an honorary member of their species, and was therefore allowed to continue unharmed. Although perhaps the truth was less fanciful: rats sense the safety of their surroundings through the movement of their own bodies. Their spatial perception was highly attuned to the width of drains, the cracks in walls, the fearful humans who moved away at great haste. Gill might have been panicked into flight, but she was weak and would not have been able to run for long. She must have stopped somewhere to regain her breath. But where?

He searched the dark square. The wind had risen to disturb the tops of the plane trees, replacing the city's once-ever-present bass-line of traffic with natural susurration. It was the only sound he could now hear. Lights shone above a corner shop. Slumped on the windowsill, two Indian children stared down into the square, their eyes half-closed by rat bites.

Edward returned to the church, slipping in behind the ragged congregation, and watched Matthew in the dimly-illuminated pulpit.

'For this is not the end but the beginning,' said Matthew, clearly preaching a worn-in sermon of fire and redemption.

'Those whom the Lord has chosen to keep in good health will be free to remake the land in His way.'

It was the kind of lecture to which Edward had been subjected as a child, unfocused in its promises, peppered with pompous rhetoric, vaguely threatening.

'Each and every one of us must make a sacrifice, without which there can be no admittance to the Kingdom of Heaven, and he who has not surrendered his heart to Our Lady will be left outside, denied the power of reformation.'

It seemed to Edward that congregations always required the imposition of rules for their salvation, and desperate times had forced them to assume that these zealous brothers would be capable of setting them. He moved quietly to the unguarded door of the wooden box and stepped inside, shutting himself in. The sense of claustrophobia was immediate. A locked room, guarded from outside. Where the hell had she gone? He sat on the futon, idly kicking at the rug, and listened to the muffled litany of the congregation. A draught was coming into the room, but not through the door. He lowered his hand down into the darkness, and felt chill air prickle his fingers. At first he failed to see the corner of the hatch, but as he focused the beam of the torch more tightly he realised what he was looking at: a section of flooring, about three feet by two, that had been sawn into the wooden deck beside the bed. The flooring was plywood, easy to lift. The hatch covered the spiral stairwell to the crypt. A black-painted Victorian iron banister curved away beneath his feet. Outside, Matthew was leading a catechism that sounded more like a rallying call.

Edward dipped the light and stepped onto the fretwork wedges. Clearly Gill had been kept in the wooden room against her will, but how had she discovered the staircase to the chamber beneath her prison? Perhaps its existence was common knowledge, but it had not occurred to anyone that she might be able to gain access to it. The temperature of the air was dropping fast now; could this have been its appeal, the thought that germs would not be able to survive in such a chill environment?

He reached the bottom of the steps. His torch beam reflected as a fracturing moon of light; the flagstones were hand-deep in icy water. A series of low stone arches led through the tunnelled crypt ahead of him. He waded forward and found himself beneath the ribbed vault of the main chamber. The splash of water boomed in the silent crypt. With freezing legs and visible breath, Edward stood motionless, waiting for the ripples to subside. Something was wrong. Gillian might have lost her reason, but she would surely not have ventured down here alone. She knew that rats were good swimmers. It didn't make sense. Something was wrong.

***

Above Edward's head, in the body of the church, the steeple bell began to ring, cracked and flat. The change in the congregation was extraordinary. They dropped to their knees, unmindful of injury, staring toward the tattered crimson reredos that shielded the choir stall. Damon and Matthew had reappeared in sharp white surplices, pushing back the choir screen as their flock began to murmur in anticipation. The dais they revealed had been swathed in shining gold brocade, discovered in bolts at a Brick Lane sari shop. Atop stood the enshrined figure, a mockery of Catholicism, its naked flesh dulled down with talcum powder until it resembled worn alabaster, its legs overgrown with plastic vines. The wheels of the wooden dais creaked as Damon and Matthew pushed the wobbling tableau toward the altar. The voices of the crowd rose in adulation. The figure on the dais was transfixed in hysterical ecstasy, posed against a painted tree with her knees together and her palms turned out, a single rose stem lying across the right hand, a crown of dead roses placed far back on her shaved head, her eyes rolled to a glorious invisible heaven. Gillian no longer heard the desperate exultation of her worshippers; she existed in a higher place, a vessel for her brothers' piety, floating far above the filthy, blighted Earth, in a holy place of such grace and purity that nothing dirty or harmful would ever touch her again.

***

Edward looked up. Somewhere above, the bell was still ringing, the single dull note repeated over and over. He cocked his head at the ribs of the vault and listened. First the trees, then the church bell, and now this, as though the forgotten order of nature was reasserting itself. He heard it again, the sound he had come to know and dread, growing steadily all around him. Raising the torch, he saw them scurrying over the fine green nylon webbing that had been stretched across the vault ceiling, thousands of them, far more than he had ever seen in once place before: black rats, quite small, their bodies shifting transversely, almost comically, as they weighed and judged distances.

They had been summoned to dinner. They gathered in the roof of the main chamber, directly beneath the ringing bell, until they were piling on top of each other, some slipping and swinging by a single pink paw, and then they fell, twisting expertly so that they landed on Edward and not in the water, their needle claws digging into the flesh of his shoulders to gain purchase, to hang on at all costs. Edward hunched himself instinctively, but this exposed a broader area for the rats to drop onto, and now they were releasing themselves from the mesh and falling in ever greater numbers, more and more, until the sheer weight of their solid, sleek bodies pushed him down into the filthy water. This was their cue to attack, their indication that the prey was defeatable, and they bit down hard, pushing their heads between each other to bury thin, yellow teeth into his soft skin. He felt himself bleeding from a hundred different places at once, the wriggling mass of rat bodies first warm, then hot, now searing on his back until they made their way through his hair, heading for the tender prize of his eyes.

Edward was determined not to scream, not to open his mouth and admit their poisonous furred bodies. He did the only thing he could, and pushed his head deep under the water, drawing great draughts into his throat and down into his lungs, defeating them in the only way left to him, cheating them of live prey. *Gill, I love you,* was his final prayer. *I only ever loved you, and wherever you are, I hope you are happy.* Death etched the thought into his bones and preserved it forever.

***

In the East End church, a mood of satiated harmony fell upon the congregation, and Matthew smiled at Damon as they covered the tableau once more, content that their revered sister was at peace. For now the enemy was assuaged, the commitment had been made, the congregation appeased. Science had held sway for long enough. Now it was time for the harsh old gods to smile down once more.

The Extraordinary Limits Of Darkness
Simon Clark

> The offing was barred by a black bank of clouds, and the
> tranquil waterway leading to the uttermost ends of the earth
> flowed sombre under an overcast sky – seemed to lead into the
> heart of an immense darkness.
> *–Heart of Darkness* by Joseph Conrad

Remember that afternoon on the beach when I told you about my expedition to Africa? Did I say expedition? If you wish, substitute 'expedition' for the word 'folly' or 'frolic.' I was much younger then, and having lived so many years as a seaman, I found my home town such a drab place that even when my brother sailors were retreating to their townhouses to work in offices and trim their rose gardens and cultivate their families, I felt this need for adventure. It was like a dull ache in a bad tooth. I didn't relish the adventure for adventure's sake. I simply knew that it was my lot in life to embark on yet another exploration, because even though I'd encounter hardship and loneliness, the alternative was worse. The wilds of the Congo are hell. The ivy clad villas of Essex are a deeper hell. You remember my yarn of the journey up-river by steam-paddle boat to find Kurtz, and bring him back to civilisation with his mountain of ivory? We found him and his ivory after a gruelling voyage. The ivory was poor quality. Kurtz had become a murderous tyrant who fed the darkest of his appetites in ways I can't even begin to put into words. I daresay even the Emperor Caligula, who hacked off his nephew's head because of an irritating cough, would have paled at the sight of what Kurtz inflicted on the natives. On the return journey, Kurtz died. We left his body in a muddy grave by the river. But we brought his diaries back with us. And it was in one of those diaries that the seed of what was to come began to grow.

As so often with these things, there is a long, involved sequence of events that ferment away in their own, dark world before we become aware of them. But the gist of it is, that on New Year's Day, 1913, I found myself disembarking at the African port of Dakar. I was as disappointed with the place as I was with my companions on my new expedition. Some men quaff their whisky in anticipation of the riotous, laughter-filled evening ahead of them. Some drink the spirit in the joyless certainty of the crushing headache and dry throat of the hangover that waits for them, come morning. I – I'm sorry to say – am attached to the latter. Dakar is a miserable town: cheaply built houses and warehouses in the modern French style. The land is flat. There are palms, there is dust. The climate manages to inflict a burning sun combined with a cold, northerly wind. My companions in adventure hadn't been to Africa before. In fact, they hadn't been further south than their wintering quarters in Monte Carlo. They insisted on dressing in a bizarre confection of white suits with feathered hats, imagining that it is the necessity of every civilised gentleman to promenade in such a way so as to impress on the African the European's godlike stature. The French crew of the ship were so richly amused by my companions strutting down the gangplank at Dakar that many of them lapsed into helpless laughter.

There were three days of wrangling with customs officers over the 14 cases of gin my expedition had brought with them (those and the rifles, pistols, blasting powder and magnesium torches) – after that, we were delivered to the train station for the five-day journey to where Kurtz had so considerately buried his riches for us to find.

And what of me? Why had I agreed to accompany these men on the expedition? I didn't know them. The offer of three percent of the net wealth of the treasure didn't really appeal. No, curse the devil on my back, it was the adventure! It was the promise of travel to Africa; it was a suggestion of sleeping in snake-infested huts in malarial swamps where hippos roared one awake in the middle of the night. That was the devil that brought me so meekly to heel in the company's British office – the one and the same company that had employed me to navigate a moribund boat into the heart of the Congo to find the despicable Kurtz. What was the alternative? Yes, yes, the alternative would be a winter at leisure in my English sitting room, with tea and buttered scones, and gleaming cutlery and spotless bedding and … oh, the crushing hand of boredom. Always boredom. Eternal boredom. Forever and ever without end …

So that is how I found myself in the company office with one of its esteemed directors, who exhibited himself behind his vast and stately galleon of a desk. There, he folded his arms so he could stroke his own elbows as he dropped the wonderful phrases into my ear. His long, grey hair fell across the rich velvet collar of his coat as he uttered those phrases – those honey-dipped phrases. 'A journey to where few white men have been … hardships will be great but the rewards greater. Three percent of Kurtz's treasures will be yours – once the value has been assessed, of course. Sail from Portsmouth on Christmas Eve. Africa by New Year's Day. You will be in the company of three gallant gentlemen, three fellow adventurers – Dr Lyman, Sir Anthony Winterflood and Henry Sanders. Sanders is a solicitor, a good, solid man, dependable as the Bank of England.'

On the voyage, my companions hadn't talked about the treasure we'd find. They spoke incessantly of the sport. The sport was the thing. In England there was sport, of course, but not the sport they favoured. They talked of a 'grand sport' to be had in Africa. A great and wonderful sport that would enrich their lives and their memories for many a year to come. They rarely spoke to me, even though I was supposedly an equal member of the team. And they rarely mentioned the rigours of the journey to come. But sport? Yes, indeed, the talk was of the fine sport to be had on the Dark Continent.

***

Toward the end of that first week of the new year, with 1912 flung on the scrap heap of time, and with 1913 rearing up in front of us like an untrod mountain, we boarded the train for our journey into Africa's secret heart. The company had chartered the train specially for us. They had no doubt we would return it to the coast laden with Kurtz's fabulous treasure. Our transport consisted of one derelict-looking locomotive – the plaque on its side advertised that it had been built in Doncaster, England in 1859. Behind the loco that was merrily spitting boiling water all over the platform was the tender heaped with more coal – although a poor, muddy coal, I noted with some misgivings. Next in line after the tender were two goods vans that would carry our treasure, then the carriage containing a cook's galley and half a dozen cabins that offered our private quarters; then at the very end of the train an elegant structure of carved timbers combined with an extravagant amount of glass. This final carriage of our treasure train was a communal lounge. Apart from the train's crew, we four would be the only passengers carried by that astonishing luxury-liner of dry land.

By the time I'd unpacked my case, washed and shaved, the train had shrieked its way out of the station. As you would imagine from the nature of the iron beast, our progress was stately to say the least. At no time did we accelerate to faster than 12 miles per hour. The terrain immediately outside Dakar is flat, open land; however, within 30 minutes, thorn trees began rising from the dry earth like skeletons frozen in time. Leaves? Yes, they must have borne leaves, but all I recall of the skeletal branches are immense, dagger-like thorns, and the way the trees multiplied quite discreetly until, whereas I'd been watching a few dozen trees sliding by on an open plain, I now saw a dense thicket of thorn trees that closed in on the track until we had no more of a view than if we'd been travelling through a tunnel. I had hoped to sit on my cabin bunk and watch elephants wander across a savannah, or be entertained by monkeys leaping through their arboreal kingdom. Yet there was nothing but thorn trees. Damned thorn trees through which we moved at our 12 miles per hour. Thorn trees that appeared to be home to nothing – not even birds.

With the view being nothing, I busied myself with my papers regarding the next leg of the expedition. In three days' time, the train would reach the end of its track; from there, we would cross country on foot until we reached a lake. Waiting there would be a sailing barque, which I would skipper to an island where Kurtz had concealed his glittering hoard. There were matters concerning the transportation of provisions that I needed to discuss with my travelling companions, so I took my map to the salon in the hope of finding them there. Of the three, however, only Dr Lyman had ventured from his cabin.

The heat in our tunnel of thorns had become formidable. Dr Lyman was seated on a sofa of plush velvet in his black frockcoat, perhaps in readiness for attracting the awe-stricken glances of any native who happened to be peeping from the thorn forest. He was a plump man with a round face and round hands that protruded from beneath starched shirt cuffs. His hair was neatly parted down the centre; the scalp revealed itself as a bright pink strip of overheated skin. His black boots were polished, as were the buttons on that frock-coat. He was astonishing, and wore a pink carnation in his lapel. On the little table beside him, a glass, containing gin and peppermint cordial, trembled from the vibrations induced by the 12 mile an hour rush through the spiky jungle. Those same vibrations made the rifle propped up against the sofa slide sideways, so he had to steady it to prevent it falling. An action he repeated frequently during the following.

I cleared my throat. 'Dr Lyman, good morning.'

He nodded, then sipped his gin and pep – he and his companions always drank gin and pep, chilled by a veritable rock of ice, so the contents of their glasses were never a mystery for me. I knew drinking liquor in a hot climate wasn't helpful to one's constitution, and so avoided it. The doctor's nod seemed to be the extent of his conversation with me. After adjusting his carnation and wiping a speck of dust from the black sleeve of his frockcoat, he returned to his silent, dignified pose, while the train chack chacked at precisely 12 miles an hour. His face became very red. Yet by an effort of will-power he checked the escape of perspiration from his skin. Dr Lyman was a man of formidable will-power. Maybe the power of his mind retarded the speed of the train. He blinked to the rhythm of the chack … chack … chack …

'Dr Lyman …' I wasn't going to be cheated of this vital discussion on logistics. 'Dr Lyman. I've been checking our travel itinerary against the map …'

'Excellent! You have everything on the nail. The company told me that you were just the man for the job. Their words to me were: he'd have everything on the nail – right on the very nail! Good work, sir.'

'Thank you, but I thought we should talk about how many native bearers we'll require for –'

'Oh, as many as you need. The company told me that you'd plan everything with aplomb. They speak very highly of you. After all, you brought the papers that belonged to Kurtz back to London.' He sipped his gin and pep; the little iceberg clunked against the glass. 'This time, they'll reward you amply, so I'm given to understand.' He nodded, satisfied that he'd granted me precious moments of his time. There you have it; this wasn't so much as an expeditional team, rather me playing Cook's tour representative to three of my social betters who wished to see something of savage lands from the comfort of the carriage.

And what a carriage. The windows were vast. The carpet underfoot deep. The carved furniture boasted an abundance of delicate scrollwork and deep upholstery. From the roof hung crystal chandeliers. This was the salon of a duchess that somehow had been gifted wheels and set rolling – rolling at 12 miles per hour, mind – through a thorn forest in Africa. As I witnessed later, a mere pull on a velvet bell rope would cause a French waiter dressed in a pristine white jacket to manifest himself into the carriage, where he would ask with the gravest of respect what meal or drink we required. Gin and pep – always gin and pep for my companions. And ice – plenty of ice! Meanwhile the train maintained its stately 12 miles per hour on a track that didn't seem to possess even a whisper of a bend. Nor did it venture upon a single break in our thorn tree tunnel.

I decided to await my other travelling companions before broaching the subject of the bearers again – although I suspected they too would quickly congratulate me on my energy and organisational skill before returning to their debate about the sport. This was 'the sport' they'd discussed so avidly on the ship. Oh, the rapture that blazed in their eyes. 'The sport in Africa is extraordinary,' they'd murmur with a disquieting intimacy to each other. 'It is quite worth the trip for that alone.' Their talk always made me weary and irritable. Hang their sport, I'd tell myself. I glanced across the swaying carriage with its chinking chandeliers to the round-faced, red-faced man. The rapture filled his eyes again. He was thinking about his sport. Sport filled him from his polished boots to the pink stripe of scalp that ran across the top of his head. Blast his sport. Blast his indolence. All this and a miserly 12 miles an hour.

The monotonous rhythm of the chack … chack … chack of iron wheels on an iron track suddenly vanished with the arrival of the other two adventurers. One, Sir Anthony, was dressed in green silk pyjamas in a style best described as Chinese; his companion, the solicitor, wore an immaculate white suit. They carried repeating rifles, while their faces wore such expressions of joy. When they spoke, it proved this was too special a time to waste on coherent speech.

'Fine animals! Six of them.' Then to me. 'Open the window man … No! No! The one on the left.' Then to the doctor. 'Your rifle! Quick! Quick! Before they run into the forest! Have you opened that window yet, man! There! Stand back!'

The doctor couldn't believe their good fortune. 'Sport,' he insisted on repeating in a daze of pure happiness. 'Is there sport? So soon? Are you sure?'

'We have our sport, gentlemen, praise be. Ready with the rifle, doctor!' The man in the pyjamas cocked his rifle and poked the muzzle through the window I'd slid back to create a cavernous aperture in the side of the carriage. I smelt hot dust and the sun-scorched branches of the thorn trees. 'Do you see them?' Sir Anthony's voice rose into high piping. 'Ah! There they are!'

Walking along the dusty borderland between the rail track and the start of the thorn trees 50 paces away was a line. A loose, undulating line of ten figures. Five men, five women – husbands and wives. It seemed they carried bundles of everything they possessed on their heads. One woman carried a dozing child in a papoose on her back. The natives were an ebony black that glistened in the sunlight. All ten were very thin; their knees appeared as bulbous oddities compared with the narrowness of their thighs and shins. They were barefoot. All were naked. Naked, that is, apart from a belt of some red material worn around their waists.

My three companions discharged their weapons with so much fervour it was as if those long-awaited gunshots had been held in pent-up frustration all their adult lives. The powder discharged the bullets at speed. But the will-power of the three men sped the lead shot to velocities that seemed to melt the air around them. They fired again and again. The men and women fell without murmur. Maybe in some undreamt-of way, they knew this was their fate. Perhaps they'd seen it in their dreams. Maybe a witchdoctor had told them to be at this place at this time to meet their destiny. They didn't cry out; they didn't flinch; they didn't react with any expression of pain or unhappiness at reaching the end of their lives on that dirt track. As the rifles discharged the tiny but swift cargoes, the natives simply knelt down in the dirt, their burdens falling from their heads, their eyes suddenly tired looking, that's all. And there they died.

'Aim for the faces,' the doctor called out with a blend of urgency and delight. The last round in his magazine enlarged upon his short statement as it demonstrated most clearly the effect of such a shot to the front of a human head. The rifle bullet popped through the face – in the centre of the flared nostrils to be more precise – before bursting out through back of the skull, resulting in the entire head deflating to perhaps half its former volume. The African toppled sideways into a cluster of weeds.

The train driver continued his majestic 12 miles per hour. The thorn trees were unbroken, from the engine a rain of soot fell on the still bodies that lay on the hot earth. The doctor permitted himself to perspire a little from his beetroot face now, as he tugged on the bell rope. 'Gin and peppermint,' he ordered as the white-jacketed waiter appeared. 'Three.' He held up three fingers. 'With ice – plenty of ice.'

***

The sport ... oh, this *sport*. The three athletes devoted soul, mind and fibre to their sport. And as the train *chacked* along the iron rails deeper into the heart of the eternal forest, they played their hardest. By the time the sun descended into a red blaze somewhere in that empire of thorns, I sat at the dining table. There I was served my *hors d'oeuvre* of salad with grilled sole and lemon. The cutlery shone, the white cotton tablecloth was perfection, and the golden honeysuckle display in the centre was amazing.

The three athletes stood at the very end of the carriage. Sustained by gin and pep, they fired their rifles for hour after hour. Mere shards of conversation reached me.

'A full six feet he was. Took two shots to –'

'The face, I say, aim for the face.'

'… their nakedness. What comes out of 'em isn't the colour of blood at all.'

'Now, gentlemen. Here's another.' *Bang!* 'See! The face!'

'A difficult shot.'

'Tricky, very tricky.'

'But admirably effective. Admirable!'

'Strikes the nail right on the head it does!'

'By Jove! Good musketry, sir!'

Men, women, old, young, lame, simple, and one with a face as fair as the Christ who takes us aloft when our toil is done. They all fell to the gentlemen's rifle-work. Mothers, bambinos, silver-haired patriarchs. Oh, I can see the Africans lying on the hot soil even now. The train chacked at 12 miles an hour. The red sunset was glorious. I picked at my fish to avoid having a bone stick in my throat; meanwhile, the doctor's bullet was a golden star that, to me, appeared to glide gracefully toward a grandma who carried a bundle of sticks on her head, and led a child by his hand. The grandma's skin was as dark as the bark of the thorn trees, her bare feet were broad from tramping over baked earth for 70 years. The golden star that was the doctor's bullet settled on the bridge of her nose, then ever so slowly melted through the skin, to continue its mysterious journey into the dreams and visions and wonders contained in her brain.

'See!' the doctor exclaimed. 'Always aim for the face.'

'You'll have to be quick, Sir Anthony, the child is running into the bushes!'

'Ah, got it!'

'Bad luck, Sir Anthony, you've only winged it.'

Chack … chack … chack … 12 miles an hour … never more than 12 miles an hour …

Going into the forest was like journeying into the underworld. The thorn trees became thicker, more gnarled, more ancient looking. And they looked less like wood than stone. It was as if the trees were formed from dark rock that had been extruded from the ground. There must have been leaves, yet for the life of me, I don't recall any leaves. Only spikes that would pierce the flesh if you attempted to walk through that deadly copse. All this and 12 miles an hour. And interminable sport.

Why didn't the natives retreat into the forest when their countrymen were being noisily despatched by the three adventurers with their repeating rifles? The fact is that those Africans walking alongside the track formed a sparse traffic indeed. Our three in their moving hide had the opportunity to enjoy their sport only every 30 minutes or so. Even though the train rumbled at a miserable 12 miles an hour, it encountered natives at intervals of at least six miles apart. So, those that were going to give their lives in order to entertain the gentlemen wouldn't have heard the earlier gunshots, let alone witnessed the stately hunt.

Twelve miles an hour. The waiter in his white jacket poured a claret for my approval.

'Very nice. Thank you.'

'*Merci, Monsieur.*'

A youth with no longer a head to call his own fell into some thistles.

Next, on my fine china plate, a row of delicately roasted lamb chops, served with saffron rice and a casserole of courgette, tomato, spring onion and blue-black slivers of egg-plant. Twelve miles an hour. The train driver sounded the whistle to spare the life of some animal sitting on the track. I saw it safely decamp into the forest. The athletes fired on a family padding along the path in the relative cool of the evening. For the first time, a reaction. A woman with pink strips tied in her hair ran after the train. She shouted in a fabulous tongue. Shouts of rage, or grief, or gratitude at the hunters returning her loved ones to the laps of the gods. I don't know. Just it was very noisy. I found a piece of eggshell in the vegetable casserole. That annoyed me immensely. To me, discovering eggshell in food is worse than finding a fly.

The solicitor felled the shouting woman with his revolver. She'd almost reached the train as it rumbled into our heart of darkness.

'Face.' The doctor's approval was heartfelt. 'Dead centre of the face.'

***

My cabin at midnight. The air was so hot it was as if you had inhaled it over a lighted stove. Still the train rumbled along at its mandatory 12 miles per hour. I lay on the bunk with the window open. There were no stars; only darkness; a colossal, overwhelming darkness. My companions must have retired to bed. Apart from the chack of iron wheels on iron track, there was no other sound. From time to time, I moved around my compact room with its expensive wood panelling. Many times I washed my face in my bathroom. I always avoided looking in the mirror. I didn't like what I saw there. Then I'd return to the bunk, where I lay staring up into the darkness. At last the train began to slow. Fantastically, or so it seemed to me, our unassailable – our sacred! – 12 miles per hour dropped to ten, then to nine. Soon we crawled. Then stopped. After 18 hours of sullen yet indefatigable progress, the train was still. All of a sudden, the iron beast that was our locomotive seemed to hold its breath. Silence! And such a silence – it was an invasive force. Ye Gods, I remember that silence to this day. I put my hands over my ears and groaned. After 18 hours of chack, chack, chack, the sudden absence of mechanical noise hurt my ears. Why had we stopped? For water or wood to feed the iron beast perhaps. Then the change was wrought ...

Our journey on the train had rendered Africa a seemingly distant place. Until then, I hadn't been able to hear the sounds of the forest, because of our locomotive grunting and clacking. This wilderness could hitherto have been a savage island glimpsed only indistinctly from the bridge of a ship. Now we were at rest, the presence – the living, breathing, palpitating, aromatic presence – of this primeval land sidled into the train. The thorn tree forest began at its regulation 50 paces from the track; that I knew; but what I sensed was entirely different. The forest crept closer. I could feel its prickling presence. Now I divined unseen forms of prodigious size lurking in the darkness beneath its branches. Even though I didn't so much as glance out of the window, I was as certain as I am of my own name that a thousand malevolent eyes had fixed on the stationary train. When we moved, nothing could destroy us. Now I had no doubt that we could be blasted to atoms by the merest flick of a lizard's tail. The window – that widely open window drew my gaze. Now a panther could leap through it. That 12 miles an hour was our magical protection. I realised that now. Without motion, we were as vulnerable as ants beneath a boy's stamping foot.

'*Marlow!*'

My cabin door bashed open. The doctor stood there in his silk dressing gown, his chest heaving, his face red in the light of the lamp he held. In the other plump fist he clutched his rifle by its barrel.

'Marlow! Quick man! You must catch him before he gets away!'

Before I could ask what was happening, the lamp had been thrust into my hand and the doctor had bundled me out through the carriage door onto Africa's baked mud.

'There he is,' hissed the doctor. 'Bring him to us!'

***

The train journey had seemed, to me, like a dream. When I found myself standing on the crisp soil, with the carriages at a standstill behind me and the light of the lamp revealing something of the tangle of thorn branches: that was when I re-entered the world of reality.

'Hurry man,' hissed the doctor. He pointed at an abandoned rail carriage that lay on its side in that naked borderland between track and forest. 'He'll get away.'

'*What?*' The irritation in my voice was plain to hear.

Sir Anthony leaned out of the carriage window in his pyjamas. 'There's a native dressed in gold. *Flush him out.*'

The three gentlemen, the blood-thirsty beggars, were armed with rifles. With utmost indignation I approached the wreck of the carriage. In the light of the lamp, I saw it was a twin of the opulent passenger carriage that bore us in luxury through the wilderness – although it had suffered here. Windows had been broken. Insects had devoured the plush upholstery. Chandeliers lay shattered in the remains of a great deal of crockery. A stink of rot. I noticed also, growing there in the centre of the wreck, a young thorn tree.

'Hurry up, Marlow.'

'Don't take all night about it.'

'Flush him out. The devil's covered from head to foot in gold.'

I moved around to the far side of the carriage to find our victim. Indeed there he was. A native boy of around 13. His dusty body was black as onyx. One foot, I noticed, was abnormally large. And he shone with gold. Gold amulets, a gold collar; he wore a cotton shirt that was decorated by oblong panels of gold. I'd never seen anyone as extraordinary. His large, round eyes regarded mine. He didn't appear afraid. He merely waited for an outcome.

'Marlow. Flush him out. Then stand back so we can get a clear shot.' Rifles cocked with a loud clicking. 'And for heaven's sake give us light!'

I raised the lamp to illuminate the child of gold. Then I advanced on him, waving my arms like a man might wave his arms to shoo chickens back into their coop. Still facing me, the boy moved slowly backward. The large foot, with unusually broad toes, caused him to limp. I shooed. He still retreated. As soon as he was clear of the carriage wreck, my countrymen would have their sport. I moved more to the right. I was a little closer now. I glanced away from the brown eyes that fixed on mine to the boy's golden adornments. They caught the lamplight with yellow flashes. Oh, they were splendid, all right. They were also cut from the sheets of gold foil that are used to wrap chocolate. Bless me, the youth had decorated himself with confectioners' tin foil. I maintained a distance of perhaps ten paces from him as I shooed, slowly flapping my arms as I did so.

From behind me came annoyed shouts. 'Out of the way, Marlow!'

'We can't get a clean shot.'

'I can't fire until you step aside.'

'Marlow … you fool.'

I maintained my flapping gesture until the boy in his gold tinfoil had backed into the forest, where the night swallowed him. Just for a few paces, I entered the fringes of that wall of thorn. Although I no longer saw the boy in my lamplight, I beheld a man. He'd stood there silently watching what had transpired. He must have been a great age. His white eyebrows and hair were a marked contrast to the ebony skin. His arms were thin as twigs and his bare shoulders were as wrinkled as brown paper. Only there was something about his eyes ... something shockingly wrong. What should have been the whites of the eyes were a bright yellow in colour. Almost a luminous yellow, like a candle flame placed behind amber glass. His face was expressionless. Then he stepped forward. He gripped my forearm in his right hand and my elbow in his left. For a moment, he leaned forward a shade to look into my eyes with that pair of yellow orbs. I fancy now that he muttered some words in a sing-song voice, but at the time I'd have sworn he'd said nothing. But memory is not fossil. It continues to evolve. After that, he melted back into the forest.

I returned to the train and the sportsmen's jeers.

'Marlow, what the devil were you playing at?'

'You ruined a perfectly good shot.'

'The face ... had it clear as day until you stood in the way.'

'And what about our gold?'

'Didn't you see how he draped himself in the stuff?'

'Where will we find gold like that again for the picking?'

In a temper I barked at them: 'There is no gold!'

The train driver sounded his whistle; steam gushed through the wheels of the locomotive as the carriage shuddered. By the time I climbed back on board, we were moving once more, gradually accelerating toward our magical 12 miles per hour.

***

With the dawn came searing brightness. The air in my cabin grew stifling; perspiration broke through my skin if I did so much as sit upright. So all that day I lay on my bunk. Beyond the window, the unbroken thorn forest slid by. Chack, chack, chack ... The three gentlemen irked me so much that I decided to keep myself absent from the salon carriage. The waiter brought meals to me along with jugs of boiled water, that being my preferred drink in a hot climate. All through that long, hot day I heard the snap of rifle shots. However, I refrained from viewing the messy results of their sport.

By the time the sun had begun to set once more, my anger at the men had increased. I found myself wrenching back the door of my cabin before dashing down into that duchess's parlour on wheels; oh, the chandeliers were tinkling merrily as the train swayed along. The flowers were fresh in their vases. Only this time, the solicitor and Sir Anthony weren't there. Instead, there was only the doctor. He sat on a plush sofa as he stared at his gin, pep and melting pearls of ice dancing in the glass on a little walnut table.

His eyes were almost closed, but he peeped through the fleshy slits.

'You've found it!' I shouted at him. 'There's no need to go any further!'

The doctor took his time to speak. 'Go rest. The journey is more arduous than I could have believed.'

'Didn't you hear me?' I wanted to hit him. 'You already have it. You've found Kurtz's treasure.'

'Have I, by Jove?' The doctor's voice was a ghost of a sound. No more than a breath. It was a miracle I heard it at all. Not for a moment did he remove his gaze from the glass of liquor.

'Do you know what Kurtz's treasure is? It's not ivory, it's not pearls, not diamonds. What Kurtz valued most – his prize possession – was his ability to commit the most savage acts without guilt. Kurtz was the consummate torturer and violator. It invigorated him. Every death he caused had the same virtue of a conscientious man saving another penny for his future prosperity. That talent for slaughter is Kurtz's gold. You've proved you have it. So, there is no need to go further. Take your wretched treasure home with you. See if you can invest it! See what kind of reward murder brings to you!'

'I'm going to lie down in my cabin,' he whispered. Then he looked at me. The whites of his eyes had turned quite yellow. It was as if someone shone a candle through amber.

Within the hour, the sun had set. In turn I visited the cabins of each of the sportsmen – those athletes that gave so much to indulge their sport.

Sir Anthony sat on his bathroom floor with his back to the wall.

When I spoke his name, he managed only by dint of great effort to look at me. His eyes – a bright yellow. It reminded me of the gold foil stitched to the boy's clothing.

The solicitor lay beneath the blankets on his bunk as if cold to his bones. I, however, found the heat stifling. He didn't say a word; instead, his tongue constantly marched back and forth across his lips. When I looked more closely into his face, his part-open eyes formed slits of an uncannily brilliant yellow.

The doctor. He sat on his bunk, his back jammed tight against the wall. He regarded the corner of his cabin with absolute terror. He was shaking violently. The fever had ransacked his body of all physical strength. When he saw me, he beckoned – such relief at being no longer alone.

'Marlow,' he gasped. 'Do you see who's standing there?'

I looked at his frock coat swaying on its peg.

He clutched at my shirt sleeve. 'You know who that is, don't you?'

I said nothing.

'It's Kurtz, isn't it?'

'Kurtz is dead.'

'Yes, he is, isn't he?' With horror, the doctor stared into the cabin wall. 'And there's something extraordinary about his eyes.'

***

They called out as I packed my bag.

'Please help me!'

'Marlow … water …'

'Marlow! Kurtz is here. He's staring at me … *Those eyes!* Marlow, in the name of God …'

The bacillus that felled the three sportsmen could, I suppose, have been in the very air. I suspect, however, it emerged from tainted water that had been used to make the ice that chilled their drinks. To make good its escape from the frigid prison, all the germ required was a little warmth.

Twelve miles an hour. That's how fast that haunted, nightmare world travelled on its track. Not fast enough to break my neck when I jumped free of it. Moments later, with both feet firmly planted on African soil, I had my long walk in front of me. Behind me, the train continued its even longer journey along that track through an entire universe of thorn trees, and I watched it dwindle into the distance – into the heart of an even greater darkness.

Stephen Jones is the winner of three World Fantasy Awards, three Horror Writers Association Bram Stoker Awards and three International Horror Guild Awards, as well as being a Hugo Award nominee and a sixteen-times recipientof the British Fantasy Award. One of Britain's most acclaimed anthologistsof horror and dark fantasy, he has more than eighty books to his credit.You can visit his web site at www.herebedragons.co.uk/jones.

Tim Lebbon lives in South Wales with his wife and two children. His books include *Dusk, Berserk, Hellboy: Unnatural Selection, Face, The Nature of Balance, Changing of Faces, Exorcising Angels* (with Simon Clark), *Dead Man's Hand, Pieces of Hate, Fears Unnamed, White and Other Tales of Ruin* and *Desolation.* Future publications include *Dawn,* a sequel to *Dusk.* He has won two British Fantasy Awards, a Bram Stoker Award, a Shocker and a Tombstone Award, and has been a finalist for International Horror Guild and World Fantasy Awards. Several of his novels and novellas are currently under option in the USA and the UK. Find out more about Tim at his websites: www.timlebbon.net and www.noreela.com

Charles de Lint is credited as having pioneered the contemporary fantasy genre. With 60 books published to date, he is known internationally as a master in his field. His writing includes adult novels and short stories, as well as young adult and children's literature. Awards for his fiction include the World Fantasy Award, the William L Crawford Award (presented by the International Association for the Fantastic in the Arts) and the Canadian SF/Fantasy Award (the Aurora).

Charles says he hopes his stories will encourage people to 'pay attention to how many special things there are in the real world.' He regards his greatest artistic achievement as 'the moment when a reader tells me that something I've written has inspired them to go out and create something of their own. Or that the story has helped them through a difficult time or inspired them to help others.'

A respected critic, de Lint is currently the primary book reviewer for *The Magazine of Fantasy & Science Fiction*. He's also been a professional musician for over 25 years, writing original songs and performing traditional and contemporary music with his wife, MaryAnn Harris. His main instruments are flute, fiddle, whistles, vocals and guitar, while MaryAnn's are mandolin, guitar, vocals and bodhran (Irish drum). For more information, visit his personal website at www.charlesdelint.com.

Alison L R Davies is a writer and storyteller from Nottingham, and her fiction has appeared in numerous magazines and anthologies. Her first collection of short stories, *Small Deaths*, was published in limited edition hardback, and her first short novel, *King of the Birds*, has recently been released. She has written articles, stories and features for a number of popular magazines and newspapers including *The Times Educational Supplement*, the *Daily Mail*, *Writers News*, *Writers Forum*, *Record Collector* and *Eve*.

As a storyteller, Alison has performed her work at venues throughout the UK. She loves to lift the words from the page and make them come alive for an audience. She runs regular storytelling workshops for adults and children. Her book *Storytelling in the Classroom* includes a number of children's stories and educational materials to be used by teachers. Her website is at www.alisonlrdavies.com.

Graham Masterton has published more than 35 horror novels, including *Charnel House*, which was awarded a Special Edgar by the Mystery Writers of America; *Mirror*, which was awarded a Silver Medal by the *West Coast Review of Books*; and *Family Portrait*, an update of Oscar Wilde's classic tale, *The Picture of Dorian Gray*, which was the only non-French winner of the prestigious Prix Julia Verlanger in France. His most recent horror fare is *Manitou Blood* and *Descendant* in the US, and *Touchy and Feely* in the UK.

Graham has written more than a hundred novels ranging from thrillers (*The Sweetman Curve, Ikon*) to disaster novels (*Plague, Famine*) to historical sagas (*Rich* and *Maiden Voyage* – both of which appeared on the *New York Times* bestseller list). He has published four collections of short stories, *Fortnight of Fear, Flights of Fear, Faces of Fear* and *Feelings of Fear* and edited the charity horror anthology *Scare Care*. He and his wife Wiescka live in Surrey, and he can be found online at www.grahammasterton.co.uk

Justina Robson lives in Yorkshire. She was the winner of the amazon.co.uk Writers' Bursary in 2000, and two of her books (*Silver Screen* and *Mappa Mundi*) have been shortlisted for the Arthur C Clarke Award. Her third book, *Natural History*, was runner-up in the John W Campbell Award and received a special citation in the 2006 Philip K Dick awards. The first book of a new and exciting adventure series is out now from Gollancz, *Quantum Gravity One: Keeping It Real..* She likes going out to coffee shops and writing. Sometimes she does yoga but not as often as she ought to.

Darren Shan's real name is Darren O'Shaughnessy. Although he is Irish, he was born on 2 July 1972 in St Thomas' Hospital, London – across the river from the Houses of Parliament in Westminster (which may explain his fascination with evil bloodsuckers …)

In January 2000 his first children's book – *Cirque Du Freak*, which he'd written as a fun side-project – was published in between his two adult books. The first book in a series entitled *The Saga Of Darren Shan* (or *Cirque Du Freak*, as it's known in America), it attracted rave reviews and much media attention. Over the next five years, Darren wrote a total of 12 books about vampires. He quickly followed his vampiric saga up with *The Demonata*, a series about demons, which will run to ten books in total.

A big film buff, with a collection of thousands of movies at home, Darren also reads lots of comics and books, and likes to collect original artwork. Other interests include long walks, watching football (he's a Tottenham Hotspur and Ireland fan), listening to pop and rock music, worldwide travel, and dreaming up new ways to terrify his readers!!!

Paul Finch is a British-based full-time writer, who works primarily in TV and film, but who is no stranger to short story markets. His first collection, *After Shocks*, won the British Fantasy Award in 2001, while his short novel, *Cape Wrath*, made the final ballot for the Stoker awards in 2002. Other recent anthologies that feature his work include: *Children of Cthulhu*, *Shadows over Baker Street*, *The Darker Side*, *A Walk on the Dark Side*, *Quietly Now* (a tribute to author Charles L Grant) and *Daikaiju* (a collection of giant monster tales). Paul has contributed regularly to *The Bill*, the popular British television crime series, while *Spirit Trap*, a teen horror movie starring Billie Piper, which he co-scripted, was released to cinemas in the late summer of 2005. Paul lives in Lancashire, northern England, with his wife, Cathy, and his children, Eleanor and Harry.

Neil Gaiman writes books and comics and films and poems and songs, and is happy that nobody seems to mind. He has won many awards and sold many books, has three children and too many cats, and wishes there were just a few more hours in the day.

Gary Greenwood's short stories have appeared in dozens of British magazines and the anthologies *Hideous Progeny*, *Raw Nerve* and *Tourniquet Heart*. He is the author of the novels *The Dreaming Pool*, *The King Never Dies*, *What Rough Beast* and *Jigsaw Men*.

He managed to survive over five years working in a Job Centre and now works as a faceless Civil Servant in the Office for National Statistics. He lives in Newport, South Wales with his wife Ly, two cats and far too many comics.

James Lovegrove is the author of nearly 20 books. His novels include *The Hope*, *Escardy Gap* (with Peter Crowther), *Days*, *The Foreigners*, *Untied Kingdom*, *Worldstorm*, and most recently *Provender Gleed*. He has also published a couple of novellas, *How The Other Half Lives* and *Gig*, and a short-story collection, *Imagined Slights*. He has written four short books for reluctant readers, *Wings*, *The House of Lazarus*, *Ant God* and *Cold Keep*, and has just begun a teen fantasy series written under a pseudonym. He lives in remotest, ruralest north Devon with his wife Lou, son Monty, cat Ozzy, and imminent second son, currently going under the name of Little.

The *Oxford Companion to English Literature* describes **Ramsey**

Campbell as 'Britain's most respected living horror writer.' He has been given more awards than any other writer in the field, including the Grand Master Award of the World Horror Convention and the Lifetime Achievement Award of the Horror Writers Association. Among his novels are *The Face That Must Die, Incarnate, Midnight Sun, The Count of Eleven, Silent Children, The Darkest Part of the Woods, The Overnight* and *Secret Stories.* Forthcoming are *The Grin of the Dark* and *Spanked by Nuns.* His collections include *Waking Nightmares, Alone with the Horrors, Ghosts and Grisly Things* and *Told by the Dead,* and his non-fiction is collected as *Ramsey Campbell, Probably.* His novels *The Nameless* and *Pact of the Fathers* have been filmed in Spain.

Ramsey lives on Merseyside with his wife Jenny. He reviews films and DVDs weekly for BBC Radio Merseyside. His pleasures include classical music, good food and wine, and whatever's in that pipe. His web site is at www.ramseycampbell.com.

Dawn Knox is married with an 18-year-old son and currently has a demanding job in the ICT department of a specialist college. She is also the administrator of the BrightLights Theatre School. Any spare time is shared between studying, writing and drawing portraits. She enjoys writing children's fiction but has recently become more interested in other genres, including horror. 'An Appropriate Pen' is her first published fiction.

Steve Lockley and Paul Lewis have been writing together for so long that it seems to be the natural way to work. Together they have produced the novel *The Ragchild* and *The Quarry,* along with the novellas *King of all the Dead* and *The Ice Maiden* and a slew of short stories. Their work has been nominated for British Fantasy Awards on eight occasions, but the prize continues to elude them. 'Puca Muc' was originally written for an ill-fated William Hope Hodgson tribute anthology and has been waiting to find a good home.

Storm Constantine has written over 20 books, both fiction and non-fiction, and well over 50 short stories. Her novels span several genres, from literary fantasy to science fiction to dark fantasy. She is most well known for her Wraeththu trilogy, and has recently completed a new set of novels set in the world of Wraeththu, concluding with *The Ghosts of Blood and Innocence*. Storm is also founder of the small publishing house Immanion Press, created in order to get classic titles from established writers back in print and innovative new authors an audience. She's currently working on several ideas for new books, as well as reading and editing a far-too-large pile of manuscripts for other writers. She lives in the Midlands of England, with her husband, Jim, and nine cats.

Michael Marshall Smith is the winner of several British Fantasy, Philip K Dick, August Derleth and International Horror Guild awards, and he will be Guest of Honour at the World Horror Convention in Toronto in 2007. Writing as Michael Marshall, his last three novels, *The Straw Men, The Lonely Dead* and *Blood of Angels*, have been international bestsellers. Current projects include writing a seventh novel and co-producing a film adaptation of one of his short stories. He lives in North London with his wife, son and two cats.

David J Howe has been involved with *Doctor Who* research and writing for over 25 years. He has been consultant to a large number of publishers and manufacturers for their *Doctor Who* lines, and is author or co-author of over 20 factual titles associated with the show. David was contributing editor to *Starburst* magazine for 17 years from 1984-2001. Since 1994 he has been book reviews editor for *Shivers* magazine. In addition, he has written articles, interviews and reviews for a wide number of publications, including *Fear, Dreamwatch, Infinity, Stage and Television Today, The Dark Side, Doctor Who Magazine*, the *Guardian, Film Review, SFX, Sci-Fi Entertainment* and the *Oxford Dictionary of National Biography*.

His short fiction has appeared in *Peeping Tom, Dark Asylum, Decalog, Dark Horizons, Kimota, Perfect Timing, Perfect Timing II* and *Missing Pieces*. He wrote the screenplay for *Daemos Rising*, released on DVD by Reeltime Pictures in 2004.

'Blackfriars' started life as an outline for the television series *Urban Gothic*, and became a short story when that project fell through. It's been waiting for a home ever since.

Poppy Z Brite is the author of eight novels, three short story collections and much miscellanea. Her most recent work includes a series of novels set in the New Orleans restaurant scene: thus far, *Liquor*, *Prime* and *Soul Kitchen*. She is at work on another book in the series. She lives in New Orleans with her husband Chris, a chef.

Twice short-listed for a British Fantasy Award, **Mark Samuels** is the author of two collections, *Black Altars* and *The White Hands and Other Weird Tales*. He has also written a short novel, *The Face of Twilight*. His as-yet unpublished third collection of short stories is called *Glyphotech and Other Macabre Processes*, and he is currently working on a full-length dark fantasy novel.

Author, editor, critic/essayist, poet and now – with the multiple award-winning PS imprint – publisher, **Peter Crowther** has edited more than 20 anthologies and produced almost 100 short stories and novellas (two of which have been adapted for British TV while two more are scheduled to begin filming for the big screen later this year), plus *Escardy Gap* (in collaboration with James Lovegrove) and *Darkness, Darkness*. He's currently busy writing story notes for *Dark Times*, his fifth collection, while working on the second instalment of his *Forever Twilight* SF/horror series, a mainstream novel, a couple of new anthologies, and another TV project. He lives about 500 yards from the sea on the east coast of England with his wife, Nicky, and an unfeasibly large collection of books, comics, DVDs, record albums and CDs.

Debbie Bennett's short fiction has been published in outlets as diverse as women's magazines, small press books and an award-nominated British horror anthology. Novels include a teenage fantasy novel due out in 2007 and an adult thriller looking for a home. She's been short-listed for an Ian St James Award, long-listed in the Crime Writers'

Association Debut Dagger Award and won several writing competitions. She's also edited and produced more books, newsletters and magazines for the British Fantasy Society than she can actually remember, and co-organised several successful fantasy conventions.

In her spare time, Debbie works as a data analyst for the police, freelances for an independent publishing company, runs a house, child and husband and does interior design when the mood takes her.

Richard Christian Matheson is a novelist, short story writer and screenwriter/producer. He has written and produced scores of episodes of television, for over 30 primetime network series, dramatic and comedy, and, at the age of 19, was the youngest writer Universal Studios ever put under contract. He has written over 20 pilots for comedy and dramatic series and had seven feature films made, including the critically acclaimed, paranoid satire *Three O'Clock High*, which the *New York Times* called 'brilliantly subversive,' as well as *Full Eclipse*, an original spec script he wrote and executive-produced for HBO; one of their highest rated films of the year. Richard also co-wrote the feature films *Loose Cannons, Paradise,* and *It Takes Two*.

He has written feature film and television projects, including three mini-series for Richard Donner, Mel Brooks, Aaron Spelling, Joel Silver, Ivan Reitman, Steven Spielberg and many others.

To date, Richard has written and sold 12 original, spec feature scripts; considered a record in the industry. Matheson is also a cutting-edge voice in psychological fiction and widely considered a master of the short story. Sixty stories are gathered in his critically hailed collection, *Dystopia*, called "Miniature masterpieces" by Publisher's Weekly.

His novel, *Created By*, has been published in ten languages.

Matheson is also a professional drummer who studied with legendary Cream drummer Ginger Baker.

Christopher Fowler lives and works in central London, and his novels include *Roofworld, Rune, Red Bride, Darkest Day, Spanky, Psychoville, Disturbia, Soho Black, Calabash, Full Dark House, The Water Room, Seventy Seven Clocks* and *Ten Second Staircase*. He is author of the

2005 British Fantasy Award winning novella *Breathe* and the short story collections *City Jitters*, *City Jitters 2*, *The Bureau of Lost Souls*, *Sharper Knives*, *Flesh Wounds*, *Personal Demons*, *Uncut*, *The Devil in Me* and *Demonized*. This latest collection included his hundredth published story, the Bram Stoker Award-nominated 'The Green Man'. Other awards include the British Fantasy Award in 1998 for Best Short Story ('Wageslaves'), and in 2004 he won the same Award for Best Novel (*Full Dark House*) and for Best Short Story ('American Waitress').

Simon Clark lives with his family in Yorkshire, where he as been a professional writer for more than ten years. He is the author of a dozen novels including *Darkness Demands*, *The Tower*, *The Night of the Triffids* and *London Under Midnight*. In addition to novels he has written short stories and non-fiction and is currently experimenting with the production of short films for his website www.bbr-online.com/nailed.

Copyright Information

'Introduction' © Alison L R Davies 2006.
Frontispiece © Clive Barker 1980.
'Foreword' © Stephen Jones 2006.
'Hell Came Down' © Tim Lebbon 2002. First published in *The Darker Side: Generations of Horror*, ed. John Pelan, Roc, 2002.
'Making A Noise In This World' © Charles de Lint 2000. First published in *Warrior Fantastic*, ed. Martin H Greenberg and John Helfers, DAW, 2000.
'Going Bad' © Alison L R Davies 2000.
'Neighbours From Hell' © Graham Masterton 2002. First published in *Cemetery Dance* Issue 38, 2002.
'An Unremarkable Man' © Justina Robson 2006.
'Life's A Beach' © Darren Shan 2006.
'Of The Wild And Berserk Prince Dracula' © Paul Finch 2006.
'Feeders And Eaters' © Neil Gaiman 1990, 2002. First published in *Keep Out the Night*, ed. Stephen Jones, PS Publishing, 2002. Originally published in different form in *Revolver*, 1990.
'Feather' © Gary Greenwood 1999. First published in *Sackcloth & Ashes* Issue 4, 1999.
'Cutting Criticism' © James Lovegrove 2006.
'One Copy Only' © Ramsey Campbell 2002. First published in *Shelf Life*, a limited-edition American anthology, 2002.
'An Appropriate Pen' © Dawn Knox 2006.
'Puca Muc' © Steve Lockley & Paul Lewis 2006.
'An Old Passion' © Storm Constantine 1996. First published in a convention booklet for *The Festival of the Imagination*, Australia, 1996.
'Walking Wounded' © Michael Marshall Smith 1996. First published in *Dark Terrors 3*, ed. Stephen Jones & David Sutton, Gollancz, 1997.
'Blackfriars' © David J Howe 2006.
'The Heart Of New Orleans' © Poppy Z Brite 2002. First published in *City Slab* Issue 1, 2002.
'Mannequins' © Mark Samuels 2003, 2006. First published in slightly different form as 'Mannequins In Aspects Of Terror' in *The White Hands*, Tartarus Press, 2003.
'Jewels In The Dust' © Peter Crowther 2004. First published in *Haunted Holidays*, DAW, 2004.
'20-20 Vision' © Debbie Bennett 2006.
'Red' © Richard Christian Matheson 1986. First published in *Night Cry* Issue 6, Montcalm Publishing, 1986.
'Seven Feet' © Christopher Fowler 2004. First published in *Demonized*, Serpent's Tail, 2004.
'The Extraordinary Limits Of Darkness' © Simon Clark 2006.

Other Telos Titles Available

TIME HUNTER

A range of high-quality, original paperback and limited edition hardback novellas featuring the adventures in time of Honoré Lechasseur. Part mystery, part detective story, part dark fantasy, part science fiction ... these books are guaranteed to enthral fans of good fiction everywhere, and are in the spirit of our acclaimed range of *Doctor Who* Novellas.

ALREADY AVAILABLE

THE WINNING SIDE by LANCE PARKIN
Emily is dead! Killed by an unknown assailant. Honoré and Emily find themselves caught up in a plot reaching from the future to their past, and with their very existence, not to mention the future of the entire world, at stake, can they unravel the mystery before it is too late?
An adventure in time and space.
£7.99 (+ £1.50 UK p&p) Standard p/b ISBN 1-903889-35-9 (pb)

THE TUNNEL AT THE END OF THE LIGHT
by STEFAN PETRUCHA
In the heart of post-war London, a bomb is discovered lodged at a disused station between Green Park and Hyde Park Corner. The bomb detonates, and as the dust clears, it becomes apparent that *something* has been awakened. Strange half-human creatures attack the workers at the site, hungrily searching for anything containing sugar ...

Meanwhile, Honoré and Emily are contacted by eccentric poet Randolph Crest, who believes himself to be the target of these subterranean creatures. The ensuing investigation brings Honoré and Emily up against a terrifying force from deep beneath the earth, and one which even with their combined powers, they may have trouble stopping.
An adventure in time and space.
£7.99 (+ £1.50 UK p&p) Standard p/b ISBN 1-903889-37-5 (pb)
£25.00 (+ £1.50 UK p&p) Deluxe h/b ISBN 1-903889-38-3 (hb)

THE CLOCKWORK WOMAN by CLAIRE BOTT
Honoré and Emily find themselves imprisoned in the 19th Century by a celebrated inventor … but help comes from an unexpected source – a humanoid automaton created by and to give pleasure to its owner. As the trio escape to London, they are unprepared for what awaits them, and at every turn it seems impossible to avert what fate may have in store for the Clockwork Woman.
An adventure in time and space.
£7.99 (+ £1.50 UK p&p) Standard p/b ISBN 1-903889-39-1 (pb)
£25.00 (+ £1.50 UK p&p) Deluxe h/b ISBN 1-903889-40-5 (hb)

KITSUNE by JOHN PAUL CATTON
In the year 2020, Honoré and Emily find themselves thrown into a mystery, as an ice spirit – *Yuki-Onna* – wreaks havoc during the Kyoto Festival, and a haunted funhouse proves to contain more than just paper lanterns and wax dummies. But what does all this have to do with the elegant owner of the Hide and Chic fashion chain … and to the legendary Chinese fox-spirits, the Kitsune?
An adventure in time and space.
£7.99 (+ £1.50 UK p&p) Standard p/b ISBN 1-903889-41-3 (pb)
£25.00 (+ £1.50 UK p&p) Deluxe h/b ISBN 1-903889-42-1 (hb)

THE SEVERED MAN by GEORGE MANN
What links a clutch of sinister murders in Victorian London, an angel appearing in a Staffordshire village in the 1920s and a small boy running loose around the capital in 1950? When Honoré and Emily encounter a man who appears to have been cut out of time, they think they have the answer. But soon enough they discover that the mystery is only just beginning and that nightmares can turn into reality.
An adventure in time and space.
£7.99 (+ £1.50 UK p&p) Standard p/b ISBN 1-903889-43-X (pb)
£25.00 (+ £1.50 UK p&p) Deluxe h/b ISBN 1-903889-44-8 (hb)

ECHOES by IAIN MCLAUGHLIN & CLAIRE BARTLETT
Echoes of the past … echoes of the future. Honoré Lechasseur can see the threads that bind the two together, however when he and Emily

Blandish find themselves outside the imposing tower-block headquarters of Dragon Industry, both can sense something is wrong. There are ghosts in the building, and images and echoes of all times pervade the structure. But what is behind this massive contradiction in time, and can Honoré and Emily figure it out before they become trapped themselves ... ?
An adventure in time and space.
SOLD OUT

PECULIAR LIVES by PHILIP PURSER-HALLARD
Once a celebrated author of 'scientific romances', Erik Clevedon is an old man now. But his fiction conceals a dangerous truth, as Honoré Lechasseur and Emily Blandish discover after a chance encounter with a strangely gifted young pickpocket. Born between the Wars, the superhuman children known as 'the Peculiar' are reaching adulthood – and they believe that humanity is making a poor job of looking after the world they plan to inherit ...
An adventure in time and space.
£7.99 (+ £1.50 UK p&p) Standard p/b ISBN 1-903889-47-2 (pb)
£25.00 (+ £1.50 UK p&p) Deluxe h/b ISBN 1-903889-48-0 (hb)

DEUS LE VOLT by JON DE BURGH MILLER
'Deus Le Volt!'...'God Wills It!' The cry of the first Crusade in 1098, despatched by Pope Urban to free Jerusalem from the Turks. Honoré and Emily are plunged into the middle of the conflict on the trail of what appears to be a time travelling knight. As the siege of Antioch draws to a close, so death haunts the blood-soaked streets ... and the Fendahl – a creature that feeds on life itself – is summoned. Honoré and Emily find themselves facing angels and demons in a battle to survive their latest adventure.
An adventure in time and space.
£7.99 (+ £1.50 UK p&p) Standard p/b ISBN 1-903889-49-9 (pb)
£25.00 (+ £1.50 UK p&p) Deluxe h/b ISBN 1-903889-97-9 (hb)

THE ALBINO'S DANCER by DALE SMITH
'Goodbye, little Emily.'
   April 1938, and a shadowy figure attends an impromptu burial in

Shoreditch, London. His name is Honoré Lechasseur. After a chance encounter with the mysterious Catherine Howkins, he's had advance warning that his friend Emily Blandish was going to die. But is forewarned necessarily forearmed? And just how far is he willing to go to save Emily's life?

Because Honoré isn't the only person taking an interest in Emily Blandish – she's come to the attention of the Albino, one of the new breed of gangsters surfacing in post-rationing London. And the only life he cares about is his own.

An adventure in time and space.

£7.99 (+ £1.50 UK p&p) Standard p/b ISBN 1-84583-100-4 (pb)
£25.00 (+ £1.50 UK p&p) Deluxe h/b ISBN 1-84583-101-2 (hb)

THE SIDEWAYS DOOR by R J CARTER & TROY RISER
Honoré and Emily find themselves in a parallel timestream where their alternate selves think nothing of changing history to improve the quality of life – especially their own. Honoré has been recently haunted by the death of his mother, an event which happened in his childhood, but now there seems to be a way to reverse that event … but at what cost?

When faced with two of the most dangerous people they have ever encountered, Honoré and Emily must make some decisions with far-reaching consequences.

An adventure in time and space.

£7.99 (+ £1.50 UK p&p) Standard p/b ISBN 1-84583-102-0 (pb)
£25.00 (+ £1.50 UK p&p) Deluxe h/b ISBN 1-84583-103-9 (hb)

TIME HUNTER FILM

DAEMOS RISING
by DAVID J HOWE, DIRECTED BY KEITH BARNFATHER
Daemos Rising is a sequel to both the *Doctor Who* adventure *The Daemons* and to *Downtime*, an earlier drama featuring the Yeti. It is also a prequel of sorts to Telos Publishing's *Time Hunter* series. It stars Miles Richardson as ex-UNIT operative Douglas Cavendish, and Beverley Cressman as Brigadier Lethbridge-Stewart's daughter Kate. Trapped in an isolated cottage, Cavendish thinks he is seeing ghosts. The only person who might understand and help is Kate Lethbridge-Stewart … but when she arrives, she realises that Cavendish is key in a plot to summon the Daemons back to the Earth. With time running out, Kate discovers that sometimes even the familiar can turn out to be your worst nightmare. Also starring Andrew Wisher, and featuring Ian Richardson as the Narrator.
An adventure in time and space.
£14.00 (+ £2.50 UK p&p) PAL format R4 DVD
Order direct from Reeltime Pictures, PO Box 23435, London SE26 5WU

HORROR/FANTASY

CAPE WRATH by PAUL FINCH
Death and horror on a deserted Scottish island as an ancient Viking warrior chief returns to life.
£8.00 (+ £1.50 UK p&p) Standard p/b ISBN: 1-903889-60-X

KING OF ALL THE DEAD
by STEVE LOCKLEY & PAUL LEWIS
The king of all the dead will have what is his.
£8.00 (+ £1.50 UK p&p) Standard p/b ISBN: 1-903889-61-8

GUARDIAN ANGEL by STEPHANIE BEDWELL-GRIME
Devilish fun as Guardian Angel Porsche Winter loses a soul to the devil ...
£9.99 (+ £2.50 UK p&p) Standard p/b ISBN: 1-903889-62-6

FALLEN ANGEL by STEPHANIE BEDWELL-GRIME
Porsche Winter battles she devils on Earth ...
£9.99 (+ £2.50 UK p&p) Standard p/b ISBN: 1-903889-69-3

SPECTRE by STEPHEN LAWS
The inseparable Byker Chapter: six boys, one girl, growing up together in the back streets of Newcastle. Now memories are all that Richard Eden has left, and one treasured photograph. But suddenly, inexplicably, the images of his companions start to fade, and as they vanish, so his friends are found dead and mutilated. Something is stalking the Chapter, picking them off one by one, something connected with their past, and with the girl they used to know.
£9.99 (+ £2.50 UK p&p) Standard p/b ISBN: 1-903889-72-3

THE HUMAN ABSTRACT by GEORGE MANN
A future tale of private detectives, AIs, Nanobots, love and death.
£7.99 (+ £1.50 UK p&p) Standard p/b ISBN: 1-903889-65-0

BREATHE by CHRISTOPHER FOWLER
The Office meets *Night of the Living Dead.*
£7.99 (+ £1.50 UK p&p) Standard p/b ISBN: 1-903889-67-7
£25.00 (+ £1.50 UK p&p) Deluxe h/b ISBN: 1-903889-68-5

HOUDINI'S LAST ILLUSION by STEVE SAVILE
Can the master illusionist Harry Houdini outwit the dead shades of his
past?
£7.99 (+ £1.50 UK p&p) Standard p/b ISBN: 1-903889-66-9

ALICE'S JOURNEY BEYOND THE MOON by R J CARTER
A sequel to the classic Lewis Carroll tales.
£6.99 (+ £1.50 UK p&p) Standard p/b ISBN: 1-903889-76-6
£30.00 (+ £1.50 UK p&p) Deluxe h/b ISBN: 1-903889-77-4

APPROACHING OMEGA by ERIC BROWN
A colonisation mission to Earth runs into problems.
£7.99 (+ £1.50 UK p&p) Standard p/b ISBN: 1-903889-98-7
£30.00 (+ £1.50 UK p&p) Deluxe h/b ISBN: 1-903889-99-5

VALLEY OF LIGHTS by STEPHEN GALLAGHER
A cop comes up against a body-hopping murderer …
£9.99 (+ £2.50 UK p&p) Standard p/b ISBN: 1-903889-74-X
£30.00 (+ £2.50 UK p&p) Deluxe h/b ISBN: 1-903889-75-8

PARISH DAMNED by LEE THOMAS
Vampires attack an American fishing town.
£7.99 (+ £1.50 UK p&p) Standard p/b ISBN: 1-84583-040-7

MORE THAN LIFE ITSELF by JOE NASSISE
What would you do to save the life of someone you love?
£7.99 (+ £1.50 UK p&p) Standard p/b ISBN: 1-84583-042-3

PRETTY YOUNG THINGS by DOMINIC MCDONAGH
A nest of lesbian rave bunny vampires is at large in Manchester. When Chelsey's ex-boyfriend is taken as food, Chelsey has to get out fast.
£7.99 (+ £1.50 UK p&p) Standard p/b ISBN: 1-84583-045-8

A MANHATTAN GHOST STORY by T M WRIGHT
Do you see ghosts? A classic tale of love and the supernatural.
£9.99 (+ £2.50 UK p&p) Standard p/b ISBN: 1-84583-048-2

TV/FILM GUIDES

A DAY IN THE LIFE: THE UNOFFICIAL AND
UNAUTHORISED GUIDE TO 24 by KEITH TOPPING
Complete episode guide to the first season of the popular TV show.
£9.99 (+ £2.50 p&p) Standard p/b ISBN: 1-903889-53-7

THE TELEVISION COMPANION: THE UNOFFICIAL AND
UNAUTHORISED GUIDE TO DOCTOR WHO
by DAVID J HOWE & STEPHEN JAMES WALKER
Complete episode guide (1963 – 1996) to the popular TV show.
£14.99 (+ £4.75 UK p&p) Standard p/b ISBN: 1-903889-51-0

LIBERATION: THE UNOFFICIAL AND UNAUTHORISED
GUIDE TO BLAKE'S 7 by ALAN STEVENS & FIONA MOORE
Complete episode guide to the popular TV show.
Featuring a foreword by David Maloney
£9.99 (+ £2.50 UK p&p) Standard p/b ISBN: 1-903889-54-5

HOWE'S TRANSCENDENTAL TOYBOX: SECOND EDITION
by DAVID J HOWE & ARNOLD T BLUMBERG
Complete guide to *Doctor Who* Merchandise.
£25.00 (+ £4.75 UK p&p) Standard p/b ISBN: 1-903889-56-1

HOWE'S TRANSCENDENTAL TOYBOX: UPDATE No 1: 2003
by DAVID J HOWE & ARNOLD T BLUMBERG
Complete guide to *Doctor Who* Merchandise released in 2003.
£7.99 (+ £1.50 UK p&p) Standard p/b ISBN: 1-903889-57-X

A VAULT OF HORROR by KEITH TOPPING
A guide to 80 classic (and not so classic) British Horror Films.
£12.99 (+ £4.75 UK p&p) Standard p/b ISBN: 1-903889-58-8

BEAUTIFUL MONSTERS: THE UNOFFICIAL AND
UNAUTHORISED GUIDE TO THE ALIEN AND PREDATOR
FILMS by DAVID McINTEE
A guide to the Alien and Predator Films.
£9.99 (+ £2.50 UK p&p) Standard p/b ISBN: 1-903889-94-4

THE HANDBOOK: THE UNOFFICIAL AND UNAUTHORISED
GUIDE TO THE PRODUCTION OF DOCTOR WHO by DAVID J
HOWE, STEPHEN JAMES WALKER and MARK STAMMERS
Complete guide to the making of *Doctor Who* (1963 – 1996).
£14.99 (+ £4.75 UK p&p) Standard p/b ISBN: 1-903889-59-6
£30.00 (+ £4.75 UK p&p) Deluxe h/b ISBN: 1-903889-96-0

BACK TO THE VORTEX: THE UNOFFICIAL AND
UNAUTHORISED GUIDE TO DOCTOR WHO 2005
by J SHAUN LYON
Complete guide to the 2005 series of *Doctor Who* starring Christopher
Eccleston as the Doctor
£12.99 (+ £2.50 UK p&p) Standard p/b ISBN: 1-903889-78-2
£30.00 (+ £2.50 UK p&p) Deluxe h/b ISBN: 1-903889-79-0

THE END OF THE WORLD?: THE UNOFFICIAL AND
UNAUTHORISED GUIDE TO SURVIVORS
by ANDY PRIESTNER & RICH CROSS
Complete guide to Terry Nation's *Survivors*
£12.99 (+ £2.50 UK p&p) Standard p/b ISBN: 1-84583-001-6

TRIQUETRA: THE UNOFFICIAL AND UNAUTHORISED
GUIDE TO CHARMED by KEITH TOPPING
Complete guide to *Charmed*
£12.99 (+ £2.50 UK p&p) Standard p/b ISBN: 1-84583-002-4

WHOGRAPHS: THEMED AUTOGRAPH BOOK
80 page autograph book with an SF theme
£4.50 (+ £1.50 UK p&p) Standard p/b ISBN: 1-84583-110-1

TALKBACK: THE UNOFFICIAL AND UNAUTHORISED
DOCTOR WHO INTERVIEW BOOK: VOLUME 1: THE
SIXTIES edited by STEPHEN JAMES WALKER
Interviews with behind the scenes crew who worked on *Doctor Who* in
the sixties
£12.99 (+ £2.50 UK p&p) Standard p/b ISBN: 1-84583-006-7
£30.00 (+ £2.50 UK p&p) Deluxe h/b ISBN: 1-84583-007-5

TALKBACK: THE UNOFFICIAL AND UNAUTHORISED
DOCTOR WHO INTERVIEW BOOK: VOLUME 2: THE
SEVENTIES edited by STEPHEN JAMES WALKER
Interviews with behind the scenes crew who worked on *Doctor Who* in
the seventies
£12.99 (+ £2.50 UK p&p) Standard p/b ISBN: 1-84583-010-5
£30.00 (+ £2.50 UK p&p) Deluxe h/b ISBN: 1-84583-011-3

ZOMBIEMANIA: 80 FILMS TO DIE FOR
 by DR ARNOLD T BLUMBERG & ANDREW HERSHBERGER
A guide to 80 classic zombie films, along with an extensive filmography
of over 500 additional titles
£12.99 (+ £2.50 UK p&p) Standard p/b ISBN: 1-84583-003-2

SECOND FLIGHT: THE UNOFFICIAL AND UNAUTHORISED
GUIDE TO DOCTOR WHO 2006 by J SHAUN LYON
Complete guide to the 2006 series of *Doctor Who*, starring David
Tennant as the Doctor
£12.99 (+ £2.50 UK p&p) Standard p/b ISBN: 1-84583-008-3
£30.00 (+ £2.50 UK p&p) Deluxe h/b ISBN: 1-84583-009-1

MIKE RIPLEY

The first three titles in Mike Ripley's acclaimed 'Angel' series of comic crime novels.

JUST ANOTHER ANGEL by MIKE RIPLEY
£9.99 (+ £1.50 UK p&p) Standard p/b ISBN: 1-84583-106-3
ANGEL TOUCH by MIKE RIPLEY
£9.99 (+ £1.50 UK p&p) Standard p/b ISBN: 1-84583-107-1
ANGEL HUNT by MIKE RIPLEY
£9.99 (+ £1.50 UK p&p) Standard p/b ISBN: 1-84583-108-X

HANK JANSON

Classic pulp crime thrillers from the 1940s and 1950s.

TORMENT by HANK JANSON
£9.99 (+ £1.50 UK p&p) Standard p/b ISBN: 1-903889-80-4
WOMEN HATE TILL DEATH by HANK JANSON
£9.99 (+ £1.50 UK p&p) Standard p/b ISBN: 1-903889-81-2
SOME LOOK BETTER DEAD by HANK JANSON
£9.99 (+ £1.50 UK p&p) Standard p/b ISBN: 1-903889-82-0
SKIRTS BRING ME SORROW by HANK JANSON
£9.99 (+ £1.50 UK p&p) Standard p/b ISBN: 1-903889-83-9
WHEN DAMES GET TOUGH by HANK JANSON
£9.99 (+ £1.50 UK p&p) Standard p/b ISBN: 1-903889-85-5
ACCUSED by HANK JANSON
£9.99 (+ £1.50 UK p&p) Standard p/b ISBN: 1-903889-86-3
KILLER by HANK JANSON
£9.99 (+ £1.50 UK p&p) Standard p/b ISBN: 1-903889-87-1
FRAILS CAN BE SO TOUGH by HANK JANSON
£9.99 (+ £1.50 UK p&p) Standard p/b ISBN: 1-903889-88-X
BROADS DON'T SCARE EASY by HANK JANSON
£9.99 (+ £1.50 UK p&p) Standard p/b ISBN: 1-903889-89-8
KILL HER IF YOU CAN by HANK JANSON
£9.99 (+ £1.50 UK p&p) Standard p/b ISBN: 1-903889-90-1
LILIES FOR MY LOVELY by HANK JANSON
£9.99 (+ £1.50 UK p&p) Standard p/b ISBN: 1-903889-91-X
BLONDE ON THE SPOT by HANK JANSON
£9.99 (+ £1.50 UK p&p) Standard p/b ISBN: 1-903889-92-8

Non-fiction

THE TRIALS OF HANK JANSON by STEVE HOLLAND
£12.99 (+ £2.50 UK p&p) Standard p/b ISBN: 1-903889-84-7

The prices shown are correct at time of going to press. However, the publishers reserve the right to increase prices from those previously advertised without prior notice.

TELOS PUBLISHING
c/o Beech House, Chapel Lane, Moulton, Cheshire, CW9 8PQ,
England
Email: orders@telos.co.uk
Web: www.telos.co.uk

To order copies of any Telos books, please visit our website where there are full details of all titles and facilities for worldwide credit card online ordering, or send a cheque or postal order (UK only) for the appropriate amount (including postage and packing), together with details of the book(s) you require, plus your name and address to the above address. Overseas readers please send two international reply coupons for details of prices and postage rates.